The Countess of Darkness

Of the Ravens of Berengar

Robin John Morgan

First published in the UK in 2023 by Violet Circle Publishing.

Manchester, England, UK.

Print ISBN: 978-1-910299-40-1
Digital ISBN: 978-1-910299-41-8

British Library Cataloguing in Publication Data.
A catalogue record for this book is available from the British Library.

All papers used in the production of this book are sourced only from wood grown in sustainable forests.

www.violetcirclepublishing.co.uk

*When people are scapegoated, and accused unjustly,
the truth becomes meaningless to most.*

*For everyone,
Scapegoated and labelled wrongly, I know your pain.*

Ariel and Bade

It felt like a meaningless statement to Ariel, and yet from nowhere, she felt her anger begin to rise. She trusted him, he was one of her oldest friends, and yet just for a moment he had questioned everything she had told him, almost as if he did not believe her. Her rage suddenly erupted as her voice rose, as she stared at Bade as he stood helpless and pale.

"What did you think…? What Bade, you thought the phantom dark Fae had come back to claim me?" Her voice rose to a shout, as her fear and anger mixed.

"You think that was the work of Bran, is that really what you thought, my lover had come to take me back?" She burst into tears.

"SHE IS NOT DARK, SHE IS THE LOVE OF MY LIFE, AND THE MOST GENTLE SOUL I HAVE EVER KNOWN!"

He put his head down, as Ariel lifted her hands to her face with her feelings of loss and fear, and wept. Bade fidgeted for a moment and took a step forward.

"Look Ariel you have to understand…." She snapped at him again in anger.

"NO, I DON'T…" Ariel lifted her head.

"You are just like all the rest. None of you have any idea of who she is, her queen snaps her fingers and all of you just jump to the same conclusion. You just assume that miles and miles away across the realm, Bran is the cause of everything we here have suffered, because of what?" She stood up.

"WHAT BADE?" He shook his head.

"It's not like that at all." Ariel gave a sniffle and lowered her voice.

"Oh, but it is… The mighty Rhiannon clicks her fingers and you have all jumped to the same conclusion as her. I have seen how Rhiannon rules, I have spent two years in the heart of her precious realm watching good people slave and toil for what Bade?"

He shrugged looking hurt and apologetic, but also unable to answer.

"I will tell you exactly what will happen in Avalon when her mighty royal highness arrives." Her anger felt like it had taken over, and even though she knew it was wrong to voice such discontent, she no longer cared.

"She will arrive with all her precious faired haired folk in Avalonia, which I might add is something beyond the dreams of everyone, it is a sight to behold, you should visit it. What you won't see though, is how all the workers, the real Fae of skill, will be rounded up and hidden in the outer reaches of the realm so as not to offend her precious grey eyes. It's so easy to place all the blame on Bran and the thousands of others, who I have watched work themselves into the ground to create such a dazzling place of glory and wonder. As she sits her privileged fat ass on her silken padded seat, every one of those workers will be shipped out of the realm and taken back to the moon realm. They are destined never to live in the homes that they built, and do you know why Bade, do you even care? Let me tell you, it's for no other reason than they were born with dark hair like me, and unlike our own queen, who is the personification of pure goodness, Rhiannon is a misguided bigot."

(Ariel. Taken from Rise of the Raven.)

Chapter One.

Lost Hope and Light.

*B*ranna stood at the top of the high tower, far above the room of the gathering, as her eyes stared out to the west. Her mind was filled with those cherished precious final moments, as the sound of Ariel's voice echoed through her mind.

"Bran, listen to me, this is not as before. Last time I was hidden from you, I was not around to remind you, but here I will always be on view, and at your side. Bran you are so clever, I know you can find a way, I have seen your notes and diagrams, I mean, they are coded but I can see how you are working to find a balance like Merlin's. Don't you see, with me here at your side as you work, you will see your reason to fight every day, and you will find a way through to a balance. When the time is right, I will be waiting for you to awaken me."

In her mind, she heard her own voice, as she tried to get Ariel to understand, and as she remembered, she spoke the words out loud.

"Ariel it is not the same, I was so alone without you, I just want us to be together always as we promised each other in Avalon." Ariel's soft loving voice echoed back from the past.

"But we will be Bran, I will always be there in your heart and in your thoughts, can you not see, we can never really be parted, our love is too strong. Bran, we have eaten a wonderful meal together, we made love, and then bathed together, it was a perfect day together for us. Remember today, hold it in your heart for me, for it was perfect and filled with love, but now I am tired, hold me until I fall asleep to dream of you. Let me fall asleep in your arms, and then do the spell, and let me rest a while. When it is done, then control the darkness, find the balance, and rule this family as an equal to Rhiannon."

$\mathcal{S}$tood alone on top of the tower, out of sight from everyone, she felt the tears run down her cheeks, and gave a sniffle.

"Ariel, I miss you so much." She took a deep breath.

"I sit with you every day, I see you as I work, but I yearn to hold you close. Seeing you sleep is a comfort, but not seeing your beautiful grey eyes, or hearing your soft voice is torture to me. I want to feel your touch again, I miss it so much. I have kept my word, and I have fought so hard to overcome much of the darkness, but it is not easy, as those who surround me grow darker and darker. I fear for the future, everything has gone wrong, this family is crumbling and I have not got the strength without you to fight to rebuild it. I feel so weary, and so tired, I could join you and sleep for an age."

The wind lifted up into the air, and her hair which was tatty and longer, rose on her shoulders, as she faced the west and her anger rose again. She knew out there in her deep halls Rhiannon was alive, and still inflicting suffering on her Fae family and friends.

"Ariel, I am so lonely, and I am starting to lose all hope, forgive me, for if I fall, Maud will rise darker and eviller to replace me. I fear there will come a time, where I will not be strong enough to stop her, and I will fall."

$\mathcal{B}$ranna had aged, she looked older, as her face bore the lines of her grief, and within her black hair, soft lines of white had appeared. It was due to an unyielding grief that had cast a dark shadow over her for ten years, since she had performed the spell and sealed Ariel within a crystal container. To a degree Ariel had been right, Branna had placed the crystal in front of the window so that it would be bathed in the light of everyday, in the centre of her large work room, deep below the castle. Each day, Branna had worked on her study of the balance between light and dark, and had moved her work table, so that all she had to do was look up, and through the double doors, she could see Ariel through the thick crystal.

It had helped keep all of her memories alive, and served to hold back the darkness within her, but it had not improved her deepest feeling, because deep within her, there grew a void of emptiness where her love for being around Ariel had resided.

Just like the early days of Avalon, when Ariel had first arrived, Branna was prone to outbursts of anger, and would snap loudly at people, and on the few occasions her temper had arisen, she had been seen to be wild and terrifying to all that were around her. The simple reason she lost control was her loneliness, her days were painful and empty, unlike her nights, which were filled with dreams of her moments alone with her precious Ariel. Her life now was one of brooding and walking round devoid of joy, not really that interested in what was going on in the castle. She spent her time in the library or her workroom, battling the darkness that fought to grow inside her, as she searched for the secret of Merlin, and complete control.

Her only companion was Roack, who she would talk to quietly alone at the top of the tower. Roack was the only one who understood her feelings of loss and pain, it had taken a long time, but in her final days, Ariel had shown Roack the truth of Branna, and through Ariel, Roack had come to terms and understood the unique balance of her and Branna.

Roack understood how the light within Ariel had given extra power through her love to Branna, and with her sealed in a box of crystal, Roack could see how much Branna had lost of her strength, and none of the others would accept it. Even now, they clung to their misguided theories that Ariel would one day destroy them all, and as a result, Ariel stayed sealed away, out of sight of prying eyes, deep below the castle.

*R*oack flew in and landed on her shoulder, and Branna came out of her thoughts, and her eyes moved to see the side of the head of the raven.

"Are they there?" Roack bobbed up and down.

"They sit, they talk, and they watch." Branna understood.

"I cannot feel her, yet she has my blood in her. You are sure she is her child; she is the daughter of Ariel?" Roack turned and looked at Branna.

"She looks a little like you, her eyes are like yours, but her face is that of the woman of light. Branna the Raven, there is no doubt, she is of yours and the woman of lights line."

"Good… Midsummer is two months away, at noon, we shall thin the veil for a few minutes, enough to let them pass, but also keep us hidden. Ariel's daughter will run free as her mother wished. You did good work Roack, I know finding her was not easy, it has taken time, but I have done all I can now for Ariel's line. The light of Enaria can shine in other worlds, and we will be safe here knowing she has left."

Roack gave a slight flap of her wings and steadied herself on Branna's shoulder.

"What if she brings the Queen of Light?" Branna smiled.

"She won't, by now she has read and understood her mother's books, Rhiannon is the last person she will run to, and I doubt she will head to Florae. With Rhiannon still on her throne, this daughter of Ariel will know their hands are tied, just as they were when Ariel returned there. No Fae will seek us out, because to do so will cause another split, be patient Roack, her daughter is free, it is all I can do for her."

Branna stared back out towards the west.

"It may bring about my end, but I will be replaced, and before that happens, you will find another companion, one more powerful than I, and I will release you to them, I have seen it in my dreams. You and I will be free, and I will awaken Ariel, and live the life we promised each other so long ago in Avalon."

"What of the child of Victor?" Branna smiled.

"She is powerful there is no doubt, but she is still young and needs to find her way. The death of her father is a deep wound, and she is unhappy with her new life, a time will come when she seeks me out, and at that point I will go to her aide."

"Things have not gone well of late Branna the Raven; you need to get her now." Branna shook her head.

"The time is not right, but it is coming, I will ensure she will know of me, and she will come, for now she is safe and out of the reach of Maud."

*R*oack was right, in the last ten years, the Berengar family had suffered some bad luck. When a politically motivated member of the Fae of moon named Galliant, rose to prominence, he began to talk of ties across the seas, which attracted many eyes, including Berengar's.

Galliant was based in Avalon, and his primary task was to attract as much trade as possible for Rhiannon to increase her coffers. The problem was, those abroad who had made excursions into the land of the Anglo's saw his attempts as a signal that the land was filled with riches, and so the men of the Norse, the men of Rome, and eventually Berengar, all set their sights on invasion.

The land of the Anglo, became a war ground, as the rival tribes known as Celt, clashed with the invaders and each other. Berengar and

Vladimir saw a country in chaos, and against Branna's wishes, they planned an assault, which would be based at Fey Castle on the edge of the lands of Gaul. Berengar left and was gone for six long years, leaving Branna even more alone and isolated, having lost Ariel.

Branna's only success was Victor, the second child of Maud, he was an intelligent man, and he took Branna's advice, and rather than land and conquer through force, he landed on the west coast of the land at a place named Tintagel, and brought with him supplies, and knowledge taught him by Branna, which held many secrets of the Fae.

Whilst Vladimir and Ivor, sailed with Amand to battle in the east of the Anglo Isles, Victor quietly won the allegiance of the local Celt tribes, and built a fortress, which became the focus of the area, where many sought protections, and Victor prospered.

Such was his reputation, he was offered and married a Celtic Princess of high standing, and after a few years, she bore him a child, whom he named Morgana.

*O*tto was outraged that his son would marry a Celt, and not pick a woman of Sachsen blood, and shunned him from that day. It was Branna's wish that all children born to the line of Berengar, were born in the castle, and so Igraine, wife of Victor was brought to the castle, and under the supervision of Filiberta and Branna, Morgana was born.

It was clear from the moment of her birth that she would be powerful, and again Branna had cast her thoughts back to Ariel, and her warnings over the birth of Rosamund, and so within a week of the birth, Branna travelled with Igraine back to the fortress at Tintagel.

She stayed for a month veiled from Rhiannon, but not wanting to leave Ariel encased in crystal left for too long in the castle with Maud, and for the first time since that night in Avalon, Roack and her separated, as Branna left Roack to watch over Ariel.

*I*t was a shrewd move, because Maud tried to sneak in, and destroy the crystal box and kill Ariel, only to find Roack holding Rajani, Maud's raven in her claws. Maud suffered great pain and withdrew, and Branna packed and returned, knowing she would never leave the castle again whilst Maud lived within it.

Within the year, Amand was killed in battle, when his head was removed, breaking the link from his raven, it dropped dead to the floor on the battlefield next to him. Ten miles away, during a battle with a Celt named Uther, Vladimir who was not tied to a raven, was slain, when he took a severe blow to the head from the sword of Uther. Ivor the first son of Maud sent his raven to attack Uther as he fought his way towards Vladimir, and with one fatal swipe, Uther cut the raven into two, and Ivor fell to the ground instantly dead.

It was a sombre time when the bodies were returned with a heartbroken Berengar, across the long bridge into the Berengar Castle, and for a long time Berengar mourned the death of his brother and grandchildren.

Branna preserved them, and placed them in state in crystal boxes, sat in their seats, in the room of the gathering. From that moment, she ruled, no other from the family would die in battle, and Berengar returned to Castle Fey, to try and regain the initiative, but the truth was, too many of his men had died, and he was losing the war.

Branna ordered him and his men back to the castle, something he resented, but he knew deep down she was right, and so for the first time in an age, the Varisci retreated, and returned home.

All eyes were fixed on Victor, the only one who had made any sort of headway, as he was married with lands, and had produced a female child to the line of Berengar, it was clear, Branna's plan had worked.

The biggest shock came when a year ago, Uther, the man who defeated and killed Vladimir and Ivor, made a pact with Victor, as he strove to bring peace to the nation, and be crowned king. Victor had been against it, but through battle and dialogue, an unstable peace was brokered.

The next clash grew when Uther saw Igraine and desired her, and with the help of Merlin, Uther had managed to find his way into Igraine's bed, disguised as Victor. As Uther took what he wanted, which was witnessed by Victor's daughter Morgana, Victor was attacked by the men of Uther, and during the battle, Victor with his raven were slain, and Igraine became the prize of the battle for Uther.

Branna was enraged when she heard, and swore to find this king and bring about his downfall, and despatched Rosamund and Lothar to go to the aide of Igraine and Morgana.

*B*ranna stood at the top of the tower, still facing west and gave a sigh, there had been many days and nights at one time, where she had stood here, knowing, below in the trees, Ariel had been living her life, having ran from the castle. She smiled, as she remembered her moments alone, sat between the two trees talking in hope that Ariel was there listening, and she remembered the day when she had turned to leave, and Ariel had stood up in the deep fern. Branna closed her eyes, and saw the face in her thoughts, those beautiful grey eyes so filled with life, her long flowing wavy brown hair, it had meant so much to see her again, how much she wished that was now.

Branna slipped her hand into her robe, and slid out a soft lace edge piece of fabric and lifted it to her eyes to wipe them, and she stopped and looked at it, understanding she had done the same then, and Ariel had smiled. Roack lifted off her shoulder, and flew into the air in front of her.

"It is growing late, you must prepare for tonight, there will be much to discuss."

Branna understood, even now Roack felt the pain within her when she thought of Ariel, she gave a sigh.

"You go ahead, I will be down soon."

Roack swerved in the air, and dropped like a stone breaking the connection between them for a while. Branna stared out into the darkening sky, closed her eyes, and remembered the smile of Ariel. She sat down and gave a heavy sigh, she had over time come to hate the gatherings, but tonight she knew was important, as she would get news from the world of men around Avalon, and this new man rising to power who had already caused so much pain for her family. She let her legs hang over the edge of the ledge, and watched the world before her under the dark canopy that was her veil, she missed the sunlight, it had been so bright during those days before Ariel had run from the castle. Walking with Ariel holding her hand, the woodland had felt so filled with life, but now it had become how she felt, dull and miserable, and devoid of life.

*F*ar down below Berengar greeted Lothar as he trotted onto the bridge, and dismounted at the sight of his father. Berengar embraced him with a large smile.

"I am happy to see you my son, how was your journey?"

Berengar had started to age, he was still tall and broad, and a man of immense strength. On his face, the lines of his age were starting to show, and yet his eyes still burned with life, and he had less of the brooding set features of his youth. Lothar, who was now a fully grown man, smiled as he patted his father's shoulders.

"We took it at a gentle pace, and enjoyed the surroundings, but I must say, it is good to be home again." He looked up to the tower, and saw the small dark figure, he looked concerned.

"I see there is no change in mother, how is she?" Berengar gave a deep sigh.

"She misses her, she misses her companionship. She has good days, and dark days, I feel she is lonely, but she resists all of our efforts to bring cheer to her life."

They started to walk along the bridge, as the horse was attended to, Lothar glanced up again.

"Why can she not just open the box and let her out, I am sure by now everyone will see that the woman of light was never a threat? From what I have been told, she lived here for an age before Uncle Otto pulled his stunt and never hurt a soul. I have read up on these Fae of Earth, it is not in their creed to harm others." He stopped and looked to Berengar.

"Can we not just let her have the woman back?" Berengar looked back up at the tower.

"I wish that was truly the answer, it pains me to see her this way, I miss the laughing and her fun loving ways. Sadly, Maud and Otto still stir up trouble at the mere mention of her, and in the past, they have caused so many problems, it made it impossible to keep things orderly. Your mother knows it is a price she must pay for the time being, although, I feel it takes much of her, in enduring the loss she feels."

Lothar understood, he had done his share of sparring with Maud and Otto, and he understood the chaos they could create.

"She should leave here for a while, just get away and take some time for her." Berengar shook his head.

"She will not do that, Maud may appear subdued, but she wants to lead this family more than ever, even now in secret she lusts to take the throne from your mother. Fear not, she will sit up there for a while longer, and then she will come down and be a little more like the mother you know."

They entered under the large gate, and walked across the yard towards the main entrance of the castle, where workers laboured with wood and stone, the castle was having yet more additions added, as the wealth of the family grew.

*T*he hall was laid out for a feast, and wealthy guests arrived over the following hours, slowly filling the place, and it was clear how large the family was growing. Many of Berengar's initial tribe, had also risen to places of power, as lords and land owners, as the family moved away from the battle fields and into trade. It was clear, that the family had dealings with all of the nations and tribes, as Gaul's, Celts, Romans and Picts of prominence mingled, and talked yet more trade. Here the rivalries of war were unnoticed, as profit, dominance and greed were the only items on the agenda, as they smiled and flirted around the table as they ate.

*B*ranna arrived late, and seated herself at the head of the table, she watched the guests with an interested eye. There was no one from Avalon, which had become a realm of trade, and yet, here in a room filled with the wealthiest and most powerful from the world of men, not one Fae was present.

Branna found the whole event boring, she had done too many in her life, and the thrill of it all had gone. When the feasting was over and everyone moved into more relaxed quarters, seeing Berengar as he smiled and flirted with a countess from Gaul, she quietly slipped out, and made her way down to her private rooms below.

For a little over ten years, Branna had resided below the gathering hall, moving from her chambers in the high tower. Below the castle, in her workrooms one for her research, and one which now contained a desk and the long crystal box of Ariel, Branna found a small place of peace and quiet, away from the bickering of the family. Sat alone with Ariel, she would write and talk, although it was mainly just her voicing her thoughts, as Ariel was in no place to answer. She looked up from her paper, and rested her nib on the edge of the desk.

"The gathering was dull my love, I find them loathsome these days, with their petty small talk and flirtatious behaviour, not one of them has a mind capable of comprehending my thoughts and theories. You have no idea how much I miss our long conversations, that would last until the small hours, I miss the intellect of your sharp mind. I had hoped there would be at least one person worth talking to tonight, but chieftains and warlords, have little ability to discuss anything that is not death and destruction." She lifted her wine, and took a sip as she sat back in her seat.

"Do you remember how we sat up late under the apple tree, and talked of the stars in the skies, and wondered where Erathhome had gone, and how Tideguyde must have tracked him down, using his trail left by his essence?" She smiled.

"We lay on our backs and held hands, as we stared at the darkness above us, and you pondered the notion of its size, and how if it was possible it was sat inside another sphere and another and so on, and we just started to laugh. It was such a wonderful moment; I have never forgotten it." She sat silent for a while remembering, and then stirred as other thoughts entered her mind.

"Ariel, I want to go back, I want to walk where you walked, I want to sit below the trees and pick an apple like we used to. I want to sit in the room we first made love in, do you miss it as much as I do?" She took her sip of her wine.

"Ariel, I want to return to Avalon to die, I want to go back to the house, and under your star of protection, I want to cut the ties with this family and Roack. There is nothing in this world for me any longer, I yearn for death. Roack is my only companion, but she does not understand the bond we shared. I have tried to explain it, but she fears the love and the light, and so disconnects from me as she has now. This… This here and now, cut off from Roack and the family, alone in a room with just you and I, this is all I have ever wanted, but not with you in a box. My love, I am so sorry, but I am not sure like this I can continue." She took a deep breath to hold in the surge of emotion within her.

"I want to find a way to take you back, and open your box in our home, we may not live long, but one hour holding you in my arms is better than this endless eternity of pain. Berengar would not listen, he has not the intellect, and his armies have failed. I mean, yes, we are still powerful, but we have been set back and the family has lessened. I lost Amand, Vlad, Ivor and Victor, they are gone, they were my strongest, and all that is left is the weakened and greedy. I do not want to start all over again, my only real hope is Morgana, she appears very bright, and I feel the power within her line, but as you know, Maud will kill her."

She drained her glass of wine, and gave a frustrated and saddened sigh.

"I no longer want this, I cannot start again, I am no nearer to confronting Rhiannon than the day I fled from the top of the rock. I feel everything has been a waste, for a little over ten years you have slept in your box, and it was all for nothing, because they have squandered it all. I wish we could talk, I know you would have an idea to help, and I feel so utterly exhausted I cannot think straight, because all I want is to meet, and make that golden queen pay, just so I can have you back again as I promised."

*H*er eyes fluttered, and slowly closed, as the tiredness of her soul dragged her into sleep. Her arm fell and the empty glass hung on the end of her arm, as it flopped down the side of the seat, and her chin dropped onto her chest. Across the room, within the glass box just below the neckline of Ariel's white dress, a pulse emitted, and a white light began to glow.

The light intensified, and as it came out through the crystal container, it fractured into colour, and long lines of spectral light flowed into the room, casting rainbows all over the walls and illuminating Branna. She stirred in her sleep, and deep within her heart, there was a sudden pulse, and it ran up through her and into her mind, Branna opened her eyes.

She felt the soft warm hand of Ariel slip into hers, and turned looking down, at the slender white arm, and the small silver bracelet. Her eyes followed it up to the long flowing wavy brown hair, and the soft caring face, with the bright love filled grey eyes. Ariel smiled.

"Welcome home my love." Branna turned, and looked at the door with the small red star of protection above it. It made no sense, and Branna felt confused as she turned back to Ariel.

"What is this, is this some sort of dream… Am I dreaming of you?" Ariel smiled.

"Bran, this is my love flowing out of me to you, I know you feel lost and alone, but I am there right in front of you, and I may not hear your words, but such is the power between us I feel you, I feel your loneliness." Branna swallowed hard.

"So, this is a dream, you are somehow in my head?" Ariel smiled, and squeezed her hand, and then reached for the handle to the door.

"Does it matter? Bran I am here, I am with you, this is what you desire, and so we are here. Come, let's see our home together one more time." She pulled, and not fully understanding, Branna followed, as Ariel opened the door and walked in.

*T*ogether they looked around at the mess, the soldiers were not tidy, cupboards were open, pots were smashed, and scattered across the room. Ariel pulled her arm, and gave a little chuckle.

"It reminds me of my first day here, the soldiers are bad, but they are nowhere near as messy as this place was when I first got here."

Branna was trying to comprehend what was happening, she wanted this to be real, but somehow, she knew this was not possible. Ariel walked into her own room, and gave a smile. The bed was made, even after all this time, the soldiers had not stripped it, although the drawers hung out, and the large closet in which she hung her dresses was open, and all her clothing lay in the bottom of it, the top shelf was empty. Ariel turned with twinkling eyes.

"Come, see… Put your hand on the top of the closet, and feel around, I know it is there, I can feel it." Branna frowned.

"Feel what… Ariel what is happening to me?" She gave a soft giggle.

"I thought you were clever, you forgot who I am. Come on, feel around and find it."

Branna's eyes lifted to the top of the large wooden closet, and slipped her hand onto the top, she slid it over the rough wooden surface.

"What am I looking for?" Then she felt it, was it a book?

Branna lifted down a small dusty hand bound book, she recognised it as the one Ariel made sat in the garden under the apple tree in her second summer at Avalon. Branna remembered watching as she stitched it together with skill, and admired how talented she was. She lifted it down and held it in front of her.

"What is this, Ariel?" She gave a big smile.

"Bran this is very special, I always regretted leaving it behind. I wrote this for you, it has a lot of very personal thoughts and feelings inside it. I cannot talk to you through crystal, I have tried, but you cannot hear my voice, but this, with this I can tell you what you need to know. Bran my love, I dreamed a lot here, I saw things and I did not know if they were real, but when I went back to Florae, when I read my mother's writing's, I knew… I knew then they were not just dreams, they were moments of things that would happen in our future. Bran, I wrote this with the runes of love. When you had that bad fever, I used your sweat and your blood and I bound this book to you, for only you will ever read it, these are things I wanted to say, these are the conversations we should have had, but we were denied them by events. These my love, are the most important words I ever wrote, because I wrote them just for you."

*B*ranna looked at the book, and she swallowed hard trying to fight back her tears, Ariel gave her a smile and slipped her arm around her, and pulled her close, and Branna closed her eyes as the yearning to be held for over ten years surfaced. She drew in every moment and second of the feeling, absorbing all of it into her being. Ariel's words were soft in her ear.

"Bran my love, you must live, you cannot go on like this, I need you to live, I need you to find your way again and defeat Rhiannon, because I am lay here, and I am waiting. Do not give up on me, keep your promise to me. Fight it Bran my love, fight the darkness and find a way through, and use the book to guide you." She felt the softest of kisses on her lips.

"I cannot do this often, it drains me, so remember this, Bran my love I am waiting, please push forward, and then release me." Branna's eyes snapped open.

"WHAT!" A voice shouted through the locked door.

"Lady Raven… Lady Raven, The Lord Berengar wants you to know, that the gathering will assemble in two hours."

Branna shook her head as she jerked in her chair and looked around, everything was as it was. She blinked her eyes and looked to the door, as her thoughts cleared.

"Thank you… Tell the Lord Berengar I will be there shortly."

"Yes, My Lady Raven." Branna took a deep breath, and then remembered.

"Is the Banquet over?" There was a moment of silence.

"My Lady, that was last night, the family gathering will start as tonight's sun sets in two hours."

"Yes of course. It is fine, I will be there."

*H*er head was swimming and confused, she sat back, and her eyes moved to the desk and she felt a bolt of shock shoot through her. There on the desk in front of her was the book, Ariel had made in Avalon, and at its side was a large red apple. Branna stared at it, not really understanding what had happened. She reached out and lifted the book, it was real, this was not a dream, but it made no sense, as she pulled it forward and held it in her hand in front of her, her eyes moved to the crystal box and she gave a slight gasp of surprise.

"Ariel, how is this even possible, it was a dream… Wasn't it?"

She looked down at the book understanding nothing that had happened, she had slept for almost a whole day, and yet it had felt so real. The feel of her hand, her arms round her waist as she pulled her close, and the softness of her lips as she kissed her. The book was in Avalon, and now it was here, none of it made sense to her.

*R*oack flew up to the window, she landed softly, and her dark eyes looked at Branna, she appeared displeased.

"You said you would warn me when the woman of light was around." Branna looked up from the book.

"What do you mean, Ariel is there in a box, you have been here hundreds of times with her there?" Roack bobbed on the window ledge.

"Next time you let her out, warn me. I will be in the gathering room when you are ready." Roack spread out her wings, turned, and flew off. Branna stared at the book, her voice was soft, almost a whisper.

"I did not let her out… Ariel, how did you do this?"

Chapter Two.

A View of the Future.

Branna had not really had the time to examine the book made by Ariel, as she had to prepare for the gathering of the family. She slipped it into her desk drawer and locked it, and then headed through the door to her bed chamber, where she washed, and changed her clothing for her attendance at the gathering.

Just over an hour later, she walked into the preparations chamber, where Berengar stood waiting, he smiled and lifted his arms to her shoulders.

"How are you, you have a tiredness about you, is it a bad day again?" She gave a smile, and lifted her hand to his.

"I am fine Beren, some days I miss her more, recently has felt harder than normal."

He gave a slight nod, in many ways he understood, there had been a great many times in the past where Branna and Ariel had sat in their room with him and shared a meal and talked. He always understood the depth of the bond between them, there were a few women in his past that he had felt close to, and so naturally could see how Branna would miss Ariel a great deal. In his mind, the bond between the two women had always been stronger than in others he saw. He felt something similar with Branna, to him she was the most important person in the castle, and yet it was not a romantic thing, it was more a deep and understanding bond of kinship. He stroked back some of her hair, from her white face and smiled.

"A day will come when we can bring her back, she is not gone forever, I will ensure it. Now come, tonight we will have much to discuss, and news to learn that will be important to the family."
She gave a nod and smiled as he moved to her side and linked her arm, and then as she took a deep breath, he opened the door to the chamber, and they walked in to see the family sat in their seats.

Branna crossed the room through the centre of the circle of seats, and sat in her red velvet seat next to Berengar. Staff wandered around filling glasses, and leaving the bottles. When all were taken care of, they left the room, and the doors were closed shut. Branna gave a nod to each of them as she looked round.

"Welcome home, to all of you, for this chamber is the centre of this family, and it has been some time since we all gathered, it is good to see all of you home amongst us again."

Otto scowled, and pointed across the room, to the new vacant chair, which had been installed recently, next to Rosamund.

"I hope that is not for the bastard offspring of that Celt bitch, we have no use of a half breed in this family?" Branna turned to him.

"That will be the seat of Morgana, who I may add is the daughter of your son Victor, and she has a right, as a family member to take her seat that awaits if she wishes to. I will remind you Otto, that is not just the rule of this family, it is my rule, for my family. There is one seat for every member, and considering the death of her father, I would have thought you would be more understanding, after all, she is your granddaughter." He spat at the seat.

"This family runs pure with our blood, not the blood of that Celt whore, Victor disgraced us by marrying her." Merwig gave a sigh.

"Oh, really Otto, the child has a line of power, it has been felt by all of us, and considering the losses we have had recently, I would say another member, especially one of the female line would be an asset. Victor's blood runs strong through her, and considering he is sat preserved beside you, one would have thought you would at least try to hold your tongue." Branna dismissed Otto and looked to Lothar and Rosamund.

"How is Morgana doing, it must be difficult for one so young, to have her father suddenly replaced by the man who ordered his death?" Lothar leaned back.

"The child is surprisingly resilient, she told me she saw this Uther enter disguised as her father, to sleep with her mother. The girl witnessed all of it, and I feel she is very intelligent, she certainly has no liking for this Uther who will be crowned king, and has a hatred for a man named Merlin, like I have never known." Branna's ears pricked up.

"What has Merlin got to do with this?" Lothar shrugged.

"The girl say's he arranged it all."

*B*ranna sat back in her seat and thought for the moment, Ariel's words flitted through her thoughts. 'A man who was created by equal parts light and dark.' Branna's mind pondered it, half dark and half light, a man of kindness, but also capable of acts of treachery. Rosamund moved in her seat and lifted her wine, her dark eyes stared at Branna.

"Morgana is gifted, even for one so young, she certainly has good insight. I wanted to bring her back here, but Igraine wants to keep her close for a while." Branna gave a nod.

"This Uther, he has taken three souls from this family, what do we know of him, and what is his connection to Merlin?" Rosamund took a sip of her wine.

"From what we can gather, the ruling council have picked this Uther to lead and bring stability, Merlin has been assigned the task of overseeing him. The Celt tribes have been locked in battle for years, the Norsemen, and the Romans have had a fight on their hands, as did we, although, Victor took a completely different approach, and he was embraced by the local Celts, which makes it even more surprising that this Uther would go to war against him. There was a treaty between them, but Victor felt Uther violated it by coveting his wife, and as you know, Victor felt deep feelings for Igraine, and so his temper got the better of him, and the treaty was broken." Maud tutted, and rolled her eyes.

"The woman was weak, she was just a pretty little maid to bed, I never understood him wanting to marry her, and as for his half breed child, I really do not know why we concern ourselves; I say cut her tree and have done with all of it, that land is worthless." Otto gave a sharp nod of his head, and agreed. Berengar leaned forward in his seat.

"I have heard this Uther is a mighty warrior, he certainly made life hard for us, is he really as powerful as they say?" Lothar scoffed.

"He only had the advantage because he was sold weapons from Avalon." Branna's ears pricked up.

"Do you know that to be a fact, did Rhiannon arm his men?" Lothar gave a nod.

"It is a well known fact, the council want unity. Rhiannon, Eve and Hearne, personally agreed with the choice for him to lead, he apparently has noble qualities. I cannot deny being in that castle at

Tintagel, I saw little of them. His table manners are appalling, I saw him as a brute, nothing more, I saw no king." Branna looked around the room at all of them.

"What more do we know about the antics of the council? I want to know everything about what they have planned, I want all of you to talk to every contact you have that trade with Avalon. We need to get as much information as possible, and I want to see every scrap that comes our way." Dagaric crossed his legs, and leaned back in his chair.

"You should have attended the gathering last night Mother, I heard that Rhiannon has a mind at some point to seat Eleanor on the throne, and move back to the moon realm. I also heard she is still looking for a Fae who unleashed evil into the realm and feels she is close. Gwendolyn is spitting out bastards in a free for all, she had another two, twins they say. She is spending a great deal of her time between Avalon and Gaul these days; it appears she is very close to Rhiannon." Branna gave a smirk.

"Do not let that fool you, Gwendolyn is as cool as Bridget, she understands Rhiannon, she will not be so foolish as to leave herself vulnerable to a political animal like our glorious golden queen. Gwendolyn wants peace, so she can build up her line, never forget she is advised by Merlin her husband, he sees all and says little." Otto stared at her.

"They are all in it together, they conspired to kill my son, the queen of your whore of light is equally to blame, and as for that pretend wizard, he is the worst of all. You head this family, what are you going to do about it?" Branna glanced at him.

"I am going to learn all I can, and then I will plan, never forget Otto, I have overdue business with Rhiannon, fear not, for once you will get the revenge you seek. I want to sit with Morgana and talk to her, I want to hear her story of the night this Uther came to visit, and then I will know better how to play things." Maud perked up in her seat.

"You will be leaving for a while?" Branna smirked.

"No, I have other means of meeting." Maud frowned.

"When will you let me use your black book, it is not fair, you are hampering my progress?" Branna looked at her, as she scowled across the room at her.

"I have told you daughter, my book was written after years of research, it was how I learned. In time you will see it, but for now, it is being put to better use in the hands of someone who can actually wield it." Maud sat back and hissed through her teeth.

"When the day comes to take over the running of this family, I will need to be ready." Branna gave a nod.

"You will be… But it is a long time off. Have some patience little daughter, your turn will come." Branna looked around.

"Is there anything else to consider?" Otto frowned.

"What about those bloody Gypsies on the rocks, I shot four yesterday, what are you doing about it?" Branna smiled.

"Nothing, it appears your shot has improved, and you are doing fine removing them for us, we all appreciate it Otto, thank you." Dagaric and Lothar sniggered, even Rosamund managed a half smile.

*F*or the rest of the time, they sat in their seats and spoke, drank wine and ate, the doors opened, and staff wandered in and out. Slowly over the night, they thinned out and headed for their rooms, Branna and Berengar were last to leave. As they walked out of the room, Branna felt a little more uplifted, the news had been interesting and given her some ideas, Berengar stopped and looked at her.

"I miss the feel of you in my arms, will you ever lie with me again?" Branna gave a soft smile, as she looked at him.

"That time will come my lover, for as you know, I take no other men. I have things on my mind Beren, and much to sort out, we have lost too much, and I need to find a way forward for us all again. Do not think I am not aware of the white haired duchess who has been lay in your room all day." She gave a smile.

"Go to her Beren and enjoy her, I will come to you soon enough." He gave a sigh.

"I miss you; I miss your laughter, and those bright sparkling black eyes beside me. I understand, I do, she was worthy, but you also had me, and yet I feel I have been set adrift never to be beside you again." Branna lifted her hand to his face, he had changed little, and still had that look of grim determination.

"Beren, our road has been a long one, and yet there is a longer one to travel still to come. We have not drifted; you are still the rock on which I stand. The battles took their toll on us, and we became parted for a long time, I need to get away from my habit of isolation, and I am trying. I feel tonight I found a focus, and I think it may help all of us, let me investigate, and I will come to you before the others to talk. Go now to your duchess, and enjoy the time you have with her." He gave a nod, and leaned down and kissed her cheek softly.

"You are the finest woman I have ever known Branna the Raven. I will look forward to the time when your soft skin lies beside mine again."

*B*ranna smiled, as she watched him walk along the corridor towards the steps that led up to the main hall. She turned in the opposite direction, and walked slowly back to the steps that led down to her personal chambers, and her work rooms, she had much to think about, and even more to plan.

Branna hurried down to her room, she unlocked her doors and slipped in, then locked them behind her again. The room was dark, and yet in the small amount of light that came through the window, the crystal box containing Ariel appeared to glow as the light covered it. She moved to her desk and lit her candle, and then slipped out her key, and opened the draw, and there was the book made by Ariel in Avalon.

She had no idea how Ariel had done this, but as she lifted it out and opened the cover, she realised that she was indeed the daughter of Enaria. In Ariel's neat writing there were two words. *'For Bran.'*

She felt a sudden surge run through her, and rise into her throat, and her hand trembled, as she placed it flat on the desk, and leaned forward into the candle light to see it better. Branna nervously turned the page, and started to read the neat lines written by Ariel.

'Bran, I am the daughter of Enaria, and I have never thought that I have had any of her gifts passed on to me. Yet, tonight as I sit in my bed, having spent the day with you making this book, I have had more dreams. You are working high on your rock, and even though I am now wide awake, in my mind is a picture of you, alone in a large room, leaning over a desk, reading this very book by candle light, and I sense the deep pain and sadness within you.

I really am not sure if this is right or I am just going mad, did I dream this, or am I seeing this? The truth is I just do not know, and yet since arriving in Avalon, I have experienced a lot of moments like this, and they feel important. Bran, are we apart, have I died and left you alone? I am so afraid that may be the case, and so tonight, I thought I would try to reach out to you, and talk to you of the things that I see when I sleep alone in the nights you work late.'

*B*ranna sat back, and took a deep breath.

"How can you see this Ariel, it was years ago, how could you have seen this moment?" She looked down and continued to read on.

'I see you sat talking alone between two trees, I have had weeks of dreams of you surrounded by tables and bottles. Last night I dreamed you were sat on a white beach, as the water rolled towards you, and you were talking to me, and yet I was not there with you. Bran my love, I have seen you hold up a small child with dark hair, from a woman lay on a bed with deep woven red blankets, and I felt the surge of power from the child, and it frightened me. I have no idea what these mean or if they are real, and so I have decided tonight to write down the things that I see, in hope that if anything should happen to me, you will not be alone.

If you are talking to me and I am not there, then know this, within these pages I have written everything I have thought, dreamed and felt for you. It is not easy to fully detail how deeply I love you, and how you have made my life so happy and content, but I will try, and I will fill this book with every emotion I have ever felt around you, so with some hope, you will truly see the full depths of my love. I know we vowed to always be together, and I want that with all my heart, but just in case, the runes hidden within this book, will bring it to you, should we ever be separated, and your heart starts to falter. I love you Bran, you are the love of my life, read on and grow strong…. Ariel'

*B*ranna bent down her head, and shook as her tears fell to her lap, she looked up at the crystal box and her eyes streamed, and through her sobs, she spoke.

"I am so sorry Ariel, I brought this upon us, it was my stupidity, and now I have ruined everything." She lifted the book, and clutched it to her heart, as she wept.

"I miss you so much, I yearn to undo it all so I can awaken you, but Ariel I am struggling to find a way. I need you so badly right now, and I do not know what to do, I am terrified the darkness will take me, and I will not be able to free you."

She felt a warmth run from her hand and into her arm, and slowly it worked its way through her whole body, and as she closed her eyes and sobbed, in her head she heard the soothing voice of Ariel.

"Hush my love, I am here in my words, I have not left you, I never truly could. Bran my love, I will always be with you in your heart, you cannot truly lose me, concentrate and remember, and feel me, I am here."

Branna saw the pictures in her mind of that day, the last day they stood between the two trees, when Ariel had appeared out of nowhere and told her to wait. It was so vivid and clear, and sharp in her thoughts, as Ariel stood before her, just a few feet away.

She took another step forward and pulled her into a kiss, and Branna felt her breath trap in her throat, and slid her arms around her, as she kissed her back. It was long, loving, and passionate, and she felt a warmth inside her grow, and closed her eyes taking note of every second of the moment. She could feel the power of the darkness as it struggled against the light, and she felt the warmth of her happiness as it filled her.

When Ariel pulled apart, Branna stood with her eyes closed, and swayed as her head felt disorientated and cloudy. She opened her eyes, and Ariel was stood back in the trees, and smiled at her.

"I gave you what light I could, make it last and fight with it. No matter where I am or where I go, know this Branna Ofmoon, my love will always be yours, for I will love no other. You are and you always will be the love of my life."

Branna flopped back in her seat and opened her eyes, she was still clutching the book to her heart, deep within her she felt the presence of Ariel. It was almost as if the memory had woken up and raged into life within her, Ariel's voice echoed in her mind.

"I gave you what you needed that day, you have a part of my being deep inside you, and it is the purest light I hold. It will fight the darkness, you will never be completely dark, for I also live within you now. Bran my love, settle your score with Rhiannon, and then release me back into your world. Read the book, seek out the answers you need."

Branna rose from her seat, lifted the bottle and poured a new glass of wine, and then she walked into her potions room, and gathered more candles. With a ring of lit candles on her desk, surrounding the book, Branna sat with a wine and began to read about every dream that Ariel had witnessed during her times alone in Avalon.

Each dream alone had significance, but they were not in the right order, but as the night passed into the following day, Branna began to see a pattern, as she noticed small glimpses of her life after she had run from Avalon. The rock splashed with blood, a small child in a village of men suffering. The long golden beach in Hispanica, the field in Bohemia filled with wild flowers, all of it was there, including the birth of Morgana, and the power that emitted from her.

The days stretched as she continued to read, and she had bouts of weeping, and even some moments of chuckles, as moments of her life with Ariel came back to her memories. One page caught her attention the most, it was Ariel's feelings the night of her return to Branna, and how she felt inside as she made love to her in the forest. It took her breath away, and she sat back in her seat, unaware it was late afternoon and she had been reading for two days straight.

"Ariel, you knew, you knew in Florae I would call to you, and you knew that you would arrive between the two trees, and we would make love again. All that time alone, and you always knew I would find you, and bring you to me."

*B*ranna was tired, so she blew out the candles, lifted the book and headed towards her sleeping chamber. Branna slept for a whole day, and appeared from her chamber feeling refreshed and walked up to the hall, where she ate alone. Roack sat on the table looking slightly annoyed, although she enjoyed the meat Branna put on a plate for her.

"Why do you torture yourself with the words of the woman of light, I feel her in those words and leave?" Branna smiled and gave a sigh.

"Roack, these words are important. Ariel is the daughter of Enaria, in Avalon she saw things she did not understand and wrote them down. Roack, she saw beyond this time, and things she saw in Avalon have come true. I know you hate it, but I have to read them, it is important to all of us, including you." The black bird bobbed up and down.

"How can the woman of light see things that help me?"

"Roack, Ariel saw things before they happened, she saw the birth of Morgana, and she predicts that she will be powerful. I have not read all the book, but if I do, some of the things I see which have not happened yet, may help us make better choices. Think about it, if we had seen the death of Vlad or Ivor, and Victor, we may have been able to stop it from happening. Ariel did not understand what she was seeing when she wrote this, but she saw things connected to us and the Merle, so she wrote them down hoping I would understand them. Roack, we can use this as a reference to ensure we make the right move and save lives to keep the family stronger."

Roack lifted a piece of raw meat and swallowed it, and then stretched out her wings.

"The woman of light wanted to protect you, I saw that, and she loved you dearly, and so I will trust in her because she wanted you safe. Read this book that hurts me, and then tell me when I can return." Branna smiled, it was possibly the first time in a long time, but the bird could sense the hope within her and that was a relief.

*I*t took over a month for Branna to fully absorb all of the meanings within the dreams of Ariel. The book gave her great hope, and it also brought moments of pain and anguish, as in between each of the dreams, Ariel wrote words of love, and devotion, which at times left her distraught and heartbroken, wishing she had not sealed Ariel in crystal. There were a few days, where she lay on the top of the crystal and looked through to Ariel's sleeping face, and wept as she spoke her own words of love. Branna found as the month moved on, she felt a great deal of regret, and wished she had said more to Ariel of her own feelings.

Making notes as she went along, Branna started to notice a pattern within the dreams, and soon realised that without understanding, Ariel had seen many of the interactions of the ruling council. It became clear through several of her visions that Rhiannon intended to leave Avalon, by placing Eleanor on the throne there, so she could return to the realm Ofmoon, and many dreams described a woman with bright blue eyes, and long red hair, who would take Roack away from Branna.

Branna worked out that Eve was playing her part in the downfall of the family, and so slowly Branna began to plan, and get prepared. One dream in particular stood out, where a young Morgana would go to war with a king, and he would be slain, and so Branna's attention moved back to home, and rebuilding her army for Berengar.

The more she read, the more it started to paint a picture of what could come, and if that was the case, Branna was ready, although she said nothing of the book to any other than Roack. She knew Maud would play her part in trying to undermine her no matter what she did, and so with a plan of action in her mind, she planned out her future to move her closer towards the death of Rhiannon, and her first job was to try and convince Morgana to come to the castle.

*O*ne dream stood out more than any, and Branna sat for a long time reading it over and over. It was the moment when Branna had jumped to the castle, and had dropped her veil of protection. Ariel had no understanding that Branna had done it to save her life, but even in her inability to fully comprehend the dream, Ariel outlined the spell, to move unseen, which was a secret only known to the Fae of Earth. It had been given to them by Eve and Hearne, for it was at heart a green circle spell.

It did not take long to work out, that Branna could sit at her desk, protected by her veil, and travel to others to meet with them. It guaranteed that she would never have to leave the castle in the hands of Maud again, and she started to practice and learn the spell straight away.

*A*t noon on midsummer, Branna took a break, and walked up the steps of the large tower. High above her realm as Roack sat on her shoulder, she looked to the west, and focused her mind.

"It is time that the truth be taken out of here and told to the world Roack. It is time Rhiannon was seen for the queen with a corrupt heart, for that is what she truly is." As Roack lifted into the sky, below the trees Ena and Dorin made their way to the outer reaches of the realm. Branna focused her mind.

"Are the soldiers clear of that part of the wood?" Roack's voice croaked into her mind.

"There is a mile that is clear, nothing from the castle stirs in the woods today." Branna gave a small smile.

"Tell me when you see them."

From high above the realm, Roack looked down into the deep woodland, where she saw the figure of a young girl at the side of a young man. She spoke into Branna's mind.

"I see them, they are watching, and waiting." Branna's eyes began to flicker with flashes of red.

"I am ready, thin the veil and let them run free."

*U*nder the trees Ena lifted her head above the deep fern, she turned as Dorin at her side lifted his head a little higher for a better look. Ena frowned at Dorin.

"It does not look any different, you are sure aren't you, because if you are not, we will die today?" Dorin gave a smile.

"Trust me, the sun is rising and you will see, today is the day." Ena was not sure; she was nervous, and pulled her bag with the few belongings of hers and her mother's that she owned closer.

"I am taking a huge risk, and this for me is a big leap of faith, I trust you, I do not trust the Raven." He turned and watched, and then he saw it, lifted his arm and pointed.

"Look, see how it ripples, get ready."

Branna stood high listening to Roack, and deep inside her she felt the struggle of the darkness and light. Forces within her were fighting, and she closed her eyes to focus her powers, and spoke quietly to herself.

"I will not fail you Ariel, no matter how hard the darkness tries to stop me."

Her eyes blazed red and she focused hard, and then in a bid to force back the darkness, Branna clenched her fists and screamed with all her might, and it wailed across the whole realm, and her eyes exploded with red light. Ena's head snapped around.

"What the hell was that?"

Dorin was not waiting, the edge of the barrier had disappeared and he could see the other side. Ena gave a squeal as he lunged at her, dragged her into his arms and then ran for all he was worth towards the area where the barrier had gone. Ena watched as it got closer and snapped her eyes shut in fear as she clung to his neck, and within three more paces, Dorin ran through the gap carrying Ena, and suddenly they were free.

He was not about to stop, he just ran down the slope moving as quick as his legs would carry him, and half a mile down the hill, he stopped, panting hard, and slid Ena to the floor. He leaned forward, and dragged air back into his lungs.

Ena stood lost for words looking up the slope back to the realm of the Raven, she glanced at Dorin as he panted, red in the face with sweat rolling down his forehead. Her voice was soft and contained her utter disbelief.

"We did it… Dorin we did it, we are free." She gave a gasp of a small laugh.

"We are actually free, I cannot believe it, you were right, and we did it."

Roack watched them lower down the valley side, and Branna saw them through Roack's eyes, and tears came to her eyes, as Roack croaked.

"It is done." Branna swallowed hard.

"Look at her Roack, she is perfect, she is so like Ariel, and yet I see myself as a young girl in her."

"Focus Branna the Raven, close the veil."

Branna gave a sniffle and focused her mind, and within a few moments the veil thickened and sealed them all in once again. Roack flew down from the sky and landed on Branna's shoulder.

"I will leave you for a while, I know the thoughts are coming." Branna gave a soft smile.

"You know me so well Roack, thank you, it was important to me I did this."

"The woman of light went into her box to save you; you have now repaid her by letting her bloodline free. What is done is done."

Roack lifted into the air, and dropped down to the lower battlements in search of snails. Branna turned, and walked down the steps and headed for her rooms, knowing that today, the power of the light within her won out over darkness. Deep below at the side of Ariel, she wept as she told Ariel that her daughter was free, and she would never be tied to a raven, and her life would be light, free of the darkness. She knew in a way that Ariel could not hear her, but it mattered to her that the words were said, and with a heavy heart and the pictures of the young woman with dark hair in her mind, she sat at her desk and wept.

*F*ar away down the valley, Ena hung from Dorin as she kissed him, and he squeezed her tight. Now the shock of actually being right had worn off, and suddenly understanding they were free, their laughter and joy bubbled up.

Dorin released her, and she slid down in front of him, her dark eyes dancing with delight. He smiled at her.

"We cannot stay here Ena; we need to get as far as possible from her as we can. Grab your bag, we have a long walk, but every step we take, is further from her, and the risk of capture." Ena gave a nod as she smiled.

"I love you Dorin, since the day we met you have been there for me, and since my mother was taken, you have been my strength. No matter what we face, it can never be as dark as it was in there, just look at the sunlight, it is dazzling." She looked up with a glorious smile and stretched out her arms, and bathed in the wonder of its brightness.

Alone in the workroom, deep within the crystal box, the pendant around Ariel's neck gave a faint pulse of light.

*T*he years moved on, as Branna learned as much as she could, and practiced the spells within Ariel's book. Uther became king, and married Igraine, and the Isles of the Anglo became settled and peaceful. Rhiannon trained Eleanor who had grown into a beautiful young woman, who was loved and adored by all. Her best friend was Gwendolyn's daughter Una, and she became her travelling companion, and often attended the court of Uther under the supervision of Una's older sister Madeline.

By the time Branna had perfected the spell to allow her to travel unseen, Morgana was fifteen years old. Uther resided at Tintagel, so Branna understood the terrain, she had never forgotten the place where she saved the life of a young child. Lothar had been useful sending back information, and Branna had a plan of the castle showing the location of Morgana's room.

She had practiced many times, and was now confident that the spell would allow her to travel the great distance unseen. One evening she prepared with Roack, and stood in the centre of her room as the large black bird stood watch, as she closed her eyes and spoke the spell in her mind. Roack watched as a mist enveloped Branna, and yet she did not disappear, her body remained stood in the centre of the room, frozen like a pillar.

"It is time to pay our respects, and embrace a new power to the line of this family. I have another little raven to instruct, now is the time when we all shall rise and strike at the heart of Avalon.

Chapter Three.

Little Raven.

Branna opened her eyes, and smelt the sea air. She was stood by the window, and turned to look into the room. A large log fire burned in the hearth of the empty room, Branna walked around looking at the bed and the clothing hung on a rail of metal, there was little to the room, although she noted the large stack of books and smiled, Morgana it appeared was well educated.

After some time, lifting items of jewellery to inspect it and sitting on the bed, Branna returned to the window, where outside the waves crashed on the rocks below. Behind her she heard footsteps and then the door opened, she turned, and saw a young woman with long black hair, and eyes as dark as Roack's, she stared at Branna.

"Who are you, I was not told of any visitor, this is my private room, no one else is allowed in here?" Branna smiled.

"Fear not child, I am of your line, well to be honest, you are actually of my line. I thought it was time we spoke, and so here I am. They call me Raven; it is nice to meet you, Morgana."

She stared for a moment, looking afraid, Branna gave another smile.

"You have nothing to fear from me, I sense the feelings of those around me, and your fear is unnecessary, I have no intent to harm you. I suppose you are my great granddaughter; you are family." Morgana appeared to understand.

"Lothar has talked of you, he favours you highly, although he says you rule the family with an iron grip." Branna walked over to the large bed and sat down; she patted it with her hand.

"This is but an introductory visit, I have asked your mother several times to allow you to visit us at our home, but she has as yet declined. I fear her new life has severed the ties of your father from her, and so I decided that I would visit here this day and meet you. I would have been here sooner, but life has a habit of preventing things."

Morgana, closed the door, and walked over to the bed and sat down. Morgana was slender, dressed in a long black dress, her complexion was pale, and she had very long black sleek, straight hair. Branna could see how like her as a young girl she was, there was a very strong resemblance to her own mother in her. Morgana looked at her with a curious look.

"I was told you were stern, and would snap at the family who did not please you." Branna gave a giggle.

"I am the head of the family, and I need to be obeyed at times, and so yes, I know when to shout if needs be." Morgana smirked.

"I have wanted to meet you, I was not sure I ever would, it is not easy to get away from here, my parents do not allow me far from home. I was not here simply because I had to escort and entertain Eleanor, she is visiting at the moment, to be honest, I just wish she would go back to Avalon." Branna gave a chuckle.

"I take it, you do not like her very much, I have heard everyone thinks she is wonderful?" Morgana gave a sigh.

"I am not like them, I am different. My title is Countess of Cornwall, she is an heir to the throne of Avalon, and will one day be a queen, and so she sees me as lesser than her. I hate how everyone fawns over her, I just wish she would disappear and not come back here, I hate her visits." Branna raised her eyebrows.

"Is she really that unbearable, well if that is the case, I shall have to see what we can do about that. I cannot have a granddaughter of mine looked down upon. You come from a line of proud Sachsens, they do not bend easily to others, and have the utmost respect shown them, as I am sure you saw often with your father." Morgana put her head down for a second.

"He died when I was just four summers." Branna reached for her hand and took it in hers, and gave it a squeeze.

"I know, it was a bitter blow to me, I spent a great deal of time talking with him before he came here. I have to confess, I favoured him highly over his brother Ivor. I liked that he was highly intelligent, we spent many a long hour in my library at home discussing his plans for life. He was very proud the night you were born, I took you out of your mother and handed you straight over to him, he had the biggest smile, he was so happy." Morgana turned and looked up at her.

"You brought me into the world?" Branna gave a nod.

"I have birthed all my grandchildren; did you not know?" Morgana shook her head.

"No, I thought I was born here."

"Oh, no, your mother is lacking indeed. You were born at Castle Berengar in the Sachsen mountains. I delivered you, as your mother was struggling, and as is the case with many in my household, I was the first to see you and I may add, the first to hold you. Your mother did not have a good time, Victor's father, your grandfather Otto, is quite the moody and bad tempered one. He has some very odd views on life and was not pleased when he met your mother, and it showed a little. Once you were born, I travelled with your mother back here, and I spent a month here, helping out, before I had to return home." Morgana put her head down, and stared at the carpet, Branna sensed her sadness.

"I did not know, mother does not talk of father's family, and I do not like my new father, he is a liar, he does not play fair. He cheated my mother and father, and it caused my father's death. I am glad you came; I get very lonely at times." Branna gave a nod.

"I am well aware of what Uther did, and one day he will pay for his treachery, have no fear, the line of Berengar always seeks justice for those who hurt our family. You are not alone, you will always have me, and in time I will show you how to talk to me without worry. Morgana, I am only here for a little while, so why don't you tell me of Uther and what you saw, and give me the details of your life here, and let me see if there is anything we can do to improve it."

*F*or the young Morgana, who felt lost and isolated in a world in which she felt she did not belong, Branna to her was an inspiration, as they sat on her bed and quietly talked. She spoke for the first time about how she really felt, she found she had someone who would listen and take her seriously.

Morgana talked of her strange feelings for the first time, and the pain she felt at losing her father, and how she thought Uther had used her mother and taken advantage of her. She talked of how she felt her mother was shamed and humiliated into marrying Uther, who did not love her, but saw her as a prize of war. Branna quietly took it all in, as the treachery of Merlin and the support of the Ruling Council and their plans to control the world of men was made more apparent to her. It was clear that Morgana was highly intelligent and motivated, and was no fool, especially when it came to Rhiannon and her family, and her corrupt rule.

It was late when Branna explained that her family line had gifts that were powerful, and how she could help Morgana understand herself better, and by the time she had to leave, it was clear, that a bond had been forged between them both. Branna saw in Morgana a great deal of the young woman she had been as she fought to survive on the Moon Realm, before she came to Avalon.

It was clear in her mind, that this was her one chance to help Morgana grow to power, but rule with a more even hand, and she knew in that moment, she would grow to mentor the young woman, and guide her in the ways of the Berengar line.

When the time came to leave, Morgana embraced her with a smile, it was clear it had been an important moment to her, and Branna assured her that she would remain in touch. When she returned to the Castle of Berengar, she had a better idea of what she needed to do. Rhiannon was her target, and after seeing some of the pain within Morgana, she could not help but feel her anger towards the golden queen grow more.

As she came out of her trance, she looked across the room at Roack sat on the window.

"It is time to begin, and with Morgana to aide us, we will finally start and strike at the heart of Rhiannon's precious kingdom. She will now feel a taste of the strength of the Raven, and I aim to bring fear to her heart and rob her of the love in her life as she has robbed me. She took my family, and now I plan to take hers."

*I*t took several days of study in the library, but Branna was making a plan in her mind. She knew Eleanor was to stay at Tintagel for some time, and so she knew just where to find her, and so began her first strike at the heart of Avalon.

She returned to her workroom filled with her potions and bottles, and began working. Roack was interested and flew down to the window and watched as she worked, and Branna made a sweet smelling paste. Roack was curious.

"What is it you make?" Branna's eyes lifted to the large black bird.

"I have a gift for a lady who is the adoration of all, nothing more. If Rhiannon wants Dark Fae, she will have one for a daughter, that is if her delicate little system can cope with it." Roack bobbed on the window ledge.

"We like this Branna the Raven; we like that we are fighting back in the heart of the light. She was cruel to us, and she will pay for it." Branna looked down to the paste as she mixed it with care.

"Many Fae have suffered because of her and her lies, this will show her the true meaning of what it is like to be dark. Half of my race are imprisoned or worked to death early in their lives, so that the golden may prosper. It is time she learned that all dark haired Fae are carriers of the darkness, and some of those of gold can also take the darkness to her."

Roack bobbed about watching as Branna mixed the paste, and then poured it into a beautifully engraved container of silver.

"All I need now is the final ingredient, and for that I need you. I want you to put a concentrated small fragment of your darkness into this before it cools, can you do that?" Roack flew to the table and landed beside the container.

"We like this idea, and we can do that Branna the raven."

Branna smiled, and walked over to the doors and pulled them closed. In a way it felt foolish, but in her mind, this was something Branna did not want Ariel to see.

Roack focused, and then as Branna turned and watched, a small amount of the darkest smoke she had ever seen, slowly came out of Roack's chest, and hovered above the container. Roack gave a squawk, and it dropped into the smooth cream coloured paste, and Branna walked over and lifted the lid and screwed it on.

"Let's see how she feels when her daughter is infected, will she have the guts to take it out of her at the cost of her own life?"

Deep down inside, Branna wondered if Rhiannon would actually do the right thing. Would she give her life to save her daughter as Ariel was prepared to, she was unsure, but it would be fascinating to see if she would?

*T*he visit from Branna, made a huge change to the life of Morgana, as several days passed, and she felt her spirits lifted. In a strange way she felt she had a connection to something other than the life she had been forced to live in court. Knowing that somewhere inside she had powers, interested her and she wanted to know more, her only problem was that within court, the only person she knew of with any kind of power, was Merlin, or Rhiannon in Avalon.

She scoured the library for anything that might give her some idea of how these powers would work, but there was nothing, and she left feeling disappointed, and walked along the high cliff path to her favourite spot that overlooked the bay to think.

Lost in thought staring out at the sea, her dark hair lifting off her shoulders, she did not notice when Branna appeared and sat down beside her. Suddenly understanding someone was there, she came out of her thoughts and jumped with fright. Branna chuckled.

"Sorry, I thought you heard me approach. You remind me very much of myself in my first days in the world of men, I sat down there, just as you have and stared at the sea to clear my thoughts and think."

Morgana turned and looked down the cliff, and the small stretch of white sand.

"You sat there, when was that?" Branna gave a nod, and looked to the spot.

"It was a long time ago. I used to live in Avalon, but I gave all of that up and came out into the world of men to discover the truth of life and learn about who I really was. I was deeply in love with someone who had been taken from me at that time, and I sat there on that beach, and thought of her, as I missed her. It was just one night, but I have never forgotten it, as that was the night, I decided to leave this land and seek a life on other continents, as far from the Fae and this land as possible." Morgana stared at the sea.

"Did you ever reunite with your lover?" Branna gave a happy sigh and smiled.

"I did, we had many years together. She is lost to me now, but not a day passes that she is not in my thoughts." Morgana turned.

"She… I thought you were with the lord of the castle?" Branna gave a nod.

"I am, I rule at his side, the people of Fae do not frown upon love, no matter what the union, they believe love is pure and should be cherished, it is something I find the world of men has to learn and accept. So, Morgana of Berengar, tell me, why do you sit alone and stare out at the waves, surely a young woman such as yourself cannot have all the woes of life on her shoulders by now?"

"Is it strange that I feel things and no one else does? I cannot explain it, but I feel things, strange things inside me, and I do not know who I can talk to about it."

Branna understood the unsettled feelings that coursed through young Fae, she too had felt something similar growing up, she patted her shoulder, and smiled.

"It is the part of you that is Fae. I am the start of your line, and in the males, the Fae part of my blood appears to have weakened, but in the female it strengthens. I was the same at your age, and my mother sat with me and explained that with time, the powers I held would come to the surface, and when they did, she would teach me all about them and how to use them. It is the reason I am here, and why I wanted you to come to my home, for soon they will surface, and when they do, I will guide you in them."

Morgana turned to her, and her dark eyes appeared to fill with life.

"I would love that, but I fear my mother will not allow it, she mourns the loss of her child and keeps me closer than ever. I went to find out if there were books, I could read, but there is nothing written about any kind of powers. Those I asked frowned and asked me to leave." Branna gave it some thought.

"The world of men fears our powers, I know of some who have been given names and tortured because of their power. Morgana, you must never let any know that you are of a Fae line, the world of men is ignorant of much, they have no understanding and fear us, for we are a more powerful line than they are. Trust me, the less they know the better. I take it the child Merlin took has not returned?" Morgana shook her head.

"My mother weeps often for the loss of her son, it is again another reason why I hate my new father. He bargained her first son with Merlin so he could have his way with her, I do not care what others say, I think Merlin is evil, and one day I will get my revenge on him."

Branna could feel the rage grow inside Morgana, as she spoke of Merlin, she too wanted to get even with him for the death of Victor, she gave the moment some thought as she stared out to sea.

"We have much in common my little raven, I too have a debt to settle with him for the loss of my grandson, maybe this is a task we could share, as he is very powerful and from what I have heard, he is very intelligent. I will think on it for a while, and when I have an idea, I will come to you. From this day talk to no one of your powers but me, for I will come to you often. For the time being, if you wish to understand powers, look to the powers of the natural world, for there are many things we can use in it. I studied the lore of the plants for many years, and in doing so, found their properties enhanced the powers I hold. Learn the cures of the land and their uses, it will be of great value to you later."

Morgana understood, and felt a little hope grow within her.

"I am glad you came to me, although I fear you may tire of my questions, for there is much I wish to learn." Branna gave a chuckle.

"I once said the very same thing to my mother, she laughed and every time I had a question, she answered me honestly. She never grew weary of me; I loved her more for that." Morgana frowned.

"Did you lose her, has she passed on?" Branna shook her head.

"No, she lives, but I cannot see her, she is on the realm Ofmoon, a prisoner in the slave labour camps of Rhiannon. She was taken in my thirtieth summer, and I have not seen her since, as was my father and brother. Rhiannon is seen as wise and beautiful, but there is another side to her no one sees, be wary of her my little raven, she has quite the sting. She will understand the true meaning of losing family that is loved, I will see to it, and then she will learn the wisdom of her cruel acts, and fully understand the power of us ravens." Morgana smiled.

"I like that you say us." Branna gave a contented sigh.

"You are one of us Morgana, you too are a Raven of Berengar, but we are few. In years to come we have a lot to accomplish, so that the likes of Merlin, Uther and Rhiannon understand that people are not their pawns to play with."

Morgana drew her knees up to her chin, and leaned forward onto them, Branna watched and smiled as she could see her thinking about what they had spoken about. She was pale and drawn, and yet her eyes as they looked out over the sea were alert, and filled with intelligence, as her hair wafted in the soft breeze behind her.

There was something about the way she watched, the sense of her being, and it stirred deeply within Branna, as she understood the loneliness within her. In many ways, Branna could see how much they had in common, Morgana stirred and turned to look at her, her eyes were bright and seeking understanding.

"Can you answer me one question, because I have thought of it often, and yet I still cannot work out the answer?" Branna gave a nod.

"If I can, I will, what is it you want to know?" She took a deep breath, and paused for a second.

"Merlin is supposed to be a powerful wizard, a man of peace, a man who can persuade other men to act civil yes, so why would he do something as underhanded as use magic to make Uther look like my father? It makes no sense to me, he is a wizard, he could have used magic to quell Uther's lust to keep the peace, and yet he did not."

Branna sat back and thought about it, the simple truth was it was a really good question, and she could not give an immediate answer. She looked at Morgana's searching gaze.

"I cannot say for sure; you are right, he is supposed to be powerful. All I can think of at this moment, is that he was part of the big plan of the council to sit Uther as king, and your father was possibly his greatest opponent. Morgana, sometimes it is the best tactic to remove possible future problems, and maybe your father was seen as a threat, because he was seen as a powerful man, and possibly as powerful as a king. Maybe Merlin thought it best he was taken out of everything as quickly as possible, the truth is we will never really know, but your question is a valid one, and it holds great merit." Morgana gave a long sigh.

"I would like to study this so called powerful magic, just to see how powerful Merlin really is, because if you ask me, he is not as wise as he pretends." Branna gave a gentle shrug.

"Then why don't you? All knowledge is power, study the white lines of time, and see for yourself." Morgana frowned at Branna.

"How?" Branna shrugged.

"Ask… You have power, but it is still in its infancy, he will sense it within you as I do. Ask, and see if he will take you on as a student."

"But what about you, will you not be disappointed with me?" Branna gave a small chuckle.

"Oh, my little Raven, anything we can learn will aid us. I am skilled, but even so, I learnt much from my Fae lover, she taught me many new things to add to my list of gifts. He will teach you things I cannot, as I can teach you things, he has no knowledge of. Learn both and balance them both, for I know for sure, that knowing both sides, will enhance your true power. I say ask him, and if he agrees, then do it."

Branna stood up and looked around, somethings had changed little over the years, and she recognised some of the area from her journey years ago.

"I have two reasons for being here today, you were my most

important, but I still have another task to accomplish." Morgana stood up and looked at her as her hair blew round in front of her face, and yet Branna's did not move, she stared at Branna for a moment.

"Why does the wind not have an effect on you, your hair has not moved, and yet mine blows across my eyes?" Branna gave a little chuckle.

"What you see is my ability to walk unseen, my hair does not blow, because where I am really stood, there is no breeze." Morgana frowned, and Branna gave a smile.

"At this moment in time, the real me is stood in my workroom in my castle, what you see is my essence, that has travelled here to meet with you, this is one of many spells I will teach you in time. Here in this form, I cannot be seen or detected. I choose who does and does not see me. Few would notice, I am glad you did though, it shows how sharp your mind is, and for magic, that is a good thing." Morgana gave a nod, it made sense to her, and Branna smiled at her.

"I have to go, but I will see you soon, take care of yourself my little raven, and learn the plant lore, it will be a big help to you."

Branna raised her hand and snapped her fingers hard, and in a flash, she was gone, and Morgana was stood alone on the path above the cliff tops, she gave a smile.

"I would love to learn that."

*I*n the busy centre of Tintagel, Una and Eleanor separated, as Una needed to gather things for her mother, and Eleanor had spied a stall covered with bangles made of shell. As she looked at the many items lay on the stall, a stranger walked to her side and looked at the jewellery on display.

"They may be hand made, but they are far too overpriced, I would be careful young mistress, this one will ask far more than the value of their worth."

Eleanor turned to the woman in black with a shawl over her head, and smiled.

"Do you know much of things like this?" Branna smiled.

"I once had a man who made these things and we traded all down the coast." She lowered her voice and leaned in.

"He was far cheaper than this, he did not believe in over pricing his items and traded fairly, this one is not, they are robbing people blind." Eleanor looked at the bracelets and bangles, and gave a nod to

Branna.

"Thank you, I will be more aware in future. What happened if you do not mind me asking, did your man leave?" Branna shook her head.

"No, he was enlisted and was killed in the war, since then I have traded my own wares alone, I did not have skill with the shell splitting. I make soothing balms, for the skin when it flares up. It cures pimples and boils and takes away the inflammation of the skin, it is a special recipe passed down from my grandmother." Eleanor seemed quite excited.

"Do you have your stand here today? I suffer at times with blemishes of red, and I have to apply a great deal of powder at times to hide them." Branna shook her head.

"I was hoping to trade, but my latest batch has to set for a day, and I was late in the making. I have only one pot, and it is not worth holding a stall with just one, I will be back in two days for the market then." Eleanor looked disappointed.

"That is sad, I would have bought some, I have a spot forming I can feel it." She rubbed the side of her face, and Branna leaned in to look.

"I see what you mean, I can see it swelling… Look I have one pot only, and I suppose your need is greater, I usually sell two for one penny." She pulled the silver pot out of her pocket, and it shone in the sunlight, Eleanor smiled when she saw it.

"The container is beautiful." Branna smiled.

"It is to my fortune that my husband made me many, I fear when the time comes and I run out, I will need to seek a worker of metal to match his skill." Eleanor handed her a penny.

"I will gladly pay a penny for such a beautiful thing." Branna gave a tut.

"Oh no, I cannot have that, come and see me on Friday and I will give you another, I believe in fairness of trade, and you are such a pretty girl. It is a fine paste that is scented, apply it just before bed and rub it well in all over the face, and when it is soaked into the skin, sleep well, and you will rise radiant and spot free."

Eleanor gave a big smile, and looked at the silver pot with excited eyes.

"Thank you for your kindness mistress, I will see you again in two days. My friend awaits and I must go." Branna smiled.

"See you in two days, and remember, rub it well all over the face, then sleep well."

"I will."

Eleanor turned and ran across the busy market to where she saw Una approaching with her older sister, she showed her the pot and told of her the woman of kindness and her balm. Una looked across the busy stalls at all the people and traders, and yet there was no older woman in black, she felt a strange tingle in her fingers.

Branna sat back in her seat and gave a smile at Roack, as she lifted the bottle and poured out a glass of red wine.

"Tonight, fear will strike at the heart of Avalon, I feel Rhiannon will be changing her plans, for by morning, she will be forced to stay sat on her pampered seat, and rethink her plans for leaving Avalon." Branna lifted her glass and took a sip as Roack bobbed on the window ledge.

"Roack, she took my parents and my brother, and now I have lost Ariel. Rhiannon has no understanding of the pains to a person to lose such love, but tonight, I will reach into her safe and protected land of the golden, and for the first time in her life, she will know the truth of fear."

"You have done well Branna the Raven, what news have you of the young one?" Branna put down her glass, and looked at the long box of crystal.

"Ariel was right, I really felt the strength of her powers today, and she will be strong. I feel she is moving at the right pace, soon she will come to us, and that will be a good thing. The council have been busy, they have meddled in many affairs, and I feel they are responsible for the downfall of Victor, and also my son, and grandson. I will watch and when I see a chance, I will strike at their heart. Morgana will be useful, we must bring her into the family as soon as she is able, although I still have the problem of Maud. Morgana will need to be protected. When Maud senses her powers, she may feel threatened, for I think we can say, Morgana will rise to be a powerful raven one day."

Chapter Four.

The Heart of Avalon.

Rhiannon enjoyed the social scene of life in Avalon, the town of Avalonia was a shining symbol of the Fae, and so when visiting dignitaries from the land of Gaul arrived, she promptly organised a banquet in the lavish and stylish hall in the Citadel, on top of the mount.

The huge round hall with its ornate glass ceiling, was decked out in flowers, and long tables were laid with the very best silverware and candelabras, and guests from all of the region were invited. Rayne and Eleanor were recalled immediately back to Avalon, and some of the high lords of the moon realm came down to attend.

Uther and Igraine with Morgana were guests of honour, and so in Tintagel with the help of Merlin, there was a quick packing of belongings, and soon carriages and horses rolled into Avalonia, and all the guest dwellings were filled.

On the white steps outside, Marshals of the Fae dressed in blue, wearing white gloves, opened doors on carriages and directed the dignitaries and guests up the steps into the Citadel, where Rhiannon in a long flowing silver dress welcomed all.

Branna had not been wrong when she told Ariel the halls of Avalon ran gold, as fair haired members of the Fae Ofmoon dressed in their finest clothes, smiled and mingled with the guests. Rhiannon knew how to entertain in style, and tables were laden with the finest of everything, from foods from every realm, to the very finest of wines.

It was a dazzling display of wealth and status, as she sat at the head of the table and talked in many languages to the guests from every nation, as dark haired members of the Fae fetched and carried the many courses of the meal.

Gwendolyn took note, as she sat with her three daughters, and remembered the words of her grandmother, for it was obvious to her, how little had changed since her grandmother had reigned as Queen of the Fae of Earth.

For three hours the guests sat and ate their fill, and then there was music, and dancing and more wine flowed. Rayne stood at the side of the large doors, watching, as Gwendolyn walked up and gave him a smile.

"Your mother is quite the host, never have I seen such a lavish affair, it is impressive." Rayne watched her across the room, as she smiled and laughed, talking to an ambassador from Gaul, and gave a sigh.

"You know my mother; everything has to be bigger and brighter than anyone else." Gwendolyn smiled.

"I take it things are still a little icy between you two?" He smirked.

"There is ice, and then there is her attitude towards me, and trust me, the ice is warmer." Gwendolyn gave a chuckle.

"You are an asset of great value, one day she will see it Rayne. My grandmother thought very highly of you, she often expressed how you had a love of your people and always did the right thing for them." Rayne smiled as he watched the dancers.

"That is the problem though isn't it, doing the right thing is not always what Mother wants?" Gwendolyn shrugged.

"How is Luminaria, I have heard you visit her often? You know, I never understood what happened with you two, she loved you deeply Rayne, and here you are still without a bride, and doing all you can to free her. I heard you petitioned your mother with her brother, on her behalf again?" For a moment, Rayne looked a little saddened as he looked into the bright blue eyes of Gwendolyn.

"Luminaria was only guilty of being honest, she does not deserve to be sent back to work the lower prisons as a captain. She did her job as sworn to her queen, and presented the truth, the problem was it did not suit the politics of my mother. She is doing well though, I admire her, she has accepted her position and carries it out with complete competence, but I feel, she deserves better. Stenlow is a good man, but he is nowhere near as good a replacement." He took a sip of his drink.

"Luminaria is a fine woman Gwen, and if she was free now, then maybe I would have considered marriage. I cared for her deeply, but I was not ready, admittedly, I was being pushed, but in all truth, I wanted something more than a career military wife. My friends tell me I am too picky, but to date I have met few I would say held my eye long enough." Gwendolyn gave a chuckle.

"So, what about Opal, I have heard you and her spend a lot of time in the forest, she most certainly has a spirit as wild as yours?" He started to laugh.

"She most certainly is wild and untamed. We do spend a lot of time together, we hunt and have mapped out the marshes, but I can assure you, we are merely good friends, I fear she may be too wild even for me." Gwendolyn turned and spotted her with her long red hair and bright blue eyes.

"She is certainly very attractive, although she does appear a little out of place dressed in fine silks, the poor girl looks positively uncomfortable." He smirked, as he watched her.

"It is probably having to actually wear clothing; I am sure she will be fine when she returns to the forest, strips and dives into the pools there."

They both stood laughing as they watched the scene, and the night was wearing on and some guests were starting to leave. For Rhiannon it was yet another glorious success, as she had once again, shown the world her power and might as a leader within the Ruling Council.

*M*organa walked down the steps of the citadel and onto the wide rock, and walked softly towards the edge, and looked out as the darkness fell, and the moon rose large and bright above the realm, reflecting in the lake below. She was hot and tired, and the feel of the soft breeze on her face felt cooling. Deep within her she felt a stirring she could not explain, almost like a feeling of dread, which flowed around her, as if something bad was about to happen.

She stared out towards the forest, sensing something she could not quite pinpoint. Little did she know that far away across the realm, stood high on the large mountain known as the Giant's Shoulder, next to an old wind battered tree, stood a dark solitary figure watching. Branna was on the very edge of the realm, on the border of the Forest of Time, far away enough to not be detected by Rhiannon, but within sight, to watch as Rhiannon yet again flaunted her prowess and power. Stood still and silent, in her long hooded cloak of dark feathers, her dark eyes watched, her voice quiet and low, so only she would hear it.

"There lies the home you robbed from Ariel and myself, and soon you will know what it is like to suffer like I have. Soon, I will take from you, what you stole from me, enjoy your night Rhiannon, my golden queen, for after tonight, you too will feel my touch, and the scratch of a raven, and all the loss it brings." In an instant she was gone, and the breeze blew over the cooling stone of white, and stirred up the dust, where Branna had stood moments earlier.

Morgana watched over the realm, as a figure walked up to her side, and she did not notice straight away. His voice was soft, and filled with care.

"Still avoiding the crowds, isolating yourself, I see? Morgana, you would have such a good life if you found a place for yourself." She turned to see Merlin watching her from his young face with his intense green eyes.

"I feel there is nothing here for me, I feel I do not belong. The king wants a son not the burden of an adopted daughter, and my mother is filled with grief from the loss of her child." He gave her a smile, but softly shook his head.

"Morgana you are so wrong, Uther cares for you more than you realise, he is trying, but you push him away. Can you not find it within yourself to allow him closer, instead of isolating yourself away from everyone?" She stared at him, feeling her insides swirl.

"Give him back his son, and then you will see, his time for me will wane, and the truth of the king will be seen by all. I have no wish to be his play thing until he produces another heir. I have the life I chose; I study, for within me I know there are hidden gifts, I just need to find them and then find my own way in this world. I am happy to be left alone, I do not want the same things as Eleanor or your children."

"You choose a hard road, especially with no one to guide you. Morgana, is it not more prudent to find a mentor, someone you could look to on the road you have chosen?" She gave a scoff.

"Like who, you? Would you guide me, and share your knowledge, would you open your world and teach me of the gifts you have and the powers you control, for that is where my interest lies? I do not want the mundane life of a lady of court, I do not want a husband, I want to learn everything about everything, and dedicate my life to study, why is it so wrong for me to wish for what any man can freely have?"

Merlin stood back and looked her up and down, he had a slight smile to his lips, she shrugged as she looked at him.

"I am stronger than most of the women here, I can carry the

weight of knowledge, is it so unusual, to be a student of the world for a woman?" He gave a smile.

"I cannot deny, I am intrigued and you have my interest. Morgana, you must realise, the study of the Whitelines is not an easy path, it is hard, and at times will test you to the core. The power of the Whitelines can place a heavy burden on a young mind, are you telling me you can seriously handle the burdens it will place upon you?" She gave a laugh.

"My mind is stronger than any man who walks here, and I will prove it." He gave a nod.

"So I see. Hmm, I feel maybe I should discuss this with your parents, you will not be able to remain at Tintagel, you will have to move here. It will be a solitary life for a long time Morgana, you will be responsible for yourself, there will be no other to support you on this journey, for there will be lessons you must face alone."

"I am already alone; it is all I have known since my father died. I have no fancy maids; I take care of myself, and I am more than capable." He raised his eyebrows.

"Alright then, I will talk with your parents, and if they agree, I will consider your request to become my apprentice. Somehow, I feel, it will be an education for both of us." She smiled.

"I will not let you down, I know this is something that is right for me, it is the life I choose."

"I shall see what the outcome of a conversation with your parents is first, and then we will talk." He gave a bow, and Morgana bowed back.

*D*eep below the mount, inside the crystal castle on the mirrored waters, there was an almighty scream. It reverberated across the clear waters of the lake sending ripples across its glass like surface and stirring the waters as they lapped along the shores. Merlin turned, feeling alarmed, and in a flash, he was gone. Morgana turned back to look at the steps, where there was a lot of commotion. She gave a sigh and turned back to look out across the realm, her mind filled with thoughts of learning the powers that would fill her mind and the emptiness she felt inside. She was looking forward to the next visit of her Lady Raven, so she could share her news.

*I*n the bed chamber of Eleanor, the daughter of the queen of the realm convulsed on the bed, her face burning red as she screamed riddled with incredible pain. The maids flustered unable to get close, as Eleanor thrashed around screaming in agony.

There was a blinding flash of white, and Rhiannon appeared in the centre of the room, a look of terror on her face as she saw her daughter writhing and thrashing out, and screaming with terror in pain. A second flash of white followed closely by a flash of blue brought Merlin and Gwendolyn into the room, Rhiannon stood frozen, unable to think, as Gwendolyn rushed to the side of the bed, Merlin at her side.

Her palm shot over the child as she thrashed kicking out with her arms and legs, as if possessed by all the demons of hell. Gwendolyn looked panicked as she looked at Merlin.

"Her mind is going to fracture; we must do something." Merlin lifted his fingers.

SNAP!

Eleanor slumped onto the bed and lay still, as black froth erupted from her mouth, as the roots of her hair turned dark, colouring her hair slowly from golden to a dark rich black. Rhiannon stepped back her hands to her mouth, her face white, and painted with a look of sheer horror. Her voice was almost silent.

"What is happening to her?" Merlin looked back at her.

"I am not sure; I have seen nothing like this before." Gwendolyn's hands were glowing white as she leaned over Eleanor, her voice contained her fear.

"We need to act fast; it is draining her life force, I can only hold her for so long. Merlin do something, or we will lose her."

Eleanor began to shake, as more of the black froth poured up out of her mouth soaking the bed, a strange gurgling emitting from deep within her throat. Gwendolyn gasped as Merlin's hand exploded with white light, and he pressed it onto her stomach.

"This is not poisoning, whatever it is, it is growing within her, her whole body is infected with something evil." Gwendolyn looked back.

"Rhiannon, do something, we are losing your daughter." Rhiannon's eyes filled with tears.

"I do not know what to do, I have no idea what it is, help me, I cannot lose her, she is my most precious gift in this world."

She fell to her knees as the door exploded open, and Rayne came charging in. He faltered in his steps as he saw the scene, and felt his breath catch in his throat. He swallowed hard as he saw his mother in tears, and Eleanor lay violently shaking as Gwendolyn and Merlin stood over her trying between them to hold her life.

He stepped forward and roughly grabbed his mother by the arm as she wept on the floor. With a huge wrench, he dragged her up and flung her at the bed.

"SHE IS YOUR DAUGHTER, SAVE HER, YOU ARE SUPPOSED TO BE THE MOST POWERFUL, NOW USE IT!"

Rhiannon crashed to the floor at the side of the bed, as Rayne stepped up and his hands exploded with light, he pushed them hard onto Eleanor.

"I beg all the lords of all the realms, if it is a life you need to take, then take mine, do not rob this land of my most precious sister."

The whole room lit up, as Rayne pushed all of his life force into Eleanor, and she jerked on the bed, and opened her eyes, as she shuddered violently, a look of fear on her face. She coughed out the filth from her mouth and tears formed in her eyes.

"Rayne, I am frightened; I do not want to die." He looked down from within the white light with tears in his eyes.

"You won't."

She smiled as Rhiannon reached over and took her daughters hand, Eleanor turned and looked at her mother and smiled, and then she gave a violent wretch, and thick black oozed from her mouth. Rhiannon's eyes opened wide and with one final jerk of her body, Eleanor shuddered no more. Rayne collapsed onto the floor completely spent and passed out. Gwendolyn turned and knelt down to him, and across Avalon a deafening wail of pain shook the realm, and the sky exploded with lights.

*M*organa stood unable to understand what was happening, all around the realm people fell to their knees covering their ears, and wailing with anguish, and softly in her ears she heard a few spoken whispered words.

"Feel the power of a Raven." Morgana smiled.

*I*n a garden, under a large apple tree, next to a tiny house, fifteen miles behind the Citadel Mount, the almost translucent figure of a woman in a long feathered hooded cloak, stood silent and still, as she looked through the window onto a messy room with a bed that had its sheets torn from it, and cast on the floor.

She lifted her hand and wiped her eyes under her large hood, her voice was soft and filled with pain.

"This was the life I should have had; this was the life I wanted. Just this, I wanted so little, and you could not let me have it. It is not much, just Ariel and me, living happily, a simple life of love, and care. Tonight, my precious queen, I have taken something as precious to you, forgive me Ariel, but she had to pay for what she did to us."

There was a soft sob, and the figure faded away into the darkness, and the garden fell silent.

*T*wo days later in the vast hall within the mount, with walls of white, with rich seems of amethyst, Eleanor, princess of Avalon lay sealed in state in a box of glass and gold. Her mother had washed her, and dressed her, covered her black hair in a wrapping of pure white, and placed her on a bed of silk.

The vast hall was filled with flowers as thousands of bouquets adorned the floor, and in the silence broken only by the water running over the statues of the fountain, there came the soft sniffles of Una, daughter of Gwendolyn, as she knelt on the floor before her lost friend, with her head down.

Around the hall, in front of every door, stood a guard of the Marshals in full ceremonial robes, their swords of gleaming silver held before them, in a salute to the fallen, some of which had tears in their eyes.

The loss of Eleanor was felt right across the realm, as every citizen wore black and wept openly in the streets. Eleanor had been a beacon of all that was pure in the realm of Avalon, and to lose her so young, was a devastating blow to the whole realm.

*T*he queen of the realm had not been seen, she had prepared her daughter, and then retired to her rooms and had remained there, her doors locked and all staff were banished. The atmosphere in the crystal castle was one of heartbreak, as the staff maintained their duties and wept as they worked.

Rayne, prince of the realm, lay lost to his state of dreams, exhausted in a bed at the home of Merlin and Gwendolyn, as her daughters sat and wept in their rooms. Branna was right, the touch of the raven would bring darkness to the realm, for even though Avalonia was still the glorious and bright white city it had always been, somehow it felt dimmer, with less light as the realm lay in a state of mourning. Gwendolyn came out of the room and looked at Madeleine.

"How is Una?" She walked into the main room with her, and Maddy gave a sigh.

"She is still up at the mount, she wanted to be alone with her. Una has taken it badly, those two were very close. Mother, how did this happen, what was it that killed her? Mel is really worried there is some strange disease in the realm, is this something from the realm of men?" Gwendolyn sat down by the fire and leaned back in the seat, she felt tired.

"Honestly Maddy, I have no idea. After the funeral, I want you to take your sisters back to the house in Morbihan. Until I can find out more, I want you girls safe. Your father and I will have to remain until we know what caused this." Maddy gave a nod, her watery blue eyes watched her mother carefully.

"I know I should not say it, but Mother, is this what struck at the heart of Florae, you know, that was an illness of darkness as well?" Gwendolyn stared at the wall.

"That was more a series of dark thoughts that led to melancholy, this was dreadful, blackness just poured out of her, I have never seen anything like it. I will not deny, Maddy it scared me, your father and I, as well as Rayne pumped a life force into her that would revive a thousand men, Rayne came close to giving his own life to save her, nothing could stop it."

"How is he?" Gwendolyn sighed.

"He is reviving slowly, but I feel it is his heartbreak and sense of loss, which is slowing his progress. Rayne needs a reason to live, and currently, she is lay in state in the great hall. I fear for him too."

"What will you do Mother?"

"I am going to talk to Sequana, I need her influence to bring me the one thing he needs to recover. I need her daughter, Luminaria, if she cannot bring him back, no one can. I had hoped Opal's visit would help, but he needs someone with a stronger connection, and she may be the only one alive who can help him now."

*U*na walked out on to the top of the mount and breathed in a deep breath of air. Her eyes were red from her tears, and she carried a small cloth handkerchief in her hands, as she slowly walked to the edge of the mount and looked down. Behind her there was a faint flash of blue, as her mother appeared at her side, Una took a deep breath, as she fought with her grief.

"Why did I not see this, I should have seen something, why did I not see it?"

"Listen my daughter, you are still young, and your powers are still early in their development. Una, do not blame yourself, there are two queens in this realm, and we did not see this either. There will always be times when our sight is blind, we cannot see everything in this world."

Una turned as her mothers' arms came around her, and she buried her face deeply into her as she sobbed deep bitter sobs. Gwendolyn pulled her close, and held her tight.

"I am sorry such pain is part of your early life, I wanted none of the pain I have suffered in your lives. Losing someone so close is a bitter pain to carry, I know, I lost my grandmother and grandfather, and also Ariel. Even now after years without them, I feel the pain." Una gave a sniffle.

"She was so young and so fair, Mother she was the kindest person I have ever known, she did not deserve this." Gwendolyn breathed out a sigh.

"I know my darling, this is the one time I wish I could offer some wisdom, but I have nothing I can say that will make this feel easier, for I too am at a loss as to why this happened." Gwendolyn softly pulled her back and looked down at her.

"Will you be alright, I am worried about you, I know how you feel things deeper than most? If it helps, Madeleine can take some of this from you." Una shook her head.

"No, I will carry the loss of my friend for life, and I shall never forget her. I will honour her in life with my memories of her." Gwendolyn understood, and gave a soft smile.

"I feel that would please her, she loved you dearly as her friend, I feel you honour her greatly my darling."

*G*wendolyn slipped her arm round her daughter's shoulder, and together they slowly walked back to the steps of the Citadel. A bright white flash erupted in front of them and Merlin stepped out looking concerned, he looked Gwendolyn right in the eyes.

"I need you to come with me, it is important." He looked at Una.

"Una my darling, I need your mother to come with me, will you be alright alone?" At their side a young lord turned, and looked at them.

"Your Highness, My Lord Merlin, if it pleases, I would feel honoured to ensure the safety of your daughter to her destination." Gwendolyn turned and smiled.

"My Lord Kane, that is very noble of you, if my daughter has no objection, I am sure that would be very well received, we thank you."

Kane offered his arm, and Una slid slowly from her mother's arm, and took his, Merlin took Gwendolyn by the hand.

"Dire things have happened here, and I am at a loss, but you must see this."

There was a brilliant flash of light, as Kane walked Una off towards the Citadel, and in another flash Merlin and Gwendolyn arrived in the bed chamber of Eleanor. Gwendolyn looked around and frowned.

"I thought the queen had sealed this room off?" Merlin winked.

"She has, but when has something like the rule of a queen ever stopped us?" Gwendolyn giggled.

"Alright, what is so important that we have to break the queens rule?"

Merlin took her hand and led her round the room, to the table with brushes and small jars of perfumes and creams.

"You must not touch it, but place your hand above it, and tell me what you sense, it is faint, but it is there."

Gwendolyn looked down at the silver container, which was elaborately etched, and held her hand above it. A cold sensation ran through her whole body and she pulled her hand away and shuddered.

"What is this I sense, for it creeps through me and makes me afraid?" Merlin gave a nod.

"I can only speculate, but if you ask me, whatever is in that container, is the purest darkness." Gwendolyn looked shocked.

"What are you implying, are you honestly saying that the death of Eleanor was deliberate?" He lifted his eyebrows as he looked at her.

"Do you have a better theory?" She swallowed hard, as she looked back at the ornate container, adorned with a raven, surrounded by scrolls and flowers.

"But who?" He shrugged.

"Gwen, there are dark deeds here, and we have an assassin in our midst. I want you out of here, I want you safe, take the children and return to Florae, and protect yourself."

Chapter Five.

The Passing of Eleanor.

Roack watched, as Branna came out of her trance from walking hidden in the realm of Avalon, she gave a sigh and looked at the large black bird sat on the window.

"Eleanor has gone, Rhiannon will now have an understanding of those she has abused in her kingdom. Roack, I need to be alone for a while, I want some time with Ariel." The Bird understood, broke the connection and left. Branna walked over and looked down at the glass box, and tried to smile, her voice was a little higher than normal.

"I saw our home, I went there, Ariel, it has not changed, it is exactly as we left it." Her eyes filled with tears as she tried to smile.

"It will need a clean up, and a bit of a dust, but it is there just waiting for us."

Her tears dropped onto the glass, as she watched Ariel's sleeping face, and she gave a sob.

"I am sorry my love, my anger got the better of me, and I took a life of an innocent. I did not mean for her to die, I just wanted her to suffer so Rhiannon understood the pain she has caused, and Eleanor died." She gave another big sob.

"I miss you; I wish you could hold me; I really need you tonight."

In many ways it was strange, because the death of Eleanor gave Branna no pleasure at all, if anything she regretted it. Her aim all along was to teach Rhiannon a lesson, but it had been a fatal one, which was not her intention. Eleanor was not as strong as Branna had thought, her Fae powers where nowhere near as powerful as they should have been. It was a miscalculation, but never the less, the lesson had been served to the Queen of the Moon, and in that she felt closer to her lifelong goal.

Rhiannon did suffer, she was broken hearted, and for a whole week as Eleanor lay in state, and the people of the realm made many visits, she remained in her room, racked with grief and weeping into her pillows. Pwhyll arrived and took a custodial role in the realm, and arranged the funeral of his daughter. With red swollen eyes he allowed Gwendolyn and Merlin to present their findings in private, and with such grave news, he informed his wife.

Plans changed, as it was decided that Eleanor should be placed in the tomb above the White Steps, high up above the Shrouded Lake, she knew it was the one place no one could enter without the express permission of the White Lord himself, and Eleanor would be safe for eternity.

Seven days after the death of Princess Eleanor, as dawn rose, two large drums set high above Avalon on the citadel mount boomed out, and began a slow beat that would echo across the realm. All over Avalon, black flags of mourning rose up the poles, and the realm was sealed to all, as the citizens of Avalon, dressed in black, mourned the passing of the child they had all called the Heart of Avalon.

Every minute, the large drums echoed, and it was a chilling reminder of the saddest day in the history of the realm. Rayne was awake but weak, Merlin had done all he could, as Rhiannon refuse to allow Luminaria down from the Moon Realm. Rayne looked pale, and tired, and had lost all of his usual sparkle, and came across as a man utterly defeated.

On the steps of the Citadel Mount, Eleanor's glass casket was lifted onto the shoulders, of six marshals, and at a sombre pace, Eleanor began her final journey of the realm, along a route lined with weeping citizens.

Before the casket walked Rayne, aided by his father, as both of them shed tears, and following behind came the distraught Una, flanked either side by her sisters Melanie and Madeleine. Behind them walked Merlin and Gwendolyn, closely followed by Hearne, Opal and Eve.

For over an hour, the procession slowly made its way along the long road, and down the steep incline into the large town of Avalonia, where the people under the guidance of Fagan, Maker to the Realm, oversaw the procession and gave a deep bow to the procession as it passed by, heading to the long dock at the side of the lake.

The whole of the dockside was lined with flowers of every colour, and a path had been cleared to allow the procession through. Flowers twenty feet deep lined the floor, up the walls spreading back into the trees, as Rhiannon stood on the long black barge, her face covered in a black mesh veil, to hide the face of a grief stricken mother. The minute arrived, and the drums high above boomed loud into the sky, as Eleanor reach the water's edge.

Rhiannon stood tall, tears streaming down her face, as the glass casket was gently lifted onto the barge. She looked down, and her shoulders shook, as she placed a hand on the top of the glass box, and laid a single white rose of crystal from her garden onto it. Pwhyll took her gently by the shoulders, as a wail of grief came out from below her veil.

No one had ever seen the slightest sign of weakness in Rhiannon in her long rule, and yet as she stood beside the casket, she broke down and wailed in a grief never seen before, and it was devastating to behold. The principal mourners lined the barge, and slowly it moved from the side of the dock, as long oars came out from below, and began to softly stroke the lake in unison. So, it began its journey, passing around the lake that Eleanor had loved to walk beside for most of her life.

*T*he banks were lined with the citizens of Avalon, workers and crafters, labourers and scribes, all dark haired, and all equally as saddened, as they threw flowers into the water as the barge passed by. In death, Eleanor had done one thing her mother never could, she had united the Fae Ofmoon, for a single event. At the castle at the northern most tip of the long island known as, 'The Fork,' blazing arrows lifted into the air, as tribute to their princess, and fell fizzing into the water behind the barge, to symbolise the snuffing out of a life.

As the barge passed slowly under the bridge at the end of the lake, in the centre of the top of the bridge, Morgana of Cornwall, stood with Lothar, looking down and watched the day's events, as they passed under it. For the briefest of moments, Rhiannon looked up, and right into the dark eyes of Morgana, and then the boat passed quietly below the wide bridge, and out into the daylight of the other side.

Morgana stood lost in thought, as the whispered words from that terrible night still echoed in her mind. Had this really been the work of Branna? She had no idea, but she knew that Branna in order to do something as bad as this, must contain even greater power than even she realised. It was a startling thought, to stand above the river and ponder if she was truly of her line, would she wield as an immense power one day?

*T*he barge drifted slowly over towards a long wooden jetty that had been built on the side of the river that edged the forest of time, and it came to a halt with a gentle bump, as the Marshals of the Fae guided it slowly into place. Standing alone on the jetty, was the single figure dressed in a long black tatty hooded robe, for he had given consent for Eleanor to be laid to rest in the room above the White Steps.

The party disembarked and stood in a long line, as the casket of Eleanor was carried from the barge, Albanlin stood before Rhiannon.

"There are no words of solace for you at this time, as words compared to the loss I feel within you are meaningless. Follow, and I will lead the way to her final resting place, where she will be watched over forever by my gaze."

Rhiannon gave a sob, and wiped her eyes under her veil, and then gave a bow to the White Lord.

"Thank you, My Lord."

He turned, and before him opened a shimmering archway of the brightest white. The Marshals stepped back, and Merlin, Pwhyll, Hearne, and Rayne all lifted the casket, and followed Rhiannon, as she stepped into the light. Gwendolyn walked close to Rayne's side concerned that he was too weak, but he had been adamant, he would carry Eleanor on her final journey, and she knew that there was no power within her to stop him.

It took but a few steps, and they came out of the light, and onto the wide ledge, where down below them in the thick mist, lay the shrouded lake. Albanlin lifted his arms, and the large golden doors gave a deep boom, as they swung open, and Rhiannon led the way.

*E*leanor was laid to rest on two ornate golden stands, as Sequana spoke the words of passing, to the sound of sobs and weeping. With bowed heads, the final words were spoken first by Eve, and then Hearne. As Rhiannon fell to her knees and wept, Rayne turned and walked towards the doors, Gwendolyn turned to him as he passed.

"Rayne, wait."

He stopped and turned; his violet eyes surrounded by the redness of his tears. He gritted his teeth as if trying to hold in his broken hearted emotion. His voice was harsh and bitter, as he spoke through gritted teeth, fighting back his anger.

"She could have saved her, and she did nothing."

His voice was loud, and his father turned at the side of the casket, Rayne stared at all of them, and then his father, as his tears began to stream again from his eyes.

"There was, and never will be another soul as pure as hers, and she is gone. I am finished with Avalon." Gwendolyn gasped, as Rayne turned, and walked towards the doorway. Gwendolyn hurried to try and catch him up.

"Rayne, please I beg of you, wait." He stopped outside in front of the white light passageway of Albanlin, and turned back to look at her.

"For what Gwendolyn, for her to start to care about anyone else in this realm, apart from herself?" It took Gwendolyn by surprise, and she took a gasp inward. Rayne shook his head.

"I admired your grandmother, she was a true queen to her people, as are you. You know well what caused this, just as do I." He turned, and stepped into the light, and was gone. Gwendolyn stood shocked, and felt the hand of Merlin, as he placed it on her shoulder.

"Leave him Gwen, he has to discover who he truly is, and that process has started, let him go, he needs this time." She turned to look at Merlin.

"What did he mean, I know as does he?" Merlin shook his head.

"Of that I am not certain, but in time, it will be revealed to all of us."

*T*he party stood for a long time, as each of them shared their final moments, Rhiannon was eventually led out of the room and through the light back to her chambers in the crystal castle on the mirrored waters. Una sat for a long time alone saying her goodbyes, as she understood, when the doors closed, she would never see Eleanor again.

Alone in the room, besides the glass case, Albanlin stood, as he unclipped the catch, and opened the lid of the casket. With great care, he removed the wrapping of cloth from the head of Eleanor, revealing her long fine blackened hair. He arranged it neatly, and then softly stroked it, and as he did, the black withdrew, restoring her golden hair. He gave a long sigh.

"Rest restored as you were in this realm my fair princess. Sadly, it was never your fate to rule, had it been so, you would have been saved. I fear now, the daughter of Enaria was right, there will only ever be one here to rule, such was your fate."

He closed the lid, sealed it, and turned to walk towards the steps, that led down into the tunnel, and the passage. Albanlin had much to consider, as he softly spoke to himself.

"Darkness has many faces, but which is the darkest, and how many will be seen before all this is done and over? I fear, the times of darkness will thicken now."

*G*wendolyn was the last one to come out of the light, and it closed behind her. She arrived in Florae, her heart filled with the sadness of the day, and was greeted by Bade as she walked to her royal apartments with her children.

"I am sealing the realm Bade, it is just a precaution for now, but until more is known of the loss of Eleanor, no one enters or leaves." He gave a regal bow.

"Yes, My Queen, I shall inform Master Elgin immediately." She gave a nod and continued on, as Bade turned and walked briskly down the corridor to the apartments of the council.

*B*ranna walked up the great hall towards her seat, Roack swooped above her and landed on her perch. She turned and sat down, the room was empty, which was a rare occurrence, and she relaxed lost in thought.

She did not notice when Berengar walked in and up to the bottom of the steps, and looked up at her with concern.

"Is it true… Does the Princess of light lay forever lost to the realm?" Branna's eyes moved to him as she came out of her thoughts.

"It is true, Eleanor is no more, and Rhiannon feels the pain of a loss of family." He gave a nod as he walked up the steps towards her.

"Was it you?" Her eyes held his, and he knew before she spoke.

"It was." He gave a sigh, and appeared to understand.

"You should have told me; it was foolish to enter that realm alone." She shrugged.

"I did not enter it, I used other means, call it a gift from Ariel. As for informing you, why should I, this is between Rhiannon and me, I am the one she hurt? You have your conquests, as you did with the Anglo Isles, I was not consulted until it was almost all arranged, well this was something I alone wanted to do." He sat down in his chair.

"Is this how it is to be between us, secrets all the time." Branna turned, and took his hand in hers.

"There was no secret Beren, I did not hide this, I planned it out openly. You have been busy of late with your duchess, I left you to her and busied myself with my own things. It is no secret I have planned for a long time to strike at the heart of Avalon. You know I visit the girl, Morgana. I will admit, I tell the rest of the family little, but you are aware of most things in my life." He gave a nod.

"I was looking for you, there is a man who names himself a Bishop, from Rome, he would wish to have words with you." She frowned at him not quite understanding why.

"What would a man of the Christian faith want with me, I have little time for their lifestyle and religion?" Berengar shook his head.

"I have no idea, but he carries a great deal of gold with him." Branna gave the matter some thought for a few moments.

"Alright, I will see this man, but it is more out of curiosity than anything else."

*L*ater that night, in the library, the bishop was shown in, and bowed to Branna, she acknowledged his welcome and sat back and offered him a wine.

"Bishop Amara, that is an interesting name, if I am correct, it has the meaning of immortal being, or one who is blessed?"

The bishop was stout in his build, with fine grey hair and a chiselled face, he smiled and gave a nod of appreciation, he clearly lived a life of wealth.

"I am impressed Lady Raven, very few understand it's meaning, I can see clearly I have visited the right place." His Sachsen was crude, so Branna changed to Italian, and spoke fluently.

"You say you seek the right place, of which you have named this castle, but as yet, I am not aware of your business." He appeared to be mightily impressed, and gave her a look of amazement, as he sat back in his seat and lifted his glass.

"My business is a delicate one, which I have been chosen to do on the behalf of the church in Rome." Branna gave a nod of understanding.

"I am listening." He leaned forward.

"The church has been led to believe that you have little dealings with Avalon, as you share a mighty distrust of them. Let me just say, they are proving to be a problem for us with the Heathens of the Britannia's. We have need of good fighters, and your men have a reputation that is worthy indeed, so I am here to find out if there is hope of some form of arrangement being brokered."

Branna sat back and watched him carefully, she could feel the deviousness within him, and had little trust of him.

"You have been misinformed Bishop." He frowned looking very surprised.

"How so?" She took a drink from her wine.

"It is true the Varisci are a fierce tribe in combat, few can stand against us, but your error is in assuming they are mercenaries, they are not. It is true we have little dealings with Avalon, but that is not through distrust, it is simply because they have nothing we need, we trade a great deal with many, and have adequate supplies of all we require."

This was news he did not expect, but Branna was aware of that, she felt a great distrust of this man, and she felt very wary. She sat forward in her seat.

"I am sorry Bishop, but we cannot help you, we have good trade if you wish to spend gold. We have the finest cloth, trade gems and jewels, the very best wines, and we can provide you with a companion to warm your bed, be it male or female, but we do not hire out our fighters, they defend what is ours nothing more."

He was clearly not expecting her response, and she could feel his annoyance. It interested her that his church wanted to wipe out the Earth Faith, she could not understand why, they were peaceful enough when not provoked. She watched as he searched for words, he considered his position.

"So, your army would not be suited to our purpose?" She smiled.

"I did not say that, I said they are not paid for fighters. If I chose to fight with these Heathens as you name them, they would not last long, but as a family we are more interested in the business we do. War is expensive, and peace is profitable for us. I have no idea why you wish to wipe out these heathens, I find them peaceable and interested in trade, and as for Avalon, Queen Rhiannon has a mighty armoury. If I could give your church any advice, it would be, steer clear of Avalon, you will not place feet on their roads easily." He understood, albeit grudgingly.

"I shall return to my church and inform them that we were given the wrong advice, but I thank you for your time, and the hospitality shown to me here." She smiled, as she rose from her seat.

"I hope you stay a little while longer, and enjoy the gifts of this house, and as I said, we have many fine things to occupy your time here. Please express my regret to your church, I would think the Norse or the Picts would be more suited to your cause of fighting, although, they would also be seen as heathen in your eyes, although gold does change minds at times."

*H*e smiled a forced smile as he stood up, and took her hand, and gave a bow, Branna gave a smile in return, as he turned to leave. He made the door and exited, and Berengar stepped out from the shadows, Branna looked across to him.

"Watch him Beren, I neither like or trust him, I am not sure who sent him here, but it displeases me. We cannot trust this church, they mean to harm us, I can feel it." He gave a nod, and headed for the door.

"He will be watched, fear not we have many eyes on him." She smiled, knowing he took her at her word, and would act immediately.

"Send a young male to his room, he became quite excited at the thought, I am sure it will make his stay here memorable. When he leaves, follow him, I want to know who he meets on the road." Berengar gave a nod and smiled, as he opened the door, and left.

*R*hiannon took several days to recover from the funeral of Eleanor, Rayne had been seen by no one since he had left. Rhiannon had ruled no guests, and the realm for now remained sealed as she met with Sequana in her private quarters to talk.

"What have you learned, is Merlin right, was this a planned attack at the heart of Avalon?"

Sequana sat, her bright blue eyes, surrounded by the flowing white hair around her face, she thought deeply of the matter.

"I cannot say without doubt, but I do trust to the wisdom of Merlin, he is no fool. My own deep look into this revealed little, no one entered this realm with malice in mind for you or Eleanor. I will say this, in my dreams and my scry glass, I see the same image always when I ask the question." Rhiannon looked at her with a fixed stare.

"What is it that you see?" She gave a sigh.

"I feel we are veiled from the culprit, but I do see dark hair and dark eyes in all that I look into."

Rhiannon sat back in her seat in deep thought, her grey eyes flashed as she wove back into her memories, she looked to Sequana.

"Morgana, what about Morgana, she was on the bridge and paid me a lot of attention? She is a loner, and tried her hardest to avoid Eleanor, she always appeared displeased to see her. Tell me, is she capable of such an act?" Sequana shook her head.

"I have searched using every method I know, and cannot get a conclusive answer, she does fit the look, with her dark eyes and her shoulder length hair, and the death of her father has left her resentful, it could be her, I just cannot say for sure." Rhiannon gave a nod, as she stood up and paced around the room.

"I cannot deny, it fits her well. I know she resents Avalon for arming Uther with superior weapons against her father, and she does spend a lot of time out of sight and brooding. The question is, does she have the knowledge to use the right plants to create such a fast acting poison? We need to know more, we do not have enough evidence, but I need to tread carefully, she is under the protections of the king. I will have to think this one through, but I will have my answers, and if it is her, she will die by my hand. What do we know of the symbol of a raven?" Sequana shook her head.

"Very little, there are a few who use it on their coats of arms, but they have not been seen in these parts for some time. Morgana was in the realm when it happened, but they were not, I suppose that says it all." Rhiannon gave a nod and smiled.

"Yes, it does, it does indeed, I think we should watch little Morgana closely, and find out exactly what she is up to."

*S*equana was to a degree right, she just did not realise that the dark eyes and hair belonged to the family line of Morgana, the start of it. Neither her or Rhiannon had any idea of where the raven came from, it would be some time before they realised just who bore that crest. As they sat together working out their truth, Merlin walked Morgana down from his cottage on the misty bank of the lake at Avalon, towards a small stone built cottage.

"It is only small, it has two rooms, and I built it initially for Gwendolyn, when she was a young princess, but she preferred to stay as a guest in my house, I suppose she preferred the company whilst away from home. As I say, it is not much, but it is a start, and as my apprentice, you will be close enough to me for your lessons, but far enough to have the solitude and the privacy you will require."

Morgana gasped, as the house came into view, her eyes wide open with excitement, she turned to Merlin with a big smile.

"This is mine… I mean, I can live here… Alone?" He chuckled, and his eyes twinkled.

"Morgana, it will not be easy, you will have to collect your own firewood, do your own chores, and take good care of yourself. I assume you can cook?" She nodded rapidly.

"Yes, cook taught me, and I do not mind, I really do not mind, this is perfect for me. Can I bring my books and things over from the house in Tintagel?" Merlin chuckled.

"Morgana, it is hardly a house at Tintagel, it is a large fortress." He held up a key before her.

"You will need this." She put her hand on it ready to take it and stopped, as her face clouded over.

"Why are you doing this, why are you being so nice to me?" It was an odd sort of question, and it surprised Merlin, but he smiled, and lowered his voice to a kind tone.

"Morgana, there are people who commit acts of kindness for no other reason than they want to, I am sure others in the past have been kind to you." She shook her head.

"No one is kind to me; they avoid me and call me strange." He gave a long sigh, and felt a jolt to his system.

"Morgana, you are a bright girl with a good future, study hard and you could be a very positive force for good, keep that in mind at all times. Now, I think we have a home to view, don't you?"

Her dark eyes danced with delight as he released the key, and she held it tight in her hand. She walked up to the door, fitted it to the lock, gave it a turn, the lock clicked, and the door swung open into a narrow passage. Filled with excitement she hurried inside, and stood in the centre of a small room with a large stone hearth, and stone floor.

Merlin followed her in, and watched her as she slowly turned around taking it all in. Her eyes covered the large fire place, the two old chairs of red, a crooked small table, the small window, and the door to a small bedroom. She walked over, and slipped back the curtain; Merlin smiled.

"Not a huge amount of space, I hung the curtain, as with a door the bed would not fit. As I said, it is not big, but with a good fire and a little cleaning up, I am sure it will feel quite homely." Morgana turned with tears in her eyes.

"It is perfect, absolutely perfect, I want to use words that will express my feelings, but I fear I am struggling with emotion currently." Merlin smiled.

"I think your gratitude has been expressed perfectly, welcome to your new home, my new apprentice." She gave a smile and sniffled, and wiped her eyes on her sleeve.

"I am deeply grateful for the chance you have given me; I will study hard, I promise."

Merlin gave a smile and turned to head for the door, he stopped and turned back to see her smiling, as she walked round stroking the chairs and the table, it was obvious it meant a great deal to her.

"You will need a short time to settle in and get adjusted, I took the liberty of talking to the maker, you will require pots and pans etc, call it a home welcome gift from Gwen and myself. There is a well at the back with good water, and this is Avalon, there is no shortage of wild fruit should you require it. I will drop some books in, as you settle in, read them, they will help you start." Morgana gave a nod, and smiled.

"I will be fine, do not worry about me, I will read all your books, and I will learn fast." He gave a small wave.

"Two weeks and we start, that will give you time to settle, and start to read."

He walked out through the open door, leaving Morgana alone in what was to become her new home. She pulled the chairs in front of the fireplace, and then crossed to the table and pulled it across to below the small window. There really was little else she could do, as she had no broom, or a bucket, and so she headed outside with her small knife, the only possession she had on her, and started to cut long fine twigs from the birch trees surrounding the house.

Within the hour, she had cut a small strip of fabric from the wide hem inside her long skirt, and after some intense work with her knife, cut a handle to bind the fine twigs onto, and fashioned herself a besom, and began the long task of sweeping out the whole house. By the time she had finished, she was red in the face and sweating, but all the floors were clean, and the debris swept outside the door.

As she stood in the doorway trying to cool from the light breeze, a cart pulled up outside, and Fagan the Maker looked down at her.

"Tis good ye are here, I have the things Father Whiteline requested for ye. Come little dark eyes and get them off the back, ye look like ye is in need of a cool drink. Tis a good thing I added cups."

Morgana unloaded as quickly as she could, placing the pots and pans on the floor, she had two of everything, including plates and bowls and two much needed cups. Once Fagan had left, she ran round to the well with her large saucepan, and winding up the bucket she filled it with water, and staggered back to the house. After several cups of water to quench her thirst, she sat back in her chair exhausted, feeling happy and contented. That night she curled on the slatted wooden bed wrapped in her cloak and slept deeply.

Merlin sent a cart to be packed with Morgana's possessions, and the following day, he collected Morgana, and travelled in his white tunnel to her home. She packed her books with the aid of some of the house maids, then returned to her new home with the few possessions she valued the most. Her house was tiny, and once the cart was unloaded, she set to work arranging things.

Morgana was smart enough to load her mattress made of duck down, and plenty of blankets, she also brought a small cabinet for her clothes. He helped her to carry all her things in, then left her to arrange her new home, and after collecting plenty of wood, which she stacked by the door, she built a fire, and made a stew with a good supply of fresh veg, and venison given to her by the cook at the castle.

By the time the darkness came, she was pretty much settled. She had no book case, so stacked her books along the wall without a window, lay the rug from her room at the castle, down the middle of the room, and hung a curtain made roughly from an old black cloak. It was not much but it was a start, and as Merlin told her, in time her life would improve and she could acquire more things.

The following day, Merlin dropped in with a few bottles of wine and the books he promised, she had been out collecting fruit, and he smiled to see a bowl of red apples on the table. The house looked completely different as Morgana gave him the tour, and it pleased him to see the effort she was putting in. In many ways, it reassured him that he had made the right choice, it was clear she was eager to work hard and learn.

That afternoon after he had gone, Morgana sat outside in the sunlight, opened her book and began to read. She was surprised to find it was hand written by Merlin, and the first chapter, was how to apply charms to veil the house and keep out prying eyes. He was no fool, and knew that Rhiannon would be watching, and he was going to be sharing certain secrets of the Whitelines, and he wanted them to remain secret. In a small note that he slipped inside the book, he instructed her to practice until she could cast a veil over the house, at which point they would continue.

Morgana sat in her chair outside and gave everything a great deal of thought, she knew Branna would visit her, but was not sure she would enter Avalon. It was important she mastered the veil as soon as possible, that way, Branna could visit without being detected. Sitting back, she felt hopeful, and knowing she was as far from court as possible, she breathed a sigh of relief and softly spoke to herself.

"Now I am free of everything, it is time for me to live and learn, and become a little raven of my own."

Chapter Six.

Rhiannon's Rule.

*F*ive days after Morgana took up residence within the realm of Avalon, Merlin was summoned before the queen. He walked into the large hall with its fountain, and walked slowly towards Rhiannon sat on her golden seat. The flowers had been cleared and as always, the long hall filled with doors along each side, was clean, spotless, and empty.

He stopped below the steps and looked up at Rhiannon, as she clapped her hands loudly.

"Leave us." Everyone headed for the doors, and he waited until the room was again empty, and all the doors were closed.

"You wish to see me?" She stood up, and walked to the top of the steps and looked down on him.

"I do, I have considered your findings over the loss of my daughter, and have looked into other avenues of investigation." Merlin gave a nod.

"What did your seer see, was it illuminating?" She appeared irritated, he knew far too much about her and the methods she used.

"It was, and she has used several methods and confirmed in all of them the same result." Merlin gave a nod.

"Which is what?" Rhiannon watched him carefully to try and gauge his reaction.

"The culprit had dark eyes and dark hair; we believe it to have been Morgana, the daughter of Igraine." He smirked.

"That is a ludicrous suggestion, how in all the realms could you possibly think it is her?"

She felt a pulse of anger rise within her, as she noted his smirk, was he trying to make a fool of her?

"Morgana is a loner, an outcast, and angry at us all for the death of her father. She has many books on plant lore, many of them on dangerous and poisonous plants. She was unguarded and free to roam, it would have been no problem for her to slip into Eleanor's room, and leave the balm laced with poison."

Merlin gave a nod, and considered her evidence, and he tapped his foot as he thought about her deductions, and looked up at her and gave a smirk.

"So, I take it you ruled out all your staff? It is no secret Rhiannon that most of the Fae of Moon with darker hair have at some point complained about their treatment. If you use the logic, you have applied here then you would have to turn the whole of the moon realm into a prison as you locked away every member of the Fae, with dark hair and dark eyes. The logic you apply is illogical."

She could feel her anger rising, as she tried to bite her lip and swallow it, she glared at Merlin who appeared very much relaxed.

"Everything points to her, she was not at the banquet, she was roaming free, she had the motive and the opportunity, and I believe it was her, and she will be punished for it." Merlin shook his head.

"Rhiannon, I know the girl is innocent. Yes, she was not in the banquet, she did indeed leave after the meal, as did I. I saw her in that room filled with your dignitaries and guests, and I felt her discomfort. The girl feels because she is the daughter of Victor of Cornwall, she does not belong, so yes, you are quite correct, she is lonely and isolated, but she did not roam free. She stood at the top of the mount and took in the air to calm herself, and then stood staring out over the realm lost in thought." Rhiannon felt her anger, she hated his smugness at times.

"May I ask how you know all of this?" His bright green eyes twinkled as he spoke.

"I watched her, I felt sorry for the girl. I will not pretend I do not carry some guilt for the part I played in the death of her father, I do, I regret it, and I wanted to ensure she was alright. I sensed her loneliness, and wanted to assure her that she was not alone in this world, so I stood at the citadel doors and I kept a watchful eye over her." Merlin took several steps forward and walked up the steps level with Rhiannon.

"I once warned you about rushing to judgement did I not? Rhiannon, you are grieving the loss of your daughter, so I will overlook your short sightedness, but I will warn you again, do not make the same mistake you made over Ariel. You allowed your prejudice to blind you then, do not repeat the mistakes of the past. I assume you examined the balm, you and I both know that what that balm contained was no plant, it was a pure form of the darkness, but there is no Ariel or Branna in this realm this time, do not rush to judgement."

Her anger was pulsating up into her, and she fought her hardest to contain it, her words were almost spat at Merlin.

"How can you be so sure; how can you stand there and prove the innocence of Morgana?" He shrugged.

"It is quite easy really, at the time of the act, she was with me, talking." Rhiannon blinked.

"She was?" He gave an assured nod, and walked along the top of the platform looking at the walls.

"She was indeed, I was discussing her future with her. The girl is very bright and has strong determination. Admittedly, she is a loner, but considering her, and what she wants for her future, that is actually a useful aspect of her." Rhiannon turned as he walked round behind her.

"How is that so?" He stopped, and looked back at her.

"She has begun her training with me to become my apprentice."

"How… When, and why was I not informed, something as important as that should have been brought to my attention and approval?"

Merlin walked back towards her slowly, his eyes were fixed on her.

"To begin with, I have given her the cottage down the road from me, she has been moving her things in and settling in. Morgana is also of the line of men, not Fae, and so therefore, not under your jurisdiction. I will also add, when it comes to matters of the Whitelines, you are Queen of Fae, not Whiteline, and so therefore I do not need your consent in order to choose and train anyone. It is right you are informed she has relocated to Avalon, and I just did that, so now you are aware of it. I have been busy of late, especially considering the concerns of your late daughter's demise, and so at my first convenience, which is now, you have been informed."

Rhiannon felt her anger starting to boil over, her voice was sharp, as she spoke.

"I am the Queen of this realm, and whether you agree or not, I should have been informed of all this sooner." He smiled.

"As I stated, I have been busy." He walked closer.

"Let me be frank with you Rhiannon… May I remind you; I served on the Ruling Council beside Tideguyde, I was one of the first, my role was given to me by my master. The White Lord himself was very specific, and there was nothing in those roles that stated that at any time, I would answer to a queen of Fae. I have shown you great respect in your time here, but never think for one second, I will bow down and answer to you, I won't. I am the guardian of the Whitelines, and the Fae have no business interfering in the business of them. I answer only to the white lord, but if you are unhappy, you are free to take it up with him, but until such time, I am the one responsible for my student, and it will serve you well, to leave her alone." She blinked as he leaned into her. He turned on the steps.

"Morgana is innocent, find another to blame, sadly Ariel no longer resides in any realm of Fae, or maybe you would like to go with Branna is alive and well, and living back in her cottage planning your downfall. Sequana may be right, but the dark eyes and dark hair do not belong to Morgana, look elsewhere."

He walked off towards the end door to the right of the hall, and left the room. Rhiannon breathed in, and then stamped her foot down hard on the floor, and gave out a squeal of anger.

"Never in my life have I met such an infuriating man, there is nothing I hate more than a smug wizard."

*T*hree days had passed since Branna had spoken with the bishop, and earlier that morning, he had lifted his bags into a carriage and left, closely followed by three of Berengar's best men.

It was late morning, and Branna was doing her rounds, checking on the staff, and talking with the heads of the tribe's soldiers, to ensure everything was secure. The conversation with the bishop worried her, and she was not sure why, but someone had told his church they were against Avalon, and had soldiers for hire. She visited all of the family to air her thoughts, and warn them all to be careful, after all, Lothar was still in Avalon, and she wanted him safe.

She had spoken to all the family, except Maud, so headed to the south side of the castle and the long winding set of steps down to her lower work rooms. Maud was busy with her bottles and jars, working away mixing up potions. Branna walked in and looked around the room as Maud looked up, she turned back to Maud.

"Your equipment has expanded; this is looking very good." She crossed the stone slabbed floor towards her, Maud looked flustered.

"I work and study hard, are you surprised?" Branna shook her head as she noticed the black leather, crudely bound book, which she assumed was Maud's spell book.

"Not at all, I have watched you always, and you have come a long way." Maud looked suspiciously at her.

"No thanks to you, why are you down here, you usually avoid this place?" Branna smiled.

"I had to learn from scratch and understand my powers before I could advance, and yes, dear daughter, I have allowed you to do the same. It may surprise you, but I am impressed with your progress, you have done well." She lifted a jar of selfheal to examine the contents.

"I am here as I am concerned that rumours are spreading about the family, so I have spoken to everyone, so they are aware of what is being said."

Maud lifted her head, her narrow eyes focused on Branna as she walked round examining the contents of the jars.

"I never discuss family with any, what is being said?" Branna glanced across at her.

"There is a rumour we are against Avalon, and have soldiers for hire, to fight their marshals. I had a visitor who wished to pay us for them to strike at Avalon, I turned him away." Maud gave a nod.

"The bishop from Rome, I saw him. I heard him in his room with those two young men, he was very noisy, but enjoying himself. I have no trust of these men with a cross, I told father, one day they will come for us and we should not trust them." Branna gave a nod.

"I am happy we agree, I have no trust of them, it is good you are wary, no good will come from associating with them. I am happy you too think as I do, and it is good Beren sees that." Maud gave a slight nod; it was not often they both agreed on anything. Branna came up close and glanced at the open book on the table, she smiled as she read the neat handwriting.

"That is a good way, but I find just a pinch of wolfsbane will enhance the result. I am pleased you are using herblore, it will aid you greatly in the future with this family." Maud gave a scoff.

"You will live forever, Roack is a purer source to be directly connected to, our ravens are all connected through Roack, I will never rule this line." Branna gave a smile as she turned back towards the stairs.

"How do you know? I may one day revive Ariel and leave with her, leaving you to rule in my stead. Not everything is as clear as you may think daughter, I have Rhiannon to deal with, after that, as yet I have no plans." Maud stared at her as she reached the bottom step.

"You will never give up all this, not even for her, you love it too much." Branna stopped and turned.

"There is one place in this world I would rather be, and if the chance ever arises to return there, I will go and leave all this to you. It is sad that you wanted to kill Ariel, and you plotted my downfall because of her, because if you had just sat and been the daughter you should have been, you would have learned that, and left her alone. You have always underestimated the power of love between us, in truth, if I could return to the life I had before all this, I would leave today." Maud blinked, as she gave a slight gasp.

"You would leave father here, and leave with her?" Branna gave a nod and smiled.

"I would, your father is a good man Maud, but we have never been in love, we have simply protected each other from the dangers posed by the world outside. This family means more to me than anything, and you grow more powerful every day. One day you will have what it takes to rule here, and at that time, knowing you care for and protect everything, I will leave here with Ariel."

She turned back, and walked up the steps back towards the main hall, and the rest of the family. Maud stood still and stared at the empty steps, unsure of what to think, Branna had surprised her deeply.

*B*ranna returned to the hall, where she saw Lothar and Berengar sat talking. She walked over and Berengar looked up, Lothar turned and she smiled.

"Lothar, how nice, I did not expect you so soon, how is Morgana?" He smiled and stood up to embrace her.

"Morgana is well Mother, she has taken your advice and has requested Merlin take her on as an apprentice, and he has agreed. She has been given a small cottage in Avalon. She asked me to tell you that she is learning the art of the veil, and when it is in place, she will let me know, so you can arrange to see her there." Branna understood and released him.

"I am pleased to hear she is doing so well; I believe she will flourish in Avalon. What news do you bring, on other matters from the realms?" He sat down, and lifted his wine.

"There is much to talk about, I was discussing some of it with Father." Branna pulled back a chair, and sat down to listen, Lothar gave her a wide smile.

"The death of Eleanor served its desired purpose. The queen of Avalon has taken to her quarters and will only meet with her seer, or the wizard Merlin. I saw the funeral, and she was very distraught, I feel you served your purpose, and it had the desired effect."

"She now knows the feelings of great loss, a loss I may add, she has inflicted on half her people for too long by separating their families." He gave a nod.

"Some say it has broken her, and she will never be the same again." Berengar leaned back against the back of his chair and looked at Branna, his face looked focused and serious.

"You struck hard, but that is not all of it, listen to our boy and what he knows of this king Uther." Branna's eyes moved from Berengar to Lothar.

"I have heard much of this King Uther, and how he snuck into the bed chamber of Victors wife, and took her. It is said Merlin enchanted him to look like Victor, what else do you know of this?" Lothar nodded, and smiled.

"It appears, the council chose Merlin to aid Uther unite the country, but Victor who as we know was a powerful man due to his deeds for the local people opposed Uther. Merlin used a lot of magic, and so did Gwendolyn." Branna frowned.

"Gwendolyn… This is news to me, what part did she play?" He leaned forward on the table, and stared into his mother's eyes.

"Gwendolyn made a sword of fable, a mighty sword of power, and placed it in the keep of Rhiannon, and it appears, she gave it to Uther." Branna gave a sigh.

"There is only one sword I know of from Fae fables, and that is the sword of power known as Excalibur." Lothar's eyes lit up.

"So you know of it? People say that if held in the hand of a king, he can never lose, and when the rumour of it reached Victor, he agreed to meet and speak with Uther. Uther had defeated and united all of the tribes of the celts, Victor was the only one left, so agreed to a talk. He met Uther, and when he saw the sword, he noted it was not Excalibur, it was Albion, he knew it was powerful. He worked out he might not win, unless he got the sword off Uther, but he knew that would not be by combat. Victor agreed to peace, but his terms were that he kept his lands as his price of accepting Uther as king, and Uther agreed." Branna listened very carefully.

"I am aware of some of this Lothar, but not the sword. I know they met to feast and when Uther saw Igraine, he desired her, which led to Merlin's involvement." He nodded.

"It is true, Victor was outraged at Uther's behaviour and lack of respect for Igraine, and they had a mighty row, which ended up with the peace pact broken, and Uther storming out. For four long weeks after that, he sat at Victor's door, and tried to battle his way in, but as you know, Tintagel is a fortress, and Uther had no chance at all." Berengar smiled.

"Victor was wise to build such a stronghold, he was a clever man." Lothar nodded, as Branna watched.

"He was, but it was his own folly that brought about his death. Uther decided to give up and leave, and that is where Victor went wrong. He waited until the darkness fell, and then went after Uther, and attacked his camp three miles away, but Uther was not there, and that is when he was killed. It is said, that was when Merlin became involved and did the charm, and Uther became Victor for a night, which is how he got into the fortress to lie with Igraine." Branna leaned back in her seat and thought, her eyes moved to Lothar.

"I know the rest, Morgana even though only young, witnessed Uther taking her mother. She told me, everyone saw him as Victor, but she could see it was not, she told me she saw Uther under the skin. So, my grandson was not just killed by Uther as I thought, Rhiannon, Merlin and Gwendolyn also played their part, Morgana will know this when I see her next. The problem is, if this Uther truly does have a sword and it is a sword of fable, it will not be easy to unseat him." Lothar gave a shrug.

"Actually, it may be easier than you think." Branna frowned.

"How so?"

"There is a lot who think that Uther is no longer worthy of the crown and plan to unseat him. They say, he has no honour, because it was he who broke the pact of peace, and stole Victor's wife and castle. There are many planning his downfall, and if we are smart, we could use them to remove Uther." Branna gave a sigh, and lifted her glass as she gave the matter some thought.

"Who do we have who is loyal?" Lothar smiled.

"Wolfhilt, Bregeran, and Manstien stayed at the castle to protect Morgana under the guise of turning their allegiance to the king. They loved Victor, and they have already told me, would play a part in the removal of Uther." Branna smiled, and looked at Berengar.

"They are good men, who are very loyal to you from the first days of your reign, I feel there is room to plan, it is time Uther paid for Amand, Ivor and Victor." Berengar smiled and lifted his glass.

"If we plan carefully, it is possible to remove him without anyone else knowing it was us." Branna gave a nod of agreement as her eyes shone brightly, already her mind was working out ways in which to trap Uther.

Lothar stood up and slid back his chair, he placed his empty glass on the table, and looked at his parents both lost in thought.

"If you aim to do this, in four weeks, Uther plans to celebrate the anniversary of his reign as king, there is to be a big banquet, and he has called Morgana to return to the castle for it. Everyone will be there, including Merlin, and I may add, a lot of the people who say he is undeserving as a king. Everyone is saying, he who takes the sword shall rule, and there is quite a line of those who feel they are more deserving, it could be the perfect opportunity."

*B*ranna returned to her rooms below the hall to think, she needed to talk with Morgana, but if she was in Avalon, she knew it would be dangerous, her only hope was that she went to the castle at least a few days before the event, she had no wish to enter the area of Avalonia, especially since the death of Eleanor, she knew Rhiannon well, and she knew that she would be far more vigilant than ever before."

Branna returned to her table in her workroom, and unlocked the drawer. She opened it and slid out the book written by Ariel, and idly flicked through the pages to see if there was anything at all that would give her an insight as to what to do. Her eyes moved up to the long box of crystal.

"I wish you were here to give me some of your insight and advice, I am unsure of what to do, I know you would talk reason, and cool my anger. I get so angry these days, I am really trying hard to stay controlled, but when my anger flares, I lose control for a while. Ariel, I need you here with me to help, they have killed my son and two of my grandchildren, and Morgana is alone, I wish I could send you to her, so I would know she is safe."

She sat back and rested the book on her lap, and gave a long sigh, as she watched the silent figure of the love of her life sleep in her box.

"Morgana is alone, but I cannot deny, I have wondered if I should go to her and help her as I have, or just leave her with Merlin. There are days I feel I have too much darkness within me, and I am fighting it for us, but I wonder if I left Morgana alone, her life would be better, I mean, I am not exactly the right person to guide her, am I? I have made so many foolish mistakes, I never understood what Rhiannon was doing, I can see now she let me study the merle because she did not care if I got infected, all she cared about was finding out more, so she could use it for even greater power. Let's be honest, what I have discovered, would make her invincible, she would rule forever. It might even make her more powerful than the council. I am so glad she never got copies of my notes, in that, my family and those trapped on the Moon Realm are safe."

*B*ranna closed her eyes, as she felt weary, and her sudden realisation washed over her. She was right, Rhiannon had seen her as a sacrificial lamb, which is why she had given her consent for her to study the merle. Once again, the true nature of the moon queen revealed itself, as Branna saw the injustice of her life. She had been exposed to the merle so that Rhiannon could learn enough to find a way to control it safely, it was clear, she had always meant for Branna to die infected by the power of the darkness.

Her stupidity and eagerness to prove that she was as worthy as those with golden hair, had become her downfall. She had been just a puppet in Rhiannon's plan to keep her fair haired race pure, and she knew she had been used. Her mind wandered as she considered it all, and then something else came to mind, and she felt her anger jolt in her stomach, her voice was soft and quiet as she looked at Ariel.

"Is that why she sent you to me, did she intend for you to become infected, did she want to kill you too to shut Bridget up?" Her air flowed out of her, and her eyes filled with tears.

"Ariel, she wanted you to die, and she wanted me to be the cause." She gave a loud sob.

"It almost happened, if it was not for Enaria you too would be as dark as me, oh Ariel, I played right into her hands, and I could have killed you too. Look what I have done to you, I have played her game and sealed you away so the truth will never be known. Rhiannon has won, she got what she wanted, she shut you up, it was all part of her plan."

Her shoulders shook as she sat helpless weeping, it was too much for her to bear, and she felt utterly lost and alone, knowing she had been the cause of Ariel's downfall.

$\mathcal{M}$organa sat at her doorway deeply engrossed in the book given her by Merlin. It had been a warm day, and yet there was a cool breeze outside, so after all her chores were complete, and with plenty of fire wood, as her pot filled with a thick stew simmered in the hearth, she moved out to her door to escape the heat of the room.

Her mind was focused on the page she was reading as she silently tried to get the phrasing of the veil charm right, and she did not notice the rider that came up the track and pulled their horse to a halt a few feet in front of her.

He dropped down from the saddle, and looked at her, his blue eyes narrowed with distrust, above his long nose and his thick handlebar moustache. Her visitor was Commander Stenlow of the Marshals of Avalon, and he was a little put out that she had not noticed he was there in a blue uniform, with highly polished buttons and sword. He lifted his hand to his mouth, and gave a loud cough, Morgana blinked, and looked up at him, he viewed her sat there in her long black dress, which was hiked up revealing her slender pale white legs to allow the air to circulate.

"I am assuming you are the new resident to the realm, Morgana of Cornwall?" She gave a slight nod.

"I am actually a countess, but have little use for it, and you are who exactly?" She closed her book on the paper marker, as he puffed out his chest with great pride.

"I am Commander Stenlow of her highness's Royal Guard of Avalon." Morgana was unimpressed, but gave a slight nod of recognition.

"Can I help you, is there some ailment I could assist you with?" He stood quite still, and appeared surprised.

"I am here for an interview with you, all new residents are vetted by the queen, but as you are probably aware, she is currently in mourning, and so I have been awarded the task." Morgana shrugged.

"Sorry I am new here; I was not aware I had to make some form of representation for myself." He gave an understanding nod, and took a few paces forward, as his horse idly grazed on the grass.

"I have been informed you are here to be instructed by the wizard Merlin, how long will that be for exactly?" She hunched her shoulders up, and lifted her hands.

"I don't really know, he will teach me until he sees fit, I suppose you would be better off asking him that." Stenlow frowned, and pulled out a small piece of parchment from his pocket and a stick of charcoal.

"I see, well this is not really good enough, the queen requires hard facts. Tell me what powers you actually have." Morgana blinked and thought about it, she looked at him with her dark eyes.

"I am not sure, I feel things others don't, Merlin has not assessed me yet, so you would be better off asking him." Stenlow frowned again, and wrote something down.

"Will you be having guests, lovers and things of that nature?" Morgana blinked.

"I beg your pardon?" He looked at her sternly.

"I have to know, if you will be entertaining others from outside the realm, if they are lovers, we assume they will be spending time here. It is my duty to protect this realm, so I need to know." Morgana swallowed hard, and looked down feeling a little embarrassed.

"I have not done those sorts of things before, no one has ever seen me and wanted to, so at the moment no, as to the future, I do not know, as I said no one has ever wanted to with me." He gave a forthright nod.

"Good, it would be prudent to keep your legs closed in this realm." Morgana felt her breath catch in her throat. He wrote something down, and looked up at her.

"Do you know how to make poisons?" She looked up.

"What?" He was watching her reaction.

"It was a simple question for a learned girl." She shook her head.

"I do not, and I am not sure that is the sort of thing Merlin will teach me." He appeared satisfied.

"It is common knowledge your father will be hosting a banquet; will you be leaving the realm to attend it?" Her dark eyes fixed on his, as she felt a little irritation.

"My father is dead." Stenlow corrected himself.

"Your step-father?" She gave a sigh; this was becoming annoying, and she just wanted to run inside and lock the door.

"My mother has written to me expressing her wish I attend, although I do not really want to, but I am to be forced." He gave a nod.

"How will you travel, using your powers or other means?" She looked confused.

"I am mortal, I will go by coach… Is all this really necessary, it is a bit personal?" He looked back at her with an expression of disbelief.

"It is young lady, I have to ensure the security of the realm, I need every detail to ensure you are suitable." She gave a long exasperated sigh.

"Look, I live alone, I do not want guests, I go into the town once a week for supplies, I eat wild fruit, hunt a little, although I am not very good at it. I collect and dry herbs to sell, as I need an axe to chop more fire wood, and I read a lot of books and study what Merlin tells me to. I do not like going home, as I hate the king, he is not my father in my eyes, step or otherwise. In truth, I want to live here quietly and be left alone, and not be interrogated by everyone who stops to interrupt my learning. That is about everything, can I go now to continue my reading, I have a lot to get through?" Stenlow wrote on his piece of parchment, and quietly spoke.

"Irritable, anti social, and prone to outbursts." She gasped.

"No, I am not, my mother raised me at court, I know exactly how to act in public." He wrote on his parchment.

"Argumentative." Her eyes fixed on him with annoyance.

"That is not true at all." He moved his charcoal, as he watched her.

"Challenging and disrespectful to authority figures."

Morgana had taken as much as she could of the pompous officer. She gave a loud huff, turned, picked up her book, and walked inside closing her door with a bang. He stared at the door, and then back to his parchment.

"Lacks manners." With that, he turned and pulled at his horse, and climbed up on to it, and then spoke rather loudly.

"Should the queen require more, I shall return."

With a kick of his heels, the horse moved and he turned it around, and then galloped back towards Avalonia. Morgana sat against the door on the floor, and pulled up her knees.

"Why won't people just leave me alone? One day I will have the power to make them do as I wish, and that day cannot come quick enough. I hate kings and queens; I wish they would all leave me to live here in peace."

Chapter Seven.

Merlin's Failure.

Branna stood high up on the tower, and observed the dimly lit woodland before her. Roack picked up the snails that crawled all over the roof just below her.

"I miss the sunlight through the trees, I always enjoyed walking under it with Ariel."

Over the last week, the realisation of what Rhiannon had done to her, by allowing her to dig deep into the merle, and finally understanding she had allowed it only because Branna in her eyes was expendable. It was clear, it was so she could learn the power and secrets to make her more powerful over the realm of moon and all the others, and it had left Branna feeling utter hatred and anger towards her and the council. No matter how she looked at it all, Rhiannon had been involved with the loss of her son, her grandson, and Berengar's brother Vladimir, and on top of all that, understanding Ariel had only been sent to her to die from being infected by the Merle, just about pushed her to the edge.

Stood there at the top of the tower, she knew that she was going to strike back, and her first target would be the king that killed Armand and Ivor. In her mind, if Rhiannon had supplied Uther with weapons, she was as equally responsible, and so was Gwendolyn for making a sword of power to fight with. If legend said only a king could wield Excalibur, then she would make sure that it was not Uther.

Morgana gave a sigh as the large fortress of her childhood came into view, she was dreading this, her life in her new home was exactly what she wanted, and she had not wanted to leave it. As the coach pulled up, her mother with Uther were waiting, a servant opened the door and she stepped down, and Igraine pulled her close.

"Morgana, I have missed you terribly." She held her so tight she could hardly breathe, her mother kissed the side of her face and released her, Uther stepped forward and opened his arms.

"I do believe you have grown; it is nice to have you back home." Morgana saw him step forward, and sidestepped out of the way.

"My home is in Avalon; I take it I still have a room to freshen up in?" She moved passed the side of her mother completely avoiding his embrace, and walked in through the doorway, Uther gave a frustrated sigh and looked at Igraine.

"You see, I try, but she refuses to accept me." She could see the anger in his eyes as he turned, and marched from her towards the door. She looked up at Merlin who sat watching.

"Even now she refuses to see how much he tries." Merlin gave a nod of understanding, as he stepped down.

"Morgana has gifts, the night he came to you disguised as your husband, she did not see her father, she saw him as Uther, she may have been young, but she has not forgotten. I doubt she ever will, he is the reason her father is dead, that is not something one easily forgives." Igraine understood, but she could not understand why Morgana could not see how Uther was kind to her.

"Merlin, her father could be hard on people, I know she saw that, why can she not see how Uther is kind and caring towards me?" Merlin took her arm, and walked her in through the doors.

"Regardless of the man he was, Morgana loved him, and so she refuses to accept what everyone else could see, it is the quality of a loyal daughter."

*I*nside the castle was busy, and filled with the activity of the servants, who were preparing for the large banquet. The central hall was vast, and already large tables had been moved to the sides of the room, where over two hundred guests would sit, and the empty floor space would be free for entertainers and dancing. Morgana headed to her room, which had changed little, apart from the fact that there were a few less items, which were in her cottage in Avalon. The bed also had a new mattress of down.

She did not want to be here, she wanted to be back in her new home, and gave a sigh of boredom as she sat down on her seat by the window. She looked out to the sea and the tall rocks, and blinked, on the headland across the bay, stood a figure dressed in all black, she gave a smile and softly whispered to herself.

"Raven."

Morgana came running down the steps with her shawl wrapped around her, her mother looked up at her, and Morgana gave a smile.

"I am going out to walk on the cliffs." Igraine called to her as she ran past her.

"Morgana, wait, I will come with you." Her voice trailed behind her.

"I am fine, I will be back soon, I want to see the beaches and the sea." Igraine shook her head, as she looked at the cook who was waiting for her attention.

"She hates being here, and yet as soon as she returns, she is off out onto her precious cliffs, I have no idea anymore of what to do with her." The cook smiled, and said little.

Morgana was breathless as she came up to Branna.

"I thought you were closer than this, that was a long way." Branna stared at the castle.

"I sense people of powers; I thought it best to move back. Come we have things to discuss." Morgana panted as they moved on down the path.

"The king is holding a banquet tomorrow night, there are many guests including Merlin and Gwendolyn, he arrived with me, she has just arrived." Branna gave a nod.

"It's better we are as far out of view as possible, to some I may be seen. Tell me of your new life in Avalon." Morgana turned her head with a look of surprise.

"You know about my new home?" Branna gave a smile.

"Did I not tell you that I watch over you?"

They came to a small depression surrounded by slanting windswept trees, and Branna walked down towards them, Morgana followed. At the bottom Branna turned to face Morgana.

"I have not got long; it is a risk being this close to Merlin. Tell me about your lessons." Morgana's eyes sparkled.

"I have to learn the veil to hide my home first, I have a book from him. I am practicing, but I find it hard." Branna understood, it did take practice.

"Morgana, you must clear your mind, and then and only then will you be able to fully create a protection that none will see into. You are in the realm of Rhiannon, to create a veil to keep out her eyes is not easy, Merlin is shrewd to teach you this first. Listen to me, when you recite the charm, you must believe it with all your heart, but you must also feel it in your whole being. It is that which will open your powers to all of it, and once applied, it will never fail." Morgana gave a nod.

"I will try when I get back, will you be able to come to me there if I do it?" Branna smiled.

"I would do it for you if I could, but he will know the difference, so I will avoid the risk. If you can do it and make it work as it should, yes, I will be able to visit you there, but only within the house, I have walked in Avalon, but only at a time when she was greatly distracted with grief." Morgana suddenly looked a little afraid.

"Did you really do that?" Branna gave a sigh.

"The spell I used was too powerful, I only intended to make her sick, but she was not strong enough to handle it, and so yes, it killed her." Branna looked her in the eyes, and her voice was serious.

"Morgana, the power of life and death is a very fine line, never forget that, it takes but a moment, and you can slip into the realm of death, always be aware of that, and try to stay in the powers of life." She nodded.

"What else did you want to talk to me about?" Branna gave a smile; Morgana was eager there was no doubt.

"There are two reasons I am here, firstly, did you know that there are those who wish to take the crown from the king? They say he has broken his word, by breaking the peace pact he had with your father, and stealing his wife and his lands. Morgana, there are plots for his death." Morgana shrugged.

"It means nothing to me, he killed my father, I hate him. If they kill him, I will not weep." Branna gave a nod.

"I needed to know, and also prepare you. If it happens, show some grief, it will make things easier on you. Just act like you are saddened, it will appease those who will be watching." She gave a nod, she understood, after all it was common knowledge, he had adopted her as his own. Branna could see the intelligence in her eyes.

"The other thing is I have brought you a gift. It is a special thing I give you, and it will allow us to talk more." Branna clicked her fingers, and a white raven flew to her shoulder, Morgana gave a gasp.

"Is that for me?" Branna chuckled, as Morgana eyed the bird excitedly.

"Morgana, there is no coincidence that I am the Lady Raven, I can communicate with these birds. If you need to tell me something, talk to the bird, and he will come to my raven Roack and tell her. She will then tell me, and I will find a way to get a message to you. As soon as you have mastered the veil, tell this bird, his name is Jarron. I cannot teach you how to talk with him, as the power would show on you and Merlin would detect it, but the bird is loyal to my family, and will always reach me." Morgana gave a nod as she watched the bird.

Branna clicked her fingers and the bird jumped onto her shoulder, and she gave a big smile. Branna shook her head.

"He likes raw meat and some seeds, let him fly free around the trees, and click your fingers when you need him, and he will come to you. Time is short I have to go, there are other tasks for me this day. Take care and learn quickly, and we will speak soon." Morgana stood and watched fascinated as Branna faded away into nothing, she turned her face to the bird.

"Hello Jarron, I am Morgana, we will be looking after each other from now on."

Morgana walked slowly back to the castle, with the bird on her shoulder talking to it. In a strange way, she enjoyed it and her mood lightened. It was almost like having a friend, something she had never really had before. As she approached the castle, Jarron flew off her shoulder, and she watched as he flew to the window of her room, she smiled, Branna had taken note of a great deal, and prepared the bird.

For the rest of the day, Morgana sat in her room at the window, talking to Jarron, whilst downstairs in the lower castle, preparations were reaching fever pitch, as some guests arrived to spend the night prior to the big celebration of Uther's reign.

It was late when Morgana fell asleep, and her sleep was deep and long. Throughout the night, Jarron sat on the ledge of the window and watched over her, his mind connected to Roack, as they spoke.

By midday the following day, Morgana was awake and ate in her room, she had brought her book given her by Merlin, and with Branna's advice fixed firmly in her mind, she spoke to herself over and over, trying to get the words right in her head. It was early evening when two maids arrived, sent to her by her mother to dress her for the banquet. They brought with them a dress made of a soft pale blue fabric, Morgana frowned when she saw it.

"What is that?" The maid smiled at her.

"This is the dress your mother has chosen for you Mistress. It is of the finest fabric; you will find it feels wonderful against your skin." Morgana looked disgusted.

"No, it won't, I am not wearing it, I brought a dress of my own to wear, I bought in Avalonia. You can take that back to her and tell her I have a dress and will dress myself; I have no need of maids." The maid looked a little panicked.

"But Mistress, the queen was very specific in her words to us, you must wear this." Morgana looked at her with her dark piercing eyes.

"Not you, or your helper or my mother the queen, have the power to put me in that, now take it and leave me before I get angry. I will dress myself in what I choose to wear, and it will not be that rag." She snatched it out of the maid's hand, threw it on the floor and then wiped her feet on it.

"That is what that is fit for, nothing more."

The maids gasped, and gave small shrieks as Morgana lifted her boot, and the dress was covered in soil stains from her walk on the cliff tops. They snatched it off the floor and hurried from the room, as Morgana gave a chuckle and then opened her bag, and carefully lifted out her black dress.

*A*s with all things Uther, it was a lavish affair, Morgana arrived late to a packed room, and Uther made a great show of announcing his daughter, she simply ignored him, and took her seat at the side of her mother. Gwendolyn watched next to Merlin from across the room.

"The rumours are true then; she really does not like him at all?" Merlin bit into his chicken leg, and chewed.

"She has said little in our conversations, but the few things she has said are clear, he killed her father and she will never forgive him for it. Uther can try, but I fear, he will never win her over." Gwendolyn watched the room with bright blue eyes.

"I can see that, I cannot deny, I have questioned whether or not we should have given him the sword. His antics of late concern me deeply, there is a great deal of unrest, and it has been growing over time. Many no longer trust him, they say he had no right to break the pact of peace with Cornwall, and a few are not happy he took his castle and wife. You need to talk with him, Uther needs to see the error of his ways, and make some sort of gesture to renew confidence in him, I fear for his future." Merlin wiped his mouth, and lifted his flagon.

"Have you seen something?" She shook her head.

"Nothing has appeared in my visions, but I have a strong sense that all will not go well if he does not make a greater effort, unrest is growing and I fear it." Merlin took a large gulp of ale to wash down the food.

"I will talk to him tomorrow."

*T*he night was filled with food, ale and wine, and soon Uther was loud and boisterous, and got louder as the night wore on. Gwendolyn noted how he banged on the table and eyed most of the women, he clearly had a wandering eye, and she watched as Igraine excused herself, and retired to her rooms. Uther laughed and jeered with his companions, and soon Gwendolyn retired and made her way with Merlin to their room. They walked together down the long corridor to check that their daughters were settled, and she looked at him.

"Morgana left early." He gave a chuckle.

"She ate her fill, and then slipped out, I fear the girl will never be a social animal, but I find it suits her. She really is applying herself; I find her enthusiasm for her scholarly activities refreshing." Gwendolyn smirked.

"Do you not fear she will use what she learns to kill Uther, I cannot deny, it concerns me, she does hate him you know?" Merlin frowned.

"She is far to meek, I do not feel a murderous streak in her, if I did, I would not be helping her." They arrived at their room and walked in, Gwendolyn walked over towards the bed and loosened her robe.

"Why do you help her, do you feel guilt for the death of her father, is that what this is, because to be honest, I never thought you would take on an apprentice?" He stood still, and stared at her with his bright green eyes.

"Am I so shallow you can see right through me? Gwen, I played a part in her father's death, I cannot say I have not thought of it, and regretted the choices I made." She gave a smile, and came towards him and pulled him close.

"We all played a part in the downfall of Victor. I made the sword that convinced Victor, he should take him seriously. Rhiannon supplied Uther and his men the weapons, you should not carry the guilt, we were trying to end the wars and bring peace. Even though watching

Uther tonight it may look unlikely, this land does have peace and the lords try to rule with a fair hand. Talk with him tomorrow, all is not lost." Merlin smiled.

"I think I will sit a while and think, I have to find a way to make him see reason."

"Alright, but do not stay up all night, you do too much at times, you also need rest occasionally." He smiled and kissed her softly on the lips.

"I won't."

Gwendolyn slipped into bed; her eyes fixed on Merlin as he sat in thought. She knew him well enough to know he would think things through deeply, and tomorrow, he would approach Uther with a calm determined and reasoned argument, her eyes fluttered and soon she was gone and slept deeply.

*T*he following day arrived, and Morgana sat out on the high battlements with her book and a bowl of fruit, she also had a small bowl of raw meat and would occasionally toss Jarron a small piece. Inside the castle, the clean up was a massive operation, as an army of staff cleaned up the mess left by Uther and his drunken comrades.

Uther was up and sat in one of the day rooms nursing a bad hangover, Igraine was nowhere to be seen, Merlin walked in and Uther raised his eyes, and gave a sigh.

"Where have you been, I have not seen you in weeks?" Merlin walked casually down the room towards the window.

"I do have other duties to attend to. You have your throne Uther, and I will remind you, I am not at your constant summons, I serve a realm with many." Uther gave a groan as he leaned back his head, and closed his eyes.

"As have I." Merlin nodded in agreement.

"And yet of late you hardly leave this castle, and your affairs of the day appear to be within the confines of a glass. Dissatisfaction is growing in your land Uther, you need to attend to it, you do not have the loyalty you once had, even your wife tires of your behaviour. What has happened to the warrior who swore to honour the land and its people, and rule with fairness and honour?" His eyes snapped open.

"My wife grieves the loss of a child that you tricked me into giving to you, where is my boy Merlin, he should be here beside me to rule as my right hand? Igraine suffers the loss, how can a king rule when his only son is lost to him?" Merlin eyed Uther carefully.

"The boy thrives, as a king's son should, he understands the plight of the people, unlike his father. You wanted victory, I gave it you, look around you Uther, look what you have and understand its meaning." Uther stood up, his temper flaring, and he regretted it immediately.

"You have a nerve to lecture me wizard, you promised me complete victory, with a sword of power, a sword you said none would side against, and yet you claim there is dissent. If that is the case, where is a real sword of power, and how do I have my victory? You took my boy; you owe me a more powerful sword." Merlin hardly twitched, as he faced the temper of Uther.

"I kept my end of the bargain, you have the most powerful sword Uther, what you have lost is your honour, it went when you decided to throw away all your hard work and betray the pact of peace you swore with Victor of Cornwall. The people saw that when you took his lands and his wife for your own. That was not my doing Uther, you did that all by yourself, to sate your lust. Tell me, was that not a betrayal of Victor, and the people who loved him?" Uther's nose flared and his face reddened.

"You have a nerve wizard, you played your part in his downfall, and yet here you stand and lecture me, having taken my boy and destroying the heart of my wife. I should cut you in half with your worthless sword." Merlin gave a long sigh.

"What exactly would that achieve, tell me, that you do not petition me for your son on your wife's behalf, because she is an annoyance to you? Victor wanted peace, it was you who walked from the table, you who enraged Victor, and you who lay siege to his castle for the chance to bed his woman." Uther gritted his teeth.

"By all the gods you are the coldest, cruellest and dark hearted of them all wizard, she is his mother, and yet you lecture me on morals and honour, where is your honour wizard, where is my son?" Merlin gave a sigh and turned.

"It is clear, you will no longer listen to reason, I shall walk in the forest and reflect on your words, and then I will return when you are of a more reasonable mind, which currently you are not. You need to think Uther, and make changes to bring back the loyalty of those that flee from you. I fear you have lost your way; it is time to find it again." Merlin turned and walked out of the room, Uther seethed through his teeth, and yelled.

"WHERE IS MY BOY, WIZARD?"

Merlin strode out of the castle, as Igraine who had heard most of it hurried into the room, and stared at Uther as he stood holding his head. She looked at him in utter disbelief.

"You said you would find out where the boy is and go to him, why did you anger him? You promised me Uther, you promised you would find out about our boy, you must make haste and go after him. Uther you must not anger him, go to him, and talk with reason, I need to see our son, hurry, you promised me Uther."

Uther gave her a frustrated look, but he had promised her, and he knew he would not hear the end of it until he went after the wizard. He stormed out of the room and yelled out loud.

"ARMOUR, I NEED MY ARMOUR, YOUR KING NEEDS TO HEAD OUT!"

Yelling and screaming with rage, Uther was fitted with his armour, and walked out for his horse, slipping the sword into the saddle. He mounted quickly, and without waiting for a protection detail, he kicked his horse hard, and raced out of the castle, heading for the forest on the edge of the mire. As he rode, he cursed the wizard, calling him names and getting even more angry, as he knew that if he returned without news of his boy, Igraine would never forgive him.

*D*eep in the forest in secret, Wolfhilt, Bregeran and Manstien spoke quietly with Branna in the trees, when she suddenly looked up and saw Merlin walking in the distance. She lowered herself, pulling the others down out of sight, as she watched between the leaves, as Merlin walked at a fast pace muttering to himself. He did not notice, and she breathed a sigh of relief. The three men who were squatting with her, signalled back to the other ten all was clear; she had spent the last hour talking and working on a plan to get Uther drunk and kill him in the castle he stole from Victor. She was about to rise, when in the distance came the sound of hooves, and the yelling voice of Uther.

"MERLIN… MERLIN WAIT, WE HAVE NOT FINISHED!" Branna turned to Bregeran.

"It is Uther and he is alone, quick, take this chance, go for him, slay him here, and then run. We will never have a better chance."

*B*regeran sent out the signals and they made their way towards the forest road with their weapons out ready, the sound of hooves was getting louder, Branna felt her heart beating in her chest. At the side of the track, she peered out from the trees, and could see Uther racing down the track on his horse, he was alone, it was the best chance they would ever have, she could not pass it up.

As the horse came up at speed, she stepped out, lifted her hand, and there was a flash of bright red. The horse reared up, and Uther slipped backwards, the weight of his armour was too much, and he fell to the earth with a huge crash. Wolfhilt was first out followed by Manstein, and they crashed down heavy blows on the defenceless king, he yelled in pain and kicked out, sending Wolfhilt reeling backwards. As Manstein lifted his sword for a second blow, Uther rose up from the ground and punched him hard with his steel gloved hand, teeth and blood shot into the air, as Uther turned to reach for his sword from his saddle.

The others saw their chance and moved swiftly out, as Uther gripped the hilt of his sword of power, he felt the pain of the swords that made contact under his armour. He squealed in pain, yet swung round wildly with the sword, taking three with one swift action, and they crumpled to the floor. On the track, riders approached as the king's guard raced towards him, but blood was starting to run from under the armour of Uther. Branna slid back into the trees out of sight, and the guards clashed with the group of assassins. Uther breathed heavily, and staggered forward away from the fight.

"MERLIN!"

Merlin stopped in his tracks, and turned around feeling a sudden sense of something wrong.

"Uther?" He began to walk back as Uther slipped on the wet earth, and staggered blindly into the edge of the mire.

"MERLIN!" He swallowed hard, feeling the pain in his sides, and gasped in more air, as he felt a weakness flow into his bones.

"MERLIN… MERLIN YOU BLACK HEARTED BASTARD, WHERE ARE YOU?"

The huge frame of the knight in silver armour, crashed through the trees. Blood ran down from under his breastplate, as he staggered, bouncing off the tree trunks. He gasped for air, as he trudged through the thick mire, and struggled up on to the rocky bank, where he stopped and breathed heavily. The red stained silver of his metal glove, lifted as he leaned onto the glowing decorated sword. He took a deep breath and gasped out his words weakly.

"MERLIN!"

He slid back the metal visor as the wizard walked toward him, down the long path from the top of the slope. In the distance the waves crashed onto the beach, on the very spot, Branna had once sat swearing her revenge. A storm was brewing out at sea, Merlin noted it, change was coming, and he needed to hurry to Uther's aide. Uther leaned on the sword, and staggered up the bank on to the solid grass, and brushed through the trees.

"You promised, and you lied. Where is my victory old man, where is the victory when there is dissent, assassins are here to kill me, how is that a victory?"

The tall armour clad warrior staggered forward, as the glowing figure in white with a blue sash exploded out of a faint violet dot in the air.

Uther pushed the sword into the floor and collapsed in front of it as his knees gave way, and he felt his strength running away with the blood that now stained the legs of his armour, and coloured the grass and stone around him. He gasped hard as the figure came towards him glowing in white, and he looked up into her eyes and pale white face.

"Gwendolyn help me." Her face carried her sadness, as she viewed the mighty king now in the final moments of his reign.

"You have squandered everything for a woman Uther. You let your hot head and your passions control you, we cannot prevent the magic that has woven around you." Her face looked down with pain and concern. He breathed heavily.

"I am dying; he promised me I would rule." Gwendolyn knelt down, as Merlin came up to her side.

"Uther you were the first to rule a free realm, free of heart and mind. You have taken everything you have wanted, and yet you have given nothing back to this realm." His eyes burned with rage.

"NOTHING…! NOTHING, I GAVE YOU, MY HEIR. HE STOLE HIM WITH HIS TRICKS AND HIS DEVIOUS WAYS. HE LIED AND CHEATED ME!" He gave a great gasp, as he felt the pain of life starting to run through him.

"I have just a plain sword, this is Albion, it is not the true sword of power if men plot to kill me, it is not enough. He promised me a better one, a sword no one would disobey, Merlin, where is the sword of kings?"

Uther gave a loud groan as he used up the last of his strength, and he pulled himself up to his feet, as the sword stood like a crucifix, its blade tip firm in the solid ground of rock.

"Where is my sword of power? You owe me a child wizard." Uther raised himself to his full height, and then pushed with the last of his dying strength.

"None will take my sword but a true son and heir." Merlin reached out his arm in alarm.

"NO UTHER!"

*M*erlin stepped forward as Uther drove the sword blade down through the rock, and into the earth, and the light of the realm exploded out of it, as the magic of the Whitelines burned it into the rock.

Uther flopped forward and hung over the hilt and gave a laugh; his breath ran from him, and he slumped forward dead. Gwendolyn stood up, the sadness of her feelings pictured on her face, as Merlin stared unable to speak, feeling the pain of the moment.

"Oh Uther, what have you done?"

Merlin watched the Whitelines lift his soul, and hand it to the crow that flew in. It shone in the beak of the bird, as the Crow of Rhiannon lifted it into the air and flew to Avalon. The first true king of the Celts in whom Merlin had such high hopes had failed. Merlin looked down with sadness as he looked at the first true king that had been given the rule of the land. His armour glinted in the sun, as he hung over his sword, the rich redness of his blood pooling in the rocky ground below him.

"Oh Uther, after everything we did and spoke of, how did it come to this?" Gwendolyn touched his hand.

"My husband, he has finally done what is the right thing for his people. All his life he has fought for his honour, and he knows in the dying breath of his life he has found it. He will not be the last."

Merlin lifted his eyes to the beautiful soft face of Gwendolyn, Queen of the White Circle, and he saw the light of hope shining in her eyes.

"I should have guided him better Gwen, he should have had Excalibur, not Albion." She smiled, and leaned forward and gave him a soft kiss.

"You did what was allowed my husband, no king could have asked for a better man to aid his cause. He could never have wielded Excalibur, that is destined for another hand, and now he has sealed the future." He looked at her with great uncertainty.

"How can you be so sure, when I feel so much doubt?" Gwendolyn pushed her white hand into his chest.

"Trust in this my husband, what does your heart tell you?" He gave a soft smile, as he looked into her eyes.

"I know that I love you." Gwendolyn smiled, and pulled him into her arms.

"Then my husband you have a good heart, listen to it, for now will come a time of new men. When next you hear those words spoken in truth, you will know the true king of this realm, and he will rule with honour. For now, only a man of the highest honour will be able to draw that sword from the land to lead his people. Watch the son, for he will be a leader of all men."

Merlin looked down on the slumped figure of Uther, and felt the sadness in his heart, he had worked so hard, and yet he felt he had failed. It was not long before the sound of riders approached, and he looked up to see the guards of his protection detail. The assassins had either fallen or fled into the forest. Merlin gave a sigh as they arrived.

"Your king is dead, the land lies without a ruler, his last words were, he who can take this sword and lift it up, shall rule. Take your king, and bury him with honour."

The men looked shocked, and fell to their knees and wept. Merlin turned with Gwendolyn and walked back up the hill away from the scene of sadness. Branna watched from afar hidden in the trees, and gave a nod to herself, and quietly spoke.

"Justice has been served this day, and for this family, which shall now rebuild and rise again as the ravens of power they are meant to be."

Chapter Eight.

Finding Confidence.

*T*he death of Uther came as a shock, as his body was carried into the castle on a board, and laid out on the long feasting table. It reminded Morgana a great deal of when her own father had died, and they had done the same with him. Her mother was distraught, and flung herself across the body weeping, as Morgana watched with unfeeling eyes. To Morgana, it felt like a betrayal, she had not wept that way at the death of her father, so why do that to the man who had slaughtered him, and taken all he had owned for his own?

Leaving her mother to weep and wail, she turned and headed to her room to pack, and one hour later she awaited the carriage at the door. Igraine came out wiping her eyes, and looked at her.

"How can you leave now; your father has just died?" Morgana turned coldly to her, as Gwendolyn stood in the doorway watching.

"My father has been dead for years, Uther was never my father, he was your husband. I am sorry he has left you, but do not ask me to grieve the man that killed my father, for I never will." Igraine gave a sniffle into her hankie.

"He was good to me Morgana, he treated me kinder than your father." Morgana gave a nod of agreement.

"Then for that I am grateful, my father was not perfect, I saw some of the things he did to you, and I am glad you were spared that, but Uther could never replace the man I admired and called father, you never understood that. My father died because Uther wanted you, and he could not have you, and that is why I never liked him. Had he faced my father with a sword in combat, and had a fair fight and won, maybe things would have been different. The truth mother, is he didn't, he snuck in here using magic and deception, and that is why I despise him. To me your worth is far more than to be the prize of a war to bed, you were born to a line of high honour, and destined to be the queen of your tribe, and with my father you were, until that dead man in there defiled you." Igraine gasped in shock, as she watched Morgana climb up into the carriage.

"Be well mother, take better care of yourself, because I value you if no one else does. Come and see me if you are in Avalon. I shall write to you." She closed the door, sat back, and the driver whipped the horse, and the carriage lurched forward, and Morgana leaned back her head and gave a sigh.

"Thank the lords that is over, I need to get back to the life I want." Igraine watched with tearful eyes, as Morgana slipped away into the distance, Gwendolyn came down the steps and took her arm in hers.

"Come, there are preparations to be made, many will want to honour him." She turned and guided Igraine back into the castle, where Uther needed to be prepared for his funeral.

*T*he sudden death of Uther, at the hands of assassins, brought a big surprise to many, and some of the lords of the land were saddened to hear the news. They feared for their lives as they had supported him, and strengthened their armouries, and defences. The simple fact was, that despite his cavorting and drinking, he was a great warrior, and he had brought peace. The country had been divided, and tribes and clans had battled, and through his strength and fair handedness, he had brought a stable peace.

Those who were wise enough, knew the story of the sword would bring conflict again, as war lords battled to take up the mighty sword and claim the rule of the king. There were also many who secretly smiled and were glad to see the end of him, for them, his about turn on Victor, had appalled them, and they had considered him unfit to rule. It was within those family's talk was rife of how they could claim the sword, and pull it from the stone.

What began in the weeks that passed after the death of Uther, grew into a large annual tournament, where all men could try their hand at winning, and earn the right to try the sword. Until such time as one man drew it out clean, the country would stagger along leaderless. Around the area of the sword, the mires were drained, the trees cleared and a large arena was built and named in the glory of Uther.

Rhiannon deemed that a king of such high standing should be buried in Avalon, and so the large rock to the far eastern side of the

Citadel, was hollowed out into chambers, and named 'The Rest' and Uther was carried up to the top in a grand procession, and finally placed within a large stone tomb, and words of high praise were spoken of his deeds and the goodness of his being. Morgana did not attend, she remained in her cottage and practiced her spell to create a veil, so that her education could continue, and she spoke with Jarron, her white raven, and her messages were passed back to Branna through Roack.

*B*ranna worked away in her rooms below the castle of Berengar, with five vials of red liquid. She had read many passages on how the blood of a king could be used to revive the body, and so after Uther had been taken away by his men, she had snuck out and gathered his blood from the pools below the sword, in an old wooden discarded goblet, and returned to the castle, to bottle it whilst it was still fresh.

That night she did the ritual alone with Roack, and dipped a fresh chunk of raw meat in the blood, and fed it the bird during the ritual, and at the same time, she drank one of the vials and felt the sudden heat in her body. Feeling suddenly exhausted, she made her notes and retired to sleep, and entered into a long deep sleep of rejuvenation, that lasted longer than a day.

When she awoke, her skin was smooth, her eyes clear of bags and dark lines, and the streaks of white in her hair had disappeared, and she had the appearance of her younger self, as she had been in Avalon. Examining herself in the mirror, she was delighted, and rushed to her table to write up her results, and without thinking, she began what would become the hunting and destruction of the line of Pendragon for hundreds of years. The blood of a true king, would extend the lives of all her family, and allow her to reign for as long as she wanted, with no fear of ever stepping down for Maud. It was a perfect solution for her biggest concern.

Branna sat at her desk in thought, she had stood back in the trees and watched as Uther pushed the sword through the earth and into the rock. The moment replayed in her mind, as she saw the rock rise from the earth, glowing white hot around the sword. Uther was from the line of men, and yet she had seen him speak the words and push his sword into the earth, what was this magic she knew nothing about?

Moving and shaping rock, was a power of Fae Ofmoon, and yet

Gwendolyn who was queen of the Fae of Earth, had made the sword, and she knew they did not do magic to go deep into the earth. Was this the power of the Whitelines, and if it was, why would Gwendolyn use it, when as a queen of Fae, she had many more powers at her command? She looked across the room at Ariel sleeping in her box.

"This Uther was just a man, and yet his blood takes away age, and he has the power to melt the rock around his sword. How is that possible, when no Fae could do that, was the power of Uther or the sword?"

It was stupid to ask, she knew Ariel could not hear her, but it did pose some interesting questions, like was this the power of the Whitelines, and if it was, was that the key to the balance Merlin had achieved with the darkness?

*A*s the news spread across the country that Uther was dead, it even reached those who had little communication with many of the country's settlements. On the eastern side of the country, there was a gathering of boats, as the people who sailed the rivers, all came together under a large canvas tent, in a field not far from the water.

Many were gathered for the once a year meal, and new faces were greeted and welcomed, as families met up and passed on news of their kin. In the midst with his uncle, was Dorin, and at his side was Ena.

It had taken a year and many months to cross the continent, and find a boat heading across the sea to the east coast, of what people called the Britannia lands. Once they landed, they used the waterways, and finally arrived at the dock, and Dorin's Uncle Dale. They travelled on his boat up the estuary for several years trading goods from meat to bread, and eventually once they reached a place, named Cambridge, they were handed over a boat that had once belonged to Cezar. It was not a big boat, but it had a good sail, and more than enough room for Ena and him, and soon they set sail, doing repairs as they went, following the others in a close group.

The boat was named 'Magpie' for it had been repaired from many things found and salvaged to better use, and Ena found a great love of the water and this strange new land they were in. After living all her life in the dimly lit gloom of the forest around the castle, here in this new world, everything appeared lush and vibrant. She would lie on deck and look up in the bright blue sky, and marvel at its wonder.

Ena was happy as she sat with Dorin sharing food and watching all his relatives and friends within the boat people tribe enjoying themselves, when she felt a soft hand touch her shoulder, she turned laughing, and looked right into the kind blue eyes of a woman, who smiled at her.

"You are very like her, you have her face, and the same aura around you." Ena stopped smiling, feeling a jolt in the pit of her stomach, the woman smiled again.

"I knew her briefly in Avalon, I used to deliver reports to her friend Bran, I sense you have her heart." Ena was really surprised.

"You knew my mother?" She gave a nod.

"I did. It was after she had left, and Bran ran, that they sent the marshals to round us up, and I followed Bran's example, and escaped before they could return us back up there. I travelled with Cezar and Crina for a while, for she is my mother's sister's daughter. I am glad you were not caught in the web that Crina was, I had thought all her family had been trapped." Ena nodded.

"We were, but we found a way out, we have only been free a short while." The woman smiled and her eyes twinkled.

"I am Bella. We should talk, come and see me, I am on the Harebell half a mile down the path from the dock, I will be here for two more weeks." Ena was not sure, but sensed no danger, she gave a nod.

"I will." Bella gave a wide smile and stood up.

"I am sure your mother educated you well, but things have happened outside her realm, and you should be in the know of them, before the light comes." She turned and walked away, and Ena sat lost in thought watching, what did she mean before the light comes?

*L*ater that night sat on the Magpie, Dorin talked about the large meeting and reunion. He was happy and upbeat, and filled with optimism and hope. He was so happy to have met and caught up with his family, that Ena did not want to spoil things. She lay in bed in the dark, thinking about Bella and her words, and drifted off into the uneasy dreams of that day leaving her mother to the mercy of her guards.

She woke late the following day, Dorin was already up and working on the boat, when she came up on deck, and sat sipping her tea. He had repaired the sail, and was reattaching it to the mast, he turned and looked back and smiled.

"You had the dreams again last night; you cried in your sleep."

She gave a nod, it was a regular thing for her, and he had grown accustomed to it, his bright eyes watched her carefully.

"I spoke with a woman called Bella last night, she came up to me, and told me I looked like my mother. She was in Avalon at the same time as her, and she spoke to her daily. Her boat is the Harebell, she told me to go and talk with her, I guess it just got me thinking again, and I had the dreams." He understood her.

"Are you going to see her, you do know she is related to my grandmother, don't you?" Ena gave a nod; she could see his concern.

"Dorin, I am alright you know? I lay awake last night for a long time thinking. I think I will go and talk to her, just to see what she says."

"She cannot tell you anything more than you know, you spent ten years of your life at her side, you know her better than anyone Ena, she is your mother… You know we cannot go back don't you? It took us ten years waiting before it was thin enough for us to get through, we cannot sit outside every year waiting, she patrols the boundaries." Ena looked down at her tea.

"I know… It's just…

He dropped the sail and walked along the deck, as she looked back up, and he opened his arms and slipped them around her.

"Ena, there was nothing we could do, they took her into the castle, the Raven was not there, she would have been taken to her vile daughter, and you know how she warned us against her? She told all of us that Maud would eventually hunt her down and kill her. There was nothing you could do, Ena you were only ten summers old." She gave a sigh and lifted her eyes to his.

"Dorin, I know that, but the truth is we do not know what happened to her. Yes, she could be dead, but what if she is not? I promised her if I got out, I would find a way to free her, even if it meant killing that whole horrible family… Hell, I want to kill all of them for what they have done, not just to my mother, but everyone else."

She snuggled into him, she was feeling insecure, it had been some time, but today she felt those feelings again, and she felt helpless.

"I want to do something; I just don't know what. She told me Branna would always protect her, and never harm her, Dorin, she could be waiting, and I am doing nothing." He gave a sigh and leaned back, loosening his hold on her.

"Look, Bella has the gift of seeing things, go talk to her, see if there is anything she can tell you, it has to be worth a try, doesn't it?"

*F*or Ena it was the not knowing the fate of her mother that prayed on her thoughts, she wanted desperately to believe she was alive, but in ten years, not a word had come from the castle. Those who worked there or traded with the castle from the nearby villages, had not seen any sign of Ariel, and no one in the castle spoke about her. It was almost as if from the moment she had become caught in the trap, she had stopped existing.

Dorin had always done his best to help her, she loved him deeply, he had taken care of her and helped her get free, and into the outside world. Ariel had spoken often of the world outside, and tried to teach Ena as much as she could about it, but once out, Ena knew it had not been enough.

Once again, she spoke with Dorin about how she was feeling, and after an hour sat on top of the cabin in the warm sunshine, he told her he had to finish repairing the sail, and whilst he did that, to go and talk to Bella.

*I*t was an hour later when Ena walked down the path towards the sail boat Harebell, Bella was on deck sat in a chair watching, she smiled when Ena walked up to the boat, and pulled herself over the rail.

"I did not think it would take you long, you have good instincts, I could feel them last night."

Ena walked down the deck towards her a small smile on her lips, but inside she was very nervous. Bella was a round woman with a happy tanned face and red cheeks. She had the brightest blue eyes, and her long silver hair was swept back in a bun. Ena felt she had a kindness to her eyes, and she also felt that Bella could see into people in ways only her mother had. Bella gave a chuckle.

"Look at you, so young, and yet you look like you carry all the troubles of the world on your shoulders." Ena leaned against the side rail.

"There are days I feel like I do, and today feels like one of them." Bella seemed to understand and got out of her seat.

"Come below with me, and we shall talk."

Ten minutes later, Ena sat below deck in a large spacious cabin, at a mahogany table that was highly polished, on floral patterned, embroidered covered seats. Around her in the mahogany fitted out room, were flowers, and paintings, and large soft pillows, Bella sat in front of her, as they both sipped tea.

"I will not waste time, I have a gift similar to those that will awaken in you, I know of the line of your mother, and whether you have seen them or not, you do have powerful gifts within you, like the veil you wear. I assumed last night that you still wear it because you are aware of her son Lothar, and the daughter of Victor, Morgana." Ena shook her head.

"I was not aware Lothar was here, and I did not know Victor had a daughter. I wear the veil because in our parting moment, my mother cast it over me, and as you know, only the one who casts it can remove it." Bella understood.

"So, you are not aware that Eleanor, daughter of Rhiannon, and also Uther the king are dead?" Ena gave a gasp of surprise.

"Her daughter is dead?" Bella gave a nod.

"Oh yes, it has sent a good few ripples through the world of men, Avalon is sealed to any not resident there, even Gwendolyn has sealed Florae. It appears Eleanor died of a horrible poison, and they are looking for the culprit." This was all news to Ena, Bella was watching her every response.

"Uther was ambushed and killed not far from the river marshes, few were there to witness it, but there were some who were unseen, who saw far more than the high ups realised." Ena frowned.

"How do you mean?" Bella leaned forward and lowered her voice.

"Let me just say, that after the body of Uther was taken away, a few men of the river who were watching, saw a woman in a cloak of dark feathers, come out from the trees, and collect the blood of the king in glass vials. We know why don't we?"

Ena shook her head, she knew of the cloak and who wore it, but she had no idea why Branna would want the blood of a king. Bella appeared to be a little surprised.

"What, your mother did not tell you? Good gracious girl, the blood of a king will rejuvenate any animal a Fae ties their life to. The Raven, has secured her youth of the bird for a long time to come."

Ena sat back and swallowed hard, her voice was soft and held her shock at hearing that. Her insides twisted as the understanding washed through her.

"I did not know, honestly, I had no idea." Bella leant forward and patted her hand.

"No matter, you know now, and that is all that matters. There are a few of us who think all the line of Pendragon will have powerful properties in their blood, and it is well known the king had a son who was taken by Merlin, but as yet, no one knows where. He by right, is now the heir to the throne, and everyone is waiting to see if he appears. Morgana the daughter of Victor is his half sister, and the question everyone is asking is, will she kill this son and seek to rule in his stead?"

Ena was not sure of what to make of it all, she looked at Bella and felt the question building inside her.

"I have to ask, why are you telling me all this?" Bella gave a chuckle.

"I would have thought to the granddaughter of Enaria that would be obvious. You are of the line of a powerful Fae mystic, if Morgana grows as powerful as some of us think, you will possibly be the only one to kill her if your mother is gone." Ena swallowed hard and shook her head.

"You must be mistaken, I have no powers, well, I dream about things that have happened and see them vividly, but nothing else, I do not make predictions." Bella smiled.

"You are young and did not have enough time with your mother, but you have gifts Ena, the Fae is very strong in you, and whether you believe it or not, you can do a lot more than you realise." Ena shrugged.

"Like what?"

"Like transform and move forward, I could see it in you the moment I met you. Tell me, have you dream walked yet?" Ena had no idea what she was talking about.

"What is dream walking?" She smiled.

"I can see it is a good thing we will all be leaving as a group, I have time, and you are in need of a good teacher. Crina and myself are linked, and dream walk together, it is where we leave our bodies, and our spirits walk side by side in another realm, where we can talk. I told her last night I had seen you, and she filled me in on your mother's story. Trust me, over the coming weeks, I will show you what your Fae powers will allow, and I will teach you how to use them." Ena was curious.

"Could my mother dream walk and transform?" Bella gave a chuckle.

"For the daughter of Enaria, it would be as natural as breathing." Ena nodded understanding and looked at her cup in her hand, her voice was low.

"So why didn't she, and bring help?" Bella sat back lost in thought.

"That is a good question, and she is possibly the only one who can say, as I cannot answer that right now."

*I*t was the one question no one could answer, the only person who knew was Ariel, who was sealed in a box of crystal, in a state of living sleep, lost to her dreams of happily living in Avalon with Branna. In truth, no one would ever really understand the bond of love between them, or the sacrifice that Ariel had made to save Branna. No one understood the way Branna fought every day to overcome the power of the Merle within her, and how she fought so hard in her loneliness, to stop her love for Ariel being engulfed by darkness.

Ena was blinded by her hatred for the family who took her mother away from her, Crina was blinded by her imprisonment in the realm, and the grief of knowing she may never see her family again, and Rhiannon by her fear, that one day the truth would come out.

*I*n a strange set of circumstances, Morgana appeared to be the only one who was happily getting on with her life, and living the life she had always dreamed of. She sat outside her door on her chair, looking at her shoes, as Fagan trundled towards her in his cart. She watched as he pulled up and smiled at him.

"Good day to you Master Maker, what brings you so far from town?"

His bushy eyebrows twitched as he leaned back on his seat, and reached down into the back of the cart.

"I have what ye ordered and paid for."

He lifted up a large axe, Morgana stood up and walked barefoot towards the cart, over the grass. He held the axe high, it had a shiny silver blade, and the back of the axe looked like a large hammer head.

"I weighted the blade a little, ye is small, and so the extra weight will give ye more force downwards to split ye logs. Tis good and sharp, so watch yeself."

Morgana gave a nod as she reached up and took the axe, she was delighted, she had been cutting sticks for her fire with her knife, but this would make a lot of difference to her ability to chop the logs she had dragged up behind her cottage. Fagan peered over the edge of the cart and looked at her feet, his bright eyes lifted to meet hers.

"What were ye up to as I rode up?" Morgana smiled, and pointed behind herself with her thumb.

"I was looking to repair my shoes, the soles have worn out, I was wondering if I could sow some cloth to them." Fagan nodded.

"Have ye heard of rope?" Morgana frowned.

"Rope, why rope, how do you fix a hole with rope?" He shook his head, and lifted a piece out of the back of the cart, and then he skilfully wound it round itself, forming a coil.

"Look, ye coil it like this, and sew as ye go." He made a circle with a hole in the centre, and then pushed it together flat so it created an oblong.

"Sew it firm mind ye, and then ye can sew on the sides, and the rope becomes a thick sole. I used to line mine with fabric, they are soft and comfy, and hard wearing." Morgana watched fascinated, and gave a smile as she understood, he grinned at her and handed over the coil of rope.

"I have plenty of rope, here, take it and try it, ye will find if ye is clever, ye can sow those old shoes to the rope and put a hard wearing new sole on them." Morgana took the rope with a smile.

"How much do I owe you?" Fagan waved his hand.

"Tis old rope, and I have plenty, take it." Morgana shook her head.

"If you do not mind, I want to pay or trade you for it. I decided the day I moved here I would stand on my own feet. I collect flowers and leaves and dry them to make tea to sell, what kind of tea do you like, I will mix some if I have it?" Fagan gave a shrug and considered the point; he scratched his bushy white hair.

"I does like rose hip, and I am partial to rose petal." Morgana grinned, and gave a proud smile.

"I have both, wait here a moment I will get some to trade you for the rope."

Fagan watched her, and gave a chuckle as she turned and rushed into the house, a few moments later, she returned with a hand sown small cloth bag, containing the dried ingredients.

"I have mixed them both together, I think you will find they blend well, and make for a refreshing drink. I am happy to trade this for the rope."

Fagan took the tea and gave the bag a sniff, it smelt divine and his eyes sparkled. As Morgana took the rope, she looked at him on his seat, her shoulder length hair blowing behind her in the soft breeze.

"I feel we have made a fair trade, and I am happy with it, Master Fagan." He gave a nod.

"Aye, I reckon I have too, I respect that Little Dark Eyes, I will commend ye to ye teacher when I see him. I shall also try this tea, and if it is agreeable, I will tell folks how good it is." She gave a big smile.

"I thank you Master Fagan, as soon as I have enough dried out, I will bring it to the market." Fagan sat up and flicked the reigns of the horses.

"I will look ye out, take care of yeself, and mind that blade, it has a fine crafted edge and is sharp." She nodded.

"I will." The cart gave a lurch, and he trundled on with a wave, and Morgana stood and waved as she watched him ride on down the road.

When Fagan was out of sight, she turned and hurried to her chair, and lifted her needles and threads, then sat down and began to coil the rope, and measure it against her foot. Sitting quietly in the sunshine, she sewed the rope together, and then attached it with her finest stitching to the soles of her shoes, and eventually sat back and admired her work. She had new soles, and knowing she had done it all herself, she felt a sense of accomplishment as she slipped her feet in and tried them on.

With the passing of Uther, Morgana had found that any hope of an allowance had gone. In truth, Uther had financed her early days in the cottage, but with his death, she was cut adrift, and so found she had to survive and find her own way. In many ways for Morgana, it was good for her, she had wanted independence, and now she had it, although the first week had not been easy. She had food, fire, and enough herbs and flowers dried, and so she had planned to trade for flour, and other dried goods such as oats and barley to live on.

For Morgana it had all felt like a fresh start, and she felt good about it, in many ways it was the start of her journey towards self reliance, and a life where she needed no other as she grew in power and became a force that all would one day fear. She had lived a life where she wanted for nothing at the castle, and everything had been handed to her at a whim, but she had always known deep down inside that she needed none of it, and here in the cottage at Avalon, she had felt happier, and more contented than ever before.

Her confidence had grown tenfold, as she embraced her new life, and was forced to think everything out in advance. She had learned through careful planning, that she could manage each day as it came, and for her, it felt like a wonderful experience. She was a survivor, and she knew that one day, she would rise from her poverty, and live her life of luxury again, but this time she would know, she had earned it the hard way.

Chapter Nine.

Next Step Forward.

*O*ver the following weeks, life continued, Igraine settled into her new life as the mistress of Tintagel, a role she found great enjoyment in. Branna enjoyed a new lease of life and returned to the bed chamber of Berengar at night, and spent her days working in her workrooms, talking to Roack and Ariel.

Crina and Cezar, hunted and organised all those trapped, and began to increase their trade with the few local farms and villages caught inside Branna's veil. Ena and Dorin readied their boat and set sail up the channels to trade with ten other boats, one of which was the Harebell. Ena met daily with Bella, and began to learn the ways of a Fae, and back in Avalon, Rhiannon had Morgana watched night and day.

*I*t was several months later when Merlin sat at his table in the late evening writing, as Gwendolyn sat sewing in the chair by the fire, and their children slept in their beds. Suddenly, deep within his senses, Merlin noticed Morgana disappeared without a trace. He sat back and smiled, and gave his head a little shake.

"My word, she has finally mastered it, I never thought for a moment she would." Gwendolyn looked up from her stitch.

"You didn't, then why did you offer her an apprenticeship?" He turned to look at her.

"She was alone, she had no goals, and if I am honest, I sensed she could be manipulated, and so set her a challenge, something to motivate her and give her a goal. It appears, she has risen to it in a way even I did not see coming. I find her curious, she is of the line of men, and yet she does have a power within her, but I was not sure she could harness it."

Gwendolyn looked up at him, with a strange look on her face.

"So you set her a test, because you did not think she could do it, I must say, that does sound like an odd thing to do?" He gave a giggle as he turned back to his papers, and lifted his nib.

"It has taken her a few months to learn the pronunciation properly and master the charm of the veil, she has really focused her mind to do it. Tomorrow, I will set her a new task, one that will focus her mind even more, and if she can achieve that, then I will move to more practical things. I must say, I do find her resourcefulness quite interesting, she made herself new shoes you know, they are quite sturdy, she improvises very well indeed."

"The girl had no shoes so she made some? Oh really, you should take better care of her, she is the queen's daughter after all." He smirked.

"She wants no help at all, she earns her keep by trading teas and medicines to passers by. I must say, she has a very good command of herblore considering she is self taught. I cannot deny, I admire her determination."

Gwendolyn put down her sewing, and stood up, she came over and kissed his cheek.

"It is late, and I shall return to Florae tomorrow with the girls, I need to consult my table, do not forget, we have a council meeting at the end of the week, so I need to get more up to date. There is unrest everywhere, and I want to look into some of it. Do not stay up too late, you need to see Morgana before you go off." He gave a nod, and Gwendolyn walked smiling out of the room, he stared down at his papers, and lifted his nib, and began to write.

*I*t was early morning and the sun was up, but the day was still a little chilly, Morgana lay asleep, curled up tight in her blanket.

'Bang… Bang… Bang!' She sat up abruptly, feeling a huge surge of fear run through her.

'Bang… Bang… Bang!'

She jumped out of bed, and pulled her cloak around her, and slipped through the hanging blanket into her living quarters. She glanced around, and then noticed the shadow at the window, and leaned forward to peer round the curtain.

Merlin stood outside the window with a hammer, holding some nails in his hand, she gave a sigh of relief as he smiled and waved.

"Good morning." She could not believe him; her heart was still pounding in her chest.

"What in all the realms are you doing, you scared me to death?" He gave a nod.

"Hmm… Yes, sorry I was not thinking, did I wake you?" She looked at him in complete disbelief.

"Of course you woke me, you are banging the life out of my window, I thought someone was trying to break in. What are you doing anyhow, hammering this early in the morning?"

She gave a shiver, and felt the cold draft run up her bare legs. Merlin watched her, and considered her remark.

"I see your point… Well, no matter, you are up now, so it is time for another lesson, congratulations, you passed your first test. Start a fire and make some tea, I won't be a minute."

Morgana gave a sigh, and walked over to the fire place, grabbed her flints and fine dry moss, and knelt down to start the fire. Merlin continued to hammer above her window. Ten minutes later and with the banging over, much to the relief of Morgana, who jumped every time he hit the top of the window, Merlin sat in her chair, sipping tea. Morgana sat on her rug close to the fire sipping hers, Merlin smiled at her.

"You have done well to master the charm of the veil, I am impressed, it is good, no one will see inside your property now, you will have the peace and the privacy to study unhindered." Morgana gave a nod.

"It was not easy learning the pronunciation, I will not deny, I struggled with it. I understand it is the language of the elders, and I can see how words have changed, I would prefer the spells to work with common speech. So, what is next?" Merlin sat back and rested his cup on the table.

"Did I mention I built this house?" She gave a nod at him.

"Yes, many times." He smiled.

"Never built one before, so I made a few mistakes. You see young Morgana, when I built it, I nailed the windows into the wall, so they do not open, and in the summer, it gets very hot inside."

She gave a smile and nodded at him, she already knew that, she had spent most of the hot days outside in the breeze.

"I have noticed, it gets a little too hot if you ask me." Merlin gave a large smile.

"That is your next task, I want you to fix the window so it opens."
She frowned.

"How is that magic exactly, does the Whitelines have a spell for
opening windows?" He gave a little chuckle.

"To apply the veil, you had to focus your mind, you needed a
power of concentration no line of men can do easily, and yet you have
achieved it. So, I want you to go even deeper within your mind, and try
to harness all of its power, for if you wish to wield the Whitelines, you
will need to strengthen your mind, and focus even harder."

Morgana gave a nod of understanding; she had found herself on
many occasions slipping into deep thought to learn the charm of the
veil.

"If I may ask, how will focusing my mind open a window?" He
smiled at her; she was very smart indeed.

"It won't, but it will help you to use your mind to focus your inner
strengths, and then, you will find a way to sever the nails that connect
the window and the wall. The leather straps I placed outside earlier
along the top of your window, will act as a hinge, and the window will
swing open. You will need a prop, and a means of fastening it, so I will
leave that to you, just make it neat."

She understood, and contemplated his words carefully, she looked
up at him and her dark eyes twinkled.

"This is chapter two of the book you wrote, isn't it?" He lifted his
cup and drained it, and then stood up.

"It most certainly is, it may take some time, but as before, when
you have mastered it, we will proceed onwards with more lessons.
Right, I have to be off, remember, focus deeper than last time, and
seek inside for your inner power to find a way to cut the nails free, so
the window opens. Good luck my dear, have fun." And with that, he
left her sat on the floor by the fire sipping her tea, she looked at the
window and spoke to herself.

"How many nails are there?"

Morgana stood up and walked over to her window, she could see
the small holes where the square headed nails had been hammered in.
Her eyes moved slowly round the frame as she counted.

"Eighteen nails, how bad did he think the storms would be?" She
gave a long sigh.

"This is going to take forever."

She turned, and walked into her bedroom, where her book lay

on the small table beside her bed. With a sigh, she lifted it up and returned to her table, sat down, and sipped her tea, as she opened the book to the second chapter, and began to read.

*B*ranna sat at her desk and looked at the book, and gave a soft smile, her eye lifted to the crystal box.

"Do you remember when you showed me how to make this?" She gave a soft chuckle.

"You giggled so much, and I did not do the best job, but you know what, I really loved that you showed me how you make your books. It is silly really Ariel, I have had so many over the years, but before I met you, I had never thought of who made them or how they are made, in a way, it made it such a special time for me. Now whilst you rest, I have started to make my own, I have made ten, and I am going to fill them with my words to you, I shall write everything I do down, and then one day, we can read them together."

She opened the book and started to write, and her face wore a soft gentle smile. Roack landed on the window and gave a shudder, she could yet again feel the deep emotions inside Branna. She spread her wings and flew off, leaving Branna with her thoughts and memories, as she wrote her new journals, which would chronicle every moment that she spent alone with Ariel in her glass box.

The candle burned down, the sun set and the soft scratch of her nib was the only noise, apart from the soft bubbling of her bottles, as the steel pan boiled up the tubes, and distilled new potions. All around the castle the air was still and calm, it was a rare occasion, normally there was always noise. Branna scratched her nib, and gave a slight sob, she lifted her arm and wiped her eyes, as she looked at the box, and the sleeping figure. She swallowed down her pain and took a long breath.

"Will this pain ever leave me Ariel, will there ever be a time when my thoughts turn to joy again? Ariel, I am missing you tonight, I really wish I could let you out and hold you, it has been so long, and even though I went to Beren's bed the other night, I only did it because I need someone in this endless misery to just hold me. I want you to hold me, how much longer should I have to endure this? I use my words in this book of parchment to tell you how much I miss you, and how much I love you, but I have no idea if you will ever read it, if I knew you would, it would help, but without you to tell me you will, I do not know."

She put down her nib, and stood up, and slowly walked to the side of the box, and leaned over to look upon Ariel's sleeping face.

"What do you dream of, do you dream of me, are you lay there remembering everything we have done? I wish I could walk in your dreams with you, I wish we could be together in them, or at least I could be in them with you, not just a memory from the past. I wish you could hear me, even that would be better than this endless bitter loneliness I feel." She gave a sigh, and wiped the tears off the top of the crystal.

"I have thought of just dropping the veil, I mean, how long will this last for? I yearn to just face her and live or die, either way, it would end this loneliness. I would either be free of the pain in my heart, or I could open your box and let you out. I should have stayed in Avalon, it was hard, but easier than this, hell, even her prisons on the moon would be easier than this Ariel." Branna closed her eyes, and leaned forward pushing her head to the crystal as her tears dripped onto the clear box.

"I miss you so much, it is torture."

She took a deep breath and wiped her eyes, and then walked slowly to her bed chamber, inside the crystal box, on the heart of Ariel, the light sparkled around her pendant, and lost in her dreams, Ariel heard a soft voice whisper.

"She suffers badly, if she does not break her melancholy, she will fail, and be dragged back by the darkness, she needs you, walk in her dreams and help her."

Branna slipped off her clothes and slipped under the sheets, and closed her eyes, above her the perch was empty. She knew Roack would not come whilst she felt this way, the connection for now was broken. Branna closed her eyes and breathed out, she felt weary and unhappy, her breathing changed as the exhaustion overtook her, and she slipped into sleep.

𝓗er breathing became soft, and her eyes lids fluttered, as her dreams were filled with the pain of her final moments, she muttered in her sleep.

"Ariel, I do not want to do this, you are the love of my life, I do not want to seal you up in a glass box." Her head rolled from side to side, as she twitched and moved in her sleep. The room filled with light, as

Branna thrashed out in the bed, and the soft voice whispered in her ear.

"Shush my love… I am here with you, holding you, dream with me my love, hold my hand and walk in the trees." Branna murmured and stopped moving, her eye lids fluttered, as deep in her mind she saw Ariel standing with her, and holding her hand as they walked through the trees.

"Bran, remember my light, I am here inside you, stop letting the darkness overwhelm you. Can you not see, it is using me to weaken you, Bran, stop thinking and feel the purity of my love for you? The darkness fills you with the painful memories of me, and you forget the joy we had. Remember that, and feel the joy as you did tonight, thinking of the day in Avalon, where you learned to make a book. Those memories are me, I am sending them to you, feel me again Bran, remember all the times I held you and take joy from it, for every moment is worth the fight." Branna stirred, and in her mind, she saw Ariel sat on the grass laughing.

"Bran, it is a small book, why are your stitches so big?" Branna giggled, as she looked up and saw the smile on Ariel's face.

"It is alright for you, this is my first, you have made hundreds, hell Ariel, I only use five stitches to hem a dress." Ariel looked shocked.

"What!?" Branna shrugged, and turned over the end of her long skirt, Ariel stared at it looking absolutely stunned.

"Bran, that is insane, how have you managed alone without knowing something as simple as stitching?" Bran gave a chuckle.

"To be honest, if they fell down and would not stay up, I glued them up with pine resin, you know if it is thin enough, and you only use just a small dab, they stay up forever."

Ariel's eyes moved from her dress up to the dark eyes of Branna, she smirked and howled with laughter, and Branna gave a chuckle, she loved to see Ariel so happy. Ariel held her tummy as it wobbled, and Branna continued to chuckle.

"It is okay for you, I bet your mum showed you, I did not have anyone, she was working so much I hardly saw her once I passed the age of five summers." Ariel sat up and wiped her eyes.

"I am sorry, I should not laugh, although it was my dad that taught me to sow, I learned making small books with him. Here let me show you again."

She slid up at her side and took the needle, and then slowly showed

Bran once again, how she marked the book with the end of the needle, to space her stitches properly, Branna smiled, and leaned onto her shoulder.

"I love this Ariel, I love this life here, I want it to last forever." Ariel glanced round at her, and her grey eyes twinkled.

"Yes, I do too, and it will, we will stay here in Avalon and live in our house, and one day to surprise me, you will stop using resin and pick up a needle." She gave a snort and giggled, and Branna smiled, it was silly really, but this felt like her best day ever with Ariel.

The light in the room faded and Branna gave a long happy sigh in her sleep, somewhere in the back of her mind, soft words whispered.

"Sleep deep my love and rest your weary soul, this will not be forever, never forget that, I will come back to you one day. Prepare for that day, for I am waiting, and do not let the darkness cloud your thoughts, fight for me Bran."

Chapter Ten.

Rumours.

Deep in the Forest of Time, a short distance from the vast area of trees that overlapped the edges of the realm of Avalon, within a deep cave under the sacred water falls of Eve, the Ruling Council met.

The centre of the cave had a large round table of stone, around which were highly decorated seats of elaborately carved marble, and the members sat in place ready, as they picked from fruit and drank from glasses of cut crystal. The blacked robed figure of Albanlin sat last, and from under his dark hood, his voice spoke with authority.

"Tell me of your realms." Rhiannon sat watching him.

"Avalon is sealed to only those who reside within it, and until I am certain of who the assassin was that took the life of my precious child it will not open." Eve looked saddened, as she reached out to her side and took hold of Rhiannon's hand.

"My Sister, we all feel your pain, and we are with you as we seek those who did it." Gwendolyn sat back in her seat.

"It scares me that this was done here, and yet there is no trace or any evidence to show who could do this, it could be any of the thousands of people who reside here." Rhiannon looked at Merlin.

"I have my suspicions, it was female, with dark hair and dark eyes." Merlin gave a sigh.

"As I have informed you, it was not Morgana, she was stood at my side, long before, during, and after the attack, and to be honest, as much as you may not trust her, I can tell you without doubt, she does not have the ability to create such a dark thing." Opal looked round.

"Morgana, she is not very social, but I do not think she is a bad person, she is not the most talkative, but she has always been polite and respectful." Hearne gave a nod.

"Fagan the Maker has talked of her, he is impressed at her determination to pay her own way and he has told me, she has worked hard on her home, and smiles with ease when spoken to." Rhiannon shook her head.

"My commander found her off hand and quite rude when he interviewed her, he reported that she was difficult and secretive." Merlin turned to her, there was anger in his voice.

"When was she interviewed and why, he has no right, did you authorise that, for she is in my care?" Rhiannon glared at him.

"She may be your student, but this is my realm, and I have every right to know who lives within it." Merlin was clearly angry.

"I have told you already, it was not her, and if you wish to make another Ariel, be warned, she is under the domain of the Whitelines, and I will not take it too kindly to have you probe into my affairs. If you desire an interview, you talk to me, and I will present her in your court."

"I rule here, and not you or any other will tell me how to run my realm. Let's be honest, she fits the profile?" He gave a loud huff, and responded with a dismissive tone.

"We have all heard that before, and we are well aware of your rule, I am sure Ariel has book loads of detail on that matter." Gwendolyn bit her lip and looked down; Rhiannon looked outraged.

"How dare you challenge my authority." Merlin stood up and stared at her, his anger very obvious.

"HOW DARE YOU CHALLENGE MINE, LEAVE HER ALONE, SHE IS IN MY CARE!" Albanlin banged on the table.

"ENOUGH!" Rhiannon sat back, and Merlin flopped to his seat. Albanlin's black hood twitched.

"I will not have this conduct in this room. I expect better of both of you. Rhiannon, you will obey your agreement with the Guardian of the lines, he was here long before you were, and has a right to the stewardship of his pupils, and you will respect it. Guardian, you will hold your temper in this room, I am aware of the oath you swore to the lines, but you will conduct your business here in a better manner." Merlin gave a nod.

"I am sorry My Lord." Rhiannon looked at the table, clearly very angry.

"My Apologies, My Lord Albanlin." His hood twitched.

"All of you, we must be more careful, the loss of Eleanor, and King Uther has served a blow to not just all of us, but the kingdoms we watch over. I understand the duties of ruling a realm, but we must be more vigilant, the realm of men is fracturing and leaderless, and we need to give them hope. Two dark deeds have been committed and yet there is no trace of either culprit, mistakes are being made, and we need to be more watchful. All of you, take these words to heart, and open your eyes wider." Hearne gave a serious nod.

"It is true, of late we have been too preoccupied, and we have let things slip, Merlin, tell us of the boy, how does he fair?" Merlin sat back in his chair.

"He grows stronger by the day, he is in good care, his time to be revealed I feel is close. The tournament has been a good distraction, and to a degree, it has calmed many down, as they await their chance to pull the sword. I am still unsure as to how Uther managed to invoke the lines of power, but it has to a degree secured a future for a one true king, and in that I have hope."

"It was the sword, I am just glad it was Albion, had it been Excalibur as you wished, no one can say as to what would have happened." Eve looked round as they all looked at her.

"What?" Gwendolyn smiled.

"You are correct, Uther was not the man to rule, our judgement was flawed, the sword is a very magical item, it will choose for us."

The atmosphere faded, as food was eaten, drinks were poured and the group sat and discussed all of the realms, and anything that needed to be done. Rhiannon was quieter than she normally was, but she felt the sting of Merlin, and her anger simmered deep within her, she knew, one way or another, she would level the score with Merlin.

*T*he days passed by, and Morgana sat in her home working on more cloth bags, to bag up her teas. Her knowledge of plants was growing, but she needed bottles for some of her medicinal cures, and so she bagged as much of her dried teas as she would be able to carry, and prepared for her Friday market. It had taken a long time to reach the sort of quantities she wanted, but with a very large stock, she felt her excitement build.

Morgana woke early in the morning just before sunrise, and lifted her big bag, and walked outside and gave a shiver. The moon was high in the sky, and the sky twinkled with thousands of stars, as Morgana turned at her door and began the long walk through Misty Bank, past the fortress on the Fork island, and towards the vast wooden bridge, that spanned the lake to the road leading up to Avalonia.

She had a long list of the things she needed, and so hoped for a good day of trade and bartering, so she could raise the funds, not only to eat, but to help build up her stock for sale, and make little improvements to her home.

On the far side of Avalonia, across from the large fortress, the grass of the fields was cut low, and wooden tables had been set up. Fagan organised the stall holders, and Morgana stood in line holding her penny to pay for her space. Fagan smiled as she walked up, and handed over her money, he pointed towards a table with a roll of thin hessian on it.

"That one is for ye, I got ye the spare cloth I had, and will trade for two more of that tea, tis a mighty fine brew, and a credit to ye. I put ye between Mavis the cake lady, and Seth the wood worker, they are good folk and promised to watch over ye. Stand ye ground, some of these hagglers can be brutal, show ye spirit and trade fair." Morgana smiled, and gave a nod as she looked across at her table.

"Thank you, I need supplies, so I will barter and trade for all I need, I am grateful to you Master Fagan, this is very new to me, but I aim to stand on my own feet." He gave her a wink, as his wild hair blew in the soft breeze.

"Ye do that, I will be watching, so if anyone bothers ye, just yell out."

*S*he lifted her bag and gave a nod, then headed over to fill her table. All around the atmosphere was one of busy preparation, traders talked and laughed as they loaded their tables and filled the fronts of the floor with wooden boxes of goods. There were vegetables and clothing, shoes and small trinkets, fresh baked bread, cakes, and a whole manner of tools and seeds to grow more crops.

Morgana opened her pack and used the fabric to line her table, she kept two of her bags of her special mixed tea back for Fagan, and displayed all her teas in rows from the back to the front of her table, and she had a fine selection, from which people could choose. All labelled with small signs made of birch bark, into which she had burned the names with a heated nail, it was very neat, and well organised.

It was not long before people started to arrive, and Mavis smiled as she sold her first bag. She traded a bag for three small cakes with Mavis, and traded tea for a wooden beaker from Seth. Morgana made some money, but mainly did barters, for veg, bread, a few small nice cuts of beef, and a small joint of salted pork. She was very happy as the day wore on, and found the residents of Avalonia to be polite, but it had not escaped her notice, that most of the traders had brown or black hair, like she did.

The day wore on, and a young boy carried round a bucket of cool water, she dipped in her beaker and filled it, he looked hungry so she thanked him and handed him one of her cakes. It was a warm day, dressed in her black dress with a small grey pinafore as she smiled, spoke politely, and served.

Everything was going well, until a tall fair haired woman dressed in rich silks, approached and eyed Morgana with suspicion, she lifted a bag of tea and examined it, she appeared to be unimpressed.

"Tell me Girl… Should I be wary of drinking this, I mean, after all, someone poisoned Eleanor?"

Mavis gasped, and Morgana blinked, not at all sure what she should say, the woman stared at her with malice.

"You are the girl living alone on the bank of the lake are you not?" Morgana felt shocked, and nodded.

"I am… I am a student of Merlin." The woman eyed her carefully.

"I believe you were in Tintagel the day Eleanor was there, and the same day as Uther when he was slain? I mean, that sounds like too much of a coincidence, and here you are, a student of plant lore and magic, it says everything doesn't it?" Morgana took a deep breath.

"If you are saying I had something to do with those, I am sorry, but you are very wrong. I have no wish to hurt anyone, especially the daughter of a queen." The woman smirked.

"But you did find her tiresome, didn't you? My daughter saw how you were dismissive with her, and she was such a fine girl, she would have hardly stood out with the common folk and sold her tat." Morgana felt panicked and swallowed hard.

"It is true I did live in the castle, but I did not avoid her out of dislike, I just like to be alone, and I would never have hurt her, no matter what you may think. To say that is offensive, and dangerous, I have done nothing wrong. I live a quiet life, collect my flowers for tea, and dry them, and a lot of people enjoy them. All I wish for is to be left alone to study, and live quietly in my home." She gave a snort.

"Your home, don't you mean Merlin's. My husband told me you were impolite, a woman of your position and reputation should watch herself. There are a few who have noticed you and are watching, we do not trust you, Morgana of Cornwall. After all, it appears to me, you are very like your father, he had the guile to face out our glorious king, and look where that got him. Take heed young Morgana, some of us of higher status are on to you."

Morgana stepped back and bit her lip, she could feel tears coming and did not want to cry, Fagan noticed and strode over.

"Prunella, what mischief are ye making now? Leave the young girl be, she has worked hard to be here, let her go about her day, I believe Stenlow is looking for ye."

She dropped the tea bag onto the table and stared at Morgana, and she felt a cold shiver run down her back. She was the wife of the Commander of the guards, she knew to say anything else would be dangerous, after all, he spoke directly to Rhiannon, and Morgana was now one of her subjects. Prunella turned and smiled.

"Fagan my dearest brother, how are you, I was asking Stenlow just the other day if you had fully established here?"

*F*agan looked at Morgana and gave a nod, he took Prunella's arm and led her away. Tears rolled onto Morgana's cheeks, she felt really scared, and she did not know why, Mavis came over and lifted a small cloth to her face.

"You take no notice of her, she is a nasty cow, she spreads gossip and rumours for the queen, pay her no heed, she is a wicked woman." Morgana gave a sniffle.

"I have never hurt anyone, that is not who I am, my mother raised me to be decent and polite. Mavis, she implied I was the one who killed Eleanor, why would she say that?" More tears rolled onto her face, and Mavis gave a sad smile.

"Oh, look at you, and you were having such a nice day, come on, step back for a moment and compose yourself. Ignore her Morgana, she is a horrible woman, everyone knows it, and no one really listens to her." Morgana nodded and dried her eyes. Seth leaned back; he was watching all the stands.

"Listen to me girl, pay her no attention, with these fair haired buggers, you have to ignore there narrow minds, because that is what they are, narrow minded and short sighted. They swarm around like they are better than any of us, but they are not, they are privileged because they have fair hair, and the golden queen surrounds herself with them. You are one of us girl, one of the normal ones, with a good heart and a clear conscience. Let her tongue flap, most folks know she spouts manure."

What worried Morgana, was she had heard Branna talk of it, and the injustice of Avalon and its queen, and Morgana for the first time really started to understand the politics of life in Avalon, and she knew that she had to stay low profile. It made sense to her now why Stenlow had visited her, and she had to ponder, did Prunella give something away, was that what his visit was really about, did Rhiannon actually think she had been involved in the death of Eleanor and Uther.

Her mind moved to the day of the funeral, and how for a moment she had looked up at her, as the barge passed under the bridge. She had thought it was odd to be noticed by a queen, but now she was left to wonder, did Rhiannon accuse her, is that what this was all about? Not knowing scared her, Rhiannon was powerful, and she was very aware now of how aspects of that power operated, and it really worried her.

*F*or the rest of the day, she kept her head down, and as the market quietened down, she began to pack up, feeling a little better. Mavis and Seth had both taken good care of her, and she was very grateful and thanked them as she packed her remaining teas away in her bag, and lifted her box of fresh food onto the table. Fagan walked up with a big smile, and she handed him his two bags of tea, she did feel a lot happier, she had good trades and some money. Fagan gave her a deep look in her eyes.

"It is good to see ye have made some spare, rainy days come, and at that time ye will need it." Morgana gave a nod.

"I have twenty pennies, it is much more than I hoped for, so I will save it, I still have bottles to get for my medicines, I hope people will buy them." He gave a slight smile.

"They will, not everyone will look down on ye, listen Little Dark Eyes, take no heed of Prunella, she is as sour as bad grapes and always has been. My old pa never liked her and scalded Stenlow often for getting wed to her. Ye stay on ye path and follow it, many today have admired ye for ye hard work, and round here, that counts."

She gave a smile and nodded, but deep down inside was still a little afraid, her gut told her to be wary, and from now on she would be. Seth had a cart to carry his wooden stock, and was heading over the bridge, so he put Morgana's bag and wooden box on it, and walked along at her side. Mavis waved her goodbye, having told her she would keep the table at her side free, and Morgana was grateful.

They crossed over the long bridge talking, and walked along the path through the area known as 'The Scree,' and after a forty minute walk, Seth stopped with a smile.

"Sadly, I must leave you here, my path lies up Needle Pass and over the mire bridges to my village of Hollow Coombe. Take care now, but you should be fine from here, look after yourself, and here, take this, I was not paying attention and it is a little crooked, but it still has many uses."

Morgana took the hand carved wooden spoon, she knew as soon as she saw it, she could use it for her large stew pan, she gave a big smile.

"Thank you, Seth, it has been nice to trade at your side, and walk with you, thanks for looking out for me." He gave a smile.

"Morgana, you are seen as one of us, and in here, we watch out for each other, I am sure you have heard, but there are two classes of citizen in this realm. Us with our dark hair, we are the lower ones, which is why, we stand by each other. I am telling you, because you are alone up yonder, if you get any trouble, follow this path down to marsh bridges and walk straight, and you will come to the village. I am always around, if you need help. Now go on, get off home and rest, and then study and work hard, and I will see you bright and early next week." She gave a big smile.

"Thank you, Seth, I am alright on my own you know, I prefer it that way, but I really appreciate your kindness."

He gave a wink, and turned his cart, and Morgana stood and watched as he walked along the path, pulling his little cart behind him. When he had gone, she shouldered her bag, and lifted her box of food, and walked slowly along the path through Misty Bank, heading back to her safe haven, her mind lost to her thoughts.

She had been back an hour, and had boiled a pan for a tea, and was preparing her meal for the night when there was a soft tap on the door. For a moment she felt a small jolt of fear. Still holding the knife, she walked to her door, and opened it slightly and peered out, she recognised Gwendolyn and pulled back on the door. She smiled at Morgana, as she opened the door wide and stepped back, and gave a bow.

"Your Highness." Gwendolyn gave another smile and stepped in; she was carrying a bag.

"Morgana, you are his student and I his wife, do not stand on ceremony with me, I have known your mother many years. I am here on an errand for my husband, and to be honest, I have wanted to see what you have done with this place. I must admit, you are brave, when he offered it me, I was appalled and told him I will use his guest room." Morgana gave a chuckle.

"Yes, it is not really a dwelling for a queen, it is more my style." Gwendolyn chuckled as she walked into the small living room, and looked round.

"You have done well, you have actually managed to put some life in here, I admire your courage." Morgana followed her.

"It suits my needs, and in here, I can be me and do as I wish, and I like that." Gwendolyn gave a smile, as she noted the books stacked up, and her pans hung on nails hammered into the chimney.

"It is quite a step down from the castle, I was surprised when he told me you wanted it, but to be honest, it does feel very cosy." Morgana walked up to the fire and swung the pot filled with water over it, and threw a few sticks on the flames.

"I know it is not much, but I see it as a start, and I have my independence here, at the castle there was always someone fussing and telling me what I should do. Here I have a space to study in peace, and I am kept busy with my chores, and I like it, I really do… Would you care for a cup of tea, I dry it myself and it is very wholesome, I have some honey if you like it sweet?" Gwendolyn sat in the only straight chair at the table with a smile.

"Thank you, yes, that would be lovely."

She watched as Morgana prepared the tea on the mantle above the fire, and then ladled the hot water into the cups, she gave it a stir with a small silver spoon, and then carried it over, and placed it down for Gwendolyn, she then took the other seat on the crooked chair, Gwendolyn watched her carefully.

"How are you doing, I was in Avalonia earlier, Fagan told me of Prunella?" Morgana breathed out, and Gwendolyn could see that Morgana was hiding her upset feelings.

"She scared me, she said things that were horrible and not true. That really frightened me because I am new here, and if that gossip goes round, people will hate me." Gwendolyn understood.

"Morgana, Prunella is well known for the horrible things she says to people, most people ignore her. Look, the best advice I can give you, is stand tall, and carry on as you have been, there are a lot of very kind people in this realm, and you may not realise it, but a lot have seen how hard you have worked, and they admire you for it."

"I mind my own business, and work hard, you know, I realise people do not understand it, but I am serious. I really find it all so very interesting, and I want to be able to learn the Whitelines, I could help a lot of people like Seth and Mavis." Gwendolyn really understood.

"Morgana, if my husband had thought for one second that you were not serious, you would not be here now, although I must tell you, at times it is not easy to be a woman with gifts in this world dominated by men, even a queen has her battles." Morgana understood that.

"Not Rhiannon, it appears to me she gets what she wants, and that is what scares me, I saw today how she uses those around her to do her dirty work. Can I ask you honestly and you will answer…? Is it true, she thinks I had something to do with the death of Eleanor, because I didn't?" Gwendolyn took a deep breath.

"She is a powerfully forceful woman Morgana, and she is used to getting her own way, I will not lie to you, Rhiannon has watched you with suspicion, and it does concern me." Morgana nodded.

"So she is telling people I did it, or was involved in some way, she thinks I am a murderess?"

Gwendolyn took a huge breath; it surprised her how straight forward Morgana was. Morgana understood better than most people realised, she glanced up at her.

"She thinks I am another Ariel, doesn't she?" Gwendolyn looked at her, and appeared a little caught off guard.

"You know about Ariel?" Morgana nodded.

"I have heard some of the stories, she was blamed like I have been for something she did not do, and it caused a lot of trouble." Gwendolyn nodded.

"Ariel was innocent, but Rhiannon felt she wanted to get even with my grandmother, and Ariel was her adopted daughter. Rhiannon used her to hurt my grandmother, it was a long time ago, but sadly, the rumours are true. Morgana, the reason I am here is because I did hear what happened today, and my husband has to go away on some very important business, and whilst he is gone, I have to return to Florae. You really will be very alone here for a while, and I did wonder if you could go and visit your mother for a while, you know, let things calm down a little? My husband has told the queen you were with him at the time, which you were, so we all know you are innocent, but for now, being out of her gaze would be a good thing."

Morgana nodded at her, she remembered the moment, her voice was low and soft as she thought.

"The problem is, she does not have to prove I did it, she has Prunella spreading her lies. It is up to me to prove I am innocent, but even if I do, who will listen, she is a queen, I am just a young woman living alone who wants to study magic? That alone will worry people. If I was powerful, I would have a voice, but I am not, and so she will win."

Morgana gave it some thought, she hated the idea of leaving her home for a while, she had settled in and felt at ease here. Gwendolyn watched her as she considered the point, Morgana looked up into her bright blue eyes.

"I will be fine here, but if you think it will help Merlin, I can study elsewhere for a while." Gwendolyn gave a smile and nodded at her.

"I think it will help, let the dust settle as it were, and let her go hunt someone else. All the council know it was not you, and they will defend you if needed, but for now, let the gossip die down." Morgana understood her.

"If that is your advice, I will make arrangements." Gwendolyn gave her a smile, and stood up and drained her tea cup. She looked into the cup.

"You know, I do believe you have a natural talent for tea, that really was a very lovely and refreshing cup, I enjoyed it. In the bag are a few things my husband wanted you to have, and I took the liberty of adding some shoes. I admire your determination, but I think you will find those a little easier on your feet." Morgana felt a pang of excitement as she looked down, and Gwendolyn smiled at her.

"We are both very proud of you Morgana, you really have proved your worth here, and I do like what you have done here. I will look forward to seeing it develop over time, and when I am here, you know, you will always be welcome at the cottage, it can get very isolating and quiet here." Morgana stood up with a smile.

"That is why I wanted to live here, I like to be solitary, it helps me focus on my study." Gwendolyn understood that, Merlin was not unsimilar.

"Alright then, think about what we have talked about, you know yourself enough to know what you will do, if you get into a bind, go and see Fagan, he will alert me." She nodded at her.

"Thank you, it is kind of you." Gwendolyn turned, and walked towards the door.

"I will bid you fare well for now, enjoy the food, it is starting to smell quite lovely."

She closed the door behind her, and Morgana turned quickly and reached for the bag. She saw the shoes and felt a huge burst of happiness, and sat on the floor, and slid off her old shoes and wiggled her toes with a sigh of relief. No one would ever understand the joy of not having to have rope souls on her shoes, rubbing up against her feet. She lifted out the plain black cloth shoes with a smile, and slipped them on, and smiled a happy smile.

"Oh, that feels so wonderful, Gwendolyn, you are a saviour."

*T*he night wore on, and Morgana ate her meal and considered everything from her day. She knew that Branna had lived with Ariel in Avalon, and then fled the country, as Ariel went home to Florae. The traders had told her, how Rhiannon had plotted to blame Ariel, and she was starting to wonder, if she had something similar in mind for her. The thought of it made her feel nervous, Rhiannon was powerful, and she really did not want to be dragged into something she had not been involved in, although, she had not forgotten the night of Eleanor's death, and the quiet voice that whispered in her ear.

Maybe Gwendolyn was right, maybe it would be easier to leave for a while, especially considering she would be completely alone and at the mercy of Rhiannon, and the thought of that did frighten her. The problem was, Gwendolyn had been nice to her, and she did appear as being a kind person, and yet she knew that it had been Gwendolyn that made the sword of power for Uther, that forced her father into a peace pact.

Merlin had supported Uther against her father, and allowed him to rape her mother, because that is what he did, and Rhiannon had armed Uther with superior weapons, and it was one of those that took her father's life. It all felt like they had used her mother and her father as pawns in some sort of political power struggle, to control everything, and in doing so, she had become the casualty. Was she right, was all of their kindness just to blind her into trusting them, so she could be used at some later point? She really did not know if any of them could be trusted at all, and that was the problem.

Morgana was starting to really understand how alone she really was, as she had no one she could trust enough to talk openly to them, it felt like the only person who had ever been honest, was Branna, and she could not walk in Avalon. She needed to see her, and she understood, when Jarron returned, she would ask him to tell Branna to meet her on the cliff tops, it was clear to her, Branna was family, and her father was Branna's grandson. It appeared, she was the only person who she could really talk to about all this, and so in her mind she started to plan a trip away.

It had been a long day and she was tired, she pulled closed the curtain on her small window, and checked both the large bolts were in her door, and then with her book and her candle, she headed through the blanket into her small bed chamber with her bag of things sent to her by Merlin.

She sat on the bed and was delighted to find a pair of leather boots, and large pile of parchment, some ink, and a small box of extra nibs, and to her delight, she found a small book on potion making. Once again, it was written in the hand of Merlin, she leaned back on her pillow and into the candle light, and opened the book and started to read. She really was extremely tired, and soon her eyes started to flutter, and they closed, as she slipped into a deep sleep.

Chapter Eleven.

Scapegoated.

Merlin had travelled to talk with the warlords and chieftains of the tribes across the land, to try and broker some sort of continued peace. Without Uther to rule, the tournaments to claim the right to try and pull the sword, were holding a delicate balance, but it was clear fractures were starting to appear, and Merlin needed to act.

Morgana's life did not change much, she cleaned her house, chopped wood, picked more flowers and leaves for teas and tinctures, and travelled to the glass maker to buy small bottles, and equipment to allow her to make more. On the days it was nice weather, she sat outside and read her book, as she tried to find a way to dig deeply into her thoughts and feelings, and summon the power to cut the nails in the window.

For all that time, in her thoughts was the threat of Rhiannon, and her accusation, it was clear, she did not like Morgana. Considering that she provided superior weapons to the men of Uther, to kill her father, Morgana also had a dislike of her that simmered deep down inside her. Morgana tried to distract herself by being busy, and focused on her work making teas and tinctures, as well as studying hard.

When Friday came, she packed her bag, and headed back to the markets, looking forward to seeing Mavis and Seth. It was early morning and still warm, and the long walk to market was hard going, but she arrived in high spirits, as she was greeted by Fagan, and saw he had placed her between her friends again. She paid her penny and headed with a smile to set up.

She was happy and felt at ease, as Seth and Mavis chatted to her as she displayed her teas, and her new tinctures, all clearly labelled in neat orderly rows. Soon she was busy as people who had purchased from her the week previous, came back with their friends and bought more. Morgana was happy and took a few moments to barter for food and goods, of which she purchased a new bigger and better made bag.

The morning moved on towards noon, and she was happy, having also made a good number of pennies to add to her savings. She was looking down adding new stock, and ensuring it was neat and orderly, when Mavis reached out and touched her arm. Morgana looked up, to see Mavis staring over towards the town. Without thinking, she turned and saw a large white horse, and on it was Rhiannon, she swallowed hard, as she saw her watching her, and she felt a cold shiver run down her spine.

At her side on his own horse, sat Stenlow, he too was watching as Rhiannon turned and spoke to him. A feeling of dread ran up through Morgana, she was alone with no support from Merlin, and she knew, without really understanding why. Trouble was coming. Morgana watched, as Stenlow gave a nod and dismounted from his horse, Mavis spoke quietly.

"Be factual, and honest, show respect and do not argue, he wants you to mess up, the queen wants to make you her example, so no matter what, stay calm."

*M*organa took a deep breath; she could feel her heart starting to beat rapidly. The crowd parted as Stenlow walked calmly through, everyone noticed and stopped to see what was happening. He walked right up to the front of the table, and Morgana stood frozen, trying her best to remain calm, but she was afraid, and under her long dress, her legs trembled. He looked her up and down.

"You… What are you doing here?" Morgana was unsure as to why he asked that, to her it was obvious. She took a deep breath.

"I sell fresh teas and tinctures, Lord Commander." He smirked, she was far more polite and less irritable than she was last time. He eyed her table.

"How?" Morgana frowned at him.

"Excuse me, I paid for the table, and people buy them from me." He gave a nod, she could see Rhiannon sat on her horse watching with a satisfied smirk, Stenlow looked up from the table.

"I meant how, in so much as you were not born here, or of Fae descent?" Morgana was at a loss; she did not really understand.

"I live in Avalon, I am a resident as you know, and as I told you last time we met, I make teas and tinctures to earn my living. I paid for the table like many others of the traders who enter this realm to trade." He gave a nod, looked back towards Rhiannon, and then turned and looked her right in the eye.

"They are invited guests for the market, they are here at a personal invitation of the queen, are you?" Seth frowned and looked at Stenlow.

"Since when has that been the rule, I know many traders and they have never been here on a personal invitation, how long has that rule been in place?" Stenlow looked at him with utter contempt.

"Are you questioning the rule of our queen?" Seth stepped back looking panicked, and shook his head.

"No, I would never do that." Stenlow gave a smirk, and turned back to Morgana, she could feel his enjoyment, as he knew everyone was watching.

"I asked you a question." Morgana felt her heart beating even faster, and she felt embarrassed, her mouth had gone suddenly very dry and she licked her lips.

"I did not know of that rule, no one told me. Master Fagan took my penny, and appeared satisfied that I could trade, so no, I do not have a personal invitation." She felt so scared, and could feel Rhiannon's eyes burning into her. Stenlow turned and looked back, he raised his voice.

"ROYCE!" Morgana watched feeling panicked, as the guard ran over and stood at attention, Stenlow looked at him.

"This woman is trading illegally against the wishes of the queen, seize her stock." Morgana gasped with Mavis.

"WHAT… NO, that is all I have, I need it to live?" Stenlow turned with a smirk.

"You are not welcome on this market by order of the queen, you are not a full resident, and you most certainly are not Fae." Morgana felt the tears as she shook her head.

"Please, I need my teas to trade, I will pack up and leave, and go elsewhere."

*T*he soldier pulled out his knife, and started to stab each of her bags of tea. He lifted the bottles, and dropped them, so they smashed on the floor. Morgana panicked and tried to snatch some to save them, but Stenlow snatched at her arm.

"Those are no longer your property, if you try to take them, I will be forced to imprison you, now step back, and do as you are told." The tears rolled into Morgana's eyes; her voice cracked as she spoke.

"This is not fair, I have done nothing wrong, Master Fagan told me it was fine for me to trade my goods, and people really like them." She gave a large sob, and Mavis pulled her away from the table and put her arm round her.

"Don't fight it dear, it is what they want, just step back, if you do anything, you will give them the reason they want to arrest you."

Morgana looked down as she watched her teas being torn open and scattered on the floor, and all her tonics, which had cost her the money she had earned, lay smashed and crushed on the floor. It was so painful, and she could not hold back her tears as they drained onto the grass. Weeks of preparation and work were destroyed in minutes, as Stenlow watched with a smug smile on his face, and all she could do as Rhiannon watched on, was bite her lip, and swallow the anger that was building inside her.

*T*he crowds parted and bowed their heads as Rhiannon slowly rode her tall white horse towards the front of the stand, Mavis and Seth bowed before their queen, Morgana lifted her sleeve and wiped her eyes, but she did not bow. Rhiannon looked down at her with utter distaste, Morgana looked up defiant and met her gaze, she fixed on her eyes and stared at her, she was the only person in the whole market still standing. Rhiannon stared at her, and Morgana could feel her hate.

"I am Queen here; bend your knee to me." Morgana stood still, her teeth gritted, her anger flowing up through her, and her eyes burned with her defiance, as she stared with hate at Rhiannon.

"You are right, you are the queen of the Fae Ofmoon, I am Morgana, daughter of Igraine, widow of King Uther, the one true king. He named me his daughter, and I am a countess, and by right of birth, Queen of the Britons of the realm of men. I am apprentice to Merlin, guardian of the Whitelines, as appointed by the White Lord himself, who by rights, is a superior within the ruling council. It appears we are equals, Queen of Fae."

There was a loud gasp from the crowd, and Rhiannon looked enraged, her horse felt it and jittered, Stenlow looked shocked. Rhiannon looked down at her, it was obvious Morgana had hit a raw nerve, her anger showed in her words.

"You may have Merlin to protect you, but you are no queen, you are just another piece of trash, forced to peddle poisons on a lower class market. You do not belong in my realm, and I want you out." Morgana held her gaze but was utterly terrified.

"I do not live in your realm, I live in the property of Merlin, which he owns in its entirety. It is his and is not classed as your land. It is independent from Avalon, as it is white line territory, and as long as he gives me the right to live there, I shall." Rhiannon took a deep breath, she knew Morgana was right, but she was very angry, and knew, that she had no dominion over Morgana.

"Get what you bought, and get off my market, the sight of you is offensive to me." Morgana gave a smile of defiance.

"As you wish, Queen of the fair." There were gasps.

"I see now why Ariel never returned." Rhiannon gave a gasp.

"GET OFF MY MARKET, YOU INSOLENT TRASH!"

*S*he pulled hard on the reigns, and Morgana knew she could do nothing, but she was now really afraid, because she had shown everyone, Rhiannon was not as powerful as she thought she was. Merlin was her protector, and Rhiannon knew she had no sway with him, as Gwendolyn had told her, he had spoken at the Ruling Council, and proved her innocence over the death of Eleanor. Rhiannon yanked hard on the reins of her horse, it pulled back it's head hard, and then turned, and she rode through the crowd. The Fae were startled, and they scattered backwards away from her, as she galloped at speed back into the town of Avalonia.

Mavis looked up from the floor, looking as white as a spirit, she took a deep breath as Stenlow walked off with his guard.

"Oh my, you may be small and quiet, but you are not far wrong, you spoke like the daughter of a queen. Please be careful, you do not show her up and get away with it, there will be repercussions, you can bargain on it."

Morgana crouched down and put her food in her bag, and then stood up and shouldered it, she looked at Mavis and gave her a weak smile, although Mavis was right, she knew that Rhiannon would seek vengeance.

"Thank you for being kind to me Mavis, and thank you for helping me, I really enjoyed being here with you, and I am grateful to you." Mavis looked at her with a sad face.

"Oh Love, I am so sorry this happened, will you be alright?" Morgana gave a nod, as more tears filled her eyes.

"I will find a way, I live in a house not Avalon, maybe I will be able to sell from there, if people don't mind travelling to me. I have a lot of work to do, so I can make teas and tinctures, so I will get busy and do what I can, then work something out." Mavis gave a nod and smiled a sad smile.

"I will tell those who ask where you are, take care of yourself, and keep on your guard."

She stood up, moved forward and pulled Morgana into a hug, and Morgana felt her tears run from her eyes, these were her only friends in the whole realm, and she had to leave them. She took a huge breath in as Mavis released her, and turned to Seth.

"Thanks Seth, thanks for helping me get my things home on your cart last week, and for all the kindness you showed me. Take care, and watch yourself, there will be a lot of bad things said, and you may get hurt by them." He gave a nod and winked.

"You have a strong spirit, and I have to say, I am proud of you, you stood your ground and all of us felt it. You might not be Fae born, but I for one see you as one of us. Watch your back Morgana, I will spread the word to give you a week, and then folks will be able to buy tea from you." Morgana smiled and gave a nod.

"Thanks Seth, you and Mavis are lovely nice people, I am glad I met you."

*M*organa left the market, and walked slowly towards the bridge that crossed the lake. She felt hurt and upset at the injustice, because she knew that Rhiannon had singled her out for no other reason than she had taken a dislike to her. The simple fact was, Rhiannon knew nothing of her, she had no idea of who Morgana was, she had just formed an opinion, and it was wrong.

Morgana thought of the few things Branna had told her, and she knew that deep down, there had to be more to the story of Branna and her time in Avalon. As she walked, she understood, that she needed now more than ever to talk with Branna and get the full story, of the real truth of Rhiannon. Life had suddenly got harder for Morgana, and her mind filled with endless questions and possibilities as she walked up towards her small home. She pulled out her key, and unlocked the door, walked in, and leaned back against it as it closed. She gave a long sad sigh.

"She is right, I am a daughter of a queen, but I am no queen, I am powerless in this world."

She turned and bolted the door, picked up her bag and walked into her living space and put her bag on the table and started to unpack it. The only good thing about the day, was she had made two shillings and three pennies, so she knew she could make it through several weeks, which would give her time to work out what she was going to do.

With a heavy heart, she put away her food, stored her meat, and cleaned up her home. She shook her mat outdoors and beat out the dust with a stick, then carried it in and replaced it on the floor. Her pan was bubbling, so she made a tea and prepared a small meal, then took her food into her bedroom, and sat on the bed alone, knowing the curtain was down, and the door was bolted. Morgana finished her meal, and lay back on her bed to rest and think, she felt tired, and as her mind wandered through all the possibilities of her current situation, without realising, she drifted into sleep.

Morgana woke with a start to the sound of hammering, she sat up in bed and looked around, in the night she had grown hot and must have taken her dress off, she was naked and sweating, it was hot in the house. She pulled her dress over to her and stood up.

"I really need to master that charm, so I can open the window."

Dressed, she tiptoed out of her room and walked to the window, she pulled back the black cloth a little, and peered out. Outside, a good way off, Fagan was hammering a thick pole into the floor, she frowned.

"What in all the realms is he doing?"

She slipped on her new soft shoes, and unbolted the door and walked out, and stopped to look down. Outside her door was a wooden crate filled with small glass bottles, at their side, was another crate filled with dry goods, such as flour, oats and even sugar. There were five large jars of honey, a large jar of dried beef strips and two large fresh loaves of bread, she had no idea what was happening. She looked across the wide stretch of grass, where Fagan had stopped hammering, and was stood wiping his brow. He gave a big smile and waved.

Morgana stepped onto the grass and walked up the fifty yards towards him, he leaned on the thick pole he had just hammered in. He looked red in the face as Morgana got close to him.

"Master Fagan, what are you doing here, and why is my door step filled with boxes of things?" He wiped his face and took a good breath of air.

"Ye see Little Dark Eyes, the thing is, a lot of folks yesterday, did not agree with what happened, which by the way, I had been called away to me shop. Had I been there, things would have been different. Ye see, the thing is, those folks on the market. Well, they is good people, and they saw how upset ye were, and well, they did not agree, so, as a sort of thank ye for standing up for yeself, they sent ye some things to make up for the damage. They hope that ye will not be put off, tis a good thing ye knows, they see ye as one of them, they does." Morgana looked back feeling shocked.

"They did that for me?" He smiled at her.

"They did, as I was saying, they is good folk." Morgana felt a lump in her throat.

"I am not sure what to say, I did not expect this, I am a little surprised, and I want to cry." Fagan gave a nod.

"Tis best ye get them indoors, the day will be hot, store them good, so they does not spoil." Morgana gave a nod, and wiped her eyes.

"I will, please tell them I am very grateful for their kindness, no one has ever been this kind to me before, and I am not sure of the right words to say."

"I think ye said it beautifully… Well, I must get on, I have a lot to do." Morgana turned and looked at the long line of poles placed two yards apart, she gave a frown as she realised, they were all along the road side.

"What are you doing?" He lifted his large hammer.

"Tis an order off the queen, Father Whiteline has a fence round his property, but not this one, so she says she wants it marked out, so ye knows what is, and what isn't her land. The poles mark the boundary, ye has a good piece of land here to garden and keep livestock, tis a good size."

Morgana understood, Rhiannon needed an excuse to catch her doing something on her land, which meant from now on, she would be confined within the lines of poles, and that would restrict her hunting abilities. She was glad to see a good stock of herbs, fruit bushes and trees within her boundary, she would need those in order to eat, and also dry for her teas.

"I am going to brew some tea, would you care for some Master Fagan, it is hot work for you?" Fagan gave a big smile.

"Tis a kind act, and I thank ye, it would be nice to wet me throat, I don't suppose ye has any barley crackers?" Morgana shook her head.

"No… I do think I have the ingredients though, maybe I should bake some." He gave a chuckle.

"Tea and barley crackers, well I have to agree, I am as tickled as a daffodil I is."

Morgana gave a smile, and walked back to her house to take in all her new things, and store them properly, and set a pan to boil for tea.

*F*agan worked for most of the day, and Morgana busied herself distilling witch hazel, to bottle. In amongst all the crates, she had found fine woven hessian, for bags, some measuring spoons, copper pipe for distilling, which was much better than the one she had, and forty small glass bottles. It was such a huge surprise to her. She had only spoken with those she sold to, plus Mavis and Seth, and yet she had been shown a great kindness, and it felt very strange to her, she had never known anything like this.

Morgana had to ponder if this was just because the queen did not like her, if the queen liked her, would they be so good with her, it was a question she could not really answer? Having watched Fagan, and sat at the door for several cups of tea with him, she could see that it was pretty clear, the queen now saw her as an enemy. Her only saving grace, was Merlin was her protector, had he not been, she probably would be in prison now.

*M*organa sat back on her chair, as the copper pipe slowly dripped over near her hearth into the large jar, the smell of the witch hazel scented the whole room, but she liked that. In her mind, knowing Rhiannon saw her as an enemy, made her think, and she remembered the words of Gwendolyn.

"You really will be very alone here, and I did wonder if you could go and visit your mother for a while, you know, let things calm down a little?" She gave a sigh.

"Maybe I should leave for a while, mother will no doubt be happy to see me, although with Merlin away, this would be a good time to see if I could visit Branna. I know she would be happy to see me, and I could talk to her, she probably will understand this better than anyone."

*T*he following day, Fagan returned to finish hammering in the poles around the property, and planked the fence to seal the boundary. Morgana now had a much better idea of how much land belonged to Merlin, and it was far bigger than she realised. It was a great relief to see that all the places she had gathered flowers and leaves for her teas were all inside the boundary, and she decided to walk all the way round, so she could familiarise herself with all of it.

Once Fagan had left and the poles were all in marking out the full property, Morgana sat down at the back of the house near the well, and focused her mind. It took her a few minutes, but as her inner thoughts deepened, she brought to her mind all her thoughts of where the edges of her land reach too, and once she had it all fixed in her mind properly, she did the charm.

The whole area of the property was hidden under a veil, it was a big task for her, and once she felt it was in place, she gave a gasp and lay back on the grass feeling dizzy, but smiled to herself. She felt Rhiannon was watching her, but now she knew, that any time she was on the land, she would be completely hidden from view, and Rhiannon's prying eyes. She could now live completely in private, and live as she chose, and if anyone did visit, she knew the queen would have no idea of why they were there. In her mind it felt like a small victory, she could go several weeks without ever leaving if she needed to, and for all that time, her life would be completely private.

*T*hat night, Jarron arrived back, and she was so happy to see him, he was tired from the long flight, so she fed him some grain and scraps of meat, and filled a bowl with water for him to drink from.

Morgana talked to the white bird, and told him the whole story of what had happened, and how she was going to leave Avalon and travel to Tintagel to visit her mother. She also asked Jarron, if Branna would allow her to visit. The bird needed rest, and Morgana carried him outside, and sat him at the base of a thick apple tree, he flew up to the branches and folded his head under his wing and slept, and Morgana decided she too would get some rest.

She locked and bolted the door, stripped and climbed into bed, and settled down, and closed her eyes. Her mind was filled with all the questions she would ask Branna, and she knew at last, she would learn the truth of her line, because she was now starting to understand everything, especially Branna's hatred of Rhiannon.

Morgana was starting to understand that Branna had some form of power similar to Rhiannon, and if she did, then she could only assume that she would one day have the same sort of power, and that fascinated her. Simply knowing she could maybe rise to match Rhiannon gave her hope, and she knew, that she had to work harder to focus and learn all that Merlin could teach her, because then, she knew, that never again would anyone embarrass and humiliate her the way Rhiannon tried to.

Understanding she was veiled in a piece of land that would provide everything for her, and she could practice unseen as she learned the Whitelines, felt good to her. If she could develop her gifts, and learn how to enhance them where no one could see her, then she understood, that would give her an advantage over Rhiannon, because she already knew most of her strengths, they had been well documented. A sudden idea occurred to her, she was going to study the Whitelines, but she was also going to study Rhiannon. In her thoughts, the more she knew, the less likely it was that Rhiannon would ever get the upper hand on her again. If the queen wanted her as an enemy, then she would arm herself, and what could be better for the task, than knowledge?

*W*ithin the royal apartments, of the large wooden house in Florae, Gwendolyn White Circle sat back in her seat, as she looked at her table of power and noted that Morgana had extended her veil. She had watched Morgana's encounter with Rhiannon in the market, and gave it all some thought, her mind wandered through all her thoughts.

"Why would a queen of such power take such a dislike to a stranger, why blame her for Eleanor's death when she clearly knows it was not Morgana?" Madeline looked up from the other side of the room.

"Is everything alright Mama?" Gwendolyn looked at her.

"You have met Morgana, what do you think of her?" Madeline shrugged.

"I do not really know her, I am not sure anyone does, she is very reclusive. At the castle in Tintagel when we were there, she did not really talk, she mainly read books. To be honest Mama, I thought she was just a sad quiet girl, I know she missed her father." Gwendolyn understood that.

"What was she like with Eleanor?" Madeline sat back.

"I do not think she hated her, I just think Morgana had one idea of how she wanted to live, and it was the opposite of Eleanor, I think both of them found the other irritating, and boring. Mama, you do not think Morgana was involved do you, because I would have felt it? I felt little around Morgana, apart from her sadness and loneliness, she cared about her father, I do not think people understood how deeply, I do, I felt it in her." Gwendolyn gave a nod.

"She was not involved, but that is what bothers me, why is Rhiannon so convinced she was? You know, she told me she thought Rhiannon was going to make her another Ariel. I have no idea how she knew about her, but to be honest, I do not think she is wrong, I feel Rhiannon has really got it in for her, and I am worried about her. You know when you talk to her, she is a very bright and likeable girl. I cannot deny, she understands things in a way few others do, she may be mortal, but she thinks like a Fae, Rhiannon could find, she picked on the wrong one."

"She is a very powerful queen Mama, I doubt there are few who can best her, let Papa handle it, he knows how to make her behave." Gwendolyn smiled; Madeleine was becoming very skilled in the ways of Fae.

Maybe Madeline was right, it was probably better for Merlin to deal with all of this, after all, she was his student, and his responsibility. She had no intention of creating a rift, like the one when she was young, and her grandmother offended Rhiannon. Even now there were still repercussions, and a distrust of the two lines of Fae. Maybe it was better to sit it out and let it all play out without any involvement, things for now between the two races were cordial and stable. With so much unrest in the world of men, it was better for there to be peace.

Chapter Twelve.

Family Roots.

Jarron flew to the window with Roack, Branna was sat at her small desk writing in her journal, she looked up as Roack flew in to her work table. Sitting back, she pushed back her long tatty mane of black hair, and viewed the birds with dark eyes.

"What news of our little Raven?" Roack bobbed about on the table, her voice was croaky and abrasive.

"She has left Avalon and travelled to her mother's home, there has been trouble for her with the queen of light." Branna tensed, hearing Rhiannon and Morgana had trouble, worried her, and her voice held a hint of alarm.

"Is she alright?" Roack's dark eyes watched her carefully.

"The queen has taken a dislike to her, but she stood her ground when she confronted her. Things are not easy, so she has returned to the castle of her mother to let things cool down." Branna gave a snort.

"Well, that won't happen, Rhiannon holds grudges for years, it must be bad if she has felt the need to go home. How is she, is she worried, does she need help?" The black bird bobbed around.

"She wants to talk, you will need to go to her, but be aware, that a young lord named Kane followed her out, Jarron has heard things about him, and it is thought he watches for the queen of light. Your little raven should not trust him, he will use charm to find out what the queen of light needs."

Branna understood how Rhiannon operated, everything she did was a power play to gain more control. It worried her that she had targeted Morgana so soon after she moved into Avalon. Her only assurance was she knew that Merlin was watching over her, although she was angry at his part in the downfall of her favourite grandson, and the part he played in his death. She knew he was powerful, and not easily fooled. She turned to Jarron.

"Go to Rosamund, and tell her to warn her about Kane, and then tell her I will meet her on the cliff paths when I know she is alone. Tell her I will be watching over her."

Jarron gave a bow, turned, and flew off the window, heading back to Morgana. Branna turned to Roack, her mind already working quickly.

"The time is coming, we must prepare a room for her, I need her here so that I can talk privately with her, we need her protected more. Tell Lothar to go to her and prepare her, we need her here before she returns to the care of the wizard."

Branna made her way out of the room, heading up to the castle to prepare. Roack looked at the long crystal box containing Ariel. She flew over and landed on it, and looked down through the crystal at the pale sleeping face beneath.

"It is good she has a purpose; she dwells too much on you of late, she must let you go, this will be good for her." Roack turned, spread out her large wings, and flew to the window, and out into the air.

Morgana sat out on the cliff top enjoying the fresh breeze as she read her book, on how to control her thoughts and focus her internal powers. She was lost in a world of her own thoughts, when she became aware that someone was standing beside her, she looked up, and saw a young man with long blonde hair, and bright blue eyes looking down at her. She closed her book as he smiled at her.

"I said, I am hoping I am not disturbing you; I feel you were quite captivated by your story."

"I was… I like to read; you look familiar, and yet I am not sure if we have met."

He flicked his long hair back, his clothing was well tailored and high quality, and he had an aura of confidence around him. She had met many like him in her life, he was very sure of himself.

"Is there something you wanted, you know, some reason for stopping?" He gave a wide smile.

"Not really, I saw you, and you looked so serene and at peace, I felt quite captivated and felt a desire to talk with you." She gave it some thought, and slipped her book to the ground at the side of her.

"Does that happen often, you know, you feel this desire to talk to people, I feel I am not that captivating, I am just a simple girl?" He looked surprised, or she felt he faked it, and was actually quite good at it.

"I have no wish to embarrass such a fair lady, but surely you do not believe that? I find you very interesting, and remarkably captivating. I can assure you, there is nothing simple about you." She smirked, and realised who he was, she had seen him in Avalon. It took little to work out what he wanted.

"You are quite good at this aren't you, how many maidens have fallen to your charm? I would imagine, it is quite a few." He stepped back and frowned.

"Madam, I feel I should take offence, you mistake me greatly." She gave a small laugh, and shook her head.

"I do not think so, I am sorry, my only interest is in study, I have no time for romance and its pleasures, although I feel the romance will only last long enough for your pleasure, at which point it will fade. You are wasting your charms on me, you would be better suited to the ladies of Avalon, I am sure their lack of learning will aid you greatly in your quest to prove yourself." He stepped back looking very upset, as she smiled.

"I feel I have wasted my walk, and it appears what people say is true, you are very abrasive with people." Morgana stared at him blankly.

"I talk straight and I do not lie, which I realise is unbecoming of the ladies of Avalon, but there again, I am not of Avalon, I merely live there. I remember you now, I saw you at the queens' festivities the night Eleanor suffered her fatal illness, and you were very busy as I remember." He frowned at her.

"How is that possible, I have no memory of you there?" Morgana completely understood him, and realised why he was here, and she had to admit it, Rhiannon was clever indeed.

"I was there all night, and I did see you fawning over several ladies, I am sorry sir, but on this occasion, your reputation arrived much further ahead of you. Be careful of the rumours, not everything spoken is true of me. I can assure you; I have the ability to point every woman you talked to out, and the order in which you did it. I am not guilty of the things people have been saying, although, I am flattered you thought I was so easy to fool, and was pretty enough to decorate your bed sheets. I must admit, I shall say from this moment, I have no interest in your skills at this time."

He was clearly very annoyed at her, and his brow furrowed slightly. Hearing the word no, must be something he does not often hear, and it angered him, he stepped back and looked at her.

"I feel I have wasted mine and your time, I shall therefore excuse myself." Morgana gave a nod.

"Time talking is never wasted, I am sure both of us have learned something, good day to you sir. It was kind of you to stop, I am sorry to have disappointed you." He turned with a pout, and strode off along the cliff top path, Morgana watched him with a smirk.

"You really will not stop at anything will you Rhiannon?" She lifted her book, and opened it back to her page, and then relaxed and started to read.

*F*agan pulled up in front of Morgana's house, to see the door and the curtain closed. On her door was a neatly written sign reading. 'Gone away, back soon.' He smiled as he saw it.

"Tis a good thing, let the waters settle a while Little Dark Eyes, ye are a lot smarter than folks see."

He jumped off the cart, and lifted out a large box containing herb plants. He walked round to the back of the house, where he put down the plants in the shade. They were nice and wet, and he made a note to keep an eye on them. Morgana's absence was noted; hence Kane had been despatched to keep an eye on her.

Rhiannon was so sure, considering his success with many of the women around Avalon, but she had not taken into account, that Morgana was very bright and well educated, and not about to be fooled by her stooge. Kane had walked back towards the castle unsure of why his charm had failed, he had never been refused in his life, and it left him feeling a little uncertain of what to do next. He knew Rhiannon wanted results, but how was he to get them?

*M*organa read for a little while, and then stood up, she did love it here on the cliffs, she turned and walked further down, along the path. She loved the feeling of the wind in her hair, it felt liberating and freeing. Out on the cliffs, she always felt like she had the space to think, she had felt the same in Avalon, but she was starting to wonder if she was really that protected in Avalon. She turned above the bay, Branna had told her she once sat in many years ago and looked down the path, and smiled, Branna was sat on a large rock waiting. Morgana looked around to ensure they were private, and then hurried down towards her.

"I had hoped you would turn up at some point." Branna stood up.

"We have to be careful; you are being watched, has Jarron arrived yet?" Morgana shook her head at her.

"Not yet, but I do know, she sent Kane to try and seduce me to give her more information, but I evaded him, I think it hurt his feelings, he is not accustomed to girls who say no."

Branna gave a slight chuckle, Morgana could see her watching all around them, she looked to Morgana, she could see how alert she was.

"Morgana, I want you to come to my home, and spend some time there, so we can talk without being heard. Rhiannon is casting her net wide to trap you, and I want to take you where no one will find us, and then show you the truth of our line. You must tell no one where you are going, wait for Lothar, he will bring you to me in safety. Will you do that?" Morgana understood, and in a way, she felt relieved, although something occurred to her.

"Does coming here place you in danger, because I do not want that?" Branna smiled at her.

"Fear not, I am hidden, she has no hope of seeing me, if she did, she would be here now. Trust in me Morgana, you will be safe with me, I will let no one harm you." Morgana understood.

"I will pack this night and wait for Lothar, and be ready, I will tell my mother I wish to visit a friend I made in Glaston; she will feel pleased to know I have one, she often lectures me on being more friendly and social with others." Branna understood her and gave her a smile, she slipped a small piece of parchment into her hand.

"We will be safe together soon, I promise."

*B*ranna stepped back and faded into smoke and was gone, Morgana felt a twinge of happiness and excitement, turned and walked quickly back up the path toward the top of the cliff.

She reached the top, and walked onto the worn track, and saw in the distance Kane was walking back towards her, she gave a sigh and carried on towards him carrying her book, it took quite some time before they met, he gave a courteous nod.

"I fear, it felt wrong to leave you, it can be dangerous to walk alone up here, so I returned to assist you." Morgana walked past him.

"I have walked here all my life, I know these paths better than you know Avalon, I am quite safe and have no need of a guide." She walked onwards trying to ignore him. Kane walked up to her side and glanced at her; he was clearly irritated by her.

"I really do not understand you, just what is your objection to me?" Morgana continued to look ahead following the path.

"I do not like to be followed or spied upon, especially by a person who reports back to Avalon and it's queen." He stopped, and stared at her as she continued.

"I am not like that, I genuinely find you interesting, and desirable." Morgana stopped and turned back to look at him stood on the path, he looked a little pathetic, she smirked.

"If I am so desirable, why did you not speak up for me at the market? I saw you there at the side of your queen, and you were sniggering along with her other supporters, and I may add, pawing at Gwendolyn's daughter. If I am so appealing, why did you not talk to your queen, and tell her, that I am not like that, and that I am a woman who is self assured and highly educated? You stood there like the rest and watched her humiliate me, but I have done nothing wrong, I have not done the things she accuses me of, and yet you said nothing. Seth who is twice your age tried to stand up for me, now he is a real man, and he wants nothing from me. I know your kind, you want to bed me and hope I will say something that will gain you more favour with the queen, well I am not yours to play with, and you have no right to try."

He looked completely crest fallen, as he stared at her, he clearly was struggling to think of what to say, she gave a long sigh.

"Look, I do not think you are a bad person, well not an evil one, I do not agree with the way you treat women. If you really want to bed me, prove your worth to me, show me that I am worth something, and you are worth my time." He gave a shrug not really understanding her.

"How would I do that; I am not sure of what you expect?" She understood that.

"Kane, go back to Avalon, and tell your queen I was not involved with either the death of Uther or Eleanor, because that is the truth. Tell her, and then come and tell me what she said." She gave a smirk, as he looked suddenly very awkward and scared.

"That is not an easy thing that you ask, the queen is convinced it was you, and she does not change her mind easily." Morgana shook her head.

"A true man would, for he would see me as worthy, and so he would at least try on my behalf, as Merlin, and Seth did, and neither of those wants to bed me, they just did it because it was the right thing to do. You see that is my point, if you truly believe what you have said to me today, you would, but I can see you do not even believe your own words. Why don't you realise you will not sway me, and go back to Avalon where there are plenty of woman who will bed you, because honestly, I never will." He gave a long sigh and looked down at the floor, Morgana turned.

"Go home Kane… Just leave me alone, which is actually all that I really want."

*S*he walked off and left him stood watching her. Morgana returned to the castle alone, and walked across the large main hall towards the steps, her mother looked up.

"Morgana, I believe Lord Kane was looking for you." She continued walking towards the steps.

"I saw him, he was mistaken in his thinking, so I left him behind." Igraine gave a sigh.

"Morgana, he finds you appealing, you should really start to consider people like him. He is well placed in society. You should think of such things, no woman wants to be left behind like a discarded flower. You know if you do not take this seriously, you will end up alone."

Morgana gave a chuckle as she stepped onto the steps up to her room, she glanced back.

"That is fine with me, I like being alone." Igraine gave a sigh, as she watched Morgana walk away, and shook her head.

"I really have no idea why I bother to try; she is as stubborn as her father."

*B*elow Castle Berengar, Branna was busy. Outside her work room, was a long corridor, on which were three doors, leading into empty rooms. Morgana had a hidden power, her full potential was still to come, but Branna feared Maud, because with Morgana's powers unleashed, it was clear she would one day be more powerful than her, and that could spell trouble between them.

Branna arranged for the largest of the three rooms to be cleaned and scoured out, and then decorated fit for Morgana to reside in. A large four poster bed was brought down, cabinets and drawers, chairs and tables, and Branna arranged them. She also ensured that there was a good supply of books, of things that would help her, she had documented a great deal of Fae magic, and she also, placed a large blank black book on the table, with ink and nibs.

With candles and a fire set up ready in the hearth, the room felt cosy and welcoming, and she felt pleased with herself as she walked around it inspecting every detail. It reminded her, of how she had once offered the room to Ariel after her imprisonment, but she had refused, opting to sleep with Branna in her own quarters. Once she was satisfied, she left the room, and headed up to the large tower to sit on the ledge and look out across the woodlands. Roack flew up to her, and sat at her side, something that in her isolation and loneliness she had always been glad of. In many ways, they had grown much closer and talked more than ever, for if the truth be told, with Ariel locked in her box, Roack was Branna's only real comfort in what had become a life of unbearable loss.

"What news do you bring to me this day?" Roack sat still, looking out across the land.

"Maud suspects you are up to something, she knows of the room, and fears you will release the woman of light." Branna smirked.

"After all these years where she plotted and improved her skills alone in her basements, even now she is still afraid of the one person who would never harm her. It amuses me Roack, Ariel always knew how important all of you are to me, and for that very reason, she would never have harmed any, it is not in her nature to kill." The large Raven turned her head back, and her black eyes looked at Branna.

"Her skills have deepened; she has grown in power. She is more of the line of Berengar, and has embraced the darkness within her core, she grows darker by the day, one day she will rise up to challenge you, you must be wary of her, if you wish to continue to rule." Branna smiled.

"She will strike at you, and try to harm you, which she hopes will weaken me, but in doing so, she will weaken all of us. Maud may have powers, but her greed for power has eaten her wisdom, she will never rule, for her favour with the tribe will not last long. Once they see how she squanders all they have achieved, they will turn on her, as the Varisci turned on Grembauld. Maud thinks she can replace you with Rajani, but we both know that is not possible, for Maud needs the charms of the Fae, and I am the only one who knows them, without them, she will fail, wither and die." Roack looked back across the land.

"You have built much here, when will you strike again at the golden queen?"

Branna lifted her eyes, and looked out to where she knew two trees marked a wide open space, in the midst of the large forest.

"Morgana will give me more information about the life of the Fae of Avalon, and when she does, I will know what to do. I think Morgana will have a role in that, for she too will soon feel that she wants to exact her revenge. The Golden Queen will push her too far, and I hope that with the knowledge she gains from the wizard, she will have what she needs to strike back." Roack stiffened.

"I thought you would join her to us, and make her one of our ravens?" Branna understood Roack wanted her within the circle of the family.

"The time is not upon us, if she embraces a raven, the wizard will feel it, I want her to learn the Whitelines, and then use them with the powers of Fae, for then, she will grow to match me, and when that happens, she will be marked as the one to replace me, for she will outshine all the others." Roack understood that, but she was wary.

"Branna the Raven, you know the power of light, it may prevent her from joining the darkness, it could cost us her?" Branna gave a nod and smiled at the bird, Roack's mind was so sharp at times, and she admired how fast the bird understood things.

"Morgana will never turn to the light, she has the line of Victor in her, and she loved her father a great deal. Trust me Roack, she hides it well, but there is great pain and anger in her over the injustice of her father's death. Morgana is very intelligent, she understands people in the same way we do, the wizard is a pawn in her game, she will use his guilt to learn from him, but I already feel within her, her lust for revenge on the wizard. Morgana will rise a raven in Avalon, long before she chooses a bird from here, but she will return one day to claim one, time is on our side Roack, I can wait."

Roack spotted a snack and flew down to the lower battlement, she snatched up the snail and swallowed it, she turned and looked up, and felt the feelings coming. Branna was looking out across the woodland, and Roack knew that her mind was drifting back in time, she broke the connection, and left Branna alone with her thoughts, whilst she walked around picking up snails and eating them.

Branna brought up her knees and leaned onto them, as her thoughts drifted into her past, she gave a sigh.

"What did you know of the Whitelines Ariel, are they the key to the balance of powers, are they the reason he can control both?" She stared at the tall trees in the distance.

"I wish we could talk, you could really help me at the moment, because I want to help Morgana. I want to show her how to create balance, if she can do that, one day she will rule all that I have built, and I shall awaken you, and we will leave here together."

*M*organa hurried up to her room, closed the door and opened the note. She sat on her bed and read Branna's words in neat small writing.

'Morgana.

Lothar will collect you at midnight, there will be a carriage near the gates, go with him, and three miles down the road you will be met. Once in the carriage, I know you know how to cast the veil, so veil yourself, when the carriage stops, get out and another girl will replace you, Rosamund will be waiting. Go with her and she will bring you to me, when the carriage arrives at its destination, the golden queen will think you are still at the castle, and it will give you enough time to come here. Remember, use the veil, you must be hidden before you arrive here.

Branna.'

*S*he felt excited, and read it again, then knowing she had to be on her guard, she walked to the fire place, tore up the note, and scattered it on the fire to burn. Morgana gave a big smile, turned to her wardrobe, and opened the doors. She had little left as most of it was in Avalon, but she took out what was there and slipped it into her bag, then walked round the room, gathering up her possessions, and packed them neatly, it would not be long, and she would be free of all of this, and back with the family of her father.

It felt strange to think of her father's family, for most of her life, they had been spoken about, but she had met few. Lothar, she knew well, he had often been a visitor in her younger days, as had Rosamund, who her mother appeared to like a great deal, but she really did not know the others. Lothar had talked to her of Dagaric, and Merwig, both of whom he appeared to have a great fondness of, but his tales of Maud and Otto worried her, she had not heard good things, especially in regard to Otto and his views of Celts and Saxon's. She felt her best path, would be to be aware of them, and see how they were with her, after all, she had Branna, and she knew that she would not allow any to insult or harm her.

Shortly before midnight, Morgana lifted her bag, and quietly snuck out of her room, the castle was silent, apart from the few guards who walked the halls and the main gates. She came down the steps holding her bag, and crossed the hall, Lothar was outside waiting. He gave a smile as she came out into the large courtyard, saw the carriage awaiting her, and felt the excitement building inside her, as she walked over to Lothar, and he turned.

Both of them walked in silence to the back of the carriage, where a guard stood watch, Lothar opened the door, and she climbed in. He passed her bag inside to her, which was strange, as all luggage was usually carried on the rack above. Lothar looked at the guard, he was a loyal Varisci who had served Victor.

"Make sure no one follows us, especially the Lord Kane, our young Lady Raven, needs our protection more now than ever." The guard gave a nod.

"Have no fear My Lord, no one will leave here before dawn, the gates will be locked and remain that way." Lothar gave a nod and climbed inside, where Morgana was sat back, and concentrating on the charm of the veil.

Within minutes, the carriage lurched forward, and headed out of the gates into the darkness, and Lothar sat back relieved.

"Remember Morgana, cast the veil only upon yourself, not me, or the carriage, we must remain visible in order to trick the queen." Morgana nodded with her eyes shut.

"I have never done it on myself, only my house." Lothar understood that.

"Just think of yourself, nothing else, then do the charm, and you will be hidden."

Morgana understood, she focused her mind as the carriage rumbled on down the dirt road away from the castle, and it swayed from side to side on the uneven surface. In her mind, she pictured herself, and held the image in her thoughts, and then spoke the charm quietly in her head. She felt a strange prickly feeling run down her spine and breathed out, and Lothar smiled.

"I feel it around you, fear not, the queen is now blind, and you are free of her gaze, enjoy this time, it is good you return home to the family, it has been too long. This is your time Morgana, your time to learn the truth of your line, it will be only short for now, so use it well and learn all you can. In days to come, this will be one of the most important moments in your life." She frowned at him.

"How so?" Lothar gave a slight chuckle, as he looked at her in the dim light cast from the candle in the brass lantern.

"The days that follow, will reconnect you to your roots, for you will learn more about your father, and what a great man he was, and how in the future, you will be able to avenge him, for this family has scores to settle, and will be a part of that."

Morgana smiled and sat back, she had never really realised that Branna and her family felt as she did, and she had never understood that she would not be alone in her task. Maybe Lothar was right, maybe it was time to learn more of who she was, and uncover the full truth of her life. The carriage slowed, and Lothar slipped forward in his seat and grabbed her bag.

"Be ready, we are almost there."

*M*organa felt the tension, and Lothar leaned out to try and see the road in front, he pulled in his head as the carriage slowed more, and the horses idled to a halt. He pulled on the lever and the door opened, and out in the darkness Morgana could just make out two figures, one came forward, and into the dim light of the carriage, Lothar smiled as he looked back at Morgana.

"This dark haired beauty has been my bed companion for some weeks now, she will finish the journey in your stead, this is where you leave us."

Morgana gave a nod and slid forward as the young woman climbed in with a smile and sat next to Lothar. Morgana climbed down and Lothar handed her the bag, then pulled the door closed and the carriage lurched forward and moved off. Morgana felt the presence of Rosamund at her side, and turned, it was pitch black.

"Take my hand and walk quickly, we are out in the open road, and need to get under cover, do not speak until we are indoors."

She felt the tug on her hand, and moved quickly, along what felt like a narrow path, it was soft earth. She could hear Rosamund breathing as she moved, walking at a brisk pace, and could feel that she was tense. It was the middle of the night, and they were out in the middle of nowhere, and she wondered what the rush was, it was so dark no one would see them.

Somewhere behind them in the distance, the sound of hooves thundered up the road, Rosamund side stepped and pulled Morgana close, she looked back behind her, as the hooves grew louder, and then she saw the light, as four blue clad riders holding burning torches rode at speed up the road. Rosamund breathed out her words very quietly.

"Stay completely still, do not move until they are past us and gone."

Morgana took a breath and held it, she could feel her heart pounding inside her chest, as she stared through the darkness, focused on the lights, as the sound of their horses got louder.

Rosamund held her tight at the end of the narrow path, which was between two lines of trees, the riders sped past, their horses breathing hard into the darkness, as they chased the carriage. Rhiannon had more than just Kane watching her, as her guards were also following her, she felt the jolt to her system, and felt the relief that Branna was indeed watching over her.

As the sound of hooves thumped into the distant night, Rosamund gave a gasp of relief, and moved back to the path, pulling Morgana gently along. No words were spoken, but soon she saw the outline of what looked like a barn, and inside a candle burned softly. Rosamund pulled open the door and hurried her inside, Morgana slipped in and saw Branna stood in the centre of the barn with a smile on her face. Her long black tatty hair flowed down her back and around her pale face, and on her shoulder sat Roack.

"Welcome my little Raven, now is the time that you came of age, and came home to your family. We have little time, so come to me, close your eyes, and concentrate on me only, for we shall travel using a gift I aim to teach you soon."

Morgana excitedly walked over to her, and took her outstretched hands in hers with a smile, Branna's eyes danced with happiness, Morgana closed her eyes, and listened to Branna's soft words.

"Focus Morgana, fix all your thoughts on me, and nothing else." She felt a warm feeling rush up inside her, and Branna breathed out.

"You may open your eyes now."

Morgana opened her eyes and blinked, she looked round feeling shocked, as she saw the dark outline of a large castle with many lit windows in the darkness. She was stood on the end of a long bridge, that stretched to the huge arched entrance, with torches burning either side, and two large stone carved ravens stood in front of each side on the floor. Morgana turned back to Branna who was smiling.

"What… How… I mean, where are we, how did you do that?" Roack flapped her wings and flew off, and Branna took Morgana by the hand.

"This is Castle Berengar, it is the place you were born, and for this family, it is our home, and a place of great safety where no one can look in. Morgana, this is the one place in any realm, where you will always be safe, this is your real home, for here lie all of your roots."

Chapter Thirteen.

Possible Futures.

*T*he carriage containing Lothar and his companion, was a large shed like building on wheels, with an arched shape roof, and a door at the back, that had a step down. It was heavy and cumbersome, even if it was tastefully fitted out inside with padded benches and back rests.

The biggest problem was the driver and his assistant sat up front, and their vision was restricted as to what was behind them. The four marshals of Avalon rode with speed, and over the hour since Morgana had been dropped off, they had gained a lot of ground, and had reached a point where they were just a few yards behind the carriage. Lothar was unaware of how close they were, as he sat close to his female companion, Agnes. He was softly kissing her and caressing her ample breast, when suddenly the back door opened, of which he did not at first notice, such was his passion.

A marshal had jumped from his horse onto the step, and yanked open the door, he stepped inside and grabbed Lothar, pulling him back hard, as Agnes squealed with surprise. Lothar acted on instinct and went for his knife, only to halt as a sword met his throat, and he froze, as he looked at the marshal.

"What the hell is this?" The marshal appeared emotionless.

"The young lady is under arrest, and has to be taken straight to the queen of Avalon." Lothar stared at him, in the dimness of the lamp light, cast by the brass lantern bolted to the wall, where a candle flickered.

"On what charge may I enquire?" The marshal looked at Agnes like she was filth.

"She is wanted to answer questions on the assassination of the Lady Eleanor of Avalon." Agnes looked panicked.

"I didn't do nothing; I don't know who she is." Lothar gave a smirk, as the marshal realised that his passenger was not Morgana of

Cornwall.

"Who are you?" Agnes looked terrified.

"I am Agnes of Cadbury; I work for my father at the Hangman's Gate Inn, Sire." He frowned and looked at Lothar.

"Where is Morgana of Cornwall, she was seen boarding this carriage?" Lothar shrugged.

"If she was, I have not seen her, the only people on this journey are us, although you know, I do believe Agnus does have a look of her. I would say whoever told you, must have been mistaken."

The marshal looked angry, as he slipped his sword back into its scabbard, he gave a nod as he looked at Lothar and then around the rest of the carriage.

"The young lord at Tintagel Castle was quite clear that he saw Morgana of Cornwall board this carriage." Lothar shrugged.

"I can only report what I know, and that is we boarded at the castle, and have been otherwise engaged in each other since, I am sure we would have noticed a third." The marshal gave a nod, and looked at Agnes who had the front of her top untied, he noted her large exposed breasts.

"Indeed, that is very apparent." Lothar raised his eyebrows.

"If Morgana is under arrest, I suggest you head back to the castle and arrest her."

He knew as well as the marshal, that Rhiannon had no authority here in the world of men, which was why they had tried to take her on the road in the middle of the night. There was no way that they would be able to get her as long as she was in the castle, and had waited for her return journey, the marshal looked a little uncomfortable.

"We will."

He turned back to the door as the carriage bumped along the road. He staggered out of the door, and closed it behind him, where the three riders waited galloping along with the carriage, one holding the reins of his horse. Lothar gave a smile and turned back to Agnes.

"Right, where were we, oh yes, I believe I was engrossed here?" He leaned in to kiss her, and took hold of her breast, as she giggled.

$\mathcal{M}$organa took a breath as she looked around the huge hall, with the wooden rails above on the balcony, under which were walls decorated with shields and coats of arms. She turned slowly, to see the huge roaring fire in a hearth she could walk around in, and the long wooden tables up against the walls. Behind her were the two large carved seats with perches above, and on one of them Roack sat watching her. She turned to Branna.

"This place is quite amazing, I had no idea you lived in a place this big, it is bigger than my father's castle." Branna gave a smile.

"I am happy you like it, but it is late, let me show you to your quarters. Your bags have been taken down, tomorrow, I will show you all of this place, and we shall talk." Morgana understood, she was tired, Branna took her hand and walked her towards the lower stairwell, Morgana looked at the large carved stairs.

"Do we not go up?" Branna shook her head.

"I want you close to me, I sleep where I work, which is in the lower rooms, they are also cooler during the hotter days. I felt you would be more at ease being closer to myself." Morgana understood, she really did not know this side of the family at all.

Branna led her down to the long corridor to her work rooms, she opened the doors and walked in. Morgana came in and saw the long box of clear crystal, containing the sleeping figure of Ariel. Branna gave a smile as she saw Morgana looking at it.

"That is Ariel, she is a Fae of Earth, and she is the love of my life, she chose to sleep, in order to protect me." Morgana looked up at her.

"Ariel… As in the one wrongly accused by Rhiannon?" Branna gave a sad smile.

"Yes, it is a long story, and one you will learn in the coming days, there is much of your family line that lie in your shadows, and whilst you are here, I will fill you in on all of it for you." Morgana looked over the box and down on Ariel's face, although she felt a chill run through her, the box clearly contained a person of power.

"She is pretty, is she dead?" Branna shook her head.

"No, she sleeps until a time when Rhiannon is no more, and all threats to her are removed." Morgana sort of understood, although it fascinated her that someone could be kept in a trance like state in a glass box.

After a quick tour around her work rooms, Branna showed her to where her room was for when she slept, and then took Morgana back into the corridor, along the corridor, and into her room. It was warm and toasty with a raging fire, and her bag was placed neatly at the end of the bed. Morgana looked round what was a very well furnished room, and liked what she saw, Branna smiled at her.

"Settle in and get a goodnight's sleep, and tomorrow I will fill you in and show you round, and give you all the correct introductions. If you need me, you know where I will be." Morgana smiled at her.

"Thank you for this, I know you took a big risk to get me here, Lothar told me. I am grateful, and this room is lovely. I am not actually used to this since I lived in Avalon, I have become solitary and isolate." Branna understood her.

"We are similar, I may live in this place, but I live in my rooms mostly, as I work. You have parchment and inks on the desk, if you wish to take notations, just relax, settle and feel at home. Welcome home Morgana, it has been long since you were last here." Morgana gave a smile, as she looked round.

"Yes, I suppose this is my home of sorts."

Branna pulled her door closed and left her to settle and unpack, and headed back to her rooms, Roack was already sat on the window waiting. Branna moved to her desk and sat down, she lifted a bottle of wine and poured out a glass, she looked at the bird who watched her.

"She is powerful, when her powers come, they will be noticed, and Maud will feel them as soon as she meets. Maud will feel threatened, which may go ill, be wary Branna the Raven, you play a dangerous game with this family." Branna gave a nod as she lifted her glass.

"I know what I am doing Roack, and I always play a careful game. Morgana will bring much to this family; I just need to make sure my daughter understands that."

*B*ranna was well aware of the situation, she had been for a while, but she knew how to handle Maud and Otto, they learned their lessons with Ariel, and if she needed to, she would make a show of force again. Morgana was a valuable asset to the family, and whether they liked her or not, they would tolerate her. Branna sat back and sipped her wine, she had a lot to think about, and even more to do, Morgana would need guidance, and she would need to control the powers that lived within her, so she could remain a student of the Whitelines, and fool the old wizard.

Morgana was tired, and it was not long after opening her bag and sorting through her clothes to hang up, that she slipped into the huge soft snug bed, and relaxed with a happy sigh, and her eyes fluttered and closed. Jarron landed on the window, and watched over her, as her soft breathing wafted across the room, and she slept deeply, knowing she was safe.

*D*eep below Florae, Gwendolyn paced round the circular room of the Whispering Falls, her mind lost in thought, the waters gave a ripple, and shimmered.

"What troubles your mind White Circle?" Gwendolyn stopped, snapped out of her thoughts by the soft voice.

"There is much that troubles me. The realm of men is fracturing again, Rhiannon appears to be on another quest to target an innocent, and on top of all that, I am asking myself, why Morgana gives me a sense of unease, and how she knows of Ariel?"

"You feel a sense of unease around the daughter of Igraine, tell me of this?" Gwendolyn walked to the seat and sat down.

"I really do not know why; she is quite likeable. I mean, the girl is pleasant and very polite, it is clear she is Igraine's daughter. She has many of her qualities, and I can feel a strong bond within her for her mother. She says little, but it is clear she is very protective of her, and yet I have a sense of unease around her."

"I trust your instincts, is she connected to the crimes she has been accused of?" Gwendolyn shook her head.

"No, I was at the castle when Uther fell, and she was there in her chambers, and on the night of Eleanor's attack, she was with Merlin. I know she had no involvement, and yet Rhiannon is obsessed that she did, and I have no idea why." She gave a sigh and sat back in the seat; the waters shimmered again.

"Rhiannon has Sequana, and she is no fool, and has strong gifts, have they seen something that you may be unaware of?" Gwendolyn shook her head.

"All Sequana saw was black hair and dark eyes, that could be one of thousands of Fae who despise her for their ill treatment, there is nothing to link Morgana, she is innocent. If anything, all she wants is to be left alone, and live in isolation to study with Merlin, which in itself is odd."

"Does she have powers?" Gwendolyn shook her head.

"No, which is what surprises me, because she is of the world of men."

"She may be of Fae descent." Gwendolyn sat forward in her seat, and looked at the floor as she thought.

"I considered it, but her father Victor was from the Germanic lands, he worked hard to build that fortress, he used no powers in its creation, and Igraine as we know is from a line of high lords of Celt. Neither have a history of any form of power, and yet she has some gifts, they are vague, and require great effort from the girl to use them, a Fae power would flow from her, and this does not, she is definitely mortal."

"There is no record of her father in the house literature, and very little of her mother, their lines are not detailed enough through the house which strives to record all the lines, and so I cannot illuminate anything at this time. My advice would be to trust what you feel, and watch from afar, and then it is possible, the truth will be revealed. What brings you unease at the world of men?" Gwendolyn sat up and gave a sigh.

"What doesn't? Merlin was so convinced Uther would rule with a fair hand, and I cannot deny, I trusted his judgement. It pains me, but I felt that the sword of legend did not belong in his hand, and so I handed Uther Albion, which is a mighty weapon for a mortal. Even with Albion he failed. I have to question, if I had given him the sword of power, would things have been different?"

"Uther wielded Albion, and yet still fell, White Circle, you know as well as any, the quality of the man is not made by the sword. The actions of the sword are dictated by the man who holds it. If Uther failed with Albion, he would never have been any more successful with Excalibur, your choice was a wise one." She gave a sigh, and felt even more frustrated.

"Without Uther, the stability has weakened, although it has for some time, and now the men attempt trials of combat to earn the right to pull Albion free and take the crown, and I fear that a lack of a champion is just creating even more instability."

"White Circle, the sword has chosen the hand to wield it, you must trust the sword, for as you know, it contains great power. Trust that it will know the hand of the one to rule, and will release itself to their aid. You must support whoever takes the sword as their own, for the power of the sword will guide them."

Gwendolyn stood up, and paced around the room, her mind was filled with all the knowledge she had gained, and in her thoughts, she knew that those attempting to take the sword were unfit to rule.

"That is my concern, and why I am here in Florae. I know these men who take up their armour in the name of ruling. I have watched them all since the passing of Uther, and I fear that not one of them has a true heart, all of them covet the sword for power and gain, none of them will rule fairly. If the man to rule is not a knight, we may never allow his hand to touch the hilt."

"You must have faith, the magic will reveal itself only when the time is right, so sit back, and wait for a time will come when one man will step up and rule, and he may not be knighted. Trust the magic, and the right hand will find the sword." Gwendolyn gave a nod as she paced.

"My husband is of the same thought."

"Then trust in him."

*G*wendolyn White Circle knew that the water ran with truth, after all, it was the heart of Florae, but it was not easy for her to trust at the moment. For several months she had found her thoughts and feelings in turmoil, almost as if her powers of sight were waning, and she was worried. The White Lord had not been seen since the council meeting, and yet events of great concern had been raised, and she did not understand why he was not more involved.

Hearne had been clear, that he did not want to interfere with the realm of Avalon, and he and Eve had been absent a great deal more than normal, as he had decided to walk the realm of men, and appeared preoccupied with many other things. In recent days, he had been seen walking in distant woodlands with Opal, it was her first time away from the realm, and she had thought that maybe he was instructing her in new tasks.

She made her way slowly up the steps away from the falls, her mind lost in thought, and walked into the large room of scribes, where Bade sat lost in thought, her movement caught his eye, and he looked up and saw her. Bade closed his large book, and stood up and bowed.

"My Queen, I hope your visit was fruitful, if I may be so bold, I feel you have been distracted of late, is there anything I can assist you with?" Gwendolyn snapped out of her thoughts and looked at him, he looked older, and tired.

"Bade, I need some advice, well, it is more I need to sound out my thoughts for a reaction, would you come to the royal apartments and bring your book." He looked confused.

"The book does not belong to the archive; it is a personal possession." She smiled at him.

"I am aware of that, bring it anyway." He gave a bow.

"If it is your wish, then I will of course oblige."

Gwendolyn headed for her apartments, Bade turned, and lifted the large book, he had no idea what purpose it could serve, but his queen had requested it, and so he felt duty bound to do so.

When he arrived at the apartments, Gwendolyn was stood next to the long polished table, she smiled as he walked in.

"Close the door Bade, I wish our conversation be private, and place your book down here."

He looked a little nervous, and at a loss as to why the queen would request such a thing. He ensured the doors were closed tightly, and feeling a little unsure he walked over and placed the book down in front of Gwendolyn.

"I am unsure as to why you would request this, all it contains are the pictures that Ariel drew in Avalon, and sent to me. She would send them to me with small notes attached, I have placed them all together in this book, nothing more."

Gwendolyn gave a soft smile, as he stepped back and allowed her closer to the book.

"I admire your dedication to her, even now you do her great honour, and I find it quite endearing of you. Bade at this time, I feel we both miss her, I really could use her insight at the moment, and yet my instincts tell me she would have already provided all the answers we would ever need. I have seen and read everything she sent back, apart from the contents of this book, and so with your consent, I would like to look upon it?" Bade appeared to understand.

"I take it, her wrongful accusation of another innocent is why you requested to look?" Gwendolyn smiled at him.

"The speed of your mind serves you well, yes, I am struggling with why Rhiannon would accuse Morgana of Cornwall, for something others have proved was beyond her ability, and yet she still insists on trapping the girl, and blaming her." Bade gave a nod as Gwendolyn opened the book to see the first drawing of the workers in the fields of Avalon.

"You fear this is the same as the Branna woman?" Gwendolyn studied the picture carefully.

"I do indeed. Sequana has informed the queen, it was a woman, with dark hair and dark eyes that killed Eleanor, and planned the downfall of Uther, and in her rush to judgement, she found Morgana a very convenient target. My question is why her, and not many of the thousands of others living in her realm?"

Bade gave a nod, as Gwendolyn turned the page and looked upon a picture of a woman brushing a skin drawn across two poles, she turned to the next page.

"Every page is a woman with dark hair and dark eyes, there is not one with a hue of lighter hair. They have the same style, the same thickness, it is almost as if on every page, Ariel has drawn the same woman, and yet she has not, she has drawn many." Bade understood.

"Yet she has blamed the one person not of Fae descent, who has the look of a member of the Fae community?" Gwendolyn stopped on a picture of Branna sat in her chair at her desk looking up, she gave a smile as she looked at it.

"Branna was a very attractive woman, and from all accounts, she was a loner and very intelligent and astute." Gwendolyn stared at the picture, Bade gave a nod.

"She also fits the description of Morgana as written by Rhiannon." Gwendolyn looked at Bade and smiled.

"Thank you, I have realised now why this bothered me so much. Branna was a loner, strong willed, confrontational at times, and yet kind to those around her. Her mind was brilliant, but she shied away from Fae life, choosing to work on her research at night, and write her reports with the door to her office closed. I think I have my answer, and once again, Ariel saw what none of us did." Bade gave a frown.

"She did?" Gwendolyn gave a nod.

"Bade this has nothing to do with looks, it has everything to do with lifestyle and abilities. Morgana is very like a young Branna, and Rhiannon fears her because of it. Think about it, she is convinced Branna brought down powers from the Merle, what if she thinks Morgana will do the same, what if Rhiannon has tried to remove Morgana before she can? That is actually a very interesting question." Bade stared at the picture.

"If I am honest, that is the first thing I have heard in all of this that actually makes perfect sense." Gwendolyn closed the book, turned and walked over to her seat, where a small table held a glass of crystal filled with wine. She sat down and looked back at Bade.

"Doesn't it just? Since Ariel's reports, we always thought she despised those of dark hair, but what if that is not really her reason for isolating her people with division, what if it was to watch and pick off certain personality types?" Bade turned.

"Loners, those who live a solitary life and have great independence, and those who are more intelligent, and so therefore more likely to vocalise their views. I really do think you are onto something, pick off those most likely to lead a revolt, and the others will fall in line." Gwendolyn lifted her glass and took a sip.

"Morgana can be very confrontational when provoked, and she is amazingly bright and has a very sharp mind. She may not be Fae, but none the less, with the support of others, she could be more than a handful for Rhiannon to deal with. In essence, she is like a younger Branna." Finally, everything made sense to Gwendolyn.

"She may not look it Bade, but talk to her, and you can see it. She is the daughter of a powerful queen, and understands the politics of court far better than most people understand. She was raised around it, and has seen far more than people realise, but not Rhiannon, she understands politics better than any. Potentially, Morgana could be a very powerful political enemy." Bade gave a nod as he understood her point.

"In Fae yes, but she is of the line of men, and they do not favour women in positions of power. She would have little power to lead them." Gwendolyn shook her head.

"Not the Picts, Norsemen, or the Germanics, they will always be led by men, but you forget who her mother is. Igraine is from a very high ranking tribe of Celt, and they share rule equally, they are the only race of men that favour woman as highly as men. To rule the land around Avalon, you need a majority of Celt tribes to back you, Uther had that, and she is also his adopted daughter. From a Celt perspective, under their rules, she has the right to rule, and that makes her very dangerous, because you would have a line of men ruled by a woman, and in theory, that would make her equal to Rhiannon." Bade sat down with a bump.

"Two queens with a hatred of each other, that would not bode well for Avalon's trade." Gwendolyn gave a little giggle.

"I must confess, I would love to let her have a go at pulling that sword, if she does have the ability to remove it, that would be a huge message to every world, it would shake the foundations of all realms to the core." Bade suddenly looked concerned.

"Rhiannon has to get rid of her and quick, if not she may have a very big political rival." Gwendolyn nodded at him.

"Yes indeed, what a shame it will never happen, I cannot deny, I would love to see the look on her face."

"Why will it never happen?" Gwendolyn sat back with a big smile.

"She wants something far more powerful than a crown; she wants to control and use the Whitelines. She will be the female equivalent of Merlin if she makes it, and that must terrify Rhiannon. Think about it, how many secrets will she be able to hide, with a guardian of the Whitelines on her tail, who hates her?" Bade gave a very long exhale, and sat back in his seat.

"Your mind is far sharper than even I realise, but I will not deny, you pose possibly the most interesting question I have ever been asked." Gwendolyn giggled.

"I think I am really going to enjoy sitting back to see what happens."

*G*wendolyn had fallen upon something completely by accident, but as she sat back, she knew she had to be right. Merlin had not spotted it yet, but Rhiannon was far quicker off the mark when it came to the political dealings of all the realms. She was indeed very powerful, and had a long reach to control and manipulate events in many realms, and if Morgana was to rise to fulfil her dream, and master the Whitelines of power, she would be a perfect match and equal to the golden queen.

Not only had Gwendolyn spotted it, so had Branna, and she was well aware that not only could Morgana have great sway on the council, she would have the ability to perfectly balance the powers of the Merle with the powers of light. Morgana was Branna's best shot for finding something that would release her from the family to live a free life again. With Morgana at her side, she could defeat Rhiannon, and then release Ariel back into the world and she would be reunited with her forever.

It was very clear, that Morgana of Cornwall, had a very bright and powerful future if she was coaxed in the right way, and Branna had every intention of helping Morgana achieve her goals.

Chapter Fourteen.

True Family.

Morgana woke up as the light streamed in through the window, Jarron was sat on the window ledge, his head under his wing. She sat up in the large snug bed, and looked around her room in the daylight, this was a level of comfort she did not even have in her mother's castle. She smiled, as she slipped out of bed, and reached for her dress, the large fire was now just white ashes, and yet as she stood close, it still emitted heat from the stone surround.

Slowly she walked round the room, looking at the large stone beams above her. The ceiling was high, far higher than those in Tintagel, and yet there was something similar about the look, which she could not quite work out. She reached the window and looked out, the land encircled the castle, but as she looked down, she could see it was set on a vast pillar of rock, set in a round void that fell away for thousands of feet. It was a long way down, and she felt a shudder and stepped back, Jarron awoke and lifted his head and stretched his wings, she smiled as he looked up at her.

"Good morning, are you hungry, shall we go and find food?" The white raven ruffled its feathers, and then flew up to her shoulder, and she gave a giggle.

"I too am hungry, come on."

Leaving the room, she saw the stone stairwell at the bottom of the long corridor, and walked nervously down towards it. She was a stranger here who did not really know her way around, so felt a little hesitant. As she approached the work rooms of Branna, she noticed the doors were open, and peered round to look in, Branna was stood by the large window with Roack, she turned and smiled.

"Good morning, I hope you slept well?" Morgana smiled feeling a little relieved.

"I did thank you; I am not disturbing you, am I? I was hungry, but do not really know my way round." Branna smiled, and walked across the room towards her.

"I was waiting for you, come, we shall eat." She lifted Morgana's hand and slipped it into her arm.

"Today I will show you all of the land that is your home, and the true place of your family's origins."

*R*hiannon turned her eyes burning with anger, she looked down on the dithering marshals stood with the young Lord Kane, who looked terrified.

"You had one simple task, nothing too complicated, watch the girl, and yet, you have no idea where she is… HOW CAN YOU BE SO INCOMPETENT!?" Rhiannon spun on her heels and looked at Sequana.

"WELL!?" Sequana shook her head.

"It is as we feared, the wizard taught her the charm of the veil. My Queen, she is no longer in Avalon, your problem is no longer residing here, in a way, this is a good thing." Rhiannon gave a snort and looked back at the marshals.

"Leave here, all of you, I am tired of looking at you." They looked relieved, bowed, and scuttled away quickly before she changed her mind. Rhiannon waited until they had left, and paced on the steps.

"Hounding her out of Avalon was not my plan, in this realm we could watch her, I wanted her caught inside her own fence line, and it looked like that was succeeding, until that bumbling idiot and his queen spoke with her. Have you any idea of the trouble we could have if she even talks to one of the Celt chieftains? Uther named her his child, she has the right to rule, and I cannot allow that, I must find her and stop her." Sequana shook her head.

"The other tribes would never tolerate that, as a warrior chieftain she could rule a tribe, but the land of men is made of many tribes, the Norsemen would never bow down to a woman." Rhiannon turned to her.

"They have in the past, there has not been many, but they hold a high regard for their shield maidens, my only hope is the Picts, they gave Uther a hard time, they would never tolerate a woman." Sequana smiled.

"See, why do you worry so? The girl is a loner, look at her, she gave up a castle and title to live in that badly built house, with hardly anything. My Queen, the girl has no aspirations to lead a country, let the men fight it out, and she will soon be forgotten." Rhiannon sighed.

"You said the same of that Branna, and yet the loner made an alliance with a powerful queen's daughter, and then unleashed hell on us. She too was intelligent, and equally as cunning as Morgana, it is almost as if the two are related, and I have no wish to repeat history." Sequana scoffed, and flicked back her long hair.

"As I have told you, if you had only given her one audience, things would have been different. The girl was bright, and she did some work of great value to you, if only we had been able to recover her real notes, you would have the power you sought. My Queen, tread lightly, you cannot allow history to repeat itself."

Rhiannon gave a nod, she moved to her seat and sat down to think, Sequana was right, she could not afford a repeat, but that did not solve her problem of Morgana, she gave a frustrated sigh.

"Why did that stupid old fool teach her the charm of the veil, that idiot has blinded us to her, and it is an inconvenience to us, how can I rule what I cannot see?"

"I feel that is the point my Queen, like you, Merlin has his own secrets. Neither of you can afford to slip."

Sequana was right, and Rhiannon knew it. Merlin had much to hide, as did she, but she had thought that her observations would at least have given her some insight to the dealings of Merlin with the girl. Once again, he had outsmarted her, and she found it irksome, she wanted just one thing that she could use, and she had thought the girl was her best hope, but she was wrong.

"That girl is in the middle of all this, I know it, and one way or the other, I will find out, no one attacks my line and lives."

*B*erengar got up from the table as Branna appeared with Morgana, he gave a huge smile as he walked towards them.

"Morgana, welcome home, I trust you slept well?" She looked at Branna for guidance.

"This is Berengar, my consort, and also the family name you should use, for you are of his and my line." She understood and turned as he came up close, she gave a bow and smiled.

"My Lord Berengar, I have heard much of you from Lothar. Thank you for allowing me to visit here." He gave out a huge laugh, and pulled her into his arms almost crushing the poor girl.

"Morgana, I am not a lord here, I am your grandfather, well actually, great grandfather." He released her, and she smiled as he took her hand.

"Come, you must be hungry, eat with me, and we shall talk."

*B*ranna stood back and smiled, as she saw the joy in his eyes, she understood how much family meant to him. She knew, like her, he would be her greatest protector. Eating was a noisy affair, as Berengar, who appeared filled with joy talked endlessly of his family. Morgana found his humour quite infectious and giggled along with him, as she helped herself, to eggs, roasted pork, mushrooms and fried tomatoes. Branna sat happily watching, feeling happier than she had in a long time.

Merwig joined them and introduced himself, and he was polite and welcoming, Gundobarld and Dagaric had left the previous day, as they had affairs to tend to, as had Ulric, who was currently in the land of Danes doing business. Morgana was happy, as she fed Jarron from a small bowl of chopped fresh meat on the table, and high above them sat on their perches watching on, Roack sat with Asin, the largest ravens within the family.

All appeared well, until up from her chambers below the castle came Maud, Branna felt her the moment she arrived, and Roack sat up straight. She walked slowly, her eyes narrowed, as she looked at the smiling young woman. Branna prepared knowing it was impossible for Maud to miss out on a chance to humiliate someone. The small squat figure approached the table, and Morgana turned smiling and noticed, the table fell silent as Branna rose from her seat.

"There you are, Morgana, this is my daughter Maud of Berengar, she is your grandmother." Morgana rose slowly in her seat, and gave a bow.

"Good morning, Grandmother, I am pleased to meet you." Maud looked her up and down, with a sneer.

"Why… Why would you be pleased to meet me, I have hardly seen you since you were born, you do not know me, so why?" Morgana frowned.

"You are the mother of my father who I loved dearly; I am very happy to meet you." Branna smiled, Morgana was indeed sharp and intelligent, Maud was slightly wrong footed. She smirked at her.

"Yet you took the titles of that murderer's line, and cast off this families name, but there again, it is to be expected of a half breed." Morgana felt the shock run through her, she swallowed hard, she had been warned by Lothar and Rosamund, so this was not unexpected. She faced out Maud, and met her gaze.

"You are misinformed, I am Morgana, daughter of Victor of Berengar, Countess of Cornwall, a title my father bestowed upon me. I carry no name of Celt origin, and the blood in my veins is my father's, which is why I left the castle to live alone as soon as was possible. I no longer reside in a castle tainted by the smell of my father's murderer; I live alone in Avalon." Branna smiled as she looked at Maud, her tone was icy.

"Morgana has no ties to any other line than this one, and as such, she will be welcome here always. Morgana has a seat here, and as you know, that means everything to your father and me. This is the home of all of the Berengar line, if she was not one, she would not be here, now sit and join us or leave to adjust your manners dear daughter." Maud understood perfectly and looked at Morgana, she gave a nod.

"I stand corrected, and thank you for informing me of your situation Morgana, excuse me, I have work to do." Branna nodded. Morgana took a breath.

"It was nice to meet you Grandmother, I hope in time, we will get to know each other better, and you will see I am the daughter of your son, for he was a great man." She gave a nod.

"He was, and he was betrayed by that worthless Celt king, he deserved better." Morgana gave a soft nod.

"I agree with you, and know that I will seek revenge for those who conspired against him."

Maud turned and hurried off back towards her chambers, she knew she had too much to lose, and could not afford the wrath of her mother. Branna sat down as Morgana did, and smiled at her.

"Lothar taught you well." Morgana nodded at her.

"He did. I did not come here to cause problems, I have yearned to meet my family, mother prevented it, but I am here, and wish to learn, and be a part of this." Branna smiled.

"You made a good start, Maud is confrontational with everyone, do not take it to heart, it is who she is." Merwig gave a snort.

"Trust me, she hates all of us, I am not sure she actually likes anyone, you did well young Morgana, never allow her to bully you, stand your ground, she will respect that. I try to anger her on a regular basis, I find I derive great pleasure from it." Berengar gave a mighty roar of a laugh, and Morgana smiled, and felt a little more relaxed.

*O*nce they had eaten, Branna gave Morgana the full tour of the castle, they walked around and Branna showed her each of the rooms, and explained how the castle ran. They spent two hours walking around, which led them slowly towards the end of the long bridge, which was the only entrance to the castle. Morgana was interested in the story of Ariel, and why she was sealed in a box of crystal, and as they walked slowly across the bridge, Branna told her story, and expressed her anger at Rhiannon. They walked off the bridge, and headed towards what was the village, on that fateful day when Branna had arrived with Berengar to confront his father and the rest of the tribe. They arrived at the site, where once, Ariel's caravan had stood. All that was left was a large blackened ring, where the heat of the fire had marked the stone floor, Branna sighed.

"This was the place; I had some very happy times here with her." Morgana looked at the black patch burned into the stones.

"I want to say I understand, but I do not, you clearly still love her deeply, why sentence her to a life sealed in a box, when it is obvious that you want her beside you?" Branna smiled a soft smile.

"My family fear her Morgana, they have never understood she would never harm anyone precious to me. Odd as it sounds, this is my family and I do care for them deeper than most realise, Ariel knew that, which is why they should never have feared her. I did not want her in a life of sleep, it was her request not mine, and not a day has passed that I do not regret granting it." Morgana shook her head.

"It makes no sense, you have been nothing but kind to me, I cannot accept this darkness is as evil as Rhiannon says, because if it was, you would be as evil as her." Branna gave a soft chuckle.

"Morgana, I am pure Fae, as is Rhiannon. The gifts of our line have in a sense helped to subdue the full powers of the Merle, and control it. My children are only part Fae, and so more vulnerable when exposed to it. It was a miscalculation on my part, one I deeply regret, for they have done things that even I find abhorrent, but as much as I have tried, I cannot stop the process, they are darker than I could ever be."

"I am not full Fae, my father was your grandchild, so that means he was only a watered down version of a full Fae, which means I have much less." Branna shook her head.

"No Morgana, the lines of power increase in the feminine, so actually, your powers would probably rival Maud's. I think your true powers are still dormant, but they will emerge in time with practice." She understood that, Lothar and Rosamund had explained it to her.

"I have no raven connected to me, so I cannot be influenced by the Merle. You say you fight this power inside you so that you can one day release Ariel, but I do not understand, if she is pure good, and as you say, this merle contains evil, will that not be a conflict between you both, and even then, Maud will still want to kill her?"

They started to walk on the path through the old village towards the woodland, Branna gave Morgana's comments some thought, and as they walked, she explained.

"Morgana, Merlin, has light and dark in equal amounts, and so he has achieved balance within his powers. Ariel understood that there was a way for me to find the same balance, which is why for the last number of years I have studied alone to try and work out how they are balanced within Merlin. If I can achieve that, then I can protect Ariel, and possibly defeat Rhiannon if she tries to attack me. It is a delicate balance, but I am working towards it."

*T*hey walked along an old path of grass, it looked seldom walked these days, from the days when Branna and Ariel would walk hand in hand down it, Morgana understood what Branna was saying.

"That is why you encouraged me to learn the Whitelines of power, in a sense, it will protect me from the darkness that may grow within me?" Branna smiled.

"Yes. Morgana the powers of your Fae line will increase because you are the next generation, but there could be a risk, the darkness within me passed through Maud to her son. If that is the case, then they could well bind to your Fae powers and increase within you, learning the Whitelines, might give you the power to completely control them, as Merlin has."

"So, the Whitelines are more powerful than that of the Fae Ofmoon?" Branna shrugged.

"I simply do not know, but Merlin has some of the power of Albanlin, and that is a much older and stronger power than that of Fae, so I suppose in a sense, yes. Morgana, the one thing I have learned is a strong mind aids the control of the darkness, Maud is far too emotional and that leads to a loss of control. You must learn to control your emotions, and not let your anger get the better of you. The one thing I know without doubt, is I have only done things of great evil when angered, emotional stability is the key." Morgana looked a little guilty as she turned to Branna.

"I had some very dark thoughts when Rhiannon tried to shame me in the market, and I got angry and was rude, and challenged her. I am sure she will never forgive me; I am seen as her enemy now; it will not be easy living in Avalon." Branna gave a slight chuckle, she had a raging anger at Rhiannon, and she could well understand why Morgana had acted as she did.

"What is done is done, but there are ways to overcome that. You spoke honestly, you are the daughter of a Sachsen lord, and a Celtic queen, Uther also named you his daughter, in theory, you could take the throne. Morgana, you are veiled to her now, no matter how important she may feel, she can no longer see into your life, that alone will enrage her. Merlin has his faults, but as his student, you will have protections, he will stand up for you." She nodded.

"He has already. I do not want to rule, if anything I simply want to be left alone. Merlin does give me some certainty to live alone in my home, and I am grateful, but he is also the man that brought about my father's death. Is it wrong to feel confused and conflicted over that?" Branna shook her head.

"Not at all, and there is a score there to settle with no doubt, but remember, he has powers that can greatly aid you, so for now, bury your anger, and focus on learning. Morgana, in the world today, are many with powers, and they make decisions that have dire effects on others, I know, it is why my life is as it is. They act without care, and it does a great deal of damage, learn from my life, knowledge is the power that will keep you alive. Merlin has knowledge you can use, learn from him, even though you feel deep resentment towards him. The time will come when scores can be settled, and in that I will assist you, I too have scores to settle with him. Your priority, is to learn as much as you can, then train, understand and practice until you are strong, then will be the moment to strike."

Morgana walked on watching the trees, thinking of what Branna had told her. It made sense to her, she knew at the moment she was powerless, and so she had to enhance her abilities, only then would

Rhiannon leave her alone, and only then could she settle the score with Merlin.

*H*igh above them, Roack was on watch, and she sensed movement within the woodlands, others were in the area. She looked down at her mistress far below, but noted that Branna had turned on the path and was heading back towards the castle, Branna was more aware of this land than any, and she had already acted. Quietly guiding Morgana to safety, she walked slowly, her mind connected to Roack, she knew of those trapped in her land and under her veil, they gave her little trouble, and when they did surface, Otto usually despatched them with an arrow.

The castle came into view, and she smiled, Morgana was taking note of everything, and Branna could see how similar she was to her as a young woman. In Branna's mind, Morgana was highly intelligent, highly motivated, and had a great desire to prove herself, and that was not unsimilar to her when she requested to take her research down to Avalon. In many ways, Branna saw Morgana as the daughter she had wanted, as Maud and Rosamund had not favoured her much, they appeared to be more like their father. Morgana was almost identical to Branna as a young girl, and it was clear that her mind worked in a similar fashion to Branna's, and that pleased her. She lifted her hand to her shoulder as they walked, and her voice was soft, almost nurturing.

"Morgana, you must never fear, I will always be there for you, and I will teach you all I know, I hope in time we will grow very close, for I have many secrets of the powers I hold to share with you. Learn from Merlin, and I will add to those powers, and one day, you may find you will rule that land of the Anglo's, as the most powerful mistress that has ever been. Have no fear of Rhiannon, her powers will fade as her line grows, and those who come after her will rule in her stead. Think things through clearly, and one day, you will hold everything you desire." They turned on the path, and stepped onto the long wide bridge, which led to the safety of Castle Berengar.

*T*ogether they walked back into the castle, and down towards Branna's workrooms, as they did, Branna asked about the incident at the market in Avalon. She had the brief details, but wanted to know the full story, and as Morgana walked at her side, she told it all in full, of how her tea had been ripped open and scattered, and all her bottles of medicines had been smashed on the market floor. Branna listened intently taking every detail into account, and as she did, she spoke to Roack in her mind.

"Roack, go to Oviskar, the raven of Lothar, and give these instructions to be relayed to Lothar straight away."

She spoke with her mind and made her wishes and instructions known, there was no way Rhiannon was going to intimidate another of her line, she had every intention of helping Morgana from behind the scenes. It was clear to Branna, she had been away too long and had been distracted, but she understood in that moment, she needed to extend her reach. It was time to look back into Avalon and the rule of a corrupt queen. It was time to begin to plan, for one day, she would meet her face to face, and then there would be a score to settle. For now, her primary goal was to ensure that no one got in the way of Morgana, she had high hopes for the girl, and she was here in the castle, it was time to teach her how to control her powers.

They walked into her workroom, and Branna walked past the crystal case that contained Ariel in her state of sleep, she sat in her chair behind her desk, and smiled as Morgana looked around.

"Tell me of the task that Merlin has set you, and I will see if I can help you hurry along your education at a faster pace?" Morgana smiled, as she turned at the open window.

"It is not an easy one I fear, for it involves using my mind to move objects." Branna smiled.

"Is that all, I thought for a moment he had set you something difficult? Morgana, for a Fae Ofmoon, that is a mere trifle of a task. Come, see, I will show you."

Chapter Fifteen.

A New Identity.

Morgana sat back, and gave a gasp of relief, it had been four days, and as she stared at the table with six long wooden nails hammered into it, she could clearly see, the first nail had risen out of the table a whole inch. Branna smiled at her from the other side of the table.

"Good, you are really starting to feel the force build inside you, but do not be in too big a hurry. Take your time, feel the tension in the nail grow, and let it build, then with your mind, release it. That is enough for now, rest a while and tell me of the potions you brew, and what plants grow in your garden."

Branna was impressed with Morgana, she was actually doing magic that was actually advanced for a young Fae, and it showed the real depths of what Morgana was capable of. One thing was abundantly clear, Morgana was at a more advanced level than Maud had been at her age. Considering her father was Victor, Branna was unsure as to why Morgana was so powerful, and she wondered if her speculation had been right. Had the darkness within her father aided the powers of the Fae within her? She could not say for sure, but she had known the night Morgana was born, a day would come when she would wield great power.

Branna had taken on the role of teacher, something she had not done with Maud, maybe it was the high intelligence, or Morgana's willingness to learn? As the days progressed, she gave Morgana seeds, and instructed her to write down in her new black book, how to grow them, process them, and then use them to greater effect in her potions. Morgana was the perfect student, and revelled in the knowledge she was learning, which in many ways reminded Branna of herself at her age. She learned fast and studied hard, noting down every aspect in detail Branna taught her in her book.

There were many plants growing in Avalon, that Morgana had no knowledge of, and Branna lifted her book, and showed her the pictures she had drawn on her arrival, and the things she had learned of their properties, many of which, were taught her by Ariel. Morgana learned better ways to brew her potions, and even more choices of the teas she could make, and the properties they held. As the first week passed, and the second approached its end, Morgana had learned a vast amount about plant lore, potions, and more importantly, she had removed all six nails from the table using only her mind. The last lesson, was to teach Morgana how to mould the things of the earth. They walked out into the old village, where Branna pointed at a large rock, and as Morgana watched stunned, she fashioned the rock into a small statue of herself. As Morgana gasped with awe, Branna lifted the six inch stone in her likeness and handed it to Morgana.

"Here, a token of your visit home, call it a little something to remember this time together." Morgana looked down at the small statue of a young woman with tatty hair.

"It is amazing, I cannot believe you can do that using just your mind." Branna smirked.

"Look behind you, it took longer to do, but before I arrived, there were no workers of stone within the Varisci. It was hard work, and took a lot of focus, but I looked out across what was a flat surface of rock, and in my mind, I imagined the image I wanted to create, and the stones cut themselves from the earth and came together as I planned them. It is a little crude, I was out of practice, but that castle is my mark on this world, my vision, and my labour." Morgana looked back with a huge smile.

"I want to learn how to do that." Branna gave a giggle.

"And so you shall, for the rest of your time visiting, that will be the task you will have, to learn how to control what surrounds you. It is a skill all Fae Ofmoon learn as children, for when they mature, they will work below the land, and seek out the things men hold as high value. Morgana, I will teach you this, for using it you will be able to create something as big as I have, and one day, you too will have your own kingdom, and also the wealth that the earth hides. That is the true power of Rhiannon, she has great stores of jewels to trade. She controls all that is dug from Avalon, that is her true power, for to control all with things of high value, is the real power in the world of men."

Morgana's time at Berengar Castle was limited, her mother expected her back, so for the last few days of her visit, she worked with Branna outside the castle, focusing her new found skill of nail removal, into the other use, of controlling the sculpting of stone. Her first attempts were crude, but as the day's past, her vision became more obvious, especially when she created a crude looking raven, which she handed to Branna with pride.

"It is not perfect, I have much to practice, but here, a raven, given to the Raven." She smiled as she looked at Branna and her voice was soft.

"I have loved being here with you, it is the first time in a long time that I have felt a true sense of belonging and less afraid of the world beyond your boarders. Thank you… For everything, I have no idea how, but one day I will repay your kindness to me." Branna smiled at her.

"I need no repayment, Morgana you are family, my family and it means a great deal to me. I too have enjoyed your stay here, and I mean what I say, I will watch over you and do what I can to protect you, and in times of need, I will be there for you. Morgana, you thought you were alone, but you are not, you are of the line of Berengar, and it is a line of great power and pride. Rhiannon thinks she has the upper hand, she does not, but let her think for a while she does, for that will buy you the time you need. Keep yourself under the veil at all times, even though your house is veiled, stay in the darkness of our golden queen, the simple act of staying hidden, will frighten her far more than you ever could with confrontation."

Morgana nodded, she stepped forward and pulled Branna into a hug, for a moment she was lost for words, but she smiled and slipped her arms around the young woman and pulled her tight, Morgana looked up, her dark eyes filled with life.

"I know you are my great grandmother, but to be honest, being here, and having you beside me teaching me, you have felt like a mother." It touched Branna deeply and she took a breath as she smiled.

"I have taught you exactly as my mother did me, and maybe I have seen you more in the light of a daughter too. It has taken time, but I am glad that you feel the bond of family here, we will learn much together in our lifetime Morgana, of that I can assure you." Morgana gave a nod and slipped back, she looked round at the castle, stood tall in the dim light on its large circular column, with its long bridge to its gateway.

"You have inspired me in my time here, and I now feel a stronger sense of purpose. I will study hard to learn the ways of the Whitelines, and if I can discover the balance within Merlin, I will let you know." Branna nodded.

"As I said, you are one of us now little raven." Morgana smiled.

"A member of a Fae family, I like that. You know, in my mother's language of Celt, it is pronounced Le Fay, meaning the fairy, which is how her tribe named the Fae Ofmoon when they first met them?" Branna gave a nod.

"I know, I was in Avalon when they first arrived, I remember your mother's grandmother entering the land with her consort, but I do believe the court dignitary Malory of Avalonia, mispronounced her name, and called her le Fey, and it made her smile, the name after that stuck." Morgana looked really surprised.

"You were there?" Branna gave a chuckle as she nodded.

"I was, the queen at that point had not arrived, so she was greeted by Sequana, and had a moment I believe with Ariel, who brought greetings from Queen Bridget Violet. I was restocking our supplies, as Ariel had her duty as an ambassador, and when we returned back to our home, she told me all about how wonderful and respectful your great grandmother was. Ariel liked her a great deal, and she told me of Malory's mishap, she thought it was very funny at the time, it became an inside joke apparently within the Citadel." Morgana for a moment looked like she was thinking, Branna looked at her, and Morgana realised.

"Sorry, my mind wandered for a second as a thought occurred to me." The day was getting hot, so Branna turned and slipped her arm into Morgana's.

"We should head back, and find cooler places, tell me of this thought that has occurred to you." Both of them started to walk slowly down the path, that headed between the large trees towards the bridge and the castle, Morgana mulled over her thoughts.

"I listened carefully when you told me your story of your departure from Avalon, and how you remember the place my father landed on your instructions. As I lay in bed, it occurred to me, that you changed your name to hide from Rhiannon, and you became Raven." Branna nodded, she remembered the moment well, Morgana continued.

"It occurred to me as I lay in bed, that in a way, you did not really change your actual name, because in the old language, Branna, means Raven. It was in a sense a joke, and it fooled Rhiannon, so I lay there thinking that I need another name. I feel it should be one I could use to hide my identity, when I am outside Avalon, because in the world of men, the name of Morgana of Cornwall, is still very much recognised." Branna understood.

"So whatever you do outside of Avalon, Rhiannon can still track you because you are well known, which means she can have you followed and reported on?" Morgana nodded.

"I want something I could use, something to hide me from her gaze, something that kept me hidden in the shadows where she would not find me, and just then it occurred to me, because I told her I was indeed a countess with the right to take the throne. Does this make sense, or does it sound silly, but outside of Avalon, if I am to achieve anything, I will need to be respected, and so what if like you, I name myself the same as what I am?" Branna frowned a little.

"I understand some of this, but as yet not all, how would you name yourself what you already are, when you are the Countess of Cornwall?" Morgana smiled.

"Cornwall was my father's title, what if I adopt the name of my mother's family? I could be the Countess le Fey?" Branna smiled a wide smile, and nodded in agreement.

"Become what you already are, a countess of a line of Fae, or fairy in your mother's tongue. Morgana it is brilliant." Morgana smiled a big smile.

"I could be dark and mysterious, with a little brooding, and act completely opposite to as I really am, and people would address me such, and the name of Cornwall would disappear from the ears of Rhiannon, which would prevent her from tracking me." Branna gave a little chuckle.

"A countess in the darkness, hidden from the eyes of the golden queen. A line of Fae she cannot rule, it really is very inspired, and I do believe it is perfect. It is a jest from the start of Avalon, and her golden realm, and will humiliate Rhiannon if it is ever found out, because honestly Morgana, I do believe it will completely fool her."

Morgana was very happy when they made it into the cool

workrooms below the large castle of stone. Branna poured them cool drinks infused with lemons and herbs. Morgana returned to her study, copying out the last of the herbal remedies in Branna's book. Branna headed into her bed chamber and returned shortly after with a long cloak of black feathers, she smiled as she held it up, and Morgana looked up from her book with a gasp.

"Morgana, Rhiannon wears a cloak of blue feathers, made from the bird of hope. She had two, and one went missing, some say it was an act of rebellion, but that is a story for another time. When I arrived here in this castle, I created two just like hers, but made from the feathers of my ravens. Here, take this one, it is a little short on me, which is why I made a second. If you are to be the Countess le Fey, you should have a presence when you enter a room, and this cloak will do exactly that." Morgana rose from the desk looking awestruck.

"It is beautiful, I can see the glints of blue in the daylight." Branna smiled as she slipped it over Morgana's shoulders.

"The long feathers on the collar I collected when Roack lost them, so these are very closely connected to me and precious. Wear this when you leave Avalon, and be a countess in the shadows."

Morgana smiled, her eyes dancing with delight as she examined herself in a tall polished plate of silver. She turned to look at Branna, and lifted her arms with joy.

"This truly is fit for a countess, a countess in the shadows."

Branna walked up to her with a slight chuckle and helped straighten the collar, and then she stood back to admire Morgana, with her long cloak of feathers, and her dark eyes and hair.

"Yes, I do believe you are right, in that, you truly are the Countess le Fey."

Morgana gave an excited giggle, and lifted her hood on the cloak to hide most of her face creating an air of mystery to her, she lowered her voice tone and spoke, with an air of mystery.

"Good evening, Lady Branna, I am the Countess of Darkness."

Morgana burst into laughter and Branna laughed with her, it was a moment of foolishness, and yet somehow, Branna could see the brilliance of the idea. Hidden within the cloak, Morgana was completely transformed, her face was obscured and most of her features were hard to work out. It was clear, no one in the world of men would know who she was, and that was a very good thing, because yet again, Rhiannon's arrogance would be her undoing. What appeared as a joke, would grow into an identity that would hide the real truth of the line of Branna, and allow Morgana to move freely out of sight of the golden queen.

Branna was pleased that Morgana was so happy, she watched, as Morgana slipped the long cloak down off her shoulders with a smile. She turned and looked back at Branna.

"I have seen her long blue cloak, what really happened to it?" Branna lifted her bottle off the table, and poured out two glasses of rich red wine, she looked up and she had a slight smirk.

"I do not know who stole it, but it appeared in the outer lands of the realm when we arrived. Morgana you must understand how hated she is on the moon realm; we are nothing but slaves and labourers. Her hatred of dark hair shows, and many have suffered for no other reason than they were born, with the wrong colour of hair. When the cloak appeared, it was taken apart, and everyone who spoke out against the queen, was given a single feather. For us at that time, working our hardest to build a realm of glory, the blue feather became a symbol of our struggle to be free. It was rumoured Rhiannon found out, which is why, as soon as the realm was built, she shipped everyone who worked on it, back to the realm of the moon." Morgana nodded; she had heard some of this on the market.

"Lothar told me your parents are still there." Branna gave a soft nod.

"They are, and my brother. Morgana no one really knows the truth of her reign, even the ruling council have no idea of the woman she is. Queen Bridget Violet knew, and she challenged her, Ariel was her adopted daughter and Bridget confided in her, which is why we were targeted. Rhiannon can be ruthless, she hides behind a fake kindness and a soft smile, but heed my warning, when she is nice to you, that is when she is at her most dangerous. Trust me, at some point, she will show kindness to you, it will not be her personally, it will be one of her minions. Never trust her, because that is when she is setting you up for a fall. Be on your guard always, and learn your craft, and protect yourself." Morgana looked at her with a worried look.

"I will be safe, I am on Merlin's land, and he will protect me." Branna smirked.

"Well, I hope it is better than that of a king, because if someone wants you gone, they will do it. Uther was not Merlin's priority, and he died that day at the hands of ordinary men. Rhiannon is a queen, there is nothing ordinary about her."

Morgana took note, she was well aware of the way Rhiannon manipulated everyone around her, and she knew as she headed back home, that when she arrived at her small house in Avalon, once again she would be alone, especially if Merlin had not returned. That evening the family assembled, all week they had been coming and going, as they dealt with the business of the family.

Branna had ruled out war, which was at the time an unpopular suggestion, but in recent years, Berengar had managed to gain a foothold within the tribes of the wealthy, and the family had made a great deal of money, and life within the castle had become lavish by the standards of the world of men. Branna's guidance, based in Fae culture, which was far more advanced than the tribes that surrounded them, gave them a status many admired, and the family exploited it with great skill.

They all sat around the large table in the main hall, which was filled with a lavish amount of food. Berengar males could really eat, and Morgana was a little shocked at how much food they devoured. The meal started with a full boar laid in the centre of the table, and by the time the meal was over, it was just bones. The only real cloud over the night had been the appearance of Otto, who had been warned by Branna, not to create discomfort for Morgana. It was her last night, and he to date had kept his word, but as they sat at the table, and he was wheeled in, Branna was called off to attend to a problem with the staff.

Maud and Otto sat side by side staring at her as she finished her wine, and wiped her mouth. She lay down her cloth after wiping her mouth, and Otto scowled at her.

"You will be gone tomorrow?" Morgana nodded feeling a little on the spot, but she was not going to give in to her fear. Merwig and Dagaric watched on with interest.

"I will be, I would imagine you will be glad Grandfather." His face twisted.

"I am not your grandfather, that would imply I accept you, which I don't." Maud smirked with delight; Morgana softly nodded.

"I remember a time when a servant was rude to me, and my father pulled out his sword and threatened them. He told them I was his daughter, and born to a proud line, for his blood was also my blood. He also told them, if his father had heard them insult me, he would have killed them where they stood, I guess he was wrong?" Otto scowled even more, and hissed through his lips.

"I raised a real man, a Varisci to be proud of, I did not want him to soil my blood with that heathen bitch he married. You are no family to me; I could never accept a half breed in my house." Dagaric sat back and took a breath, he glanced at Merwig, who was watching Morgana's reaction carefully, she simply smirked, and gave a nod.

"I have Celt blood, but just not any Celt. My mother is a queen of great status, to be honest, Uther was not worthy of her, but my father was, his blood line was a noble one as was hers. You talk of half breeds, yet your brother married a woman of the line of Fae, would that not make your wife a half breed too?" Merwig smirked, and made a little gasp. Otto banged on the table, as his face reddened with anger.

"How dare you… This family has the purity of the Sachsen line, not the trash of your gutter whore mother." Morgana smirked, her voice was soft and calm, she had no intention of being threatened by Otto, Rosamund had briefed her well.

"It is not pleasant to hear truths, is it? You talk of purity, and yet Branna, the head of this family who is bound to your brother, is considered of the most inferior of lines in her race, which is why she fled the realm of the golden queen. You talk of purity, how many peasants did you rape before, you tried to rape a Fae, and she took the use of your leg? It appears to me, when it comes to your bed, you prefer half breeds and women of a lower status."

He clawed at the arms of his wooden wheel chair, as his rage erupted, Maud stood up in her seat, and leaned on the table, her eyes narrowed.

"You may think you have the upper hand, but to me, you are just a petulant child. Hide behind the skirts of the Raven, but a day will come when she is far too frail to protect you. I know that you hold gifts, I feel them, but be warned, if you challenge me, I will destroy you little raven. My Fae blood is far purer than yours, so be warned, you may think you have the upper hand, but you fool no one here. I am watching you, step lightly around me." She leaned back, and looked at Otto.

"Come my love, there is a foul reek in the air here."

She gripped the handles of his chair, and with a hiss of her teeth as Otto scowled, his face still a deep red, Maud spun the chair and pushed him away. Morgana looked round the table, to see Merwig and Dagaric watching, she gave a shrug.

"Volatile, isn't she? Rosamund told me she was terrifying and I should be wary, but if that is her best, I must wonder what all the fuss was about?" Dagaric sat back, and laughed as Merwig leaned forward.

"It is wise to be aware of them Morgana, they know who is watching, and they know better than to test the rule of my mother." Morgana turned as she saw Merwig look across the hall, where Branna stood watching as Maud wheeled Otto away. Morgana turned back to Merwig.

"I am my father's daughter, I must stand on my own feet and fight my own battles, I understand Maud's resentment of me, but she has no fear, as much as I love this place, I have no wish to rule here. One day, I intend to build a place of my own, and that will be my kingdom, Maud can take all of this, I have no interest in it, other than my visits to my ancestral home."

Dageric sat forward, he had a look of his father, he was wide and muscular, and carried the same chiselled face of sternness about him. Like the rest of the Berengar family, all of them had long black hair, dark intense eyes, set in intense whites. Their skin was as white as snow, which gave them an ethereal appearance. All of them were very well groomed, Dagaric especially, with his perfectly curled hair, manicured finger nails, and very neatly clipped sideburns and moustache. Morgana could clearly see, that she had many of the families' qualities.

"You are very much like Victor, you do have his spirit, but my brother has a point. Maud does not care where you covet, you have gifts like our mother, and she will always see that as a threat. It matters not what you wish young Morgana, one day she will confront and challenge you, it is who she is."

As the night drew on, Morgana had a lot to think about, she headed to her room, and packed her few things, including the small statue of Branna into her bag. She slid into bed and lay back, part of her was feeling saddened, and yet she was looking forward to leaving. As fun as the castle was, and having time with Branna had given her a great deal of joy, she also missed her tiny house, and she knew it was time to head back.

In the back of her mind, she considered Dagaric's words, and his warning that Maud would one day challenge her. It felt a little strange, she was no threat to her, and yet she understood, that even though she was her grandmother, Maud was second to Branna, and all females were a threat. Would she one day no matter what she did, have to face Maud in a confrontation? It made no real sense to her, but as her thoughts drifted, it was clear, just like Rhiannon, Maud had to be seen to be superior, and in order to do that, she would have to make an example of her.

Lying in bed thinking of her home in Avalon, she felt a little bit of apprehension creep into her. She had left her home and headed to Tintagel to be with her mother, knowing Rhiannon had her in her sights. The night of her arrival at the castle, the queen of Avalon had tried to capture her, and it worried her. Branna had been more than clear, she needed to keep a low profile, and avoid the minions of Rhiannon at all costs, she must learn from Merlin, which would in turn enhance her powers of Fae. She drifted into an uneasy sleep, and her dreams were filled with the angry face of Rhiannon at the market, as Morgana challenged her authority.

*B*ranna sat alone lost in thought, looking at the glass box before her, where inside Ariel lay in her long sleep.

"I will miss her my love. I have grown deeply fond of her in our time together. These last weeks have felt like I had a real daughter, someone I can connect with and talk to, like I did you. She is young, and yet so intelligent with the same desire I had to prove myself. You would like her, and take her to your heart as I have, for she is so like I was at her age. I really do feel like she is perfect for this family, and strong, her will matches mine in every way." She lifted her glass and took a sip, as her eyes moved over the crystal box.

"You were right Ariel, Maud fears her, and she should, Morgana has the right mind and determination to lead this family, but in that I have many concerns. Maud has been less aggressive than I thought she might be, and that does worry me so, for I know her, and I know when she is as subdued as she has been, she is at her most dangerous. I fear Maud will make an attempt to attack Morgana, and the time is not right, Morgana has lots to learn, and she will learn it, I will ensure it." She took a long breath in as her thoughts drifted, her eyes locked on the box, as she considered her feelings.

"Ariel, I do not want her tied to a raven, I do not want her to make the same mistakes I did. Morgana could be the person I wanted to be, the woman I wanted to be for you, untainted, free of darkness, the one member of this family who does not have blood on her hands. I wish you were here to help me guide her, I have little trust of Merlin, I know you did, and I could use your words of wisdom in this matter. It will be hard to watch her leave tomorrow, I would prefer she stay here, free of Rhiannon, and under my care. She will learn the Whitelines, and I am hoping through that, I will find the answer to the balance within Merlin, for if I do, I can open your box, and bring you back to me, and we will be free of everything." She gave a long sigh, and leaned back on the chair, closing her eyes, her voice was soft and quiet.

"To be free of all this, the castle, the family, and all the pretence, I would give anything my love, anything at all. Oh, you have no idea of how much I dream of being in Florae, or some other realm, just you and I, with a small house and garden, and an eternity of living peacefully together, I would lay my life on the line for that. If Morgana grows as powerful as I think she will, one day, my dream could be realised, and I will be free of the darkness forever."

She gave a long sigh, and her breathing changed slightly, her wrist which was limp on the desk holding the glass, slipped back, leaving the empty glass on the desk, and flopped to her lap, and Branna drifted into a deep sleep, to dream of a life with Ariel.

High above the castle, Roack sat watching out over the domain of her mistress, muttering quietly to herself.

"I hear you little fat raven, I hear your curses and your plans, the Raven Branna will never allow you to harm the little new raven, she is very precious to this line. Be wary, little fat raven, for I will protect her also, she has the Raven Branna's power. She does not know it yet, but if you attack her, I will touch her and release a darkness upon you blacker than you have ever known. The Morgana, will rule this line when Branna the Raven makes her choice, I will ensure it."

Chapter Sixteen.

Back to Avalon.

Morgana felt emotional as she ate breakfast, Berengar smiled, as he leaned towards her, and lifted a cloth bag from his side, and placed it beside her on the table.

"The Golden Queen may make life difficult, but continue to stand your ground. I believe your late step father paid you an allowance from his estate, which was right and proper as a member of his household. As your grandfather, and your true line of blood, I aim to match him. This bag contains currency of Avalon and your homeland, it will aid your recovery, and allow you to continue in your study." Branna smiled as Morgana's eyes filled with tears.

"I have no words Great Grandfather, and the kindness I have had bestowed upon me here has robbed me of them." He gave a gentle smile and nodded at her.

"You have no need of words Morgana, we are family, it is what we do for each other. I believe in loyalty and support, and you have mine and all of this families support behind you. The Golden Queen has robbed this family of precious souls, and we aim to repay her one day, and if our money helps keep you safe from her and healthy in your study, it is the best use of this family's fortune. Never forget who you are, never forget you are one of us."

Morgana nodded as she sniffled and wiped her eyes, Branna patted her hand.

"We know how tough she can make things, and it appears to us, she wishes to starve you out of her realm. Morgana, we will make sure that never happens." Morgana gave another sniffle and tried to smile.

"I love my place of birth, and have felt great love here shown to me. This is the first time in my life I have felt a part of something, part of an actual family." Berengar gave a reassured nod.

"That is because it is true, this is your family and you do belong amongst us."

It felt strange to be told that she belonged here, she was family, it was something since the death of her father, she had forgotten. Since his death, she had felt like she was an inconvenience. Uther had tried, she admitted that, but his behaviour towards her when her mother was not present, was very different, and it was clear, he would have preferred to trade her for his real son.

After breakfast, with Branna at her side she took one more look around, and Branna took her up to the top of the tower, where she showed Morgana where she would sit to look out above the forest. Morgana marvelled at the view, which reached out for miles, she looked up at the sky, and Branna smiled.

"I am surprised you did not ask me sooner, that is my veil of protection and the reason why Rhiannon will never find me. It covers all of the land of this family, not only does it keep prying eyes out, it prevents anyone here leaving without my consent. This Morgana, is my Avalon, I rule here as a queen, they call me the dark queen, but that is because they do not know me." Morgana nodded.

"The ones Otto shoots at?" She smiled and gave a nod.

"I sealed the realm to protect us from her, but in doing so, some people were trapped. I have no mind that they are here, had they been respectful and started dialogue with me, I would have allowed them to leave. They chose to oppose me and fight against us, and so they remain here sealed in. It is silly really, they took care of Ariel and I have always been grateful to them for that, Ariel told me they were kind to her, and she even told me they were nice people. I have no issue with them, and if they would swear an oath of peace, I would help them leave, but it would be a great risk, as they would probably run straight to Rhiannon, and I am not yet prepared to face her, when I am, she will know."

Morgana understood, she now knew the full story of Ariel, and so she really understood Branna a lot better, and why her hatred of Rhiannon was so strong.

"If I have learned anything living in Avalon, she means to get what she wants, and she has the power of those in the right places to do it on her behalf. I have no doubt, if Merlin is not there when I arrive back, I will see some rough days." Branna gave a long sigh.

"Morgana, do not concern yourself, all that matters now, is that you learn from Merlin. When you return, study hard, and live a quiet life, I have been thinking a great deal whilst you have visited. The way I see it, Rhiannon has tried to pen you in, but I have seen plants at Tintagel that will be of use to you, collect them before your return. Lift their roots and take some back to grow in your garden to increase your supplies, and never forget, you also have access to the one place she has no rule, and within that place, there are many special plants which will aid you." Morgana frowned, and turned to her.

"What place do you speak of, for I am not aware of one?" Branna gave a small smile.

"The Forest of Time is a special place, and not within the realm of Avalon. There is no physical barrier, but if you were to walk down the Queens Road and over the bridge, stay true to the path, and you will walk under the trees of the great first forest, within that realm. There are many special plants, including the White Star, they have deep healing properties, learn them and use the knowledge you learn well." It was clear Branna had a vast knowledge of Avalon, and she knew it would serve her greatly.

"I will look them out, when I return, I am grateful for all the help you have given to me, I will not let you down." Branna smirked.

"I did not think you would, I will watch over you, even as we speak, my arm has reached into Avalon on your behalf." Morgana was unsure how, she had no idea of the messages that had been sent to Lothar, and he had been busy in the outer regions of Avalon.

*I*t was market day in Avalon, and the traders had just finished setting up for the day, as the town of Avalonia came to life and people came down to trade. Between Mavis and Seth, the table of Morgana was left empty, in a gesture of allegiance to Morgana, and it was noted by all of the people who came down to buy their teas. Lord Kane, with two of the marshals who tried to capture Morgana, approached Mavis as she served three members of Fae with dark hair, she glanced at him with his two companions, as she bagged up the cakes and loaves for her customers. Kane approached and pointed at the barley loaves.

"I have come for my mother's order." Mavis looked at him.

"What order would that be then?" He frowned at her looking puzzled.

"What are you talking about, I come every week for two barley loaves for my mother, it is a regular order?" Mavis narrowed her eyes and shook her head slowly, as Seth watched on with a smirk.

"Sorry young sire, I have no recollection of an order, and I have sold clean out of barley loaves." Kane looked astounded, and pointed at the table where there were ten in a row.

"Have you lost your senses woman? I can clearly see ten, I want my mother's two loaves, she sends me every week." Mavis casually shrugged.

"I am sorry young sire, those are already paid for and sold, I am waiting now for them to be collected, I have no more barley loaves left to sell. Please tell your mother how sorry I am."

He was lost for words, and had no idea what to say. It was clear that this market woman had no idea of whom he was, or the status of his family, he dithered on the spot.

"Are you telling me that you are refusing to sell me my order?" Mavis smiled.

"As I said, I have no recollection of an order, if I had, it would be here, and it is not."

"This is outrageous."

*H*e gave a long huff of exasperation and turned to look down the line of stalls. Lord Kane, whistled and caught Fagan's attention, and frantically waved him over towards the table. Fagan walked up with a smile.

"Ye requires me, Lord Kane?" Kane nodded abruptly, and raised his arm to point at Mavis.

"This woman refuses to sell me my usual order. She clearly has barley loaves for sale, and yet she insists she had sold them all. As market supervisor, I demand you instruct her to serve me."

Fagan stretched his jaw and rubbed his chin, he looked at Mavis stood looking resolute, then turned to Kane.

"Tis a right pickle ye are having, but if she has sold out, I am not certain as to what I can do fer ye." Mavis smirked, Kane snapped his head round, and pointed aggressively at the table as his temper rose, and his face began to redden.

"THEY ARE RIGHT THERE; CAN YOU NOT SEE THEM CLEARLY, YOU OLD FOOL!?" Mavis shook her head at Fagan.

"They are sold awaiting collection." Fagan gave a nod, and looked at Kane.

"They is sold awaiting collection, ye should have come earlier. Tis good business to come early, and tis thee ups and the downs of trade, ye will have to wait, but be earlier next week." Kane gave a long angry sigh, and looked at Seth, he knew he was not going to win.

"My mother needs new wooden spoons; please tell me you are not sold out too?" Seth gave a shrug.

"I got none, I ran out of wood." Fagan smirked, as Kane stared at him with rage in his eyes, it was almost like he was going to explode, he took a huge breath inward.

"HOW…THE WHOLE REALM IS SURROUNDED BY TREES!?" Seth frowned at him.

"I don't cut wood from live trees, I use seasoned dead wood, my spoons are the talk of Avalon." Kane looked down at his table and the four rows of neatly carved spoons, and pointed angrily.

"WHAT ARE THOSE THEN?" Seth looked down.

"Bad forks, I thought I would sell them off cheap." Mavis blurted a laugh, and turned her head away quickly, Fagan wore a smirk, Kane looked outraged.

"They are very clearly spoons, and I want them, if they are cheap, how much are they?" Seth did not bat an eyelid.

"Ten shillings…. Each!"

"WHAT, ARE YOU INSANE, I COULD BUY 100 FOR 10 SHILLINGS?" Seth pulled his lip and stood resolute and calm, he gave a soft nod.

"Well then, go buy them, that would indeed be a good deal, I would take it." Kane narrowed his eyes.

"Are you mocking me, you trash?" Fagan looked at Seth, who suddenly looked very serious, as Seth put his hands on the table, and leaned right over it, his eyes looked angry as he gritted his teeth.

"You listen to me young lord, and you listen good. You may think you rule the roost with your airs and graces around here, but just remember who it was that built this place, and who is the real life blood of this place. I do not trade with sneaks and philanderers, especially those who hurt and spy on my friends. Your money here has no value, we may be trash, but are still free to choose who we serve, and you are not one of them." Kane stepped back, and looked at Fagan with a gasp.

"You heard him, he is violating the agreements of trade, I demand you arrest him?"

Fagan frowned and stuck a fat finger in his ear and gave it a wiggle, pulled it out and looked at the end of his finger.

"Sorry young lord, I heard nothing, ye have no idea of thee wax that builds in me ears hammering metal all day. Now, what was ye saying?" Kane was stunned.

"They are refusing to serve me, have him arrested, her as well, and if not, I will demand you are arrested too."

*T*hat was not his smartest idea, Fagan's eyes narrowed, he was a tall muscular man, and he leaned right over Kane and stared at him with an ice cold stare. Kane swallowed hard and stepped back, Fagan was far larger and very imposing, his voice was low and held malice.

"Ye listen to me young lord, ye may think ye have power, but trust me, bigger and richer than ye have fallen to thee scythe that hangs in me shop. Ye think ye have favour with the queen, but trust me, if ye tries telling tales on any of these good folk, or spreading more rumours bout little dark eyes, ye will find secrets creep out about some of the ladies you have tucked in ye bed behind ye fiancée's back." Fagan nodded slowly, and Kane took a deep breath.

"I have no knowledge of such things; I think you mistake me for another." Fagan smiled.

"Ye have learned wisdom this day, tales to the queen run from many roads, and all mine go past my mother and brother, never forget who they are. Ye money has no value here, think of that the next time ye tries to trap an innocent girl." Kane swallowed hard.

"I do not know what you mean." Seth leaned back off the table.

"I heard Tintagel is a nice place, especially the walks on the cliffs… Aye lad, we have our own sources, and they talk much of your behaviour." Kane looked at Seth, and then back to Fagan.

"This is outrageous, I am a man of status in this city." Mavis nodded.

"That you may be young sire, but it is us who make the food, and your status means nothing when you are hungry, and that goes for any who hurt our friends." Seth gave a nod, as Kane, looked slowly around, all the traders had stopped, and were watching him carefully, he stepped back from the table.

"Fine, you will regret this, all of you, wait until my mother hears of this." Seth gave a sniffle and wiped his nose on his sleeve.

"Go tell her, her money will have the same value as yours if there is trouble, and there is sixty of us."

With a loud huff, Kane barged through the crowd and walked off, Mavis lifted a barley loaf off her table and handed it to Fagan.

"There you go Master Fagan; this one is on us." Fagan gave a big smile.

"Ye all walk a fine line, watch yeselves." Mavis nodded.

"If they keep her off this market, they will learn, you cannot eat gold." She smiled as Fagan took the loaf.

*T*he day had slipped past, and the time to leave was closer, Branna had spoken a great deal to her, and as she packed her bag ready, Morgana felt a little sadness creep into her. Branna smiled as she walked into the room, where Jarron sat with Roack on the window ledge. Morgana tried to smile, but was finding it hard, it had been the best two weeks of her life in recent times. Branna gave a soft smile.

"You have your book, remember hide it well, even Merlin must never see it, for there are things in there all Fae consider secret, even me. Work hard Morgana, and learn your craft well, for as you learn more, the powers will come to you. Remember, keep your Fae side veiled in the ways I showed you, Merlin, and Gwendolyn will not see it that way, so you will be protected. Learn each day and practice the things I have shown you in secret, and you will find a renewed confidence. Now… Close your eyes, and focus on me." Morgana gave a nod.

"Thank you for everything, I feel less alone knowing all of you are with me." Morgana closed her eyes and focused her mind, and Branna softly took her hands.

"This is not a goodbye; this is a new beginning my Countess of darkness."

Morgana smiled as she felt the sensation run through her, and she opened her eyes to see Branna, and behind her was the barn, where Rosamund stood waiting. She took a deep breath, Branna stepped back.

"You know what to do, and now Morgana of Berengar, you truly know who you are, go live, go learn and become a raven of our line."

As Branna smiled, she faded away, and Morgana felt a twinge of sadness, Rosamund smiled at her, which was rare.

"Did I not tell you of how remarkable my mother was?"

"She truly is the queen of all ravens, I feel my life has changed with my knowledge of her, and I will serve her with deep loyalty, for she deserves nothing less." Rosamund gave a nod.

"Come, your carriage is waiting, we will see you back to the castle, you will have a few days here before you return to the golden realm."

*M*organa spent three days at the castle with her mother, she walked the cliff tops and gathered herbs, and lifted several plants to take back to Avalon with her. Igraine felt that Morgana had changed, she appeared happier, less brooding, and she smiled more. Morgana evaded all her mother's questions about where she had been, her simple response was, 'up the coast with my friend,' and she said nothing more.

When the day finally came to return to Avalon, Lothar joined her for the journey, he had rooms at the tavern in Avalonia, and intended to stay for a while and keep watch. On the journey to Avalon which took them almost all day, he told her of the traders and how they had shown great support to her. Morgana was pleased, but it also worried her, for she knew that would make Rhiannon even angrier, which for her was not good news.

They set off in a black carriage, one more suited to the use of Queen Igraine, Morgana folded her black cloak and placed it at her side. It was to be a longish journey, so she settled back, her thoughts caught in wondering what would happen when she arrived home.

They had travelled for almost an hour when the coach started to slow, Lothar got up and leaned out of the window, he pulled his head back in quickly, and looked at Morgana.

"It is her marshals; they have stopped two coaches and appear to be checking who is on them. I am sorry Morgana, but she is still determined to get you outside of Avalon." Morgana smirked.

"I am prepared. Give me your rings, and hurry."

Lothar frowned as she stood up in the carriage, and pulled the long black cloak of feathers around her shoulders, he had no idea at all what she was doing, she held out her hand.

"Lothar… The rings, hurry." She pulled up her hood, as he watched on, slipping the golden and jewel encrusted rings from his fingers.

"I cannot deny, I am at a loss as to how you think this will help… Please do not barter them, I love these rings." Morgana gave a giggle.

"Trust me, and you shall have all of your rings returned. When they approach the carriage, I am the Countess Le Fey, do you understand that? Let me do the talking, and just go along with everything I say." He nodded, as he handed over the rings.

"I trust you, as does Branna, and that is good enough for me." She smiled.

"Sit back, stay calm, and let me lead, Branna and I have talked of this." He gave a nod looking pale as the carriage slowed to a halt, Morgana sat down and pulled the hood forward hiding her face, feeling a little nervous.

*O*utside, two marshals walked from the back waiting carriage towards the black carriage of Morgana. Lothar leaned forward in his seat to try and see what they were doing, moments later, there was a tap on the door, and Lothar slid further forward in his seat, and leaned out of the window. The marshal looked up at him.

"Name your passengers, and open the door." A low husky voice from within spoke loudly.

"Lothar, who is it that disturbs my peace? I thought I was quite clear; these roads are not safe and we do not stop. I will not be late for my audience with the queen." He swallowed hard and looked back.

"I am sorry my lady, there appears to be marshals of Fae on the road."

"Well, what do they want, tell them I am in a hurry to meet with their queen?" He looked down at the soldier.

"My lady, the Countess le Fey is not pleased with this waylaying of her journey, she has an audience with the queen of your land on business, and it is best not to displease her." The marshal looked nervous.

"You have to open the door so I can see the occupants, I am sorry my lord, it is our queens order." Lothar frowned.

"We are not in Avalon, why does her authority apply here? My lady will not be pleased about this, she is heading there now." The marshal looked even more nervous.

"You are heading to Avalon? Please my lord, just open the door, and let me see how many ride with you." Lothar gave a long sigh.

"On your head be it."

He turned the knob, and the door swung open. The marshal took a breath in, as he looked inside, and Morgana sat with her hood of black feathers over most of her face. He could just about see her chin, Morgana did not wait, she slipped out her gold and jewel encrusted hand and waved at the marshal, her voice was low, coarse and bitter sounding.

"I hope you have a good reason for this rude intrusion? What is your name, I shall be speaking to your queen?" He stepped back quickly looking pale, and very afraid.

"I apologise your Ladyship, I had to do as ordered, please make your way, we will not delay your journey further." He grabbed the door, swung it shut, and waved to the other marshals.

"Let this one through, it is the Countess le Fey on her way to see the queen." Lothar gave a nod, and the marshal smiled nervously.

"On you go my lord, go with speed."

The driver whipped at the horses, and the carriage jolted forward, and the marshals in front signalled to the driver to pass the two waiting carriages down the side of the road. The carriage rumbled past, and Lothar sat back in his seat with a gasp of relief.

"Well played, I will not deny, I was worried for a moment, if I let those marshals get you, I would have suffered a fate worse than death, when I got home." Morgana slipped down her hood, with a slight giggle.

"I thought this may happen, which is why I kept the cloak out of my bags. Branna thought it would be a good way to move unseen, and she was right." She handed Lothar his rings back, and he chuckled as he looked at her.

"You have her spirit; I see it clearly." Morgana gave another little giggle and sat back, wrapped snug in her cloak.

Lothar was dropped off at the top of the Queens Road, where Stenlow observed him. Lothar winked as he got out, and the carriage then travelled over the large wooden bridge and through the scree towards Misty Bank, and her small cottage. Arriving home felt familiar, it was strange really, as for over two weeks she had lived in luxury, and yet as she walked into her empty little house, she felt a huge sense of relief, and happy to be back.

Her time was busy, she stocked up the fire, lit it, and placed a pan to boil for tea, and then carried her large stuffed bag into her bedroom, and started to unpack. That night she ate a meal at her table, and as the sun faded, she lit a candle, and rolled back her rug. Using her axe, she prized loose a floor slab, and dug away at the dry hard earth beneath it. It took a great deal of time and effort, but as the moon rose high, and she cleaned out a small cavity below her floor, she felt the excitement build within her. Under the veil and out of sight of all prying eyes, Morgana cleaned up the cavity and lined it with soft dry cloth, and then placed into it her new black book wrapped in a silk cloth. This book was special, it contained all she had learned from Branna, and contained plant lore, and some exercises to increase the potency of her mind.

Just like Branna, Morgana had begun her journey into learning her craft and increasing her powers. She had also started what would become a dual life, one spent learning the power of the Whiteline, and the other, her secret hidden Fae life, the life of a raven. She had no idea where it would lead to, but she knew that after years of searching for something that she had no idea of what it was, she felt she had finally found it. It was her real identity, and the person she naturally knew she was meant to be. Morgana, was a raven of Berengar, and after her time with Branna, she aimed to copy her, and become one of the most powerful.

With the stone back in place and her book hidden from view under her rug, she washed her hands and then headed to her room. She packed her cloak in a small trunk, which she slid under her bed, and as she lay back on her bed in the candle light, she gave a soft smile, and whispered quietly to herself.

"Morgan le Fey, the Countess of Darkness… One day Rhiannon, you will face me, and pay for the pain you have caused me."

Chapter Seventeen.

The Queens Decree.

It was early morning and Morgana was snug and warm in her bed, her eyes were closed but she was awake, as her memory of two days prior played in her mind. It was one of her sad days, those days when she looked back and remembered the past, and this morning she had awoken from a dream of her father. Two days earlier, she had stood at his grave stone and placed a posy of wild flowers below it.

"I miss you father… I went home, I met your grandmother Branna, and she has given me help and advice, I understand now the tales you told me of her wisdom and kindness."

The tall white stone had weeds at its base, and she crouched down, pulled them free, and wiped the stone with her hand to brush off the dust.

"I know you are not really here, Berengar told me of how they buried a beggar with her father's swords here, and your body was taken back to the castle, but this is all I have here of you. This is the place I have always visited, and today I miss you and wanted to be close to you, and so I am here. I brought you flowers, I know that is strange for a knight of great power, but it is all I can do for you." She gave a sniffle and wiped her eye.

"I swore revenge for you, and I aim to get it, Uther is slain, and Rhiannon is next, it was the weapons that she gave to Uther that defeated your men. When I am done with her, I aim to remove Merlin, for his part, and then Gwendolyn for making the sword that convinced you to make peace with a traitor. I swear this again to you father, I will have my revenge for your death."

Morgana blinked, and opened her eyes as she came out of her thoughts. She did not feel like doing much today, her mind was preoccupied, and she had to make up the fire, although it was not really that cold, but she needed to make a drink and eat something.

She slid out of bed and wearily made her way into the main room, and knelt by the hearth to restock the wood.

Once the fire was burning, she dressed and headed around the back to the well. When she had filled her large stone jug, she turned, and noticed all of the plants, rooted in small woven sacks, in a line close to the wall in the shade. Morgana smiled as she saw them, and recognised them as the herbs she used for her medicines and teas, one had a hand carved fork tied to it, and she lifted it up with a huge smile. There was no doubt it was from Seth, and it made her feel better, she had awoken feeling so sad, and yet here looking at the fork she was feeling a little of the cheer she had felt whilst at the castle.

Feeling better, she brewed some tea and cut a slice off a large loaf she had bought at Tintagel, and added large chunks of fresh cheese, for her first meal of the day. Having eaten her fill, she cleaned up, grabbed her bag, and headed outside. Today she felt she wanted to explore, so turned at her gate, and followed the road in the direction of Merlin's cottage. It was a nice day, and cooler than it had been, so due to her mind filled with thoughts and memories, she decided to take a walk and give herself time to think.

*I*t was not long before she passed the cottage, and turned down towards the bank of the lake, which she intended to follow to make her way towards the end of the Queens Road. It took longer than she expected, the lake was far bigger than it looked, but soon, she found herself stood on the edge of an ancient treeline, which she assumed was the start of the Forest of Time. She looked up the long road that led deep into it, and saw how the large trees leaned over with their wide canopies to shade it. Beneath the trees she could see the tall coloured grasses and small flowers, and in her desire to see them up close, without realising she wandered into the forest, not really thinking of where she was or what she was doing.

Morgana crouched down close to the small white star shaped flowers, they were beautiful, and she felt her breath catch in her throat as she reached out and touched one. It was a plant of powerful properties; she could feel it as she happily stared at the small sweet smelling flower.

"They are beautiful, are they not?"

Her skin tingled, and she looked up and gave a slight gasp. Morgana rose quickly and bowed her head, as before her stood a woman of unrivalled beauty, with long flowing red hair, pure white skin, and the most intense violet eyes. She wore a long cloak of red, edged with golden leaves.

"My Lady of life, please forgive me, I was distracted by the wonder and enchantment of this flower." Eve's voice was warm, soft and caring.

"The White Star, is the only thing my brother gave to this or any other realms. It is a flower of great beauty and enchanting to behold. I do not blame you for admiring it, I often do myself. I know of you little Morgana; I have heard of your woes in the land of the Queen of the Moon. I take it you came here to collect plants to furnish your garden?" Morgana swallowed hard and shook her head.

"No My Lady, I would never take what was not given. I awoke feeling a sadness in my being, as the past overwhelmed me, and I wanted to walk to clear my thoughts, and I am not sure why, but I ended up here." Eve smiled.

"The forest of my husband is indeed a place of great beauty, and I feel you were drawn here out of need, for within this realm, you will find the peace to ease your heart. There is much here that would aide you, and all but this one plant, could be harvested for your garden, this sadly only grows within the boundaries of this forest, and to move it, would bring about its demise." Morgana understood, Branna had told her of the flower.

"I would not do that to something of such great beauty." Eve gave a small chuckle.

"You may take some of the flowers, for I hear you wish to aide those who live within the Moon realm with tinctures to ease their ills. They are very potent, so use them with great care." Morgana looked down at the flower.

"I am grateful, and yet, I do not wish to spoil this place, for I feel it would lessen the beauty of it." Eve gave a smile, as she walked towards Morgana.

"Then hold out your palm, you show such respect for my husband's forest, and it will be rewarded." Morgana lifted her hand and looked at her palm, her hand trembled slightly.

"I am unsure as to why My Lady." Eve watched with intense violet eyes, and waved her hand softly, and Morgana gasped, as in the centre of her palm, a small plant appeared and grew two tiny leaves.

"Treasure it and nurture it, and lay its feet within the boundary of your garden, for it is a plant of high value that will aid your quest to comfort the sick." Morgana could feel her breath lost in her throat as she looked up at Eve.

"I feel at a loss for the words to express my joy, this will do much good for those who come to me." Eve gave a smile.

"You have chosen a hard path to walk, Merlin is not an easy man to be apprentice to, and the queen at times is overruled by her passions. Know this little Morgana, we have addressed your cause with the queen, and your innocence has been proven. Stay resolute in your quest to do good for these people and you will be rewarded greatly, it is a straight path, but one that can be easily strayed from. Stay true to your path, and go forth with my blessing and help those with great need, the life of the earth will always aid you in the cause you have chosen." Morgana looked at the small plant, it had grown a third tiny leaf.

"I will head home with great haste and plant this where it will get the sun and the rain, and yet be protected beneath my large apple tree. I shall tend it with great care."

"If you do, and stay true to your cause, it will flourish to aid you. Be warned, this is one plant a veil of the Fae cannot hide you from, stay true to the values of a healer, and it will thrive." Morgana looked up and gave a huge smile.

"Thank you, My Lady, I am working hard with all Merlin teaches me, and already using it to help others, and I will honour this flower in my tasks." She nodded.

"May your worries and troubles ease as you walk back, go in peace with my blessing."

Morgana stood and watched as Eve walked slowly into the trees, which she was sure bowed their branches down as she walked beneath them. She looked at her hand and the tiny white flower that had opened within her palm, and was filled with delight. She turned, and hurried back to the path, to make her way back towards the lake as fast as she could and hurry home, to plant her new plant in her garden.

As the day passed and the sun started to slip down in the sky, Morgana sat outside at the back of her cottage, and watched her freshly planted plant. It had grown many leaves, and was adorned with many white buds, and she was delighted. As the sun fell and the darkness descended, she was feeling much better and sat at her table having eaten a small meal, and looked at the books that Merlin had given her to read, one in particular caught her eye. Lifting her candle, she headed into her bedroom, and sat back to read Merlin's hand written book on symbolism, and its uses with spells.

*I*t was very late when she drifted into sleep, and the book slipped out of her hand. High above Avalon, Rhiannon stood on the steps of the citadel and looked up at the large clear moon, her mind filled with thoughts of her daughter, and her heart heavy still from the loss. Lost in thought, she did not notice the shadowy figure dressed in a long tatty hooded cloak as he approached the base of the steps. He stopped and watched her for a second.

"I feel the loss you hold within you; you show your daughter great honour." Rhiannon took a deep breath, and looked down.

"I have a realm to watch, and yet my heart feels the pain still, I am a queen, and have my duty to those who depend on me, and yet there are moments such as this one, which I take as my own." The hood twitched.

"You have always taken on much of the weight, and it is a burden you could have shared with your son, he was willing to shoulder it should the chance arrive." Rhiannon gave a scoff.

"I fear he will not walk easily back into this realm, and even if he did, I am not sure his shoulders are that strong." Albanlin took a step up onto the first step.

"I never understood why you did not give him the chance, Rayne cares for these people, he would work in their interest to help them." Rhiannon gave a chuckle.

"I am sure he would, he would back up the traders, and join them in their stand against my allies."

"They stand for one of their own, if I may, it has always been a quality you have admired amongst your people, would you care to enlighten me as to why you have changed your stance?" Rhiannon looked down and smirked.

"You use words well, my stance has not changed, and they do not stand for their own. The apprentice of your guardian, is not Fae." He took another step up, and stopped.

"I did not mean Fae, I meant poor." Rhiannon lifted her face, and eyed him carefully.

"If you come to play word games with me, you are wasting your time My Lord, I have not the patience tonight. Speak your thoughts directly as you would normally, your visits here are never without reason." Albanlin took another step up.

"Your people suffer in poverty, and yet this is the wealthiest of all the realms, your heavy heart I feel has clouded your judgement."

"How so?"

"The girl is innocent, I am aware of who she is and what she is capable of, and it is not murder. You are a queen of this realm, and she is simply an apprentice who is eager to aide your people, she is no assassin." Rhiannon lifted her head and looked out over the cliff tops.

"You know this for sure?" His hood twitched.

"I do." She turned her head and looked at the hood that obscured his face.

"How so?"

"The darkness that ate at your daughter could not be touched by one of the realm of men, it would devour them completely. Whoever did this, had a strong power within the light, for like my guardian, they would have to carry both light and dark, and she does not carry that amount of darkness within her. She is innocent, you should have seen that, and yet your heart is clouded by the loss, and so your eyes were momentarily blinded." Rhiannon gave it a moment of thought.

"Nevertheless, I have no trust of her, and it is I who rule. Maybe the girl is innocent, but give me one reason why I should trust her, because if truth be told, I do not." Albanlin gave a slight chuckle, as he turned and looked out across the realms.

"She is the daughter of a queen, and named by a king as his kin. You more than most know how things work, she is intelligent, and a day will come when she realises her value. Tell me, would you have the power of a queen with powers in the Whiteline for you or against you, for a time may come when you will be forced to choose? The path you walk, may determine the outcome, and you should consider your steps carefully. Enemies of all are plenty, is there really a need to create more?"

"I am not convinced she will rise to great power; she lacks the mental capacity. Your suggestion is foolish."

"Tell me Queen of the Moon, when did you last hear of a mortal being able to cast the veil of shadows over them, for I know of just her? The task Merlin set her alone was to learn the language of old, then use it with great power of her mind to create a veil to hide her.

She is hidden from all, does that alone not show of her ability?”

"It is a spell Fae children learn early in their life; it is not that hard if children of ten summers can do it.” His hood gave another twitch.

“And yet, in your own words, you admitted, she is not Fae.” Rhiannon flicked her wrist dismissively.

“This is foolish, what would you have me do, reinstate her on the markets to quell their rebellion?” Albanlin, began to walk down the steps away from her.

“To be seen as a fair queen, and one who rules for the greater good, by bringing peace, is an admirable quality, it enhances reputation and power.” He faded into the night, and was gone, as Rhiannon watched on and gave a sigh.

“I have no time for this foolishness, it is absurd to even consider it.” She turned and walked back towards the large doors to the citadel, and the steps to her chambers below the surface.

It was mid morning and the sun beat down on the cottage as Morgana woke from a deep sleep. Her mind felt groggy, she slipped out of bed, and walked into her room to light the fire. The room was already hot and stuffy, as she blinked in the bright light, she had not drawn her curtain last night. Yawning she knelt down and made up the fire, to brew her first tea of the day, it took longer than normal, as her mind felt weak with the amount of information she had gleamed from Merlin’s book.

Morgana stood up and looked at the window, the heat in the room was rising with the fire. She yawned again, and thought of the nails, and then without thinking, she flicked her wrist, and there was a loud cracking noise, and the small window bumped on the frame as it swung lose. She was not fully awake, so without thinking, she grabbed the wooden spoon off the table, and propped open the window, and took a deep breath, as the cooler air flowed into the room. Whilst the water heated, she headed back into her bedroom, and pulled on her long black dress, then headed back to brew her tea as the pan started to bubble.

She sat and had her first meal of the day, sipping her herbal tea, and slowly waking, understanding she had solved Merlin’s task with a mcrc flick of her wrist, and it baffled her. At Branna’s castle she had struggled for days, and yet in a moment of not thinking, she had naturally achieved something that she had thought would be a difficult task. Her mind slipped back to her moment of telling Branna of the task she had been set, and Branna's voice echoed in her mind.

"Is that all, I thought for a moment he had set you something difficult? Morgana, for a Fae Ofmoon, that is a mere trifle of a task, come see, I will show you."

Morgana stared out of the window, where Jarron sat in the tree watching the floor for beetles and snails, her voice was quiet as her thoughts formed.

"A mere trifle for a Fae, and yet the blood in my veins is only part Fae, watered down by my mother of Celt origin, how can I do something so easily, when in truth it should challenge me?"

She gave a sigh, it was a mystery, of that there was no doubt, and yet hadn't Branna told her that the power of a Fae grows stronger with each passing generation of female? Was Branna right, was this force within her she had been warned to keep hidden more powerful than possibly Maud? There was no doubt she needed answers, and the only person she knew could help her was Rosamund, and her lodgings were outside of Avalon in the large settlement of the world of men. She needed to talk to her, and get as much information as she could, and at the moment, with Rhiannon watching her constantly, she thought to keep busy and appearing to be doing her own thing, may calm her down. The large town Rosamund was in was named Glaston, and it had a market, and considering she could not trade here, she thought it would be better to be seen trading outside the realm.

As the morning wore on, she busied herself preparing new stock, she had teas to bag and tinctures to make, and she also had the problem of how she would get her goods to market? The day wore on, and there was still no sign of Merlin, and so she picked up his book and turned through the pages to the next chapter, as she decided she was not going to wait for him, and would continue her study alone.

The whole chapter was based on the language of the ancient runes, their uses, and their pronunciation. It irked her a little as she had struggled so much with the first task, which had forced her to work out the sounds of the words alone. She gave a long sigh as she looked at the hand written page.

"Why was this not the first chapter, seriously, how disorganised is this wizard?" There was no point complaining, what was done was done, so she sat back, and began yet another step towards learning more of the abilities of her teacher's powers.

As the evening came, she took a break and went out to check on her herbs, which she watered and was thrilled to see her plant given her by Eve, had grown even more, and had more buds swelling preparing to burst into bloom. As she walked around the side of the house with her pail of fresh water, she heard the hooves of a horse, and glanced down the road, her heart fell when she saw the blue uniform of Commander Stenlow.

"What now, will this man ever leave me to live in peace?" He rode up to the gate of her home, and she walked down the rough dry path to look up at him.

"Commander, is there something more I have to answer to?"

He eyed her with suspicion, and then slipped his hand inside his tunic and pulled out a parchment with the royal seal on it. Leaning down he handed it her, and Morgana frowned as she looked at it.

"What is this?" He sat back on his seat, and puffed out his chest.

"Her royal highness, Queen Rhiannon, has considered your plight, and has deemed that your removal from the markets was unjust. In her divine wisdom, she has deemed that as a resident of this realm who has aided her people, that you deserve the benefit of the doubt. Other traders have stated your case and have expressed that your manner and fairness of trade should be considered. Having done such, the Queen in her almighty wisdom has granted you a temporary special status, which will allow you to trade on the markets within this realm. That is her token of willingness to show compassion to all the people of her realm, and allows you the privilege of selling your goods at the market."

It did not take too much to work out that her faired haired dignitaries had whined and complained due to their inability to be served goods, and so she had been forced to change her mind in order to appease them. Morgana smirked, as she looked at the seal.

"I feel honoured, when do I have to respond, I would like a little time to consider her proposal?" Stenlow looked utterly flabbergasted.

"Respond… Proposal, what in all the realms do you mean? Young woman, this is a huge honour, have you any idea of the status you have there as the only trader not of Fae lineage?" Morgana shrugged as she looked up at him.

"Tom the wheeler is not Fae, neither is Greg the wine maker, they come from Glaston to trade, and there are a few others from Glaston, so it is not like I am the first is it now?" Stenlow furrowed his brow.

"Young lady, I fear you do not quite understand, no one turns down the offer to trade here, you have no need to respond, you turn up and conduct your business." Morgana nodded.

"Really, I was considering the big market at Glaston, I thought I may buy a horse or small cart or something and try there, which is why I want to consider it, I would like to visit Glaston and see what it is like before I choose a market that suits me." He snapped.

"It is Avalon, no one in the world of men will buy your products, they are uncouth, and have no taste for the finer things." Morgana smiled at him, and softened her voice.

"Why Commander, what a sweet thing to say, I had no idea you had sampled my teas and felt them worthy of such compliment. Thank you, I am deeply touched." He looked really uncomfortable and his cheeks reddened a little.

"You are expected to show up and trade."

With that, he pulled on the horse's reins, and the horse turned, and he rode off at speed as Morgana gave a little chuckle, and looked down at the sealed parchment, her mind was made up, she was trading in Glaston.

She lifted her water pail, and carried it with the parchment inside, where she placed the parchment unopened on the small side mantle of her fire place. Jarron was asleep, she felt she would leave him, and closed her window, bolted her door, and lit a small candle. Morgana curled up in bed with her book, and felt a tinge of happiness, Rhiannon had backed down, as she had been seen to be unjust, and to Morgana, it did feel a little bit like a minor victory. She was absolutely sure, that at some point she would visit Seth and Mable and thank them for standing up for her, after all, it had taken guts to face those who ruled and make a stand for justice.

She lay back on her pillow and gave a happy sigh, she would mix up some special tea with all their favourite flavours, and put them in bigger bags to show her gratitude. She would make a point of going to see Seth and thank him in person, and hope he could give her the directions to Mable's house, so she could visit her too.

Chapter Eighteen.

Harsh Facts.

*T*he day started early, and Morgana was up and hard at work, as she sorted out her teas, and made two very special bags of tea up for her friends who had shown her such support. She worked with a smile, knowing that Stenlow would return her response, and she was excited to see more of Avalon, and thought that Seth may be able to help her find a means of transportation to Glaston market.

She carefully packed her bag, and with a skip in her stride, she locked her door, and turned right at her gate onto the road, and headed down towards the fork, that would take her in the direction of Seth's village of Hollow Coombe. The walk was far longer than she realised, as she walked into the marshes, filled with tall grasses with long flower plumes, with wide wooden bridges, that wove between the dry mounds of earth surrounded by water. The day was heating up, and the air was thick and humid, as she wiped her face several times. The air above her was filled with flies and flying insects, and as much as she tried to stay positive, she felt it was a dreary place, and could not understand why anyone would want to live in such a dreadful place.

After an hour she stopped on a wooden bridge, and knelt down to dip her small cloth handkerchief in the cooler waters below the bridge. Standing up she wiped her red face, to cool it, and took a look around her, which was not that easy, as the tall seven to eight foot canes of the grasses blocked out most of the view, although she saw smoke, and gave a sigh of relief.

"Thank the Gods, there is an end to this walk, why would Seth want to live here, there is nothing but flies and bugs?"

In many ways it should have been obvious to her, and as she lifted her bag back onto her shoulder, she remembered her time at the castle with Branna, and her words came back into her thoughts.

"Morgana, you have dark hair, you are the same as all of the others she sees as lower value. Have I not told you, of why they call her the Golden Queen? Those of dark hair will always suffer as I did, hidden from view so as not to offend her grey eyes. For that alone we were pushed away from her glorious and glowing white paradise of Avalonia, to uphold the vision of Queen Rhiannon the golden and the fair. She is a fake, a pretender and riddled with her devious and evil political thoughts of yet more power."

It was a sobering thought as she remembered the bitterness of Branna, and yet it felt strange to her. Branna loved her people, and hated Rhiannon, for the very reason that her people were persecuted for no other reason than the colour of their hair. It was clear the more she lived in Avalon, the more she started to resent those who ran the glowing white capital city, Seth and Mable had both been genuinely kind and caring people. As she trudged on her thoughts drifted as she thought of Uther, he too had been a fake, a so called man of high honour, and yet all he had done was get drunk and cast his eyes on other women. She could never prove it, but she was sure he had taken others to his bed when he lived in the castle. She looked up, and the path appeared to cross a bridge and split into two forks.

She stepped onto the bridge where a young boy sat at the far end with a fishing line. She walked up looking at the forked paths, unsure of which one would lead her to her destination, and stopped at the young boy. He looked about seven summers old and was dressed in rags, he appeared to be unconcerned with her and watched his line, she smiled, even though he was not looking.

"Excuse me young sire, but do you know which path I would take to Hollow Coombe?"

He looked up from his line, and then lifted a thin arm and pointed at the path to the slight left.

"That way, you don't want the other, that will take you to the scary realm and death." She nodded and swallowed hard, as she looked at the path that wove away to the realm.

"Thank you, I most certainly do not wish to go to my death, especially in a scary realm." He gave a nod.

"No one does, they say the little people down there fill your head with nightmares and you die of the frights." Morgana lifted her eyes and looked again at the path, and felt a shudder run down her spine.

"No one does, I thank you for your good advice."

He turned back to his line and watched as a little cork bobbed on the surface some way up the calm stream. Morgana took a quick pace forward off the bridge, and with a glance at what she knew was a scary path, she walked onto the path for Hollow Coombe.

*T*he walk to the small village took about another twenty minutes, and she was amazed that each week, Seth would load up his cart and pull it all this way, surely it would have been easier to use a horse? With the village in sight, she gave a sigh of relief, and her pace quickened.

The village was just a scattering of old stone or wooden houses, that were not set in any kind of organised order, and all had small fences with gardens of food growing in them. Morgana stopped and looked around, there were around twenty houses of one form or another, but there appeared to be no sign of a carpenter's house. There was a blacksmith, a weaver and a basket maker, all with clear signs above their doors, Morgana turned around to where a large man stood watching her. He gave a nod in her direction, he was tall, and very broad with dark short cropped hair. His eyes were dark and untrusting and she felt threatened by them, she tried to smile.

"Greetings, I am looking for Seth the Carpenter, would you know where I would find him?" He stood in a firm resolute stance, and it made her more afraid of him. His voice was deep

"We know who you are, you will not find Seth here, he is gone." Morgana did not understand.

"Where… I am looking for him?" The tall man just stared at her, and she could feel his dislike of her.

"Be off with you, have you not caused enough pain to this village?" She looked around and did not understand, others had come to their doors and were staring at her, and she started to feel a deep feeling rising up inside her, and it was danger.

"I do not understand, why have I caused you pain, I live alone and mind my own business? Seth was my friend, I worked at his side on the market, and he was kind to me." The tall man took a step forward, and she felt tense.

"Aye, and that was his problem, because it was that which brought upon him his untimely death, he should have listened to the queen and ignored you."

"WHAT!?" She could not believe what she was hearing, and she felt the tears welling her eyes.

"He is dead… When… How?" The tall man took another step forward, and she noticed the long knife in his belt as his hand slipped down to it, his voice showed his hatred and anger.

"I told you begone, had Seth not got involved with you, he would be alive now." He lifted his arm and pointed to the far end of the village.

"You see that smoke, that was his place, and her soldiers came and burned it all down with him still inside with his wife and kids. That is on you sorceress, you are the reason his family are gone, burned to a crisp no soul would recognise because he refused to serve her favourites. Him and the others, all of them have been snuffed out. Begone, or you shall suffer the same fate, you are cursed and no kin to us, no one here will aid you." She stepped back as the tears flowed onto her cheeks, he took another step forward, and she knew he meant to harm her, but she stood her ground.

"I did not want this, I cared about him, he was my friend, I did not want the traders to make a stand for me, I was not going to trade again." A huge sob came up her throat, as her tears dripped to the floor, and her voice dropped.

"I did not want this, I was not here and if I was, I would have told him to stop, I would, he was my friend." Her tears rained onto the hardpacked floor, and she felt the pain of her insides rip through her, this was not her fault, she never wanted this. He just stared at her with no feelings at all.

"Get gone, and leave us be, you are not welcome here. If not, I will slit your throat and burn you on the embers of his house."

*M*organa felt heartbroken, as she turned and clutched her bag, and ran back down the path, away from the village, back towards the wide wooden bridge, as the man's words echoed through her thoughts.

"Him and the others, all of them have been snuffed out."

What others? She ran onto the bridge, passed the small fishing boy, and over the bridge back into the tall grasses, going as fast as her legs would carry her. She had no idea how long as her grief consumed her, until she could run no more, and she crashed down to her knees, still weeping bitterly with a pain that consumed her whole being, as she gasped on her knees, and wailed with pain into the hard floor.

Unaware of all around her, she did not see the rider who rode along the path, and came to a halt before her, and slid off his saddle to the floor. He walked quickly towards her and crouched down pulling her into his arms.

"Morgana, I am here, I have been searching for you." She felt the embrace of Lothar as he pulled her close, and she pushed her head into his shoulder, and wailed more, feeling the pain tear her apart inside as she mumbled.

"They said it is all my fault, Lothar it was not, I did not do anything, I was not even here." She cried harder, as he pulled her closer with a sad look on his face, his voice was soft.

"They know that Little Raven, but who else could they blame, they cannot speak out against their queen, to do so, they would suffer the same fate? All of them live in fear, it is her way of ruling, that is who she is, did my mother not tell you this?" She gave a sniffle.

"They were the only friends I had here, I cared for them, they were so kind to me." Lothar nodded, as she slipped back and looked at him with red swollen eyes.

"That is why she did it Little Raven, you are a threat to her rule, she had to make an example to all of them." She took a huge breath and tried to swallow.

"Lothar why, I am not a threat to her, I have no wish to rule anywhere, not even the castle?" He gave a sad smile.

"Little Raven, you are the daughter of a royal line, I know you do not understand all this, but Uther named you daughter. It matters not what you think, what matters is how others see you, and to a queen, especially one as powerful as Rhiannon, you are a great threat to her rule." She shook her head.

"But why, I do not want that, I just want to be left alone?" He lifted her up off the floor and held her gently by the shoulders.

"Morgana, Little Raven, you are so like my mother, and that is the problem, and even though your true powers have not come forth yet, one day they will. The queen does not know why, but she has felt threatened since the day you came here, and that is her own Fae powers sensing a rival to match her, she was no different in the way in which she treated my mother, and Ariel to that degree. As long as you live, she will feel threatened, but you are under the care of the Guardian to the Whitelines. It is why my mother encouraged you to learn here, Merlin will protect you until you are strong enough to defend yourself. The queen cannot harm you, as it would fracture the whole alliance of the council, and so for now all she can do is isolate you, and her tool for that, is fear." Morgana understood that.

"Lothar, I am not scary, no one should fear me." He gave another smile.

"No, not yet, but one day if my mother is right, you will wield great power, and that is when the queen will cower at the mention of your name. Little Raven, you could be a great threat to her, and if my mother is right, one day you will be." Morgana shook her head.

"Branna is tied to Roack, I never will be, I am no threat to anyone." He nodded and took her hand.

"Come, I will take you home, pack your goods, I will be taking you to the market, and my mother wants to talk, we shall be gone for a few days, which might be best."

Lothar lifted her onto the horse, and walked her back through the marshes away from the village, and Morgana felt the sadness surround her as he explained, that other villages had been attacked and houses burned. It was clear to Morgana that everyone who stood up to the queen, had been eliminated in one big sweep, and all of the other traders would now fall in line, and do as she told them. She knew for sure that she would not, she would trade anywhere that was not Avalon, not one grain of her tea would pass the lips of a fair haired Fae.

Once home, Lothar made her bolt her door, and told her to get all her goods for market ready and he would return shortly to escort her to Glaston in the realm of men. She was feeling calmer, but still had a ball of hurt within her. She filled her small wooden crates with her jars, and packed her teas carefully into sackcloth bags which she had made especially for transporting them, and then once done, she sat on her bed with her book and tried to read.

Her thoughts could not focus as she remembered Mable and Seth, and soon her tears came again, as her anger and heartbreak swirled together inside her. Although she was not fully aware of it, very much like Branna, her anger was starting to work on the powers of Fae buried deep within her, and she was starting to increase in the powers that she held.

*I*t was several hours later, when Lothar appeared with a small cart. He helped her carefully load everything, and as she sat on the cart, he made sure her cottage was locked, then jumped up beside her and flicked the reins. The cart lurched, and they made their way around the lake and onto the Queens Road. It was late afternoon when they passed through the curtain of light that was the entrance to the realm, and they travelled up the road past the farm, and onto the road towards Glaston.

The journey was not very long, and two hours after leaving they arrived in the sprawling town, which was far bigger than Morgana had expected. On the outskirts was a large tavern with stables, and Rosamund was waiting with booked rooms. Morgana was shown to her room to settle in, which was basic, but better furnished than her own cottage. After a little time, she was taken to Rosamund's room, where Branna stood waiting with a smile, Morgana felt her tears as Branna pulled her close.

"Come Morgana, we have much to talk this day, see we have food, sit with me and eat a good meal, you feel thinner, and need more substance to you." It took a while for her to settle, and only she ate, as Branna was just here in essence, and had eaten at her castle, Branna sat with her and began to explain things to her.

"Morgana, soon your powers will come, and they are to a degree bound for now, which will help hide them from the others, but you must understand that they will sense something from you, and it will unnerve them when they are around you. They see it as your status, you are the adopted daughter of a King, but not just that, your mother comes from a line of powerful druids, and within that, she too has some powers even if she does not realise it. The Golden Queen is aware of this, because she makes it her business to be, that woman has her eyes on everything, and it is within that she is afraid of you."

Morgana swallowed her food and lifted her wine glass, and took a sip to rinse the inside of her mouth, before swallowing.

"But Branna, I have no wish to rule over anyone, I really am no threat at all." Branna smiled.

"You are missing the point, Morgana this has nothing at all to do with what you want, and everything to do with what the Golden Queen wants, which is complete dominance. You are failing to see the world from her point of view." Morgana shook her head and frowned.

"How?" Branna sat back with a smile.

"You are considered a mortal, and also a king's daughter, you have more influence than you realise, and when your brother appears, he will be seen as Uther's replacement, which puts you as a future king's sister in a very powerful place in court." She wrinkled her face.

"I have not seen my brother since his birth, and I hate court, I never want to be at one again."

"Morgana, times change, and you will too. You have to look at the bigger picture, this land of men is changing." She shrugged.

"How so?" Branna gave a little chuckle.

"The world of men was divided, and Uther hate him or not, united them all, and now the country is fracturing all over again. The land needs leadership, and we have heard from Gunther a good fighter in our forces. He has one hundred men that were separated in the battles, and were left behind when Berengar moved his forces back. They have settled and taken brides from this land, and they have become accepted and influential within their own hamlets and villages. They are well placed to support your brother, and we are sending more of our people to join him, this land already has men of the Norse living here, the men of Rome are pulling out, but there are still a lot of isolated pockets, that opposed Uther, and they will your brother. I have spoken with Berengar and Hengist is on route with more of our forces, arriving with goods and skills, soon this land will become a land of mixed peoples. Morgana, now the Romani lords have fallen and their forces pushed back, many men of your mother's line, are rebuilding old fortresses, and the leaders of old are growing unrestful as they did before Uther. War will come again, and you are placed highly in this land, and could be seen to be as powerful as a queen, it is the Golden Queen's greatest fear, as we think, she wants control of the lines of men also."

It made sense to her, Rhiannon craved power and control, and liked to be seen as the most powerful, but none of that mattered to Morgana, she simply wanted the power to be free of everything.

"Rhiannon is Fae, she would never be tolerated in the realm of men." Branna sat back.

"The men of Rome were, and be honest, she has greater fighters, better arms and enough gold to bribe all of the leaders of the tribes. Her arm of influence extends far already into this realm, it would take just a snap of her fingers to seize control. You have no idea how much influence you have, Gunther has talked to many who hold you in high regard, and if your brother does come forward, a day will arrive when you will be the closest person to the new king. A few well chosen words in his ear, will undo all of her influence."

"I am not as sure as you are, and I really do not want to be as involved as you think I should be. Can I just come and live with you, I can be happy at the castle?" Branna gave a smile, she understood, she had seen the difference in Morgana at the castle.

"I would love nothing more, but at this time Morgana, you need to be here, you need to master the Whitelines, for they hold a very important key to balance, and if you can achieve that, then you can live anywhere in the world you wish to." Morgana gave a sigh.

"It matters not what I do, it feels like everywhere I live, except your castle, is a prison."

*M*organa finished her meal, and both of them moved to the chairs, as Branna enquired as to where she was at with her lessons. Morgana showed her book, and the chapter on the old language, and how to pronounce all the words, Branna smiled softly to herself, Merlin was indeed shrewd.

"This is good, he obviously wants to move you forward so he must be impressed. It is clear he has set you two tasks to measure your mental capacity." Morgana looked at her.

"Why is that important?"

"Morgana, it matters not how much power a person has, mental ability from a strong mind is the most essential aspect of all powers. Look, Maud has a strong power, and yet after years of study, she is no nearer her goals, and that is because she allows her emotions to run wild. Maud has not the mental capacity to hold back her emotions and focus her mind, and because of that she will always lose control. It was Ariel who taught me how the queens of both Fae lines managed to focus their minds on each issue they faced, and I may add, it was the strength of Bridget Violet and her ability to control all that was happening within her, that ultimately saved her people, even if it cost her what remained of her life." She reached out and took Morgana by the hand, and gave a small squeeze.

"Morgana, Merlin is clever, let him teach you, as Ariel taught me, strengthen your mind, and never lose control, for it is within that skill, that one day you will rise to rival me." Morgana gave a small laugh.

"I am not sure about that, you hold great power according to all that know you, Lothar thinks you could match Rhiannon." Branna smirked.

"Lothar is very loyal, he is my youngest and I do love him so, and he is not completely wrong, I do hold a great deal of power, but the time for us to face is not yet."

"Why not?" Branna sat back in her seat.

"Never forget, at this moment the golden queen is not alone, she has around her a council who are just as powerful. To face her at the moment would be folly, even though many of them know of the corruption of the golden queen, they turn a blind eye to it. If she was attacked, that would appear like they also were being attacked, and so they would rush to her aid. This is a game of careful moves, and I am smart enough to see the game and play very carefully, once she is isolated, that is when I will strike, and not before. My plans have always been a long game, and it is I who have dictated the pace, I will strike when she least expects it."

It made sense to Morgana, and she was impressed with Branna and how she thought. It was more than clear now that she was part of some political power struggle, she turned to Branna.

"Rhiannon aims to use me the way she used Ariel, doesn't she?" Branna gave a huge smile, and nodded her head.

"I see why Merlin has set you these tasks, you have a sharp mind, and I can see now that you are starting to understand your position. Ariel too ended up caught in a trap set by the golden queen. Although, I must warn you Morgana, Ariel had the protection of a queen of Fae, you however do not, which is why the closer you are to Merlin, the safer you are, and the golden queen is very aware of that."

It was a long night, and as Branna hugged her goodbye, Morgana felt the sadness inside herself. She returned to her room and climbed in bed, lay back on her pillows as the memories of her days trading on the market of Avalon passed through her thoughts. She closed her eyes and felt the anger grow inside her, Seth and Mable were simple traders, and ordinary members of the Fae community. They were both kind and caring people, and Rhiannon had given the order, and they had been murdered on her command. Morgana turned in her bed and curled up, and slid down under the blanket, and as the candle flickered, she gave a soft sob into her pillow.

*L*othar stood out on the roadway, outside the tavern, Rosamund stood at his side.

"You heard her, she thinks Morgana could be as powerful as she is, and I cannot deny, I have to ask the question, where will that leave

Maud?" Lothar shuffled his feet with his discomfort.

"I will not deny, I wish mother to rule for as long as possible, I have seen how Maud and Otto rule, and I want no part in that. Morgana is not like mother; I am not sure she has the edge to control the family, but there again, her true power is being bound within her, as mother is trying to protect her, so for now we do not know." Rosamund gave a nod.

"Maud has had no teacher, her attempt to seize power from mother has worked against her. Morgana is clear, she has no intention to rule, and she has mothers help to educate her. I fear a time is coming Lothar where we may be forced to choose sides between Maud our sister, and Morgana, our niece." Lothar shook his head.

"I will back neither, I have no wish to be caught in the middle, and will not deny, maybe it is time we told mother to let Ariel out of her box." Rosamund shook her head.

"That path is folly, if she lets Ariel out, it will start a war in the family, and I fear if Ariel is released, mother may leave with her, and hand over everything to Maud, and I am no supporter of that. We need to keep Ariel exactly where she is, it has brought an unstable balance, yet it is balance all the same. We need to be careful where we walk in this, mother is right, this is a game we all need to play with great care."

Chapter Nineteen.

Keeping the Peace.

As Morgana set up her stall with Rosamund at her side on the large market in the town of Glaston, in Avalon, Rhiannon watched as the traders set up their stalls. She turned to Stenlow, as he sat on his horse, at her side watching the few visitors to the market place.

"Where are all the traders, this is just half of what we normally have? This looks ridiculous, go and find out what is happening."

Stenlow dropped down from his horse, and then walked across the white road towards Fagan as he organised the shoppers and traders. He walked up to him and Fagan turned and smiled, as Stenlow pointed, and was very abrupt.

"Where are the traders, the queen is not happy, and where is the student of Merlin, she was told to be here?" Fagan shrugged, and then scratched his chin.

"Well, tis a thing to be sure, but this is all ye have. If ye are asking what I is thinking, well then, they is either dead or afraid." Stenlow frowned.

"What do you mean dead?" Fagan turned, and looked at the soldiers across the way.

"Ask ye soldiers, they was the ones that killed em." Stenlow appeared shocked, he turned on the spot, this was news to him.

"I know nothing of this." Fagan gave a long breath of air out, and scratched his chin again.

"Well, if ye wants the answer, you better go ask, after all, ye is in charge of em."

Stenlow felt his anger rising as he ignored Fagan, and just walked off back across the road towards the Marshals standing around. As he approached, the captain came to an abrupt salute, Stenlow looked him up and down.

"Is it true, are the traders dead?" The captain appeared confused.

"Yes sir, it was the queens direct order… I thought you knew sir?"

Stenlow was visibly shaken, he was for a moment lost for words, as he felt a shudder run down his spine, and he struggled to find the right words as his mind spun. His voice lowered more in surprise.

"What… All of them?" The other marshals were all looking at their captain, who nodded, and appeared to be a little confused that his commander did not know.

"We were instructed by the queen to take out all of the traders that refused to serve the residents of the town sir, I still have the order here." He slipped his hand inside his jacket, and pulled out a sheet of parchment that bore the royal seal, and handed it over to Stenlow, who took it with a slightly shaking hand.

Stenlow looked down at the order, it was clear and very precise, and the instruction was there, to kill all supporters of the student of Merlin, and quell any others from rising up in a rebellion against the queen. There was even a list of names, and it was not a short list, Stenlow looked up from the list.

"Some of these traders have families, what has become of them?" The captain pointed at the order.

"We took care of all of them sir, that is what the order demanded, it was the queens wish." Stenlow felt weak as the realisation of what had happened sunk in.

"You mean all of them, some of them had children." The captain nodded.

"Yes sir, all of them, that was the order."

Stenlow handed the parchment back, and felt sick, the captain leaned forward, close to Stenlow, and lowered his voice.

"Are you alright sir, you look a little pale?" Stenlow gave a nod, took a breath and stepped back.

"I am fine… Yes fine, the Queen asked I checked, what has become of the student of Merlin." The captain shrugged.

"The outer guard reported she left the realm yesterday sir, she reported she would be trading in Glaston and would be away for a few days." Stenlow gave a nod, in a strange way, he was relieved to know she was still alive.

"Alright Captain, carry on, her majesty does not want any outbursts in the market, ensure everyone continues their business respectfully." The captain saluted.

"Yes sir!"

*I*t felt like a long walk back towards the queen. Fagan, who had been informed of all the ugly shocking details, watched him from across the road. He knew his brother well, and he could clearly see how deeply this had affected him. In many ways he was not an unkind man, if anything, he was pompous, and severely dominated by his wife, but he was at heart a gentle person. Stenlow appeared sickened, and that look of disgust he wore, he had seen on Luminaria's face a few times before she finally left her post, and was returned to the moon realm. Fagan understood the politics of Queen Rhiannon better than any, he had been in Avalon almost from day one, and had overseen a great deal of its construction, and he knew Branna very well back in those days. He had never expected it, but there had been many days when he felt he understood her better than any, and he did not disagree with some of her views.

Stenlow approached the queen as she sat high up on her gleaming white horse, she looked down at him with a smirk.

"Well?" He took a deep breath, and swallowed hard to try and regain some of his composure.

"In a bid to quash the rebellion, those who were not killed are afraid to come, the student of Merlin has left the realm to trade in the realm outside, your highness." Rhiannon scowled as she lifted her head and looked across the market.

"She is impudent, she challenges me in my own realm, and then has the nerve to refuse to trade here at my request, one day she will face me for her insult and she will fall. On the bright side, there will be no more rebellious behaviour in future, I will have order, and I feel we have established it clearly now. Your men did well, let them know of my gratitude."

Rhiannon kicked her heels, and her horse lurched forward, and Stenlow stood looking lost for words, as he watched her slowly ride the line of remaining stalls, so all the traders could see her. They bowed their heads and looked at the floor, not as a mark of respect, but to hide their fears. The news of thirty whole families burned alive in their dwellings, across twelve villages within the realm had circulated fast, and there was no one left brave enough to look her in the eye.

The young boy holding the horse looked at Stenlow, as he stood frozen looking very pale indeed.

"Are you alright sir, you do not look well?" Stenlow snapped out of his thoughts, and looked at the enquiring boy.

"You can take the horse back to the stables, I think I will return to my desk for a while, I am not feeling quite as buoyant as normal, it is tiredness, I am sure. I will ease my legs and rest in the office should I be required." The young boy gave a nod.

"Yes sir, you do that, don't worry about your steed, I will take good care of her." He gave a sad smile.

"Thank you."

*F*agan understood full well the difficulties of the job his older brother had, he had seen his sister suffer the impossible requests of the queen, and struggle with her conscience because of them. Such was his disgust at his sister's treatment, when the queen requested he fill his sisters' shoes, he managed to talk his way out of it, by explaining how there was still a great deal within the realm for him to oversee. When Stenlow had been named as Luminaria's replacement, he had thought that if anything, things would settle down, as Stenlow was incapable of being as strict or regimented in his approach to the queens' whims. It was now clear, the queen understood Stenlow better than he realised, as she had bypassed him, and sent the orders directly to the captain of the guard. Knowing that Stenlow would be incapable of ordering such things, and it was yet another example of how ruthless she could be, to have her every single request carried out. It was clear, if Morgana wanted to rise up to challenge Rhiannon, she was ready, and there was no length she would not go to ensure she came out on top, even if that did mean taking the lives of her own people.

*G*wendolyn sat in her royal rooms within the large House of Scrolls at Florae and looked at Bade in shock.

"What… You mean, all of them?" Bade gave a solemn nod.

"It is distressing news, but it has come by way of our ambassador, and she is very shaken by it all. She has requested she be brought back to Florae, and replaced, Councillor Alder has already requested the position, it would not be hard to replace her. In regard to the lost souls, the letter details what she witnessed, and it is disturbing reading, are you really quite sure you wish to read all of it?" Gwendolyn nodded, and took the sheets of parchment.

"What news of Morgana, is she still safe?" Bade gave a nod as he let go of the parchments, and Gwendolyn took them from him.

"She decided to avoid the markets, and has travelled with her uncle to trade in the town of Glaston, and if I may take the liberty, I feel she is safer there at the moment." Gwendolyn nodded.

"Yes, I believe you are right, let me know when she returns, I have many things to organise, but I wish to travel back soon before heading back over to Morbihan." Bade bowed and stepped back.

"Yes, My Queen."

He spun on his heels, and headed towards the door to leave the queen in peace to read, although having read the document in full twice, he was not sure the queen would approve, and felt she may find the details of the report disturbing. Gwendolyn sat staring at the parchment but not really reading.

"How could you do this, what has happened to you? There was a time in my youth I idolised you, and now look at you starving for power and control of everything. I fear my grandmother was right, I can never truly trust you, the only side you care for, is your own."

*T*hree days passed, and Morgana returned having had two days trading her goods, and she had made a great deal more money than she expected. The town of Glaston, was a busy place, there were many who also came to trade in Avalon, and they had a great deal of silver to trade, some of which they spent at the market in Glaston.

She arrived back mid morning, and Lothar drove her back to her cottage, and dropped her off with her stock. He helped her unload, and then headed towards Avalonia, where Morgana had asked him to purchase some timber planks and posts for her. He had advised her on route home, to try and avoid the large town of Avalonia in order to stay out of the queen's gaze.

She had an axe, but required a saw to cut trees into planking, and she knew she did not have the strength to do that. With the extra money she had made, she invested in timber, knowing it would help those who did most of the work around the central town. Getting Lothar to order it and have it delivered, took her out of the picture, so she knew the trade would be welcomed. She was also aware that to cut trees outside her fence line would give the queen a reason to single her out, and without Merlin, she did not want to confront the queen alone.

Morgana settled back into her life of quiet study, she stayed within her boundary, cleaned, and dug in her food garden, and read the books of Merlin. It was a difficult task, as she tried to understand the pronunciation of the old language and also the symbology of everything connected to the world and the Whitelines. Each night, after her evening meal, she would bolt her door, roll back her rug, and get out her black book, to update her knowledge, write the advice Branna had given her, and copy out chapters of Merlin's book.

A week later her timber arrived on a large cart driven by Fagan. She was greatly relieved when he helped her unload it all, and stack it neatly at the side of the cottage. After they were done, Morgana thanked him with barley crackers, and a new taller beaker of tea, she had bought four new beakers at Glaston. She sat outside with Fagan on the two chairs from her cottage, she had the one that wobbled, and as he smiled and chewed his food, Morgana asked the one question that had been in her thoughts for three days.

"Are the rumours true Master Fagan, did she really have everyone from the market burned alive in their homes?" It was a hard question to answer, and he swallowed his food and thought for a moment.

"Tis a dark deed that has been done, and I is sorry that ye saw some of it. What ye has to realise, is that here in this realm, no one can question her rule. It matters not where ye were born, or what ye were raised to believe, under Fae law, to question is death. They chose to make a stand and disobey her direct command, and to a queen of Fae, that is not to be tolerated." Morgana gave a nod.

"I understand that, but to murder them in such a horrible way, how can she be allowed to do that, could she not have fined them, or given them jail time?" Fagan gave a sigh.

"Ye is not wrong, and many have said those very words, I know Stenlow would rather have had them punished rather than killed. He has taken a leave of duty for a week to calm down, it has taken his stride and that is fer sure. See, Little Dark Eyes, tis like this, she commands and controls everything, and in return, she ensures safety and survival for all, I know they moan and complain, but be assured, them is the lucky ones. Up there, well, they is the ones who know hardship. They should not have questioned her and found other ways, had they done that, they would have lived. Tis a sorry tale fer sure." Morgana felt the sadness build inside her, and shook her head slowly.

"It was wrong, I have no care what she thinks, Seth was the kindest man, and Mable, she was so loving and worked hard for her children, I am sorry Master Fagan but I cannot accept what she did, I simply cannot, and I feel responsible, if I…"

The sob came up, and her tears rolled into her eyes, as she looked down. Fagan lifted a large hand and gripped her shoulder gently.

"It was not ye fault, they made the choice and they knew the risks, and they did what they did because they knew in their hearts that the queen had to see her wrong doing. All is not as is seen Little Dark Eyes, and hope does come of all this." Morgana gave a sniffle.

"How, how can the death of good people bring hope? I am sorry, but they are now terrified of me and say I am cursed, and none of them will buy from me now. There is no hope, the queen killed it when she burned down their houses." Fagan smiled, and took a sip of his tea.

"Tis a strange tale, ye see, the thing is, eleven villages had burned out houses, and twas twenty Marshals did the burning. Some of them back marsh villages have a lot of folk who do not agree, and so ye cannot have twenty Marshals in eleven villages at once, ye see what I am saying?" Morgana frowned and shook her head.

"No… Not really." He gave a slight chuckle.

"The thing is Little Dark Eyes, as ye know, there are two kinds of folks living here, and that is two kinds of thinking, one thinks one way, and the other thinks different. No matter what, word travels faster than a leaf on a stream, and so, when one house burns, words sweeps quicker than the flames, and one young woman many years past, showed that there is more than one door to this place, and not all of em have eyes on em." Morgana thought she understood, as Fagan nodded at her and gave her a big smile. She thought it through carefully and spoke slowly as she put things into place.

"If I understand you properly Master Fagan… Are you saying that when they hit Seth, the others were alerted and left for safety?" Fagan gave a bigger smile.

"Ye has a good mind, and fast. Ye see the report said, all the houses were burned, and anyone inside would have been killed and burned to death, the words matter more than the act." Morgana gave him a shrewd look.

"Are you saying that the marshals knew the houses were empty?" He took a swig of his drink.

"Aye, I is… Ye still have a long way to go before ye understands things round here. The marshals swear an oath to protect the life of every member of the Fae, tis an oath they live by. Our Lumi suffered because of it. Ye bang on the door, and if no one answers, ye burn it… Ask any marshal, they will tell ye, all the houses burned, and anyone inside burned with them… Tis the right words that matter." Morgana gave a smile and nodded.

"If anyone was inside, they burned, that does not say for sure they were, and so the marshals carried out their orders to the letter without harming any of their people. I am happy knowing that, I have felt such pain thinking they died because of me." Fagan gave a gentle nod.

"They knows, the word is out about how upset ye was, but I will warn ye, it did damage, there are many who fear being seen with ye, it is not ye, tis her, they fear what she will do." Morgana gave a nod.

"I understand that, she has to isolate me more to prove she has all the power, it is alright Master Fagan, I understand how she works and how she rules, I saw that with Uther too, he bullied many to rule." Fagan drained his beaker, and placed it carefully on the floor.

"Things need to get done; I must be off." He got up from his seat, and she stood up with him. Fagan gave a smile, and nodded.

"Ye will be fine now… Ye knows, the path ye have chosen tis a hard one, here will never be an easy life, no one would blame ye if ye moved on?" Morgana understood him, he was a strange but kind person, and she knew he had her best interests in mind.

"I knew the path I was taking and the difficulties involved, I am grateful for your concern, but I will be alright here under Merlin's protection. It is hard some days, but others, are so wonderful it makes the difference."

"Aye, that tis life here alright… I shall be on me way then."

Morgana waved as he climbed back up onto the cart, and he turned and trundled back down the road towards the bridge back to Avalonia. Knowing some of them had escaped helped, and it came as a big relief, what she did not know, and neither did Fagan, was Rhiannon was two steps ahead, she knew her own people better.

*O*n the outer reaches of Avalon, where there were paths out of the realm, something she only knew because Branna had been tracked all those years ago. Since that time, a tribe from the world of men, had been paid to kill anyone leaving. Mable, Seth, their families, and all the others that fled, lay slaughtered and buried where no Fae would ever find them. The only person who knew the truth was Rhiannon, even Fagan had no idea, and as Branna had told Ariel many times during their time together.

"Our golden queen always gets her own way, never forget her primary instinct is she is a political animal, and one way or another, she will always get her revenge."

*T*he following week was a busy one, as Morgana focused on her home. She tapped two pine trees for resin, and had bought a wire saw, which was a long piece of rough wire with a wooden handle at either end, which she pulled backwards and forward across the timber to cut it. It was hot hard work, and she sweated, even with the window open it was warm. She had thought of trying the trick Branna taught her on how to shape stone, but when she tried it, the whole timber board exploded into a million splinters which fired at her, and terrified her.

Having learned her lesson, she took the longest and hardest route of using the saw. Three days later feeling exhausted, she had finally built a long set of shelves that ran the whole length of the wall. After a lot of rearranging, she placed all her pots, jars, and books on the shelves, and even had a small vase with some wild flowers in it. One shelf near the bottom, had a long double row of glass jars, into which she placed the dried ingredients for all her teas and tinctures, and it looked impressive, she had far more than she realised.

Feeling very happy with her work, she moved her table over, so that it sat directly under the window, and fixed the wobbly leg with resin and a good nail, she did likewise with the chair, and now all her furniture was stable. With the off cuts, she fashioned a small stool to sit on when she cooked at the fire, and made a tray to carry things to the table. In her bedroom, she put up two shelves above her bed, which were not completely level, but it gave her a place to store extra books and things. On her wall opposite her bed, she hammered in a row of nails with the back of her axe, and then hung up all her dresses, then made a small box with a rough lid to slide under her bed to store precious things in. It was not much, but to Morgana, it felt special, and her home felt a lot more organised, and even more like her own place of privacy.

*T*hree days after she finished, Gwendolyn arrived at her door. Morgana welcomed her in, and after she praised Morgana for her improvements, Gwendolyn sat as Morgana made her a tea. Gwendolyn told Morgana of how she had heard what had happened, and how sorry she was, Morgana accepted it, but said nothing of what Fagan had told her, she handed her a tea and sat down at the table in front of her.

"Can I ask you something, and you will answer me honestly?" Gwendolyn looked at her with bright blue eyes.

"If I can answer Morgana, it will be honest, what is it you wish to know?" Morgana sat back and considered her question.

"I know there was trouble between your grandmother and Rhiannon, was it her disapproval of Rhiannon that caused it?" Gwendolyn was a little surprised, it was long ago, and few mention it these days, even to her it was a distant memory.

"That is in the past, and there are many who wish to keep it that way, no one wants a repeat of those times Morgana. I must admit, you interest me, for you are surprisingly well informed. I will not deny, my grandmother spoke her mind, and she spoke honestly and from the heart, and yes, it did cause a great deal of trouble. As to what she said, the only other person I know of who she confided in, was my adopted aunt Ariel, so no one these days really knows the whole truth, not even I." Morgana shrugged at her.

"People talk, and some things are not as lost to the past as you think." It was a fair point.

"If they do talk Morgana, I can assure you, it is not to me." Morgana looked up with dark eyes.

"Why would they?" Gwendolyn felt a little jolt of surprise as Morgana looked at her with her intense eyes, almost as if she could see deep inside her, Morgana gave a sigh.

"I mean no offence, but you have fair hair, and you are a queen. I have realised since coming here there are two kinds of people, the fair, who have everything, and the dark who have little. They have no trust of any with fair hair, and if you think about it, you cannot blame them." Gwendolyn had to agree, she had heard Ariel talk often of it. Morgana looked at her cup and her voice lowered.

"I hate her, I hate the way she rules from her seat and thinks she is better than everyone. I hate the way she hurts anyone she considers inferior, like me." It was understandable, and Gwendolyn could feel the power in her words, even though they were spoken softly.

"Morgana, be careful, I understand, I really do. I have seen this before, and it does not end well." Morgana nodded and looked up at her.

"You mean Branna, you were a young woman at that time if I am right?" Gwendolyn nodded, Morgana sensed her apprehension, and gave a small laugh.

"Even you fear her, I can sense your distrust of her, you hide it well, but here you are under a veil, Merlin made me learn it for this very reason, I know that now. He knew didn't he, he knew she would attack me?" Gwendolyn sat back in her seat.

"Morgana, none of us have forgotten that time, even now we do not know really what happened to Branna. There is a part of us that hopes she got away and lives happily with Ariel, because the hatred Rhiannon holds for her consumes her, and if she ever returns, she will die the moment she arrives back. Morgana, you must understand, you do have a likeness of her from what we have been told, and when it comes to Rhiannon, that is not a good thing, her grudges never fail, they grow bigger with time." Morgana nodded.

"I have heard the stories and I have cast the veil on my person as well, but you already know that. I want to be safe when I leave this cottage, and without Merlin here, it is the only protection I have. I will not deny, I hate her for what she has done."

"Morgana, be careful, I will share with you something that Ariel told me. She stayed with me alone in a private retreat I had at the time. Like you, as a young princess I said the very same thing, having seen not just Ariel, but my grandmother suffer. Ariel told me, hate is a powerful emotion, that brings up strong feelings that cloud the mind. It is wiser to distrust than hate, for hate is the door that opens up into the darkness, and that is a path of destruction. I have never forgotten that moment, and knowing she was the daughter of Enaria, the most powerful seer of all the Fae, I took heed of her words, and I have remained in control of my emotions and retained the clarity of the mind. Learn from Ariel, she was far wiser than she realised."

Morgana understood, Branna had said something similar, although, Ariel was her lover and had probably given her the same advice.

"I understand what you say, and I work to strengthen my mind every day, and I am far stronger than I was. I guess my life is harder than I thought it would be, I do not mind chopping wood and cooking. I enjoy living here and fending for myself, but it also feels like she has singled me out, and I do not know why, I just feel she will do everything in her power to destroy me."

Gwendolyn knew she was not far wrong, but as to how to respond she was unsure. Morgana was bright, there was no doubt, the intelligence in her eyes, and her use of words showed that. In many ways it bothered her, but was not able to state why. Morgana gave a loud sigh and sat back in her seat.

"Do Druids have powers… You know, like the Fae do?" It took Gwendolyn completely by surprise.

"I am not certain; I know my husband holds them in a very high regard. Why do you ask, I must admit, I am intrigued?"

"My mother is a queen of a long line of Druids, I often heard my father tell her, her Druid powers captivated his heart, and he was powerless to act. I was thinking about it the other day, and I pondered as to whether I may have some. After all, I have managed to do two of Merlin's tasks, although it was not easy and took a lot of focus. I know Druids contemplate and focus their minds; I wondered if I had some of that."

Gwendolyn was actually impressed, even she had never considered it, and it did actually make a great deal of sense.

"I cannot say for sure; I have had little interaction with them, they do tend to live secretive lives. My husband has spent a great deal of time with them, maybe you should talk to him, it could explain a great deal about your abilities, after all, few of the realm of men could achieve what you have."

It made sense, and Morgana made a note to talk with Merlin, if he ever came back, he had been gone for some time and had not given her any instruction at all. He did not say when he would return, so she had no idea how long it would be.

"Do you know when he will return? I am doing my lessons and learning the things he told me too, but if I do that before he returns, should I just carry on with the next task in his book?" Gwendolyn smiled, she knew Merlin so well, and completely understood Morgana.

"I cannot say when he will return, all I know is he has travelled to many places, even beyond Mancunium, and had matters of great importance, he was nervous to leave you alone. I would think it would be best to follow his book and progress as you are able, and then when he returns you can discuss it with him. Sadly, I am Fae, and my line has its secrets as does his, so I have no idea what his full plan for you was. Do your best, and keep trying until he comes back, I feel that is the best path for you." Morgana nodded; it made sense to her.

"Thank you, I felt it was best to ask, you know, just in case?"

Gwendolyn gave a little titter; she had done the same so many times around Merlin. The time moved on and it came time for her to leave. She wished Morgana good luck, and headed for the door, she smiled as she waved from the path, and after she had walked out of view, Morgana closed her door and slid in the bolts. She walked back to the table to clear up the pots to wash, as she thought of her afternoon, and as she turned with her bowl, Jarron landed on the edge of the window, Morgana smiled as she looked at the white raven.

"You were right Branna, Gwendolyn can feel something. I feel it too, and I think it is clear, she does not fully trust me, I see now how she managed to keep the peace with Rhiannon, she does not trust her either."

Chapter Twenty.

New Line of Power.

Over a year passed by, and Morgana grew settled into her solitary life. Every two weeks she travelled out of Avalon, to the markets at Glaston, where she had become very well known for her teas and tinctures. She then travelled back to her cottage with a good supply of goods. Her garden expanded, and was filled with rows of vegetables and herbs, she even had a horse, and a chicken coup from which she collected the eggs every day.

Her growing business brought her in more money, so much so, she had no need of the money Berengar had given her. She bought lime to make paint, and painted her whole cottage, and fence, in a gleaming bright white. It did not please Rhiannon, who had wanted to isolate her to a breaking point, but all alone with little contact with the rest of the Fae, under her veil of protection, Morgana thrived.

Her study advanced, as she managed with some help from Branna, to master the language of old. Her next chapter was all of the different runic symbols, in which she could write many different languages. Rosamund who was exceptionally skilled in writing helped her a great deal, and Morgana advanced into spells, some Merlin's, and a few of Branna's. Her powers were still bound with the spell Branna had cast on her, so it took her a long time to master each one, but soon, she could place a defence on her cottage when she was away to protect it, and managed after a lot of trying to understand Merlin's crazy writing, to cast a stun spell, which would serve her in cases of self defence.

Another aspect of her learning, was taking the advice of Branna, and in a new smaller book of parchment, she made note of all of the news of what was going on around the country. The unrest was still growing as the influence of the Romana wore off, and the true lines of the past resurfaced to take power. Most of the good achieved by

Uther was wearing off, and the land had become divided into many territories. Berengar's men had really settled in, and formed treaties with the Celts, and on the east coast they were starting to thrive and take up a great many territories, which most appeared to be ruled by Hengist. To the west, a powerful leader named Voltigern controlled a great deal of the Celt lands, and in the middle, in the area known as Mancunium under the Romana, A selection of war chieftains squabbled over the land, which had been renamed Mercia.

The country was fluid and there were outbreaks of local attacks, but the south was relatively stable with few clashes, although new leaders came and went, and it was clear, that the country was becoming more and more unstable, and some of those who had been left to their own devices, had grown greedy, and wanted more than their fair share. Trouble was brewing, and Morgana had become skilled in predicting who was weak, and who was powerful, to such a point, she could predict the events to come.

In her isolation she had not really noticed the changes she had gone through. Her face was pale and under her eyes was dark, she was still slender, and her hair had grown considerably longer. Her face had lost some of its childish features, and she was looking more and more like the young Branna who had once lived in the realm. She muttered to herself a lot as her only real means of conversation, of which talking to Jarron was an integral part. Her plant lore was at its peak, and with Merlin's book to guide her, she had expanded her use of plants to mix in with some of the healing spells, as she made up her own concoctions and recipes. Her most worrying aspect was that in having the means to cure, if she worked her recipes backwards, she found the means to cause ailments, and in some cases death.

The most noticeable feature of all, was she also found at times, she became very impatient, especially when she had news of Rhiannon and her dealings with the Fae. Her anger towards the golden queen had not lessened, if anything, it had grown more intense. None of this was helped, when news came to her that her mother was having difficulties at the castle in Tintagel. It appeared a group of war chieftains had been meeting, and under the rules of their clans, a widow was only entitled to a dowery of one third of her dead husband's property, and she still controlled everything that had been left by King Uther, including the castle.

She hitched her horse to her small cart, loaded her bags, locked her cottage, and then cast a defensive spell, before making her way towards the road out through the doorway of light, and into the realm of men. The Marshals had come to know her well, they heard the rumours that she was a sorceress and dangerous, but in truth, she was always polite and respectful, and they had warmed to her. Morgana had heard all the rumours also, and in many ways, she ignored them, but also found them useful, as she had grown quite solitary and so it helped keep people away from her.

It took her two days to get to the castle, of which Rosamund who had a reasonable relationship with her mother came along for the ride and change of scenery. Her arrival brought her mother to tears, and she wept for almost an hour as she told her daughter of how she was being forced to give up the castle. Morgana sat in the main hall and grew angered as she was told of the lords and how they had sent men to intimidate her mother, and apply pressure, in order to gain the prize of the castle.

By the time darkness came down, she was blazing mad, and retired to her room and talked to Jarron of her anger and how these tricksters were trying to take what was not at all Uther's, but her father's. She informed Jarron to fly to Branna and warn her men were trying to take what by right, was Berengar land.

*T*he following morning, she bathed in a tub of hot water, something she had not done in several years, as she readied herself for the men who had threatened to return with their final demands. She had prepared well, and had bought a very high quality dress of black, and she fitted the rings that had been given her by her father, they were gold and of the highest quality, and then having washed it, she brushed her matted hair, which was painful, and made her even more angered, as it hurt a great deal. By the time she was done, she was actually very surprised at herself. Morgana inspected herself in a large sheet of highly polished metal, and she was very surprised to see herself, almost looking like a lady of court. She had aged a little and it showed, her twenty eight summers gave her more a mature look, and one of authority.

The talk of the castle was all about the tournament to pull the sword, something of which Morgana had little interest. She ate and checked on her mother, who was busy with Rosamund, Lothar arrived with six burly men, who he informed Morgana were all loyal to her father still, and they would help protect her mother. He was also accompanied by yet another female, who he excused to his room. Morgana retired to her room to read until needed, and took a few moments sat at her windows looking out over the cliff tops. She missed them, and wanted only to walk on them, but she needed to be here in the castle to help her mother, so could only stare, yearning to feel the wind through her hair as she walked on the path above the crashing waves.

It had been over an hour, when the clatter of hooves echoed up from the gate below, and she put down her book and looked down. A group of ten riders had come into the courtyard, one of which was dressed in great style, and she assumed was the man that was trying to force her mother out. Behind him, was a crowd on foot, it looked liked he had gathered together many of the locals to aid his cause. Morgana felt her anger rising, this had gone too far, she jumped up and hurried to her door.

*D*own below in the great hall, Igraine stood behind Lothar and his men, as the tall lord faced him with a stern face and raised his voice, as behind him the people jeered, and Igraine wept with fear.

"She has no right, under the law, she is only entitled to a dowery of one third, this castle is no longer hers. I have given her time, but it wears thin, she must leave and now, and if she still refuses, then we have come to throw her out." Lothar watched him unphased.

"What is going on?" The lord looked up and saw Morgana standing at the top of the stairs, she looked powerful and imposing, Morgana took a step forward.

"Who is it that forces their way into the queen's home, and makes demands of the widow of King Uther, name yourself?" The room had fallen silent, as the well dressed lord watched as she reached the middle of the stairs.

"I am the Lord Cecil de Bergerac, and who do I address madam?" Morgana nodded, she recognised the name and understood who he was, he had fought many battles, and stolen large pieces of land.

"I am the Countess of Cornwall, Morgana of Berengar, and Pendragon, and named daughter of King Uther, and I fear sir, you are very mistaken, and quite incorrect. You will apologise to your queen, for this castle was never the castle of Uther Pendragon, it was the soul property of Victor of Berengar and Cornwall, until Uther possessed and occupied it illegally." He looked completely surprised, as muttering arose quietly behind him.

"Uther was King, but he is dead, and I fear you are mistaken, this castle was taken as a prize of war, won by his hand in fair combat." Morgana felt her anger pulse within her.

"FAIR COMBAT, WHEN WAS SNEAKING INTO A CASTLE DISGUISED AS ANOTHER MAN FAIR COMBAT? UTHER WAS NOT EVEN ON THE BATTLEFIELD WHEN MY FATHER WAS SLAIN, HE WAS HERE RAPING MY MOTHER!" Her eyes flashed with her anger, and for a moment, tiny flickers of red light glinted in her pupils. He was clearly shaken but stood his ground.

"It matters not Lady Cornwall; this property was owned by the king…" He had no time to finish, as Morgana erupted again.

"OWNED BY THE KING, SINCE WHEN?" She hurried down the long stair.

"Have you seen this castle, have you seen the houses and places of trade that exist within the protection of the walls? This place is filled with the souls of those who support this land, do they also not count, as your lust for more land strips away at your senses?"

Her eyes burned with her anger, as she moved quickly, the full force of anger showing on her face. The crowd behind Lord de Bergerac moved back a little, he stared at her resolute.

"I did not come here to bandy words and split hairs; this castle is no longer hers."

He lifted his hand and pointed at Igraine, and she shrunk down behind Lothar. Morgana felt her blood boil, and her face grew whiter and more fierce.

"HOW DARE YOU SHOW SUCH DISRESPECT TO YOUR QUEEN, GET ON YOUR KNEES BEFORE HER, AND APOLOGISE!"

Without realising her arm came up, and just as she had with the nails in the window, she flicked her wrist, and his belt buckle broke. His sword clattered to the floor, ringing out as it bounced off the stone. Morgana's eyes blazed with her anger as she came down the final steps, and stepped onto the floor of the great hall. There was no doubt at all, she looked terrifying. The gathering of locals saw the sword fall, panicked, and took several paces backwards. Morgana walked towards her mother, she could feel the power growing inside her, and it felt filled with elation, and her confidence soared.

"How dare you enter my home and disgrace it with your unworthy presence, if my father was alive, he would cut you in half with one swipe of his sword. By what right do you name yourself lord? I know who you are and the men you have slain in your greed for more land. My mother is of a noble line that ruled this land long before you, Uther or the Romana walked these soils. You are not fit to lick her boots, and yet you sneak in here with your threats of power, you are as dishonourable as Uther, the only difference being you still wear your armour. I was named daughter, and all I have to do is put out my hand and pull out that sword, for it will come out for me…. You dare to walk through those doors with an empty hand, and no sword of a true king. Get out before I raise a hand and cut you in half with my mind, as I am also the apprentice of Merlin the wizard."

He stepped back as she marched right up to him, and he stepped back leaving his sword where it had fallen on the floor. Morgana's eyes glowed with a soft red, as her fury simmered inside her, she stood close, and glared at him in anger. The mere mention of being the apprentice of Merlin was more than enough, and a great many stood behind him, turned and fled. Cecil de Bergerac looked frightened, as Morgana leaned in, and with a low voice she spoke.

"I could blink and rip out your heart, and show the world the evil that lives within it." Her eyes flared a deeper red with her anger.

"NOW GET OUT!"

"ENOUGH… MORGANA, ENOUGH!"

She looked up, and over the shoulder of the Lord de Bergerac, she saw Merlin standing looking furious next to a tall blonde young man. Merlin looked very angry indeed, as his eyes fixed on her, and she knew she had done wrong. He looked around at those who were still left and muttering.

"All of you… leave now!"

He turned, and looked back across the room as Morgana stepped back and pulled her mother close. Merlin watched her closely as her temper faded, and she took a deep breath, and filled her lungs to calm herself faster. Merlin turned to the young man who looked nervous and uneasy.

"Show them."

He swallowed hard and pulled apart his cloak, and there slid into his belt was the gleaming sword of Uther. Morgana felt her breath catch in her throat, as she realised it was the sword from the stone, the one Uther had pushed into it on the day of his death. The moment felt surreal, almost like a dream, and she was not sure what to do or say, this boy, man, whomever the hell he was, had Uther's sword. Had he pulled it from the stone, because if she was quite honest about it all, he did not look strong enough to chop wood, let alone pull a sword that had defeated every knight for a good few years?

It took a moment to sink in, and then suddenly, de Bergerac, went down on one knee and bowed his head, and so did everyone else, and Morgana was left standing looking at the young man, who appeared terrified as he stared at her. Merlin gave a little chuckle, as he watched her reaction.

"Morgana, this is your brother… This is Arthur."

"MY SON!"

Igraine released herself from Morgana, and ran across the room, pulling him, looking very shocked in her arms, and wailed out with joy. She was lost for words, and was the only person apart from Merlin left standing, even Lothar had gone down on one knee and had his head bowed. Her mind swirled as she tried to make sense of what was happening and find the right words, they came out, with the only thing she could think of.

"How… How Merlin, is that possible?"

*S*uddenly, there was little time for anything, the word was out, and those who had been at the tournament came in their droves, as Merlin ushered Igraine, de Bergerac, Lothar, Rosamund, and Morgana into the back private room of Uther to explain just exactly what was going on. It appeared Arthur had been raised by a miller, and his son Kay had wanted to gain his spurs and become a knight, and Arthur had volunteered to be his squire. In the excitement and the rush, and having discovered Kay's sword had been left behind, Arthur did the obvious, and simply pulled Uther's sword from the stone and handed it to Kay.

There was doubt and calls from the knights that somehow Merlin had tricked them raged. So, the sword was pushed back into the stone by Arthur, and several large burly knights tried to pull it and failed. Arthur was then asked again to take the sword, and he took hold, and pulled it out with zero effort, and a new king was made.

*T*here and then twenty knights swore their oaths to serve the new king faithfully, and several of the richer lords, left, proclaiming that

Arthur was illegitimate as he was not even knighted. Merlin quickly removed him to the castle of his birth, in order to protect him, and take account of who was in favour and who was against the new king. Merlin as always was dramatic and yet eloquent, and went on for almost an hour, before it was hurriedly decided there should be a feast, and time to talk with all those aligned to Arthur, the new boy king.

Morgana felt all of this was too much, and took leave, heading to her room to try and understand everything that was happening. The maids delivered her meal to her room so she could eat alone, as the news sunk in, as the brother she had always known she had, was suddenly in her midst, and she was not too sure, where that left her.

It all felt like more than she could handle, as suddenly the castle was filled with the noise of knights and servants, and it reminded her a great deal of her childhood in a castle run by Uther, the man who murdered her father, and raped her mother. It was a few hours later when there was a tap on the door and Merlin entered. He looked at her as she sat on the wide window bottom with the window open, reading. She lifted her eyes from the page to look at him.

"I thought I would find you here, I am surprised you are not packing your bags." Morgana, took her hand off the book, and pointed to the far corner of the room.

"I have done so already, I leave at dawn with Lothar, Rosamund is staying to help my mother." Merlin nodded, as his eyes crossed the room, to the bags, and the neatly stacked pile of books and parchments.

"You feel you do not belong here, and need to leave?" Morgana looked at her page, and continued her reading

"I don't… Well not now the new heir of Uther has shown up with his supporters. I prefer the quietness of my home, where I can study in peace there." Merlin understood, and took a step forward.

"How are your studies going, I saw you mastered the second test, when you used it to cut the belt free from Lord de Bergerac? Considering your emotional state, I am surprised you did not cut him in half." Morgana's eyes did not leave the page.

"My emotional state had nothing to do with it, my mind was focused on the spell, and as you saw, it was applied correctly." Merlin turned, and walked up the room as he thought.

"Yet, once the spell was cast, you allowed your temper to get the better of you." Morgana turned the page, and looked over the top of it at him.

"I disagree, had my temper got the better of me, he would be dead now, and as you can see, he lives." Merlin turned and looked back at her.

"Morgana, this is not a game of wit, losing control is the path of darkness. The lessons and skills you are learning, are not the wooden swords of a child's toy, they are very dangerous weapons of power." Morgana lowered her book to her lap.

"I am well aware of the skills you are teaching, I have studied and struggled and worked hard to master your teachings, and I may add, had to do it alone. Tell me Merlin, if Rhiannon Queen of Fae turned up at your door, and demanded you throw out your wife and children, and give her your home, would you control your temper and remain calm and oblige her? This is my home, my castle, my father built this with his bare hands. It was never Uther's to possess, I was the heir to my father, it was mine, and he stole it. Now Uther is dead, it belongs to its rightful owner, which is me. That half Gaul lord, born as a bastard to a Britannic warrior, and stealer of lands to sate his greed, has no claim to this castle, it was my fathers, and now it is mine, and my mother will live here until her last days in it." Merlin gave a sigh.

"Morgana, I do not disagree with you, I knew of de Bergerac and the trouble he was brewing, which is precisely why I brought the boy to the tournament." She gave a titter.

"He is hardly a boy, he must be at least twenty three or four summers. Why did you not let me know? You abandoned me, and left me there with that harpy sat on her throne spewing her lies about me, and trying to hound me out of what I see as my home in Avalon… Why, did you not send word to me?" Merlin gave a nod.

"It was wrong of me, and in that I am sorry. Gwendolyn assured me that you were doing well, and she told me you had continued alone in your studies, which was pleasing to me, it showed commitment and dedication, and you need those. I am indeed impressed with your progress; however, you must focus deeper and not allow your emotional state to rule you. Morgana to wield the Whitelines, you can never for a second lose your intention, for it is that, which will guide all that you do. I saw the power contained within you, and I was greatly surprised, but it was edged with the darkness of your thoughts, and you can never allow that to happen again." She gave a sigh.

"I am sorry, and as you have seen, he is unharmed, but you have never understood the most important aspect of who I am, and you need to." Merlin frowned, and stopped in his tracks.

"I don't… Explain it to me then?" Morgana closed her book with the parchment marker in it, and then stood up to face him.

"I am the daughter of the man you arranged to be killed, and that woman down there, you allowed that animal to rape is my mother. She is all I have left from what was my real life, the life you helped steal." Her face was so white and so serious, and yet he could feel the power of her devotion, and he felt the guilt creep back in, she took a breath and lowered her voice.

"I am sorry, I truly am, and I want to be a great student for you, but Merlin, you have to understand, she is and has always been a queen of high stature, born of a line of the highest druids in this land. Everyone in this country who is true to the old ways holds her in the highest esteem, and yet you and the rest of that council bargained her for that brute as a prize of a fight." She smirked.

"It makes me laugh, you, Gwendolyn, and Rhiannon, and the rest all planning away to find one worthy of rule, and you picked him… Him… Down below me is a woman of such worth, everyman true to the old ways would have followed her, and she would have ruled with a fair hand. Uther called her a bride worthy of battle, it was such an insult, all of you had it backwards, he was not worthy of her, he should have gone down on his knees and begged forgiveness for his insult to her, as should all of you for aiding him. Queen Igraine is a real queen of power, and was long before you found Uther, and that is the point, none of you treated her with the respect she deserved. My father did, he built all of this in honour of her, as he knew she deserved nothing less."

Merlin watched as the tears welled in her eyes and ran onto her cheek, and in many ways, he suddenly understood her. He finally felt like he was seeing the real truth of her, the real blood of her family line. For so long, she had been a very quiet, yet bright and highly intelligent student, who lived in a rough cottage, wore hand repaired shoes, and toiled in her house chores. Yet standing there, in a dress of high quality, with her hair brushed and neat, she stood with such power of her line, and he realised, Morgana of Cornwall, was indeed the true daughter of a great queen. He looked her in the eyes and gave a slight nod.

"You are right, and you do your mother great service in your loyalty to her, and I believe had he been here, your father would be immensely proud of you this day. Morgana, I owe you an apology, I have done your family a great disservice, it is one I do and have deeply regretted. I hope you can see that for my part, I have tried to correct some of my wrongs." She lifted her hand, and wiped her tears off her cheek.

"I will always defend my home, never think for one moment that I will allow any, be it man or woman to take away the house of my father, I won't. I am aware of the power of the words I think and the spells they create, and I am, and was in control. I am tired, it was not an easy spell, and my focus drained me. It has been a long day, with much activity, I feel I shall rest a while, in the peace of my room."

Merlin gave a nod, and excused himself, he had much on his mind, and he had been surprised to arrive and find Morgana so easily using the power of the Whitelines with such skill. In truth, he had never expected her to so easily take command of it, and he did wonder, if maybe there was some truth to the secret power of the Druid leaders of their sect. It was the only thing that appeared to make sense, she was mortal, and yet had embraced the forces of light so easily, and he knew, as soon as he had seated the new king, he would look into it.

*F*rom the moment the young king had been revealed, riders were sent to the four corners of the country, to spread the word, some to rejoice, and some to plot. Many leaders had profited from a land with no ruler and no taxes, and they were not pleased to know that this new young king would change things. They had built their corners and expanded their lands, and they feared this new king, like Uther, would make demands that would lessen the contents of their coffers.

In the castle at Tintagel there was a great celebration, as the knights of great reputation met and swore an oath before him to help him adjust and take on the role destined for him. Meanwhile, back in Avalon, a rider came at a fast pace up the Queens Road to report to Stenlow. He was hurriedly taken into the large hall of the queen deep below ground and covered in dust, he bowed to the Queen Ofmoon, and held up a sealed parchment.

"My Queen, I bring great news."

The queen looked down from her seat, feeling bored and uninterested. She leaned forward and held out her hand, and Stenlow took the rolled parchment and walked up the steps, bowed, and held out the scroll to her hand.

"Great news, well that would make a change, what could be so great as you interrupt my time?"

She broke the seal, and unrolled the parchment to read, her eyes opened wide, as she read the message from her marshal stationed in the village close to the castle. Her face showed no sign of joy, as she read the events of the day, whilst the rider stayed low on his knees, awaiting a new command, Rhiannon noticed and looked up.

"Go rest and eat, I may have need of your services, leave me, both of you."

Stenlow and the rider both bowed, turned and headed for the door, they were almost there when Rhiannon lifted her gaze.

"Commander Stenlow?" He stopped and turned.

"Yes, My Queen."

"Where is that girl, is she still at the castle?"

"I believe she is, your majesty." Rhiannon nodded.

"It appears she will not be wearing a crown anytime soon; I want to know the moment she returns; it appears her half brother has appeared, and has been accepted as the new king. We will need to arrange a reception, send me my planning officials, as is tradition, we will show hospitality to the new king." He gave another bow.

"As you wish, My Queen." He turned back to the open door, and left, Rhiannon sat back with a smile.

"Well, my little apprentice, it appears your wings have been clipped, you may be pronounced daughter to Uther, but it appears now you will be side lined for Uther's real bloodline. You are nothing more than a dead Saxon's child now, a mere nothing in the eyes of others, just another mortal with bad manners and no respect, and that makes you fair game for sport." She gave a sly smile, and looked down at the parchment.

"A new young king to the line of men, Uther was difficult, but this one, he is young and impressionable, and in that I feel, Avalon will welcome him with open arms, and of course, the very best of counsel, in the ways I feel men should be ruled. This is great news; I feel the coming months could be quite entertaining."

*B*ade sat at his desk writing, further down Master Elrond sat with a group of four of the elder council talking quietly, whilst looking at a parchment. Up the long hallway, Gwendolyn walked with her Ambassador from Avalon.

"The new king will require a great deal of guidance, and Merlin will be busier than usual. I feel that now she will be pushed aside, The Queen will feel her authority grow, and that could bode ill for Morgana. I wish to know anything and everything that may occur, I do not want that girl exposed and alone. Rhiannon has an axe to grind, and if there is one thing I learned from my aunt, it was to trust her less when she is being welcoming to new leaders. Watch her for me, Merlin is far too preoccupied with the realms of others at times, and he becomes forgetful. There is no one there to aide her."

Ambassador Alder bowed to her, and made his withdrawal. Gwendolyn walked out of the hall, and across the large open space of the lower hall of scribes, Bade noted her and stood up, Gwendolyn smiled.

"Lord Bade, it appears the son of Uther has found his way to the throne, so I must depart for Tintagel to meet with my husband. I will be leaving my daughters here in the care of the realm, please inform them when they rise, I have no wish to disturb them at this late hour." He gave a bow.

"Yes, My Queen… If I may for one moment take a little of your time, I have looked into the subject you mentioned." Gwendolyn stopped, her attention fully on him.

"Indeed, and what have you learned?" Bade lifted a sheet of parchment off his desk.

"It does appear that there may be some truth to Lady Morgana's thinking. This line her mother hails from are seen as great mystics, and are reported to have great powers, although it is difficult to ascertain what exactly. They appear to be a secret sect, who hide their secrets from others, they are not keen to share their methods from ages past, which is not untypical of many lines of power." Gwendolyn smirked.

"Indeed, it is not wise to give too much away. Thank you Bade, it does answer a question that has been bothering me, because no ordinary mortal could achieve what she has, it explains much of what I have witnessed. It places my mind at rest, as I have questioned her abilities for some time now, and now I have my answer."

He gave a smile and bowed as Gwendolyn pulled on her cloak, and then she headed for the two large wooden doors. Gwendolyn felt that she had to get to her husband and meet this new king long before Rhiannon did. Of that there was no doubt, because if she was right, she knew the queen of the moon would try to take over, and control all of the events surrounding his crowning.

Chapter Twenty One.

Shadows of the Raven.

Morgana retired early, and slept deep. She arose just after dawn, and came down to find something to eat. The cook was up and preparing for the day, so made her a meal. She took her food, and sat alone in the main feasting hall quietly eating, when down the stairs came Arthur. She looked up and sighed as she chewed her food, he gave a nervous smile as he approached her, Morgana lifted her hand.

"If you are hungry, there is food." He nodded and sat down, and lifted a cob of bread.

"Thank you. I am told you are my sister, but I do not feel I have met you." She understood, for her it was the same. All her life she had known that she had a half brother, but seeing him, had shocked her.

Without his cloak he did look broader, Merlin had mentioned he had worked in a mill, and it was clear he was no stranger to hard labour. She looked at him as he chewed, he resembled their mother greatly, which in a way pleased her, as he did not have the rough brutish face of Uther. Unlike her, his hair was fair, and he had intense blue eyes, not unsimilar to their mothers. Morgana swallowed and lifted her goblet of water, and took a sip.

"We met, you were a day old and I held you in my arms, then Merlin arrived and you left, and none of us have seen you until yesterday. I suppose all this must feel very strange for you?" He gave a nod.

"I rose from my slumber yesterday morn a miller's son, and today I find myself proclaimed king. I am very uncertain as to why me." Morgana nodded at him and tried to smile.

"You are the son of Uther, this was always ordained for you, I suppose with Merlin, Gwendolyn and our mother, you will have good advisors. Fear not, you will not be alone in this task." It made sense to him, he lifted more bread as he watched her, Morgana shrugged.

"What?"

"What about you, Merlin told me you have insights others do not have, will you not advise me also?"

Morgana gave a chuckle, Merlin was cunning, of that there was no doubt. She thought for a second, and then looked across the table, he did not look anywhere like a king, if anything he looked terrified.

"If you want my advice, be nothing like Uther, actually care for the people. Instead of pandering to the rich lords of the realm, do what is right for those who live under them. Do that, and you will have the love of those who live in this realm. Listen to mother, she knows the people and understands the greed of the rich, ask her questions, she will always answer you honestly. That is the best advice I can give." He looked like he appreciated it.

"Can I ask you questions when I need to?"

"I live alone in Avalon, I have little to do with this realm, when you visit you can call on me. Avalon is not like this place, it is markedly different, and so is the queen who rules there, one piece of advice I will give you now, is never trust her. Queen Rhiannon is a powerful queen, and she will be overwhelmingly nice to you, but trust me when I tell you, her kindness is merely to distract you from seeing her real goal. She will try to influence every decision you make, but it will never be to the benefit of your people, it will always be to hers." She slid back in her seat and smiled.

"I have to go; I see Lothar is finally ready." He looked surprised, and appeared a little shocked.

"You are leaving so soon? I had hoped we could talk more, and learn of each other?" She stepped away from the table.

"I live alone in Avalon, it suits me, I do not like a lot of people around me, and you have many. Come alone and we will talk, until then, good luck."

Morgana turned and headed towards the doors, where Lothar waited just outside at the side of the cart, her things had been loaded and she was ready to leave. Morgana wanted to get back in her cottage safe, and had no wish to play a part in the court of a king. She had learned many years ago with Uther how dull court was, and she had no intentions of repeating the experience.

*M*organa left and returned to the life she knew best, albeit isolated in her cottage at Avalon. In many ways, having Arthur appear,

Morgana realised her mother had been saved as the new king would take up residence at the castle, and that would prevent any of the lords from taking it away from her mother.

Back home in her cottage, things got back to normal very quickly, she grew her food, dried her herbs, and mixed up teas. During the day between working, she studied and moved through the chapters, as she met Branna on the days she went to the markets. Their talks were long, as Branna gave her ideas and tips and taught her how to adapt the spells to alternative uses. Every night before she went to sleep, she wrote in her black book of all she had done and the experiments she had conducted alone.

The country had fragmented deeply after the death of Uther, and so as the young Arthur appeared, warlords and those who had managed to sweep up the land as their own appeared reluctant to accept the rule of a king again. Within weeks of his arrival, disagreements and fights broke out, and the country stood on the brink of war. Merlin was stuck at Tintagel with Arthur trying to sort out the mess, and guide the young king, although none of this mattered to Morgana, who was far too busy with her studies, and her daily duties.

Most of her life had become secretive, she bought all her goods from Glaston, grew most of her food, and even had many supplies such as wood or nails collected by Lothar or Rosamund in the world of men, which she then brought back in her cart after her market days. Rhiannon fumed, as Morgana appeared to have nothing at all to do with the people of Fae, the rumours that she had circulated had grown. Where Morgana had once been considered one of them, now they all feared her. Fagan was saddened, he had not seen her in a long time, as he no longer had orders of goods to deliver, and on those days where he stood on the market and heard people talking, calling her strange, mad, and dangerous, he did what he could to snuff them out.

Arthur's greatest supporter was Leodegrance, who had served Uther with great loyalty. He had a strong and well respected reputation, and when he swore allegiance it swayed a great deal of the local lords, extending from his land in Cornwall, up to the River seven and Gloucestershire. Along the southern coast there was still a Romana presence, who took no rule from anyone but Rome, and the Saxons sent by Berengar lived peacefully under their own rule. In the north, many of the lords and landowners refused to budge, and stood against Leodegrance, and resisted his requests to unite behind the king.

Heated words moved up and down the country, and many of the lords opposed to Arthur, decided it was time to put an end to Leodegrance in order to quell any support of the new king, and so armies were raised and headed south, in the direction of Cornwall and Carmliarde. It felt like dark times for the new king to be, he had not even sat on a throne, and already over half of the country was refusing to accept him. Merlin and Gwendolyn advised him, but he was unsure as to what to do, and felt caught in a trap.

As always there was pressure from Avalon, the Queen of the Moon felt her need to impress, and requested the new king attended a welcoming ceremony on his behalf. Merlin advised him that it was indeed a shrewd move, and Rhiannon would be a powerful source of support. The whole company were offered the finest rooms in the citadel, and packed up, then headed to Avalon. A messenger was despatched to Morgana, in which a letter from Arthur requested he speak to her on his arrival at Avalon, to which she agreed.

The day arrived and she washed and dressed in her best black dress, and accompanied by Lothar, she was taken by a covered carriage up to the top of the Citadel Mount, where Merlin was happy to see her. She looked a little paler than she had, and he questioned as to her health, in which her response was that she had simply been working hard, but ate well and was taking good care of herself, he was not convinced.

With servants and knights, of which a large group had developed around him, Morgana found all of it far too much to cope with, compared to her solitary life in the cottage, and she suggested she show him Avalon from the top of the Citadel. Arthur agreed, he appeared a little bolder than she remembered from her meeting at the castle. They walked out, down the white steps and onto the vast plain, that made the top of the rocky range that was Citadel Mount, and as they walked, Arthur told her of the problems he faced with the country, and the rebellions of the high lords. He explained his fears of potentially losing Leodegrance, and yet had no idea of how he could help him. Morgana understood his problem, as she stopped and looked out over the large lake below the high cliff. The sun was high and warm, as it illuminated her pale skin, her hair gently lifting and blowing behind her in the warm breeze. Morgana gave the matter a moment of thought, she glanced to her side to see he was watching her.

"You are my half brother, we have different fathers, and yours was once the king. He is buried over there; you should visit him before you depart."

She lifted her arm and pointed at what had been named, 'The Rest.' It was the large chamber hollowed out from the wall of rock.

"I think the question to ask yourself, is what do you want to do? Your blood is that of a king, it runs in your veins, and whether you believe it or not, it was that blood that allowed you to pull his sword free." He nodded his head understanding.

"I am not used to this; I am more suited to carrying flour and sacks of grain." She smiled.

"Then you have a gift no king has ever possessed, and it is a mighty gift." He frowned not understanding her.

"How so?"

"You lived amongst the people who will become your subjects, you understand their lives and their struggles. Tell me, if the mill you lived in was under threat, what would those of the village around you do?" He understood what she was implying.

"They would give us aid, and stand with us to defend the mill." She gave a smile.

"It matters not if it is a mill or a crown, as king, you act like a villager, and you defend it. I know Leodegrance, he was a supporter of Uther, and when Uther lost his way, he did all he could to convince him to change his ways. Arthur, he is a good man, and his support of your crown places him at risk, help him." Arthur understood and smiled.

"You are right, but I knew that you would tell me what was right, it is why I asked for you to be here with me." Morgana turned and looked out across the valley of Avalon.

"You could have been wrong; I could have given you bad advice." He shook his head.

"You would not do that." She gave a slight chuckle; he was innocent in the ways of the world.

"I am not sure why you would think that, you really know very little of me." Arthur stood at her side, and viewed the scene out over the cliff into the valley that was Avalon, he appeared a little more relaxed.

"I remember walking into the castle with Merlin, and watched you defend your place of birth in a manner befitting a queen. You could have ruled, I am sure the sword would have come out for you also. My father named you his daughter, you had a right to take the throne." She could not help but smirk.

"Maybe one day I will, maybe I will let you do all the hard work and rebuild the land, and then when you least expect it, I will overthrow you and take it all for myself." He gave a laugh.

"I do not think you will do that; I think your heart lies beside the grave of your father. Morgana, I aim to repair the damage done to his castle, there are parts that have fallen into disrepair, but it will never be more than the place I was born. In my heart and my mind, the castle is yours, taken from you by my father, no other hand will own it but yours, I swear it."

It surprised her to hear it, Merlin had educated him well. In a strange way, as she stood at his side, she felt that he could very well succeed where his father had failed.

"Arthur, when I was a small child, my mother once said to me of my father, he has a soft heart, and a strong arm. It took me a long time after his death to understand that, but now I am older I do. My father loved me dearly, he cared for me more than any other ever has, and he was a mighty warrior, had Uther faced him in combat, Uther would have lost to him. My father took care of the people, which is why they loved him and why they were so loyal to him, he defended them at all times. If you really do intend to rule, love your people with a soft heart, but never flinch when it comes to defending them, keep your arm ever strong. Leodegrance has supported you with his absolute loyalty, his people are also yours, so use your strong arm." He looked serious as he thought about it.

"How would I do that?" She turned, and started to walk back towards the Citadel, and he walked at her side.

"Your mother, and you also, come from a long line of the finest warriors, call to them, you are going to be their king, and they are kin. Gather all who support you and march in defence of your subjects, and protect them, show them all the power of a true king, for if you truly are the one to rule, it will show." She felt like he really understood her words, his face had a look of determination on it.

"Your advice is similar to Merlin's and I feel more confident knowing you think something similar; I am grateful to you sister." It felt strange being called that, but she smiled.

"Arthur, Rhiannon is a powerful queen, and skilled in her ways of gaining power. Watch her tonight, see how she smiles and charms those around her. Learn from her the skills of a true political animal, for you will have use of such skills in the future." She stopped, turned to him, and looked him in the eyes.

"Be wary of her, flatter her, and be cordial and grateful, but do not let her influence your decisions, for if you do, she will one day take everything in payment for her services. Remember, you are to be the king, and you are her equal, never forget that, and never bend to her, a king never kneels before a queen."

They arrived back at the base of the steps, and she stopped, and took him by the shoulders, and looked him deeply in the eyes.

"From this moment little brother, keep in mind my defence of my home, our place of birth. Emulate me, and rule with a strong arm, but when it comes to your people, keep your heart soft, and your rule will never be forgotten." He gave a smile, and nodded at her.

"I will never forget watching you, I felt inspired to know you were my sister." She gave a chuckle.

"Go, it looks like you are needed, and I have tasks of my own to attend to." She let him go, and watched as he walked up onto the first step, where he stopped and turned, and looked back.

"Will you not stay for the feast?" Morgana laughed at him.

"The only thing that the queen and I have in common, is our hatred of each other, I dine alone, I prefer it that way."

$\mathcal{S}$he felt he understood, as he walked up the steps, and she thought he looked much better dressed in clothing more fitting of a king. He was still young, but he did have a presence around him, she felt it, and in her mind, she pondered it. Morgana turned feeling that he may be a relatively decent king, after all, Uther was a pig, with no manners, and Arthur appeared to be a lot more respectful. Maybe King Arthur would achieve his father's goals, in truth she did not really care, as long as she was left alone to live as she wanted, it mattered not if he succeeded or failed. She turned to the path, and felt she would walk for a while on the top of the mount, it had been a long time since she had walked up here. As she started to walk, behind her came the voice of Merlin.

"Arthur cares for you, he values your opinion."

Morgana stopped and looked back, to where Merlin stood in his long robes, he appeared to have aged a little, although his eyes still glinted, and he still had a sense of youthful exuberance about him.

"Arthur does not really know me." Merlin gave a little nod as if agreeing with her.

"Does anyone?" She smirked.

"I think not… He has a good heart, but I fear he may be foolish, and yet I feel he will be good for the people, I hope you guide him better than you did his father."

"He admires your inner strength, which is why he requested to speak with you… Morgana, you could play a vital role at his side at court. Will you not join with him, and aid him, his task will not be easy, there are many already plotting to overthrow him?" She understood that.

"I gave him good advice, it is up to him now, he is the one to rule not me. I have other plans, but will always answer if he calls out to question."

"And what advice did you give him?" She smirked; he knew full well.

"I told him to reach out to the blood of his mother, for in that line is the strength his father never had. The Celts of our ancestors grow strong, it would be foolish not to call to them for aid, they are kin, and in that they are bonded." Merlin appeared quite surprised.

"There is great wisdom in the advice you have given him, I must confess, it is something I had overlooked." She gave a sly smirk.

"That is why I advised him to reach out to them. His mother is a queen of high standing, they will rally to his side and provide the strength that he needs. If he aims to rule, it will be the blood in his veins that sustains him, not promises from weak lords who only side with him to increase their own power." Merlin gave a little laugh as he looked at her.

"I do believe you are growing up, maybe I should have let you try the sword and rule?" Morgan turned with a nod of her head.

"That is not in my plans, but maybe one day I will, you never know. I have things to do, enjoy the feast." She was about to walk when he called back.

"You should stay, it will be good for you to reacquaint yourself with the life of court. Morgana, living alone can take its toll." She understood that better than he realised.

"You could possibly be right, the problem I have with the feast, is my hair is the wrong colour for the company it keeps. I have plenty of food and books to read, I will be fine."

Morgana walked off leaving Merlin to ponder her, she had changed, she was more mature, and did indeed have a more commanding presence to her. There was no doubt in his mind, had she taken the throne like she once argued with him that she could, he felt, she would rule as a powerful queen to the lands.

He was not wrong, the power within her was growing, the addition of the Whitelines was strengthening her, and her hidden Fae powers were awakening from the bonds placed on them by Branna. It would not be long before the full forces of the Fae raced up within her, and mixed with the power of white.

The last time Morgana had walked along the top of the Citadel Mount was the night Eleanor had died, and she had asked Merlin to teach her, since that time her life had changed, and would again soon. Her destiny was approaching, and she had no idea of what that would be, all she knew was, at some point she would rise up from her toil in the cottage, and start her life renewed, and when that happened, it would be her turn to take what she wanted, as she grew in power to match that of her nemesis, Rhiannon, the golden queen of Avalon.

Far across the other side of the wide plains of Avalon, on the high flat top of the mountain range known as, 'The Giants Shoulder.' The faint figure of Branna watched with a smile, and spoke in a low voice.

"You play the game well my little raven, and you have grown very strong, even here I feel your strength. A new king will come, and that will distract them all, and it is in that time you will rise to become the raven you truly are. I feel my legacy will be secured on that day, and a time for me will come thereafter. It is a time to plan, for retribution will visit this realm, and a payment will be owing for every soul lost from the line of Berengar. It is almost time for Avalon to pay its debts to the line of the raven."

Branna watched sensing all of Avalon knowing she was safe, as she was on the mountain, which was part of the Forest of Time. On the very edge of the cliff, Rhiannon's gaze was halted, and Branna also wore her veil of Enaria as taught her by Ariel, and yet she was not as hidden as she thought she was.

In the trees to the side of the Giant's Shoulder, Eve stood frozen, her eyes focused as she tried to work out what the strange sensation she was feeling was. Her head turned slowly as she tried to make sense of it all, her voice soft and quiet, as she focused her thoughts.

"What is this feeling, and why does it worry me such? I feel you, but you are hidden to me and I do not understand that. I sense you in my realm, where are you? Come to me and show me who you are. Why is there darkness clouding my senses, who are you, and what do you want, and why do I feel I should fear you?"

Eve took a deep breath, and filled her lungs, as she felt the powers from her line build inside her. Something was wrong, not quite right, she had felt this before, but it was only fleeting. Stood in the woodland under the cover of the trees, she let her breath flow from her lungs, and closed her eyes, as her focus became intensified by her powers from the start of time.

In her mind images appeared, as she walked up the high pass, as if looking for something she had never encountered before, and so therefore had no idea of what it was. She could feel it, it was faint, but it was there. In her mind she saw the stunted trees, and worn path of white stones, the breeze that came over the cliff top gently brushing her skin, and all the time she breathed deeper, and allowed her true powers to flow from her, her thoughts questioning her every idea.

"I know you are here; I feel you, hide if you must but I will find you. No life can be hidden from me, for I am the source of all that has flowed from this land."

The pictures in her mind flowed behind her eyes, and deep down in the woodland where she stood like a pillar of stone, she raised her arms out to her sides, and began to glow in a deep fiery red. The true power of Eve was visible, as all the plants lifted their heads of flowers, and exploded into bloom.

"Show me who you are, and why you are here, let me see what walks in my realm and hides its form from me."

The whole of the woodland was lit like the dying sun, as the red light expanded out from her. In her mind she came along the top of the bluff towards the old worn tree of great age, and just for a moment, she felt a strong pulse ripple through her, and gasped.

*B*ranna stood hidden below her veil, as she focused her mind on Morgana as she walked down from the high path of the mount, back towards the lower rocks, known as. 'The Scree.' Branna's eyes and thoughts were focused on the spot where Morgana walked, as she sensed the feelings of her as she walked away from Merlin and the king. She was completely focused, and unaware of the faint red figure that walked behind her.

Eve sensed the spot, and in her mind her head moved and she saw the faintest glimmer of a life. It was veiled, but not enough to hide from her. She walked up behind it and lifted her arm to touch it, and take hold. Branna suddenly felt her, and spun around to face the red ghostly apparition of Eve as she reached out for her, Eve's voiced echoed over the mount.

"GOT YOU!" Her hand touched Branna's shoulder, and Branna felt Eve's power engulf her, her arm came up in defence and there was a blinding flash.

Roack watched, as Branna gave an almighty scream, and was engulfed in a flash of red light, she jerked, and then flew backwards across her workroom, and crashed into the wall. Down in the woodland under the trees of the ancient Forest of Time, Eve gave a scream, and in her mind, there was a blinding flash of light, as if the lightening had exploded from the sky, into her head. She staggered backwards as another blinding flash exploded behind her eyes, and she saw the huge outline of the giant black bird.

She hit the floor hard with a grunt, and her eyes snapped open, she looked up to see the sky illuminated with lightening, and the large black bird fading above the trees, and she took a huge breath inward, as in her mind a sinister croaky voice spoke.

"We are not yours!"

Eve lay on her back as a cold shiver ran through her body, and she took a huge gulp of air, and stared up between the trees that had shuddered. She watched the leaves falling towards her, as if the trees wished to cover her in a layer of protection. Calmness washed into her from the shock of it all, she had no idea at all what she had encountered, but the voice that spoke in her head frightened her.

As guests in their carriages headed up the steep road towards the top of the mount, dressed in their finest attire, few saw the flashes of light, and the black bird. To them it was nothing but a rumble of thunder in the distance, a common occurrence of no real concern.

Morgana stood frozen at the bottom of the path, she had seen the large outline of Roack, and felt the power of both Eve and Branna that had surged through the air.

"What is she playing at, is she insane, why come here? I must hurry."

Morgana hurried onto the path, that wove through the rocks to the woodland path, back through to the road that left the bridge and ran up towards her cottage. She really had no idea what was happening, but she felt panicked, and picked up her pace.

*R*hiannon stared at Sequana, as she stood in her large hall, dressed in a gown of sumptuous silver that glittered like the stars, her long golden hair flowing around her shoulders and down to the base of her back.

"I know you felt it, tell me, what did you see?" Sequana took a deep breath and let it flow out of her, her voice appeared ethereal and distant.

"The sky paints itself in black birds, the touch of life reels in the forest, and darkness swirls through the sky above the Giants Shoulder. The unnatural walks amongst us, cloaked in death, as it watches with envy the living."

Sequana gasped, and her eyes snapped open, she swooned slightly, and she staggered to regain her balance. She breathed in deeply and then corrected her stance, and breathed out. Rhiannon looked at her confused.

"What do you mean, death stalks the living, the other realm can only connect in the thin places, and the Giants Shoulder is not one of them?" Sequana took another breath, and reached for the back of the chair.

"That is what I saw and felt." She sat down and leaned back regaining her strength. Rhiannon watched her carefully, Sequana looked at her with bright blue eyes.

"Be wary my queen, I cannot be certain, but I feel there is a darkness that walks amongst us that seeks your death. I felt it, I felt it so strongly, and I will not deny, the darkness that filled the void within it, was terrifying." Rhiannon swallowed hard, and felt a cold prickle run down her spine.

"Was it Morgana?" Sequana shook her head slowly, and her voice lowered to a soft whisper.

"No… Whatever that was My Queen, it was not mortal, and it was not living in any sense that we know of."

Rhiannon took a deep breath and stepped back, and gave a soft nod, in a way she understood that, she had dreamt something similar after the death of her daughter.

"Stay alert, I want to find it, and when I do, if it is possible, I aim to kill it forever."

Sequana gave a nod, and took in another huge breath, for the first time in her long life, she had encountered something that truly scared her.

"I feel My Queen, that you are the only one who has the power to do so."

Chapter Twenty Two.

Coming to the End.

Like all things in the realm of Avalon, Rhiannon ensured the new king had a lavish affair, and guests from all over attended. Having attended several with her daughters, Gwendolyn grew weary of them, although for Madeline, Una and Melanie, they were large occasions where they could interact and become accustomed to the lifestyle they would have as ambassadors to the realm of Florae when they were older. Gwendolyn smiled, as Una danced looking very happy with Lord Kane. He stepped forward as he looked into Una's violet eyes.

"It has been impossible to get away, I must see you soon." He stepped back, and Una smiled, the group moved forward, and she moved up close.

"I know, but you have to understand, I also have duties in Florae, I am free here for several days, when can we meet?" The group of women moved back again, and the men stepped forward.

"I want you now, I cannot withhold my desires to hold you for much longer." She gave a slight giggle as the line of men moved back and bowed. Gwendolyn looked down at Melanie, who was smiling.

"Why are you not dancing, Mel, you should mingle, and get to know people?" She looked shyly at the men across the room.

"I will in time, Mother do not rush me, I am still a little nervous, I do not have the courage of Maddy or Una, I find this all too fussy, and confusing."

Gwendolyn gave a titter, she could understand that completely, she too had been overwhelmed as a young girl, her grandmother had laughed at her for being terrified of the gentry.

"It is quite alright, there is no rush, we will have you back in the trees and fields of Florae soon enough, where you can wander off alone and draw in the peace of your serene meadows." A broad young man dressed in dark blue, with long light brown hair approached them both, he bowed very politely, he spoke with a slight twang of a Scottish accent.

"Your Majesty, Lady Melanie." Gwendolyn smiled.

"Lord Tor, I see our new young king has given you grace to take a break and introduce yourself, what can we do for you?" He looked a little nervous as his eyes moved towards Melanie.

"Your Majesty, I came to enquire as to whether you would allow me the honour, of escorting Lady Melanie, onto the floor to dance?" Melanie gasped in complete surprise, and went a very deep red colour and looked down, Gwendolyn tried not to laugh.

"My Lord Tor, I feel that is very noble of you, and I am sure my daughter would be delighted to join you in a dance. Although, I will warn you, she lacks practice." Melanie looked up with a gasp.

"Mother!" Lord Tor smiled.

"It would be my greatest honour to teach her, if she would allow me?" Melanie appeared confused.

"It would… Why?" Gwendolyn smirked, as Tor looked Melanie in the eyes.

"Why Lady Melanie, surely you know?" She looked even more confused, and shook her head.

"I fear, I do not." He smiled at her.

"You are by far the fairest maiden in the realm of Avalon tonight, I would be honoured to have you dance with me."

Gwendolyn bit her lip, as Melanie went even redder, and stood dumbstruck. Gwendolyn lowered her arm to Melanie's back, and gave her a slight shove, and she jolted forward.

"Why Lord Tor, the compliment you pay my daughter is very gracious, and well received." He bowed.

"It is sincerely meant Your Majesty, and I am honoured."

Gwendolyn giggled as Tor led her daughter who looked utterly panicked out onto the dance floor, she looked around to see the king and Rhiannon in deep discussion with Merlin. She was not surprised, no doubt Rhiannon was trying to convince them to crown him at Avalon, and she hoped that Merlin would not agree to it. Outside in the darkness, Una slipped into a waiting carriage with Lord Kane.

*T*he new king was the guest of Rhiannon for four more days, but no one saw any sign of Morgana, she stayed out of sight, and headed to market a day earlier, much to the frustration of Arthur, who questioned Merlin and Gwendolyn as to why she had to trade, when she was in fact the sister to a king? It was hard to explain, and only Gwendolyn could speculate.

"She is fiercely proud of her father's line, and she wants to prove she is worthy of it. From the very little that has been documented, when he arrived at these shores, he brought goods and supplies. We have a parchment at Florae written by one of the landowners just down from where he landed, he writes of twelve ships filled with all kinds of goods, which he distributed to everyone. He was a very generous man, and when he built the castle, as you have seen, he built an entire town within it to house the people, and provided them with trading spaces, he was a big believer in trade of goods. Morgana grew up with that, and I think in some strange way, she feels she must do this, to understand her father better."

To a degree, it made sense, she was very independent, and Merlin admired her for it. There was no doubt in his mind, Morgana was intent in forging her own path, his problem was, she was so secretive, he had no idea at all what that would be.

*L*iving in the cottage, time slipped by unnoticed, as Morgana, continued, with the occasional visit from Merlin, who set her more complicated tasks, and informed her of her brother's affairs. After the large feast arranged by Rhiannon, he returned to the castle at Tintagel, and set about organising an army. True to her advice, he looked to the Celt warlords of his mother's line, and found they were eager to assist, and Arthur started his first military campaign in defence of Leodegrance.

Arthur came out of the battle victorious, it appeared he was talented with a sword, and as a result, those who opposed him submitted, and swore allegiance, Merlin was very relieved. It took almost a year before Arthur was crowned king, and Morgana once again trekked back to the castle, and witnessed his crowning, and much to her surprise, his marriage to the daughter of Leodegrance. She was fair and beautiful, and in many ways, she was pleased for her half brother, Guinevere appeared to be perfect for him in every way.

Since the night of the lightening, Rhiannon had appeared too busy to worry about Morgana, and much to her relief, she found she could move around Avalon far more, as she explored most of the realm unhindered by the rules of the queen. Her exploration brought her great rewards which she reported to Branna, as one of them, was a hollow rock, lined with quartz. Morgana handed her a piece as they sat in the tavern bedroom, Branna took it with a smile and rolled it in her palm.

"This is very high quality, and has properties that will serve you well." Morgana looked at it as it sparkled in the light in her hand.

"How will this serve me well?" Branna handed it back to her.

"If you use the stone shaping skills you learned on your first visit to me, you will be able to smooth it and polish it, and then you will have a room that becomes a sightless room." Morgana frowned.

"Sightless… How do you mean?"

"Ariel's box. Morgana no eyes or powers can pass through crystal, especially this one, it is one of the best to hide behind. The golden queen will never penetrate this, and neither will Eve, or even Albanlin. If you use the powers of Merlin's Whitelines to create a door no one can see, then inside this cave, you can do any form of magic you wish to, absolutely no one will see it, or feel it. It will be a sightless room."

Morgana suddenly understood Branna's thinking, once inside, and with the right protections outside, no one would ever be able to find her or disturb her. She smiled as Branna watched her.

"We have another blue feather. It will give me somewhere Merlin, Rhiannon or Gwendolyn will not be able to sense, as we can meet right under her nose, and even her seer, the mightiest in the land, will not have the power to see inside."

"Morgana, the alchemy you have learned with Merlin, is powerful, and hard to hide, and if you use the alchemy I have shown you mixed with it, then you will have a very potent power. You will indeed become a very powerful little raven." Morgana understood.

"My time to part with Merlin is coming." Branna sat back and gave her a very happy look.

"Tomorrow you will not trade on the market, we have something I wish to show you. I want you to leave and head back to Avalon, and as the sun sets, I will meet you. Walk to the outside of the town of Hollow Coombe. Just before the town, you will see that the road separates into two distinct paths." Morgana thought of the little boy fishing, and his words echoed back in her thoughts.

"That way, you don't want the other, that will take you to the scary realm and death." Branna looked at her in a questioning way.

"Do you know of this path?" Morgana nodded.

"I have heard of it; a young boy called it the path to the scary realm." Branna understood.

"He was not completely wrong, it is known as the 'Chimerical Forest,' to some, and 'The Hidden Realm of Sleep,' to others. Morgana, I have studied this place, it is a place like no other, a place where the Fae can dream walk. I walked there often in my days at Avalon before Ariel came to me. I mapped it out as a place to escape if I needed it." Morgana thought for a moment, and looked at Branna.

"Chimerical, that has the meaning of many, a mixture, beasts of two parts, is this place created from many parts, what does it have to do with sleep?" Branna loved the way her mind raced, her mind was such an inquiring mind, and lightning fast when working things out.

"You are right, chimeric, means to create of mixed parts, and in a sense, the creatures that live there are, they are both flesh and spirit, that can change form and carry precious gifts of great power." Morgana was very interested.

"Power, what power?" Branna gave a little chuckle at how eager she was.

"The power of dreams… Morgana, it is a power all lines have coveted, but the problem is the realm is so complex, it is easy to become lost and lose track of time. Mortals who enter will die, and those of Fae who walk there in the flesh, risk losing their direction, and become trapped inside and eventually become lulled into sleep. Time hangs in the air there, age runs slower than anywhere else, and there is one charm, that only the line of a queen or mystic know, and its power derives from that realm." Morgana was dying to know, and she slid forward towards the edge of her seat.

"What is this charm, can it help me?" Branna flicked back her mane of long black tatty hair, and her dark eyes sparkled with mischief.

"You have seen it, you know of it, for it is the very same charm that preserves Ariel in her long box… It is the charm of endless sleep." Morgana felt a huge pulse of excitement pass through her, and her voice was soft and quiet.

"Endless sleep." She looked up at Branna watching her with a fixed smile.

"Branna, this place, it is a prison to those of power." Branna nodded softly.

"To those who do not know the way out, for the doors move at will, and there are only two that are fixed, but so powerfully hidden, even Merlin will struggle. It would take him an eternity to find a way out again. Morgana, as far as I know, I am the only person who has ever mapped it out, and I can tell you now, the ground is rich in minerals of every kind. I have thought of living there when Rhiannon is dead with Ariel, for no one will ever find us there, and you too could build a castle of your own, and use your alchemy to its greatest advantage there." It sounded perfect.

"I feel there is one problem though, if it lulls you into a permanent sleep, will it not do the same to me?" Branna gave a soft chuckle.

"There is a way to sustain life there, for there is one charm that can be done using the life form of a small creature that lives there. It is rumoured that Tideguyde did it, but she was so afraid that her secret would be known, that she wrote the spell in code, and only one person has ever cracked it." Morgana suddenly realised, and felt very surprised.

"YOU?" Branna nodded; Morgana felt a huge burst of excitement. "How?"

"When I volunteered to go to Avalon, I requested to continue my study into the Merle in my spare time. The golden queen noted I coded my notes, and asked if I was good at cyphers. I told her I was, as my father was highly gifted, and he used them as games when I was a child. At the time, I did not know of Tideguyde's code, the golden queen was the first after she left to find it, or at least she thought so. Enaria had also found it, and copied it down. The golden queen handed me the ancient parchment, and I struggled at first, but eventually worked it out." Morgana gave a sigh.

"You worked it out for her?" Branna gave a cackle of a laugh.

"Do you really think I am that stupid? No, I changed it slightly, so it was not eternal sleep, just a temporary sleep. Well, ten years, which in the scheme of things is quite a short span of time, but long enough to get done what is needed." Morgana understood, and actually, she felt that Rhiannon was a little bit dumb at times.

"So, what happened?" Branna shrugged.

"She tried it out and it worked, and granted me the freedom to choose my own place of residence, as long as it was out of sight of her gaze, and I was commissioned to research the Merle in my spare time. I added the charm to my book, and Ariel found out I had a copy, and was confused, because her mother had told her she was the only person who possessed it. Morgana, Ariel sleeps, there is no one who knows how to lift the charm or be protected from it, I am the only one."

It made Morgana's head spin, as the endless possibilities ran wild in her head, and then she suddenly realised something, and Branna noticed her face change as she thought of something.

"What about Eve? She is the source of life, she is immune to almost everything, she cannot be killed." Branna understood.

"She cannot die, but she can be restricted to just her essence." Morgana was intrigued.

"Tell me more."

"Eve is the source of all life, and with Hearne she created all things, but the one thing she did not create for herself, is her living form. The golden queen knows this, she has researched deep into the arts of the council. In order to crack her code, I needed to see some of the things left by Tideguyde, which were in the golden queen's own personal library. Whilst researching, I found a document, that contained a mixture that would rob a council member of its outer body, and poison the spirit in such a way, it could never inhabit a body again. In the realm where they came from, it is a form of punishment, that diminishes the spirit, sort of like crippling a mortal so they can never walk freely again." Morgana shuddered.

"Eve has shown me kindness, I know she is on the council, and they all plotted my father's downfall, but I mean her no ill will." Branna reached out, and patted her knee.

"Fear not, for that is not a task for you. Merlin, aided Uther, Gwendolyn made the sword, and the golden queen gave his men the weapons that slayed your father, those scores are yours to settle, any others will be with me. Although, the golden queen is mine, I have sworn an oath to face her and defeat her, and I mean to do so. Rhiannon the great golden queen, will die by my hand alone."

*F*or the first time since the death of her father, Morgana understood that her time was truly coming. For what had felt like an age, she had hidden her grief and her desire for revenge, and as she sat with Branna, a new plan was forming in her mind. She now had the means to finally face those who brought about her father's early demise, and robbed her of the life she should have had.

The powers of white that flowed through her body from her years of learning and struggles, as taught her by Merlin, were about to become tainted, as the power of the Fae was released inside her, but before all of that could happen, she had much to prepare.

*T*he following day, Morgana, returned alone to Avalon, and headed to her cottage to prepare. She was busy cleaning up as she had to wait until the sun started to fall in the sky, before she could meet with Branna.

Her pan was on the boil, and she was busy sorting out her jars, when there was a tap on the door and it opened, she turned to look, as Merlin entered.

"I was in the area, and have need to see you."

He looked around at the new longer table and the second set of shelves, all lined with dried products for teas and tinctures, and also the alchemy she had been learning from his book. He smiled appearing pleased with it all.

"I must say, this place has changed a great deal since you first came here. I am highly impressed Morgana, you have greatly surprised me and lived up to your oath. I hear there are many in the realm of men that have found themselves cured with your tinctures. You have achieved more than I ever thought possible, and so felt a reward was in order."

She was suspicious and confused at the same time, he was cunning she knew that, and so was very uncertain as to what he intended.

"What reward, you have never talked of a reward, you have said that to work hard and stay focused was reward in itself. Why now do you appear with promises of things I know nothing of?"

Merlin gave a hearty laugh, and slipped his hand inside his pocket of his long black robes.

"You are far too suspicious, that is what comes of all these years alone in the realm of a queen who does not trust you. I have always told you, that you need to get out more and mingle, you know Morgana you are still young, and there is much to learn in all of the lines of creation. I fear I have taught you all I can, and now it is time, exactly as it was with me when the White Lord released me, to enter the world and become who you were destined to be. Morgana, you are now officially a fellow of the Whitelines."

He lifted a white cord out of his pocket on which was a glowing white orb, and he smiled as he reached up, walked behind her and slipped it around her neck.

"This will connect you always to the Whitelines of Time, no matter where you go, it will give you the power to use your skills to the aid of all. I remember the day the White Lord handed me mine and told me to continue to learn as I lived, for your life will also be extended whilst you wear this talisman, and you will have a good ten lives to study and bring more knowledge to our line."

He tied it on safe and walked around to face her, he looked very happy and pleased with himself. She stared at him trying to understand what he was saying, and blurted out the first thing that came to her mind.

"ARE YOU THROWING ME OUT?"

Merlin exploded with laughter, and it was a few moments before he could contain it, as Morgana stared at him, not understanding why this was so funny to him. She felt panicked, it was not much she knew that, but this had become her home, her safe haven, a place people were afraid to visit. Even though it was a little rustic and rough around the edges, she did actually really love the place. This felt hers, the home she had dreamed of as a young girl in the castle growing up. Merlin wiped his eyes on a large stained handkerchief he had dug out of his pocket as he continued to giggle.

"Oh dear… I am sorry… I fear that felt most amusing. Morgana, you made me laugh in a way I have not done for a time, but fear not, you can live here as long as you wish to. I have informed Rhiannon that I have gifted you the house as a token of the effort you have put in to making it habitable." He took a huge breath inwards, and stifled his giggles.

"I know what this old cottage means to you, and I would never take it from you. Morgana, you have earned every stick and brick it took to build it, I may have put one brick on top of the other, but it was you who have made it a home. It is yours, with my token of respect and best wishes. Now is the time for you to walk out there and learn more, it is a task only you can do, and I cannot teach more, which is what the White Lord told me on the day he set me free in this realm, and I wish you my heartiest best wishes for your success. There is one final lesson, which is simply this." He paused for a moment as if finding the right words, and then gave her a serious look.

"Morgana, the following years will guide you forward onto your true path. Now more than ever it is important that you maintain your focus, for the path you follow must be a straight one. It is easy to be seduced by the world outside, and as much as you may resent him, Uther is a lesson well learned. At first, he was a very noble man, but with the power he had, he was seduced, and it led him astray. Morgana, to go astray with the powers you now hold, for that gem on your neck is more powerful than even you realise, will bring chaos to this world and many more. Walk true, for if you fall into the darkness and become seduced by its powers, I will have no choice than to join with the White Lord and destroy you. I fear, for myself, that will be quite devastating, as I have grown very fond of you." He smiled, and she saw the kindness in his eyes, and she nodded to him.

"I understand, and for what it is worth, even though you were hardly here, I too have grown a fondness for you too." It was right for her to say it, even if she did not completely mean it, the moment passed and he became the same old Merlin again.

"Good, I feel quite uplifted, and there is much to do. Your brother has made a request of me, and asked if I would invite you to join him in four days' time, he has something he would wish to show you. I hope you will oblige him?" She gave a nod.

"I will if he really wants me to, how is he, I hear stories of him and the love between him and Guinevere, it appears he has done much to bring peace and the people prosper?" Merlin appeared quite joyful.

"Indeed, he has, he told me he would honour his pledge, and keep a strong arm and a soft heart, and in that he has lived up to his word. He has a circle of good people around him, and I cannot deny, his love for Guinevere is strong indeed and runs right through to his core. I feel they set a good example to all of us." Morgana smirked.

"As I have told you, I am not of that interest, I doubt many men could handle me." He gave a wide smile and turned.

"I fear you are right, well then, four days, I shall meet you here at noon, until then." The door banged and he was once again gone, it was a familiar ritual between them. Morgana smiled and looked down at the white jewel.

"All that effort, and all I get is a tacky bead on a twine, no wonder there is only two of us, no one would toil such for this." Merlin popped his head up at the window and she jumped.

"By the way, the pan is almost dry, quick, before it melts!" Her head snapped round, and looked at the fire, where the last of the water was turning to steam.

"Oh hell." She moved swiftly and grabbed a cloth to lift it from the fire, she turned to look back, but he was gone, which was typical of him, and she smiled, as she set the pan down to cool.

"Finished, somehow, I thought there would have been a second volume to follow."

She turned to the table, and the old book was gone. Morgana gave a long sigh, he must have leaned in through the window and took it, maybe it was a good job she had copied it all into her own black book.

When the pan cooled enough, Morgana boiled more water and made herself a beaker of tea, and walked over to sit at her table. She sipped her tea, and smiled as her mind filled with memories of that first day in the cottage.

"Not a huge amount of space, I hung the curtain, as with a door the bed would not fit. As I said, it is not big, but with a good fire and a little cleaning up, I am sure it will feel quite homely." Morgana turned with tears in her eyes.

"It is perfect, absolutely perfect, I want to use words that will express my feelings, but I fear I am struggling with emotion currently." Merlin smiled.

"I think your gratitude has been expressed perfectly, welcome to your new home, my new apprentice."

She gave a giggle, and ran her hand across the table, which was old and stained from her years of use, mixing and drying teas on it. It no longer wobbled, neither did her chair, the room had been so empty when she got here, and now it was full, and even though she did not realise, it was as equally packed as Merlin's that was below his own cottage further up the road. For over ten years she had worked her fingers to the bone in order to survive here in a land that had turned on her, and yet even so, she had come a long way and was a very different person. The young girl filled with hopes and dreams had gone, she was wiser, stronger, and held within her a great force, and in many ways, that was due to Merlin, and the kindness he showed her on that very first day.

It felt strange knowing she was free to do as she pleased and no longer under his protection. In a strange sort of way, he had been good to her, and protected her as her father would have done, and that caused her a problem inside. She looked at the room, with the old stone chimney, and the roughly laid stone floor, and she understood her feelings.

"I wanted to kill you for what you did before I came here, but I also owe you much Merlin, for without you, I would have been stuck in that castle forever, and be less skilled than I am today. I will repay you by growing more powerful than any who have wronged me ever thought, but you will not die, I owe you that much… No, you will sleep for eternity, and dream of the darkness that entered you in your moment of weakness, and allowed you to betray my father. For your dark deed, I will repay you with one of the darkest of mine."

Chapter Twenty Three.

Unnatural Magical Forest.

Merlin's visit, left Morgana lost in thought, in many ways it felt like the end of something important, she had researched the Whitelines deeply, and had struggled a great deal with it at times. There had been days where her mind hurt so badly, she had feared it would fracture. On those days of mind pain, she had stayed in bed and rested with closed eyes and slept. In the last year there had been a lot of those days. Branna had explained that it was due to her real Fae powers being bound, but assured her the time for her powers to be set free were upon her. Soon, she would help her release herself from the bonds, and feel the true power of her line for the first time.

For Branna it had been more out of concern, she had seen how Maud had been completely seduced by the darkness, and she wanted to avoid that with Morgana, although the Whitelines had worn on her mortal side, and she had suffered moments of concern, as she had worried her mind would break. Through Morgana, Branna learned a great deal of the Whitelines, and there had been weeks and months where she had been able to slow the process of the Merle within her using the charms and spells of Merlin. To a degree, some would say she had learned equally as much of the Whitelines as Morgana had. In her long times locked away with Ariel in her workrooms, she had been experimenting to find that elusive balance that allowed Merlin to control both powers equally.

She was very surprised to find, that some of Merlin's spells included sex magic, she had laughed at the time and could not imagine him with Gwendolyn doing such things. For her, it was not a problem, she had used similar Fae sex magic in her ritual to join with Berengar in the pact they had sworn that fateful night in Bohemia. It prompted her return to Berengar's bed, where she advanced her powers, something she knew Morgana had not as yet done. Some of the spells required the blood of the dead, Merlin's book suggested the fallen in battle or from those who had died of a natural cause, as long as collected within half a day, the blood was potent. For Branna there was no shortage, as Otto frequently shot the people who hid in her realm, or Maud killed them in her sadistic sexual practices below the castle.

For many years Branna toiled, inching closer and closer to her objective, which was full control, so that she could face Rhiannon, and release Ariel from her crystal box. She found Merlin's notes confusing at times, but his mind rambled so much, his writing matched it, and she was not aware of how close she was getting to finally unlocking the secrets of the Merle blended with the power of the Whitelines. She lifted her head, and rubbed her eyes, and looked at the crystal box.

"I feel closer, but at times I feel I am further away, does that make sense my love?" The room was as silent as the grave, and she gave a sigh.

"I am missing something and I grow impatient, which just frustrates me, as I want to release you." She stood up and stretched her back with a groan. Then walked slowly over the box and looked through the plate of crystal. She placed her hand over Ariel's heart.

"I remember lying in bed feeling your heart beat, it gave me such calmness, as your warm soft skin radiated your heat through my hand. I am missing you today, I know I am close, but something just does not fit, and I know if you were here, you would see it. You always saw the things I missed. Ariel, I know I am so close, and it drives me to insanity, because my yearning to pull you out of there and hold you, is unbearable." The flap of large wings announced the arrival of Roack, she turned her head to look. The bird landed and bobbed its head.

"The time is upon you Branna the Raven; the little raven will be walking towards you." Branna nodded.

"Alright Roack, I will leave shortly, stay here in this room and do not leave, Maud is in a fouler mood than normal, she will crave blood shortly." Roack bobbed up and down.

"I have summoned the raven Rajani to come to me, there will be no fear of death for the woman in white."

Branna gave a smirk, she found Roack odd at times, she was one hundred percent riddled with the Merle, and yet she found the bird was loyal to the protection of Ariel in ways she had never expected. Branna lifted her black shawl off the back of her chair, and slipped it over her shoulders, as she looked at Roack on the window ledge.

"The doors are locked, I shall not be long, watch over her for me."

Roack bobbed about as Branna was engulfed in swirling smoke and disappeared completely. This was a realm Branna could walk in as herself undetected, as none of the powers could see her, this realm was the ultimate veil to hide everything.

$\mathcal{M}$organa hurried along the path, she was not keen on being seen by the residents of Hollow Coombe, she had not forgotten her last visit, and had no wish to confront anyone today. She reached the fork and turned onto the path that led through the tall grasses as Branna had instructed her. It was hot and humid in the marshes through which the path wove, and it felt unpleasant and stifling, as damp clouds of mist encircled her. She understood why no one came here, it was very unpleasant to fight her way through the tall grasses.

She was nervous as the sun was falling behind her, and she went as fast as she could, but the lumps and bumps of the path made walking difficult, as she also had to use her arms to push past the tall canes of the thick grass. Suddenly she stepped out into a clearing and stopped, there was a space, square in shape, where there was no tall grass, and yet each side of the square was a wall of tall grasses. She looked at the floor, there was nothing, just short tufts of fine grass, and no sign of a path to follow anywhere. She looked around her, feeling concern rising within her.

"Which way do I go now?" She looked behind her, and then heard Branna's voice.

"This way." She turned, and there stood Branna in front of her, half in and half out of the grass. Morgana smiled feeling greatly relieved.

"I was worried, I thought I had lost the path." Branna gave a big smile.

"Everyone does, which is why at this point they always turn back, and never go further. Come, it is this way."

Morgana walked over, and followed Branna into the grass, and within a few minutes she walked out into what looked like a gigantic forest, with trees taller than anything she had ever seen in her life. She breathed in deeply.

"Branna, this place is amazing." Branna smiled as she walked onto what looked like a huge wide path several yards in front of her.

"Come, see, this is a realm like no other."

Morgana joined Branna on what was a path, at least fifty paces wide, and she was staggered to see it went on for miles and miles, and faded into the distance. She turned around and it was the same in that direction, she could not believe her eyes.

"How big is this place?" Branna shrugged.

"I am not sure anyone knows, it is as wide as it is long, but it will take you years to walk from here, to the far end." Morgana gave a slight chuckle.

"This place has a lot of potential." Branna gave a smirk.

"It does indeed. Morgana, here you can be as free as a bird, there are no prying eyes, and no ears to listen and inform on what we do." Morgana was already thinking that.

"I thought the Fae dream walked here, what about them?" Branna turned, and pointed into the distance.

"The place they walk and meet is that way, and from what I can work out, it would take three months to walk to it without stopping or resting. This part is completely free of everything, apart from the Sandlings."

"What are they?"

"They are like small children; they are the dream spirits I talked about. They are strange looking and highly colourful little things. They have big eyes and cannot speak, so they use a series of nods and quiet squeaks. They say that they charm the dreams within themselves, to form them into orb like crystals that float, by singing to themselves. Sandlings are the creatures I spoke of, they are sort of mortal, and spirit at the same time, trust me, you will know if you spot them."

Morgana understood, she had heard talk of them as a child, her mother had told her they would carry her dreams to her. She looked all around at the trees.

"Are they easy to find, you said they were the key to living here?"

Branna slipped her hand into her pocket and pulled it out with a round glass like sparkling orb in her hand, and Morgana marvelled at it.

"They are not easily caught, they can fade to appear as if not there, but when you do, push your finger into their forehead. It causes them great pain and is not pleasant, but it forces them to change into their dream magical orbs, which can be used to make a spell. It is that, which will allow you to live here unharmed." Morgana eyed the orb carefully, Branna placed it into her hand, and Morgana looked up at her.

"How do I make this spell?" Branna pulled a piece of parchment out of her pocket.

"This is the document I copied from the golden queen's library, you say the incantation over a bowl with the other ingredients, and then crack it as you would an egg, and tip the contents inside. The liquid it makes is golden, drink it, and you will be protected always in this realm." Morgana took the parchment and looked at it.

"This is dark alchemy, and you say you found this in her private library?" Branna nodded.

"Morgana, she plays pure well, but if you ask me, she is more corrupted than even I am. Never ever trust her, always be on your guard, she is the most dangerous person in all the realms, and never make the mistakes she made. Never think you know it all, and never think you can control everything, I am the greatest example of how a queen of so called great power can be fooled, and out witted." Branna appeared so serious, it gave Morgana a shiver, Branna smiled and relaxed.

"I have made many mistakes Morgana, I have great power but I am a fool also. I did not think, and that moment brought a darkness so deep it consumes me. I would give up everything to take it all back to have one pure moment with Ariel again. The golden queen believes the myth she created about herself, never make that mistake and think the myths of us are true, for that is her path. The truth is, the power you hold is untainted, never tie it to a raven, never let the darkness touch it. Be strong as you have been, and yes, avenge your father, for the injustice he suffered and the pain it caused you. Never be like her and think you have it all, because the truth is, the power is so vast, you never will." Branna lifted her hand, and pointed into the deep ancient woodland.

"Here, there is all you will ever need, and it will sustain you, and give you the peace to live free, use it well." Morgana looked up and smiled.

"Well, there is plenty of timber for building, so that is a good start." Branna scoffed.

"You do not need timber for building, this is a magical place, your powers here will be enhanced, look."

Branna crouched down, and with one finger, she pointed at the dirt floor. The ground gave a shudder, and then a fine shaft like a rod came up out of the floor. It was smooth and polished and looked like a cane." Branna looked up, and winked at her.

"It is basalt, and dark as death, normally it is the hardest stone to work, and yet here in this place, there is so much magic, you can work it like clay in your mind, and do anything you like with it. When you are finished, it is solid and hard."

Morgana instantly understood, her mind was racing, and the possibilities were endless. Between them, they could build an entire realm of their own, Branna read her thoughts and feelings and smiled at her.

"Morgana, I brought you here as it gives you a place of complete privacy. I have no wish to reside here, my home is really Avalon, it is where I desire the most to be. For now, it is beside Ariel, for I never wish to be separated from her again. This, all of this, is for you, here you can fulfil your dreams, and when it is built as you wish, you can connect it to any part of any realm you wish to, so you will be able to appear and disappear on a whim. Here you can learn who you will be for the rest of your life, there are no ravens in this realm, just you my little raven, it is your realm now."

Morgana understood, but felt saddened by it, she would love to have shared such a huge place with Branna. She knew in her heart that together they could achieve everything their hearts desired, and that was the problem. Branna desired only one thing, and it was currently at Berengar's castle sealed in a crystal box. Morgana gave a sigh.

"I understand, I do, in many ways I envy you Branna, I do not think I will ever have a love in my life such as yours." Branna gave a nod.

"You will… It will take time, I was once a loner and she walked up to me and climbed up on my cart, and from that moment, I knew she would be beside me forever. There is time, all us Ravens attract a person of great loyalty at some point, it is written in our stones."

"I am not sure I will notice to be honest. I am always too busy to really take note of people."

It made some sense to Branna, she had been the same. She was so tied up in her study, she really did not care that much for people, and then Ariel arrived, and everything changed.

"There is time my little raven, even you in your isolation will one day look up and there will be someone who will strike your interest, it will happen. Now come, I need to instruct you on how to get in, and get out, I have not as long as I would wish, and will need to return soon."

*T*ime in the forest is strange, and passes quickly, or slower, it depends on the forest. For Morgana, it was a full day later when she got home, and yet she had felt like she had only been there less than half a day. Branna assured her, it was normal and in time she would be able to control it. She advised Morgana to plan in earnest, and start to prepare as soon as she returned from her visit to her brothers.

Lay in her bed in the dark, her mind focused on how she would create her new place of rule. She wanted it to be impressive, not at all dull as her cottage looked, she wanted something on a grand scale, something that announced her presence. She lay in the dark and closed her eyes, as she tried to relax and think of something she could build with her mind. What she knew was, it had to be precise in her thoughts and she would need to create every detail in her head before she attempted to build it. She took a deep breath, let her mind run wild, when suddenly something occurred to her, and her eyes snapped open.

"I could build another castle, yes, something like my father built, something that showed I lived in there." The brain wave exploded in her head, and she sat bolt upright.

"I could build a castle with a huge raven on it, and it would be all black basalt… The Raven's castle, that would do it, if anyone did get in and saw it, the huge bird would look so frightening, no one would come near it."

She flopped back on the sheets and her mind started to work, and raced as detail after detail flowed through her mind, it would be something no one would ever forget.

*A*s Morgana dreamed of her future, Branna sat at her table reading through all of her vast notes, she took a break and sat back as the candles flickered, and rubbed her eyes. Morgana had told her of the visit from Merlin and the words he had spoken, and she had felt a pang of concern. On her arrival back in the castle, she had gone straight to her books. Her eyes lifted to the crystal box, and she saw

Ariel within, lost in her sleep.

"Is too much power a bad thing my love?" She lifted her glass and took a sip.

"Is that what has caused all this, the golden queen took too much and it unhinged her mind? I do not fully understand the power of the Whitelines, I know it is more powerful than both of our lines of Fae, should I worry about Morgana? I really could use your sharp mind tonight; I fear mine has been dulled by tiredness."

She got up and walked along the edge of her table, heading towards the crystal box, holding her glass.

"Was Merlin right to worry? I have seen how the darkness has unhinged the mind of Maud, she is half mortal and half Fae as is Morgana. Will a power so pure clash with her mortal side and bend her mind to breaking point? I need to know, for if it will, I have to save her, I have to make sure she does not fall foul to the magic inside her." She leaned against the box and leaned over to look upon Ariel's sleeping face, and smiled.

"There are days like today, when I want to open your box and simply climb in, and have Morgana seal us in together and sleep free of this weary life at your side as I did in Avalon. The end of each day was such bliss for me, I would slide into the bed at your side, close my eyes and all my worries and fears would leave me. I could use that today, to simply be free of all this in your arms, now that is a dream worth having." Branna placed her hand on the box above Ariel's heart.

"I wish you could hear me, just knowing you could, would ease my weariness. I am growing to care for Morgana like she was my own, she is everything I wanted from a daughter, and yet I fear the power will crack open her mind and destroy that part of her that still holds the innocence of a child. There are parts of her that are so like I was when I was young, learning from my mother. Her hard work has worn on her, and she should be praised for it, I feel it is a mighty achievement, but I sense part of that very clever and likeable girl are being lost to the strain. I want to save her Ariel, I do not want her mind to fragment or splinter, for I have seen the effects of that in Maud. I do not want her to be tied to a raven, I want her to be free of darkness, and free to have a clear open mind, I want her to be truly free like I dreamed of." Branna looked down at the face beneath the crystal, and smiled.

"We were truly free, weren't we? We ran naked through the

woods and swam in the river, and we lived such a wonderful life, just you and I, and no one else to interfere."

The emotions flowed up inside her and her eyes filled with tears, as she looked at Ariel, her hand tightened on her glass, as a huge wave of emotion came up inside her. Branna felt her anger boil, and she stood up quickly and turned, and launched the glass through the doors.

"AND SHE TOOK IT ALL AWAY!"

It smashed into her work table filled with bottles, and exploded with all the other bottles, sending shards of glass shooting in every direction across the room, smashing and exploding on the walls. Branna stared at all the glass as it rained to the floor, as her lip started to quiver, she fell to her knees, and pulled her hands to her face, and wailed into them.

"All I ever wanted was to be left alone with her, I asked for nothing, I just wanted to be alone and free with my Ariel, why could you not just leave me alone? Why did you have to force this on me, why Rhiannon, did you hate me so much you just had to destroy the only happiness I had ever known… WHY DID YOU!?" She wailed into her hands, her deep bitter sobs echoing around the room, her voice weak and feeble, as it slipped through her tears.

"You knew… You knew it would get me, you knew about the Merle, and yet you allowed me to become infected. You were supposed to be our queen, like Bridget, you were supposed to love and protect us all, and yet you cast me out into the darkness." She lifted her head and looked at the ceiling, as if looking at the sky.

"YOU ARE NO QUEEN RHIANNON, YOU ARE A HATEFUL BIGOT, DRIVEN BY YOUR OWN WORTHLESS VIEW OF YOURSELF… I HATE YOU; I HATE YOU FOR WHAT YOU HAVE DONE TO ME, AND I WILL NEVER FORGIVE YOU!"

She drew in a deep breath, and snorted back her tears, as she breathed in deeply and tried to regain her control. Inside her, she fought her hardest to push back the darkness that was driving her rage. She clenched her fists, and gritted her teeth, and took a huge deep breath, and fought back the anger that was trying to consume her. Branna wearily lifted herself up, and wiped her eyes, and gave a snort, as her breathing started to regulate, and she felt the calmness flowing back inside her. She walked back to the table, the shattered glass crunching under her boots.

"I will fight you and the darkness you gave me, and I will never let you take Morgana. She has Jarron, and he is pure and untainted, I will never perform the right to join her, I will die before I allow that. I am the mistress of this house my golden queen, and I rule this land, it is mine, and your sick mind will never worm its way in here. I will never condemn another to this life of pain and darkness, so get ready for a fight, because I will not let another member of this house fall to a raven for your amusement." She wiped the glass off the book, and hurriedly flicked through the pages, Branna was determined to protect Morgana at all costs.

*T*he next two days were busy, Morgana collected up herbs and set them out to dry in the sunlight, inside flat reed woven trays, which she covered in mats. What was already dry she bottled and labelled, and with a happy smile, she collected and filled a jar full of the precious white flowers from the plant Eve had given to her. When the morning arrived, she packed a small bag of some belongings, Merlin had not told her how long she would be.

He arrived as always with a happy manner and big smile, and appeared to approve of her dress, which to be honest was quite plain, and as always, black. He gave her a nod.

"Morgana… There is great truth in the words you have spoken, in the eyes of many you are seen as a queen, for your mother is a queen of great standing in her family's culture. It is time you stepped out of this dusty old cottage, and took your first steps into a different life, a different kind of world, and so, with your mother's aide, you will finally meet a part of your family you know of, but as of yet, not associated with." Morgana frowned, and looked behind her at the floor.

"This cottage is not dusty; I clean it every day… Who are these people I have to meet, and why do I have to?" He smirked.

"Morgana, it is time… You cannot live here forever, surely, even you understand that there is a wide realm out there waiting for you to discover it? I fear at times you are impossible, Morgana, expand your horizons, I am quite sure there are things out there which will fill your mind with wonder. Now come, or we will be late." She gave a sigh, and picked up her bag.

"Where are we going to anyhow?" The wide white tunnel opened in front of her.

"It is somewhere quite special; I am sure you will appreciate it."

She took a step into the tunnel.

"Vague facts from such a precise man, why does that bother me so?" Merlin gave a chuckle; she was far too intelligent for her own good.

Morgana and Merlin walked out of the tunnel into a dense thick woodland, where up the path there was an old wooden dwelling, Morgana turned to look at him.

"Where are we, because no king would live there? That place is worse than the one I live in; did you build that too?" Merlin laughed, and shook his head.

"I fear your impatience is showing, and no, that is not my work, I am actually quite good with wood." Morgana gave a sigh, and set off walking towards it with her bag.

"I have seen the window, and the roof beams in my cottage, you give yourself too much credit Merlin." He strode along at her side with a chuckle.

*T*he house was set on stilts, and had a wide deck in front of it with three wooden steps the full length of the house front. The roof was made of thick thatch, and extended out right over the deck, casting a subtle shade over the heavy wooden door. It did not look as bad up close as it had in the distance, and Morgana noted it was far better workmanship than Merlin was capable of. They stopped at the steps, and Morgana turned to Merlin.

"I will leave you here Morgana." She looked at the house, and then back to him feeling confused.

"Are you not staying with me, why am I here?" He smiled.

"This is the residence of a Druid queen and her maidens; I am not permitted to enter. Your mother waits within for you, and she will explain everything. I feel this will be a good experience for you, as you follow in your mothers' footsteps, and unite with her family." He turned and started to walk away, and she stood feeling puzzled and unsure, and watched him lift his arm.

"Good luck Morgana, and for the sake of all the gods, try to enjoy yourself."

His white tunnel exploded open, and he walked into it and it closed behind him. Morgana stood alone, unsure of what to do, behind her was a creak, and she turned to see a young woman dressed in all white with long flowing blonde hair at the open door, she smiled and spoke with a heavy Welsh accent.

"Lady Morgana. Your Highness, would you care to enter?"

She looked back down the road, there was no hope of returning, so she gave a sigh, and took her first step up towards the deck.

"Is my mother here?"

"Yes, your highness, this way please."

Chapter Twenty Four.

Ritual.

*I*nside the house was far nicer than Morgana thought it would be, her mother saw her and came over quickly to her, as Morgana looked around at the very well upholstered furniture, and hand carved tables topped with marble slabs. Igraine was very happy that Morgana had actually come.

"Morgana, I am so pleased you came, this is an important aspect of our family, and one you should be involved in." It all appeared to be very strange.

"Involved in what, this is a hut full of women, what is it you expect?" Igraine took her arm.

"Morgana, in this family we are thought of highly, we come from a line of great people with very strong traditions, and some of them are very important." She gave a sigh, and looked at her.

"I know you have your own views and have become a strong woman, but for me, and this family it is an important spiritual step… Please go along with this for me, I do ask so little of you. Your father really understood this aspect of our family, he even encouraged it." She looked afraid that Morgana may bolt for the door, Morgana shrugged at her mother as she looked around.

"I do not really know anything about this part of the family, so I have no idea what is going on." Igraine smiled, and walked her down the long room.

"You will not remember but when you were a new born child, we came back from your father's home, and then he brought us here. He took part in a blessing ritual for you, and he held you up to the moon with great pride, and swore he would always protect you. It was a special moment I have never forgotten, Morgana, whatever you may think, I did love him deeply, and I was devastated when he died." Morgana nodded at her mother.

"You stopped talking about him, I always loved listening to you tell me of his deeds, I thought you had stopped loving him, and focused yourself on Uther." They walked into the room that was to be hers for her stay, it was very nicely furnished.

"Uther was not always easy, neither was your father, this world sets impossible standards for men and they feel they must have to live up to the ideals of being strong and powerful. Your father had a different side that only you and I ever saw, you know the man he was, you know of his gentle kindness." Morgana smiled at her mother and gave a nod.

"I loved him deeply, I still do, and I miss him. I get so angry because they all just decided he had to get out of their way, and when he wouldn't, they plotted to kill him. I can never be accepting of that." She sat on the soft bed; it appeared her mother understood.

"Morgana, here in the heart of this family, we are all equals, and in that, like myself, you hold a very high position. Your father's actions when you were blessed made clear his intentions, that you should be given the status of a future queen to these people. It was his wish, that you were recognised. Morgana, this is not the Ruling Council or the Fae, this is the truth of those who have walked these lands long before the Romana's or the races of others that have come to these shores. This is the true line of this land."

She considered the point, and it made some sort of sense to her, and she could see that this was very important to her mother.

"I understand, I have no idea what is going on here, but I am loyal to the family of my father and your family, and I will play my part." Igraine smiled.

"Rest a while, and the ceremony will begin soon. We do not eat until after the proceedings, and then we shall feast in style." That felt a little disappointing, she was actually quite hungry.

*T*he wait was two hours, and Morgana could feel her tummy rumble, when finally, flanked by two hand maidens, Igraine led her out of the house and down the path to the edge of the lake. They stood on the edge of the water that flowed down from the mountains, through a circular hole in the rock, and dropped to the stream that fed the lake. It felt calming and peaceful, and she could smell the richness of the earth all around her, it was late afternoon, and Igraine turned to her.

"Morgana, this is a sacred ritual, we have to cleanse ourselves first." The two handmaidens walked past her completely naked, and walked into the water. Morgana gasped and pointed.

"Why have they disrobed?" Igraine gave a chuckle.

"Really Morgana, I did not think you were so prudish."

Morgana gasped as her mother pulled off her dress and tossed it to the floor, and walked naked into the water. She stood on the bank and swallowed hard.

"I am not, I have days when it is hot that I don't bother with clothes, but Mother, it is not with others."

Igraine shrugged as one of the handmaidens attended to her and with a cloth started to wash her back, she appeared so calm, natural and embracing of this, yet Morgana felt nervous. Morgana took a deep breath, and loosened the ties on her dress, she had never done anything like this at all. Feeling embarrassed it dropped to the floor, and hiding her most intimate parts with her hands the best she could, she hurried into the water, and gave a shriek, it was freezing cold.

She waded in until it was above her breasts, and stood violently shivering, as one of the maidens approached her, and slapped a cloth on her back and started to rub. Morgana leapt out of her skin, and looked back, the young maiden smiled.

"You have beautiful soft skin." Morgana nodded, feeling terrified, was she to become as Ariel was to Branna, she had no idea?

If the truth be known, she needed a bath, most days all she could do was wash from a pot basin in the cottage, and she began to relax as Igraine handed her a soft cloth, and she washed herself thoroughly. When she was done, she looked to her mother.

"What do we do now?" Igraine turned, and pointed across a stretch of water.

"We head there, and will be met by others." Morgana looked to the bank.

"What about our clothes?" Igraine smiled.

"Leave them, we will be provided a robe over there."

She was not keen, that dress had cost her six pennies, but with a sigh, she turned and walked along trying to hide her nakedness under the water behind her mother, who appeared to be quite at ease. On the bank, a group of women stood waiting with fresh robes, they were white, which was not something she agreed with, but what choice did she have?

*H*er mother walked almost casually out of the lake, and was greeted by the women, and had a robe fitted over her. Morgana watched feeling nervous, there was no way she could slip out unseen, and did not feel anywhere near as calm as her mother was. She had no choice, so trying to hide what little dignity she had left, she hurried out of the water and two of the women dressed her, as her cheeks turned pink. She jumped feeling startled when the young woman started to dry her, it felt embarrassing knowing that she was being wiped in places, only she had ever touched, and decided there and then, she was never having a maid in her future.

The dress was slipped over her head and pulled down, then clipped in the shoulders, she looked down at it, it was a nice style, but she hated the fact it was white. As she looked down and noted her goosebumps, she felt a heavy cloak placed gently onto her shoulders, the maiden lifted her hair, and allowed it to flow down her back, and she gave a sigh of relief knowing she was dressed and hidden again. Igraine smiled at her.

"You look nice."

She did not feel it, she felt awkward and slightly panicked, she had never done anything like this, especially showing her naked body to others.

"I am feeling a little ashamed, mother, how can you be so calm showing yourself as we did?" She gave a little titter.

"Morgana, we are all women, and we are all natural creatures, do not be ashamed of your body, it is who we are." She shook her head.

"I am uncomfortable." Igraine gave a slight frown.

"Have you lost your chastity?" She felt instant panic, and shook her head vigorously.

"Mother… You should not ask that… And no, I have not, I realise I live alone, but I cannot be involved with those things whilst I study."

Igraine sniggered and bit her lip, somehow, she felt it was very amusing to see her daughter, who could be so fierce at times, suddenly look shy and nervous, and very shocked.

"I think it is quite sweet, although you know daughter, a pie left on the shelf goes rotten in time. You should be a little more accommodating, and allow at least one man a taste."

Morgana hung her head and turned scarlet with her embarrassment, this felt worse than Stenlow, when he asked. The handmaidens both smiled, they obviously had knowledge Morgana had yet to learn.

$\mathcal{M}$organa was happier when they started to move. They followed the path as the light in the sky started to dim, here in this woodland the trees were very thick and dense, and the ground was covered in a thick carpet of moss. It was so dense, that it muffled the sound, and the woodland felt sort of eerie, and she had to admit, almost sacred. Up ahead torches flickered, and she tried to see what was in front of them, but it was obscured, by what looked like a large stone wall. As they drew closer there was a low murmur, almost like chanting, and she assumed that whatever it was, there was a lot of them.

There was at least two hundred of them. Morgana walked out of the trees and was confronted by a large circle of what she assumed were druids, all robed and hooded in a way that hid their faces. The sound she had heard was low and rumbling, almost like the waves of the sea in the distance. The tall grey stone she thought was a wall, was actually a doorway, and it was at least ten feet high, made out of two massive wide pieces of granite, on which was a thick rough hewn lintel.

Igraine reached out and took her hand, and she turned her head to look at her, she was ashamed to admit, but she felt scared, and needed her mother's support. It felt like Igraine understood, and she squeezed her hand, as she guided Morgana into the doorway, and the handmaidens fell in behind them, and then Igraine stopped. Morgana took a deep breath and swallowed.

The circle of people was huge, and at the far end was a stone table, in front of which was a hooded druid. As soon as she had appeared in the doorway, the murmur instantly stopped, and everyone turned to face her, and went down on one knee, and bowed low. Morgana had no idea at all what to do, her mother leaned in and quietly whispered.

"Do not be nervous, in their eyes, you are a queen to be worshipped and admired."

She could feel herself breathing quickly, and her legs trembled a little, it felt intimidating to be treated like this by so many. For years she had lived in her cottage avoiding everyone, and to see this many people in one place, was a great deal to try and comprehend. Igraine gently squeezed her hand, and walked forward, and Morgana followed at her side.

Both of them walked slowly towards the druid by the table,

although he was still bent low to the floor. Igraine walked her to within five feet of the kneeling man, and then stopped, the handmaidens were right behind her. Morgana was breathing fast, this was all so strange and different, it worried her. The man rose from his knees, and said something in a different language, it was one she did not know or understand, and Morgana glanced to her mother, who simply smiled.

Igraine released her hand and stood at Morgana's side, and the druid spoke, and all around her, the people kneeling rose up with similar words, and stood in the huge circle all watching her, and she felt really uncomfortable, as she breathed in and out, trying to keep her oxygen flowing to her lungs. Igraine moved slightly to the side as the druid in front of her, who she thought could be a priest or something, turned to the stone table, where two oil lamps flickered. The two handmaidens came to her side, and gently slipped her cloak off her shoulders, revealing her white dress that was clipped at the shoulders. It was a little breezy, and she could feel the cold chill on her body, the dress was not that thick.

Unsure if the trembles were nerves or the cold, she tried to stand still, understanding her mother must have done this at some point in her early life. Knowing that helped, because her mother was still here, so she knew she would live. What happened next almost paralysed her.

The clips on her dress were released by a handmaiden, and her dress fell down to the floor leaving her stood completely naked, with over two hundred people looking at her. Her reaction was natural, she gasped out in surprise, and realising she was nude, she moved her hands to cover herself feeling shamed. Her mother's spoke calmly and quietly.

"Do not hide yourself, you have nothing to feel shame for, you will be anointed, and purified, in what is a sacred act. Morgana, we are all creatures of a natural world."

It was easy for her mother to say, she was not naked and being stared at, as her face burned red with embarrassment. The priest turned and began to speak, and did not even look at her body, he talked quickly and held a bowl, into which he dipped his finger, which contained a blue coloured paste. He lifted his hand and with a finger, drew a line across her forehead and then on her cheeks, nodded, and turned back round to the stone altar. He lifted his arms and spoke words loudly, and all the others replied in almost like a chanting prayer.

Morgana faced forward, terrified of looking at anyone whilst stood naked in front of them, she felt humiliated and really frightened for the first time in a very long time. The druid turned, looked her in the eyes and said something she did not understand, her mother leaned in.

"Morgana, kneel."

Her legs were shaking so much she was not sure she could, but unlocked them, and slowly descended. In many ways it helped, as she felt it did hide her womanhood a little, she looked up at the man, who gave a nod to her, and then dipped his hand in a small bowl, and he spoke in a very fast language. He touched her head, the sides of her face, and above her eyes, with what she thought was some form of fragrant water.

The large circle of people all started to speak in unison, she had no idea what they were saying, but it felt like some sort of prayer. She knew nothing of what was happening, all her mother had said was it was important, and so she had agreed to go along with it. Although, if she had known it meant being stripped naked before two hundred men, she never would have come. The priest raised his arms and spoke loudly, and suddenly, the beat of drums began.

They started slowly as the priest turned holding what looked like a wine jug, he looked down at her and spoke, as he waved it above her head, and the drums started to beat fast, and as they did, all the watchers joined in stamping their feet on the ground. The rhythm got faster and faster and the crowd started to chant. The priest looked down and lowered the jug, it was clear he wanted her to take a drink. The rhythm was getting faster and faster as the drums beat and the feet stamped, and the crowd chanted, none of this made any sense to her as she did not understand a word they were saying.

She could no longer see her mother who was now knelt behind her, and the jug lowered as the beat echoed with chants and suddenly it was at her lips, she could smell the strong alcohol smell as the jug tipped, and she leaned in, opened her mouth and the liquid past her lips, and burned into her mouth, catching her breath.

Morgana almost choked as the jug tipped in more, and she pulled back her head and had no choice but to swallow. It burned into her throat as she coughed, and the beat was faster than ever, and as she tried to recover her senses and breathe in, the priest spoke, she looked up, as his palms came down and pressed onto her face, then slid. His hands had some sort of liquid on them, and he smeared it down her face, neck, and down over her breasts, towards her stomach, she flinched with shock as he touched her breasts, and then felt him push onto her stomach and she gasped with completely surprised shock. Morgana looked down and saw the glistening red on her breasts and realised, her eyes opened wide, and she looked up as she spoke.

"Is that blood?"

He leaned in to her, lifted a small round pot saucer and FUFF! Powder hit her square in the face, and she recoiled back in total shock, as the powder drove at speed into her eyes.

*T*here was a blinding flash behind her eyes, and Morgana recoiled backwards, and her mother caught her by the shoulders, and lowered her slowly to the floor. Morgana was blinded and utterly terrified as the drums suddenly ceased and all fell quiet. In her head, all she could hear was her pounding heart and her breath as it rushed into her mouth at speed, and then flowed back out.

Her mind was filled with flashes, as she twitched and jerked on the floor, and inside her head, pictures started to form. She had no idea what had happened, somehow, she was locked inside her own mind, everything on the outside world had been shut out and closed off, as Morgana's mind took control.

In the wide circle, the robes had been flung off to loud cheers and everyone was dancing around the circle, chanting and singing, whilst on the floor, the naked Morgana twitched and jerked, her legs wide open and her arm spread out wide as in her head she wrestled with the truth of who she was. A wooden low bed on legs was carried in, and gently the handmaidens picked her up, and laid her on the soft sheets, as she writhed and jerked, out of control and afflicted with spasms.

Behind the table of stone, bonfires ignited as the people danced naked towards it, and the bed was lifted by six happily chanting naked men, and Morgana was carried towards the fire, where they lifted her up and danced around the large roaring fire, cheering and singing, the red glow of the heat lighting up Morgana's white naked glistening skin. Round and round the fire they danced, Igraine was lay on the edge of the stone table, her legs spread as the priest pounded into her, and the handmaidens writhed on the floor below as they felt the thrusts of two of the other men.

Inside Morgana's head, unaware of what was happening outside her body, and the dancing and celebrating, all was quiet as the pictures flowed, Gwendolyn looked defiantly at Merlin.

"It is Albion, it is good enough." Merlin shook his head.

"He was promised Excalibur." Gwendolyn stared at him, her eyes burning with intense blue.

"If he is the one true king, he will have no need of any sword, both Rhiannon and I rule our lands, and we carry no weapons. Is the world of men and the army of Rome so powerful that he needs a sword of power to feel like a king? I am sorry, but I feel strongly that he should not have Excalibur. He has not earned it." Merlin shook his head.

"He needs it Gwen, Cornwall will not back down if he does not have it." Gwendolyn looked resolute.

"Cornwall is a man of honour, he is no fool, when he sees how many back Uther, he will come to the table. Cornwall has a lot of lands and people in his care, he will strike the best deal for them." Merlin looked very angry.

"He needs to show Cornwall he has the authority."

"Merlin, he is backed by the Ruling Council and two lines of Fae, and he has Albion, how much authority does he need?"

Morgana felt a pulse run through her body, and jerked, the pictures faded as the voice of Rhiannon echoed into her mind.

"Send Uther the weapons, he is becoming an embarrassment, dress five ranks of our Marshals like his men, and send them in mixed with his rabble, that will take care of Cornwall's men." Morgana jerked. Eve's voice echoed off the walls around a room.

"This is getting us nowhere, Uther must withdraw and enter talks again, he cannot just take a woman that is not his. Merlin, you must talk with him and bring reason."

"I fear my Lady of Life, it is not quite that simple, Uther is not at this current moment reasonable, he demands Igraine."

"Then what shall you do, lure out this Cornwall, and then what… Slay him?"

"My Lady, that may well be the best idea yet." Morgana lurched, and almost rolled off the bed as inside her head bright lights flashed across her eyes. Rayne screamed at the top of his voice.

"SHE IS YOUR DAUGHTER, SAVE HER, YOU ARE SUPPOSED TO BE THE MOST POWERFUL, NOW USE IT!"

Eleanor screamed out in wild panic, and Morgana's brain exploded with more pain, she lurched on the bed, and spasmed, as they still carried her roasting hot sweating body around the fire, as she lay locked in the hell of seeing the past.

In her head, she could hear the battering of large thick doors below the rampart, and her father shouted and jeered from the top of the tower.

"YOU WILL NEVER TAKE THIS CASTLE UTHER. YOU HAVE NO HONOUR AND BETRAYED ME. BRING YOUR COUNCIL FRIENDS, EVEN THEY CANNOT HELP YOU." Maud and Otto yelled from the balcony.

"HALF BREED BITCH, YOU HAVE NO BUSINESS WITH THIS FAMILY, WE DO NOT WANT YOUR TAINTED BLOOD IN OUR LINE." Maud stared at her with hate.

"Do not challenge me little raven, I will never let you rule here, one day you will face me, when your raven is not here, and I shall drain your blood and drink all of it. I am the only one to rule when she leaves, no half breed could ever rule here."

For an hour, Morgana fought with her inner demons, as they showed her the truth of all that happened, and how Hearne, Eve, Rhiannon, Merlin and Gwendolyn plotted the downfall of her father. She screamed out in wild agony, as she felt the pain of the loss of her father one hundred times over, and she jerked and shook on the bed, when suddenly in her mind a white face with grey eyes and long light brown hair looked in and smiled.

"Shush my little raven, be at peace, rest your mind, for it needs to be healed. I will not let them take you from Branna, she needs you." Morgana's eyes snapped open.

"ARIEL!?" She sat up abruptly, and took a huge long breath. "Huh!"

All was silent, and she was in her bed in the wooden house, dressed in a white garment. Her hand came to her chest and she looked down expecting to see blood, she was washed and cleaned. She took another deep breath, her head felt heavy and groggy, and her throat was as dry as dust. The door opened and she squinted as the light flowed in, and lifted her hand to shield her eyes. One of the maids walked up to the bed, smiled, and reached for a jug, she poured a beaker full of water and handed it to Morgana.

"It is nice to see you awake."

Morgana took the beaker and lifted it to her lips, she sniffed at it before drinking, and was relieved it was just water. She swallowed it greedily, feeling the life come back into her throat so she could speak.

"What happened to me?" Morgana handed her the empty beaker, and she refilled it, then handed it back.

"You were given a ritual of anointment, and made a leader of the clan, which you now hold sway over. Your brother is king of this land, but we do not take the rule of someone not of our line. You are seen as the true heir, you came first, and to us, that is all that matters. You have now seen the truth of all that has happened, we will stand with you, in all that you do."

Morgana nodded, she did not understand all of this, she was just glad that she was alive. A picture of her mother had flashed in her mind, of her being taken on the stone table, Morgana felt worried, and tried to compose herself, but she had to know.

"Was I touched by a man… You know, did anyone…?" The maid shook her head vigorously.

"No, My Lady, that is not permitted, you are still quite pure and untouched." Morgana nodded, she was very relieved, the maid gave her a smile.

"You must be hungry, if you wish to rise and dress, I will send for food."

Just the thought set her stomach off, and it gave a loud whine, and the maid gave a small giggle as she turned and headed for the door, leaving Morgana alone with her thoughts. She took another drink from the beaker.

"Who were they, I thought they were druids, but that was no ritual I have ever heard of?"

*M*organa dressed and entered the large room, where she sat alone at the table, and was served food, and she ate hungrily. She had been surprised to find it was the following day, and that had been in her trance or whatever it was for over twenty hours. The strange thing was, that now she had awoken fully, her mind felt rested clear and sharp. She could recall memories from the event clearly, which made no sense to her, because she had thought she closed her eyes and lived in her mind. She could see the pictures in her mind, almost as she had left her body and was looking down on them. It was a shock to see her mother gyrating in ecstasy as the priest pleasured her, and the handmaidens, both straddled over men, thrusting their hips and leaning back with looks of sheer pleasure in their eyes.

Was this the sex magic Branna had talked of? She really had no idea, but she could see hundreds of men and women, all dancing and cavorting in sexual stances with each other everywhere, never in her life had she thought such things could happen, and yet they had.

When she had eaten, she sat out in the sunlight on the deck and relaxed and took the air, as she tried to understand why this ritual of truth had shown her what it had. The maid came out of the door to her side with a tray, and her thoughts halted, as she turned and the young girl gave a smile.

"I have made you fresh tea My Lady." She placed the tray on the small table next to her seat, and stood up.

"The Lady Igraine, asked me to inform you that she had travelled on ahead to meet with your brother, she will send an escort to collect you shortly." She went to leave and Morgana raised her arm

"Wait a moment, can I talk with you, is that allowed?" The young maid gave a smile.

"We serve you mistress; you can ask anything." Morgana was a little relieved.

"Would you sit with me a while, I have questions. Do you have a name?" She sat down in the chair opposite, and looked at Morgana, she appeared relaxed, which Morgana was relieved about.

"I am named Gerta. What else would you like to know?" She leaned forward, and poured out a tea for Morgana.

"Last night, the ritual, were those druids, or was I mistaken?" Her head gave a slight nod of understanding.

"Your mother told you little I see. Some of those who were there are or were druid, but all of us were all aligned through the house of your father. We served him, and that is where our loyalty lies. The union you saw was of many ancient lines of faiths, joined as one by your father and mother." It surprised Morgana.

"My father, you mean Victor of Cornwall?"

"Yes, My Lady, all the heads of our family's hail from the land of Berengar. They came here with your father, settled here, and raised families of their own, all of us in one way or another are related to a member of the Varisci Clan, and all of us swore allegiance to the Raven. When your father married her majesty, queen of her Celt house, we came together in one union to serve the same house. It was your father who brought with him the gathering." Morgana frowned.

"The gathering, what is that?"

"It is the ritual we had last night, a ritual he brought and blended with the faith of this earth. You are of his line, and we anointed you into the line of our clan, you are the new heir to rule after your mother. You father knew of the druid practice of worship, which in many ways was similar to that of his tribe, and so when we all came together in one cause, we adopted the ritual of the gathering into our customs." It interested Morgana.

"I knew of none of this, I did not even know that there were people still loyal to him." She gave a warm smile.

"We know this, Uther tried to destroy much of the efforts of your father, but he would not break our spirit. On your birth, and your return from the homeland, it was during the gathering that you were anointed by your father, in the same way his father did him, and his father before him." Morgana was very surprised.

"Berengar told me none of this when I spoke of my father." She smiled.

"It was Lord Berengar who passed the order to protect you, which is why we waited until Uther was gone and his heir found. We have watched over you for some time, and have admired how you have forged your own path as your father did. My Lady, you have a very loyal force behind you, all we wait for is the word, and we will all stand beside you. We all swore an oath last night as you knelt before our clan's spiritual leader, that we will fight for you." Morgana was now starting to understand, in a strange way, many things now made sense, especially her mother's behaviour.

"My mother told me she was loyal to my father, I had not realised how loyal, I see now the truth of all things." Gerta gave a broad smile.

"My Lady, she did suffer, she loved your father dearly, but she could not show her grief in public, as she had been given to Uther. There are many quiet hours alone, where we helped ease her pain, and helped to make a good show of loyalty for Uther. There were many days where cook had to hold her back as you spoke your mind about Uther, she wanted to join you in condemning him, but that would have caused many problems. We helped search for the son she bore, but alas no one could find what Merlin did with him, and so she kept up her appearance until he was slain." It made sense.

"Was Uther slain by the clan?" She nodded.

"He was, the Lady Raven was there and ensured it was done properly. Justice needs to be paid, and we have played our role and will continue, until all with blood on their hands have paid the price of their treachery."

The sound of hooves echoed down the long woodland road, Gerta, rose from her seat, and gave a bow.

"That will be your escort, I shall bring your bag out to you." Morgana smiled.

"Thank you, Gerta, I appreciate your support of my mother." She gave another bow.

"It is our pleasure My Lady, she is our queen and dearly loved."

She headed off to get the bags as three horses with a carriage came up the road and slowed as they pulled in front of the house. A tall knight slipped off his horse and bowed at the base of the steps.

"My Lady Morgana, I am Gawain, and sent buy the king to escort you to him." Morgana stood up, and looked at the other two armour clad knights.

"I will not be a moment, I am awaiting my bag, how far is it from where the king resides?"

"It is but an hour by carriage My Lady." She nodded, as Gerta came out and handed her the bag.

"Thank you, Gerta, we will talk again, I promise."

Chapter Twenty Five.

All Equal Men.

*T*he carriage pulled up, and Morgana looked out of the window, across the wide expanse of area, where large wooden scaffolds filled with men, who laboured at huge stone walls. The fields to the side were littered with tents, in between which, small forges had been built, and blacksmiths hammered away creating what was required for the build. It was loud and noisy, as the air was filled with the sounds of thousands of chisels and hammers, pounding away in a random sort of way, that beat to several differing rhythms. It was not hard to work out, Arthur was building a castle, and it was huge.

The carriage door opened, and she got out of her seat as Gawain beckoned her forward. She stepped down from her carriage, and he smiled at her.

"Impressive, isn't it?" She looked up at what was the unfinished archway into the castle, and then looked along a large front wall leading to the turret.

"It is big, I take it this is the thing my brother wanted me to see?"

Gawain led the way, with a big smile and talked of the years of work that had gone into it. It was the work of the father of Bedivere, who was a man of skills when it came to building, and how when it was finished, it would be the envy of the whole country and set Arthur above the rest. Who was she to argue, after all, she had Tintagel?

The central court yard was already paved in smooth cobbles, that led across the yard to the large inner completed castle. She walked up the steps, and in through two huge heavy wooden doors made of the best green oak, and across a wide hallway, with steps either side, cut with precision from granite, leading up to the rest of the castle. They went under the balcony that the stairs ran up to, and through another two large doors, into a vast hall, which housed a fireplace as big as her cottage, containing a roaring fire. It was clear, Arthur was building to impress, and he was winning.

Down the sides of the great hall, which towered above her, long lines of tables in dark wood ran in a line, and at the far end, on the only one that ran across the centre, people were sat deep in conversation, one of which was Arthur. He lifted his eyes and saw her, and his face broke into a smile, and he stood up.

"Morgana!"

Arthur came out from behind the table, he had filled out a little more, and he actually looked very refined in his neat well tailored clothing, he certainly looked kingly. He walked down the hall with his smile and as she approached, he pulled her close to embrace her.

"It is so nice seeing you, I am so happy you came." She gave a faint smile, as she noted the others, including her mother who were sat with Guinevere.

"You asked and I came, is that really such a surprise? Merlin said it was important to you." He stepped back, and was very happy.

"I see too little of you, I would like to see more of you." She gave a nod, as he opened his arms.

"So, what do you think?"

He looked around the large room, he was obviously very happy. She followed his gaze along the walls festooned with banners of the heraldry of every clan and family aligned to him, she had seen others that looked very much the same, just not as big.

"I am impressed, it is a mighty achievement." He appeared to be very happy, and slipped her arm into his.

"Come, I will give you the tour, I have a wish to spend time with my sister."

With that, Arthur guided her out of the hall, and as he showed her around, he talked of the years of work, that had built a castle that would house thousands, and how in the grounds, there would be a market to allow many to trade and prosper. He showed her the halls and corridors, and talked of how it would be a beacon to all to join him, as he would truly be a king of his people. This would be where all the country could travel here to voice their concerns to their king, and know they had an ear that was listening. She felt it was very noble of him, but did enjoy seeing his enthusiasm. Eventually they ended up at the top of the tall three storey central castle, and walked out onto the battlements, where Arthur leaned on the wall, his blonde hair fluttering in the slight breeze, and he turned to her.

"I took your advice sister, a strong arm and a soft heart, I am building this so all the country will know I am here at their service." He still had that youthful element about him, and she smiled.

"I am very pleased to know you will be a ruler with an open heart, but I have to ask, why could you not do that from Tintagel?" He smiled, as he leaned on the wall.

"Morgana, there were many that opposed me when I came to this throne. Oh yes, they bowed and swore their undying allegiance, but I could see in their eyes, that their intentions were just on the surface. I want to prove to them, that I will rule with a fair hand, and their problems are mine, and their lands are safe. In time they will see that I aim to make this country strong again, united against common enemies, and through that, they will know I was the right one to rule."

She thought his motives were very honourable, but she understood the politics of life much better, she knew what the ruling class were really like, she saw it in action on the markets and in Avalon.

"It is a grand dream, and I hope you do it, but Arthur, is it real, do you honestly think that men of great power will change so easily?"

Arthur stared out over the land towards the sea that crashed on the rocks in the distance, and she watched him, trying to understand if he actually believed his own words, his voice was soft, and showed his care.

"I have to try Morgana, I have to unite these people, so the likes of the Romans never land, and take all for themselves again. For too long this land has been divided, and that has been its downfall. I wish this land to unite and rise up from the waves and be glorious." She noticed the crucifix hanging around his neck.

"Will being a man of this Christ help, there is also great wisdom in the old ways of this land?" He gave a chuckle.

"Merlin told me you would say that. I suppose you will not understand, but the words of their book inspire me to be a greater man than I am, I found a deep connection with them, and wish to use them. I want to lift up those in need and show compassion to those who deserve it, and through the teachings of this Christianity, I have learned ways I can do that." It made some sense, and she had no wish to spoil things.

"I hope then, that you succeed in your task, for if you do, your name will live on forever." He turned, and his blue eyes shone with his joy.

"I am glad you are here, we do spend so little time together, you have rooms here, I had them furnished especially for you. Morgana, I know that your studies mean a great deal to you, but can you not study here also, for I would wish to see more of you?" It was clear he had been speaking to Merlin.

"I am here am I not? I can make no promises, I live a solitary life of peace, and here it is very noisy. I have always been a loner, I do not blend well with the people of court, and there are so many here, but I will promise, that I will put in more effort and try to see more of you." He gave a big smile.

"I would wish that, come, let me show you to your room, I hope you like red velvet, it is all the fashion, Guinevere insisted it was used to upholster your room?"

*H*er room was far superior than anything she had known, it even rivalled Tintagel. It was very clear that Arthur had every intention of creating a shining example for his rule, it was hard not to be impressed by it all. She settled in, and started as she meant to go on, which meant dismissing the dress maid. She had no use for a maid to put her clothes on, she was quite used to doing it herself. The room had a large wooden cabinet for her to hang her clothing, and when she opened the door, she found a rail filled with dresses, all black and very well tailored. One or two were far too extravagant for her tastes, but there was three or four she really liked, and she decided she would keep them.

The day slipped on, the room had a large window of new glass, and it was clear allowing the sun to pour in, she liked it a great deal, and pulled up a red velvet chair, and sat with her journal, and inks, and wrote down her thoughts. Down below, Arthur was planning his reason for his great gathering, and in the hall, many men worked hard assembling what would become the centre piece of the room. Below in the kitchen, an army of cooks slaved over what would be the first banquet to be held in the castle of King Arthur. It would be the first of many, and set the tone for his leadership and rule of the land.

Later that afternoon, everyone was called down to the great hall, and Morgana who met her mother on route came down the stairs to find the large doors to the hall closed, and everyone was gathering outside. Bedivere and Ector stood by the doors, Morgana stood waiting impatiently, viewing the scene, there were far too many people for her, and she hung back.

Arthur had built around him a core of the knights that had sworn their oaths to him, there were twenty four in total, but his main core of those he trusted most, was only twelve, and Morgana paid them great interest, especially Lancelot, who was considered the most noble of all the knights. What caught her attention, was the way he looked at the queen, and also, her response. Morgana knew little of the ways of love and romance, but she was keen eyed and read the signs of men's and woman interests, and from the gossip at the markets it was clear to her, many secret liaisons happened outside of the bonds of marriage. She may have been wrong, but it appeared to her, Guinevere enjoyed the attention Lancelot gave her a little too much.

*T*he doors were opened, and everyone entered to find Arthur in high spirits, stood before a huge round table that had been built right in the centre at the top of the great hall. It was a vast table with twenty five place settings all clearly marked in black and white, wide triangular panels were inlaid into the table, in black and white wood, all fitted to look like an equally divided cake. It was beautiful there was no doubt. Arthur stood before it filled with pride, he withdrew his sword of gold and laid it on the table, and Morgana stared at it, she knew Uther's sword, she had seen it every day as a young girl in the castle, and that was not it. Everyone gathered around the table, as Arthur lifted his voice.

"As promised my noble knights, a table to match no others!"

He smiled a great smile, and it amused Morgana, he wanted to show all of the people how he cared for them, and yet he had the finest of everything, and she wondered if he remembered anything of his days at the mill. Arthur leaned on the table, and looked at the knights gathered around it.

"This is a table where we all sit as equals, not kings or lords, but as men, everyone equal in the qualities we bring to this table, and where all have a voice to speak only the truth. Come, lay your swords on the table, and let us sit as men, as we will every day from here on in, and debate the days and things we may achieve." Arthur sat down, and all the knights withdrew their swords and sat with him.

It was a moment many would remember, as drinks were poured and food was served, and the ladies gathered around the edges on fine chairs with tables to discuss their men. Morgana had little interest in that, and slipped back up the stairs and sat on the large wooden balcony, slightly back, on the seats in the dim light, and viewed the affairs from above alone. She could not deny, she found it all fascinating, although she was finding it hard to see how this was any different from Rhiannon, she too surrounded herself with those of power. She sat watching, taking note of everything, when Gwendolyn appeared walking up the steps, she came onto the balcony and smiled.

"I thought I would find you up here, I would imagine all of this is too much for you, too many people." Morgana sat back in the chair.

"I can handle people if they are the right ones, I am just not one of those." Gwendolyn gave a chuckle.

"I can understand why Merlin chose you, it may surprise you to know, you both share a lot of similarities."

"I am not unhappy you know; I just wish to live a different life to some." Gwendolyn sat down at her side.

"Your brother is happy, he appears to be achieving a great deal, we all feel he will be a good ruler." Morgana nodded.

"He has a good heart, and means well, but when he talks of equal men, I fear he may be losing sight of some men. The cost of that table, would feed many villages for a year."

"I believe it was a wedding gift from his father in law, it has taken some time to create the right space for it." Morgana turned, and looked at Gwendolyn.

"Was his sword a wedding gift also?" Gwendolyn smirked.

"I take it you have not heard the gossip; the tale has become well known? When Arthur met Lancelot, he would only let him pass if he could win in a fair fight. Arthur took him on using Albion, but he lost his temper, as Lancelot was so skilled, and in his anger, he used an unfair shot, and it broke the sword. I cannot deny, none of us expected that, but there again, Arthur learnt an important lesson, and humility." Morgana turned her head away.

"So, you gave him Excalibur, a sword you would not even allow his father to hold." Gwendolyn looked surprised.

"Did Merlin tell you of that?" Morgana turned back to face Gwendolyn.

"I saw it in a vision, since studying I have had them. You were right not to hand the most powerful sword to Uther, but I fear a sword does not maketh the man, Uther should have taught you that." Gwendolyn frowned at her.

"That is a little bit cynical Morgana, Arthur is not just a man, he is the symbol of what all men can be." Morgana gave a slight shrug.

"It is not cynical; it is a fact. My brother talks of all being equal, and in one sense he is right, men can only be men, it matters not what is in their money belts when it comes to their behaviour." Gwendolyn sat back.

"You have piqued my interest, share with me your thoughts, I find them curious." Morgana watched the two groups below.

"My father fell to a man for no other reason than a future king's lust, and whether you want to believe it or not, that cross around my brother's neck, may speak of deeds of honour and chivalry, to his new god. It may even be a symbol that stands for all that is valiant and good, but when it comes to the affairs of men and women, one thing will always take control, for it is the one thing everyone has that rules them… Their desire. A woman and man alone, will always look to their carnal instincts, and that is the one thing that will never change. A woman brought down Uther, and it is likely a woman will bring down Arthur. Look at them Gwendolyn, watch how the women preen and pander to the men, and look how the men enjoy it. There will be many interactions in secret with all of those people, there already is when you know how to see it."

"How can you be so certain Morgana, is that a vision also?" Morgana scoffed at her.

"It is not a vision, it is right there, and anyone with open eyes can view it. My brother should take his mind off his castle, and place it back on his wife, she yearns for a child, and he needs to supply one. I wish to have no part in any of this, because if truth be told, had it not been for the lust of an uncouth brute, I would not be here, and neither would any of this, for my father would still be alive. I trust in the natural world, and your husband allowed me to look deeper, it matters not what clothes they wear or what metal hangs from their belts, they are men and they are woman, and already nature is starting to play its part. Take a good long look down there, for it has already begun."

Gwendolyn leaned forward in her seat, and looked through the wooden rails of the balcony, and down below, she noticed how the ladies distracted the eye of those men they admired. Morgana stood up.

"I admit I have little carnal knowledge, and I know only a little of this new Christian faith, and it's God. What I do know is that the old ways recognised the human appetites of the people, and celebrated them. This new Christian way does not, it suppresses them, and I fear that may be the spark that starts a fire, and brings ruin. I am weary, I will take a rest before supper, please excuse me, Lady Gwendolyn."

Gwendolyn nodded and sat back, Morgana made her way out of the balcony and up to her room, and Gwendolyn remained sat in the shadows, alone with her thoughts, she gave a small sigh.

"You fascinate me Morgana, I find I am quite intrigued by you, for in you there is deep wisdom for one so young. I find I am caught in your words, but I cannot help but wonder, if there is a spark to start a fire, will you be the one holding the flint?"

*S*upper reminded Morgana very much of her time at Tintagel with Uther. The wine flowed and the fire roared in the hearth, and there was much rowdy mirth, and loud laughter. She had eaten her fill, and had drunk the wine, and was finding her thoughts slightly clouded by it. In a bid to clear her head, she excused herself, and walked up the steps in the direction of her room. As she entered the corridor, Sir Lot came up at her side.

"Lady Morgana, with your consent, I would escort you safely?" She felt a little cloudy, but looked in his direction.

"Am I unsafe in my brothers' home?" He gave a wide smile.

"I am sure you are quite safe; I find my pretence in order to speak with you, has been somewhat revealed." She gave a little giggle, which was quite unlike her.

"I feel the need for some air, but prefer the battlements, I find the air high up more refreshing. If it pleases you, I will allow you to escort me and ensure my safety, which will keep up your pretence." She giggled again, and surprised herself.

Lord Lot walked at her side and spoke of the castle, and made the odd jest of the problems occurred during the building, to which she found herself giving small chuckles. This was not at all like her, and she wondered what had become of her, and dare she say it, she felt happier than she had for some time. They reached the battlements and walked out, the cool air hit her and she breathed in deeply, Lord Lot watched as she leaned on the wall, and her head fell back, her hair cascading down her back, as she looked up at the full moon and drew the air.

"I love the night."

She felt wild and free, and so alive, she had no idea what was happening to her, but she felt a deep wild feral energy flowing through her. Lord Lot came to her side and looked down upon her.

"I feel the night suits you best, especially in the full light of such a radiant moon." She smiled and started to giggle.

"I am as wild and untamed as all nights, I ponder Lord Lot, your admiration is obvious, but are you really a knight of such standing, that you think you would tame me?" He frowned.

"I have not the slightest inclination to tame you good lady, I am enamoured by the freedom of your spirit." She smiled; he was good.

Her mind filled with the pictures of the gathering and all of the people that writhed naked and unashamed as they unleashed their carnal desires, and she felt a heat grow within her body, and it was something she had never felt before.

"Tell me, in truth, I am different, I am like nothing you have ever met before, and you feel the challenge of conquest, nothing more. Be honest good sir, you wish to ravish me as you would any other maid that has crossed your path?" He stepped back, and looked shocked, she knew it was fake.

"My Lady, I can assure you, it is the furthest thing from my thoughts." She gave a loud laugh and looked at the moon, her feelings of wildness coursing through her.

"What a shame, I have need of a brave knight." She laughed out at the shocked look on his face. Morgana chuckled as she up righted herself, and smiled at him.

"You have a face to attract ladies Lord Lot, walk me to my room, I feel the air has added to my mood."

He gave a nod, and offered her his arm and she took it with a smile, she was feeling quite giddy, and a little unstable. He walked her back to her room, and stopped at the door, and released her arm, she was still feeling very hot as she reached for the handle, he gave a polite bow.

"I shall bid thee a good night, My Lady." She opened the door slightly.

"My Lord Lot, I find myself in a predicament, I asked my lady dresser to leave me, and I require the aid of another to loosen the ties. I feel I need more air, and am in danger of becoming faint, due to the tightness of my garment, would you please offer your assistance?" He looked unsure.

"My Lady, I am not sure that would be prudent. I could go and retrieve your dress maid if you would wish that?" Morgana smiled.

"Have you aided a lady in the loosening of her garment before?" He looked guilty, and like he did not wish to say, she gave a giggle.

"I find myself embarrassed, but yes, I have." She swung open the door.

"Good, I need help now, so please, if you may, I cannot wait much longer."

She stepped into the room, and Lot looked both ways, and then stepped in, and Morgana closed the door. Morgana walked over to the side of her bed, and turned her back to him, as he stood by the door looking nervous. She felt happy and giddy, and was enjoying herself. She lifted her long hair and pulled it over her shoulder, revealing the back of the dress.

"Please hurry My Lord, I find I am struggling to breathe."

*I*t was not a lie, in her mind she could see the pictures of all of the people as they pleasured each other in the firelight, and that picture of her mother, lay naked, as the priest pounded into her. She took a deep breath, her breathing was much faster than normal, and her body felt like it was igniting. The image of her mother played in her thoughts, as she felt Lot take hold of the ties, and start to undo them, the pictures of her mother's lust filled face, her lidded eyes smouldering, played in her mind, never in her life had she seen such a look on a woman's face. In truth, she wanted to know what that was like, she wanted to experience that, and know the pleasure that enhanced the sex magic of her kind. She felt the dress give slightly, and it loosened around her breasts, and slid down revealing the top of her white pink bosom.

"Is that enough My Lady, to ease your breathing?"

The dress slipped more and she turned to face Lot, his eyes instantly fell to look down, as he admired her, and she liked it, he wanted her and she knew it, and she knew, she wanted him. Morgana took a small step forward and reached up, and pulled him close and kissed him. It was the spark to light the fire between them, and he snatched her towards him, and kissed her with a passion, and she felt a huge surge explode inside her.

The dress fell to the floor as she kissed him hard, and as his hands started to wander, she pulled at his tunic and top. He was touching her, exploring her, his warm rough hands tracing her shape and contours with every inch of his hands, she felt the fires of wild abandonment growing inside her. His shirt came off and his pants fell, and his hot naked skin pressed into hers, and she was delirious with desire, as her hand moved over his soft skin, never in her life had she felt anything like this.

He pushed her slightly, inching her backwards, as she felt his arousal growing, she wanted him, she wanted this like she had never wanted anything more in her life, and it surprised her, as her feelings exploded all over inside her. Was this the true power of magic, was this what Branna had told her about, the potency of the forces that could be unleashed through the spirit? She did not know, all she knew was her body was burning and she felt tingles and sensations she had never known in her life, as she clawed at him and kissed him, dragging at his skin, with the wildness of a feral beast.

They fell backwards onto the soft bed, and he was on her, kissing her breasts and sending tingles and explosions throughout her whole body, it was glorious, as she scraped her nails into the back of his scalp, as his hand felt the warmth between her legs, and without even thinking, her legs naturally opened to allow him access to explore her. She felt like no words could ever explain, as his fingers toyed in her wetness, his other arm came under her as he lifted his head with a smile, and lifted her, pushing her back up the bed. Her breathing was coming in gasps and spurts as she looked down as he climbed on the bed and moved up to her, and she saw his extended manhood for the first time.

Her head flopped back on the pillow, as her legs opened wider, and she yearned with all her desire for that moment, that moment when she would truly become the woman of power she aimed to be, and gave him the purity of her youth. The moment arrived as she felt him arrive at her opening, as he ravished her at her neck, she reached over and grabbed him under the arm, her lust for him to enter driving her insane. Morgana pulled, and he entered, and she rolled back her eyes, and tilted back her head, as in her mind, explosions mixed with the slight pain, and her body instantly arched upwards, with a wail.

As she writhed and gasped for Sir Lot as he pounded into her, Morgana understood the power of what Branna had told her. She could feel the force of energy inside her building, and it was far more powerful than any spell she had ever cast with Merlin. Was this the true nature of the darkness of the human spirit? She did not know, but as the forces within her built and she felt she was losing control, she knew, this was something she had every intention of surrendering to, she wanted it to engulf her, she wanted to feel the rawness of its nature, and she wanted to capture it, and direct it in the power of her spirit.

The moment came fast, as her body lost control and reacted, with her head back, and as her stomach lurched upwards, Lot stiffened, his heat entered her, and at the very same moment, her mind exploded with light, and her eyes, that were rolled back in her head flickered with a dark red light. Her wail was not quiet, it came out of her like a banshee, and for several long seconds her whole body spasmed out of control, and for the very first time, Morgana felt the true power of a raven.

With a gasp, Lot fell forward, and collapsed at her side, his breathing rapid and fierce, she smiled, and strangely felt a completion wash over her, she was truly a woman now. Her eyes closed as she regulated her breathing, and felt the vibrations softly coursing through her entire body. Lot's movement alerted her to his presence again, and she opened her eyes and turned her head to him, he was red in the face, but breathing in a little better. He swallowed and lifted his head slightly.

"I feel you were right, there is no man alive who can tame what flows through you. Never in my life have I known such wildness of passion, you are without doubt, a queen amongst women." She turned her head back and looked to the stone ceiling, she was still very hot, but breathing better, and she felt utterly drained.

"You are right Lot, I am a queen, but one day I will be more, for I shall be the queen of all the darkness. The nights shall belong to me, and I will be a raven of the night, the darkest raven that has ever took flight." She closed her eyes and felt her body swirl in calmness, as Lot drifted, and she spoke softly and quietly so only she would hear.

"All men may be considered equal little brother, but no man is enough to rule me." Her breathing was calm, as she relaxed, and she drifted into a deep sleep.

Chapter Twenty Six.

Clashes of Family.

When Morgana woke up, Lot was gone, which to a degree, protected her reputation, as there were many who would see what they did as shameful. It was ironic in a way, considering the amount of extra marital sexual activity Morgana knew about. She had intended to leave within the day, but considering the night previous, she was unsure, and even though her head hurt from the alcohol, she hoped there would be a repeat performance.

Morgana got her way, Lot returned for four more nights running, before he had to head out to visit the northern reaches of the country. Arthur had men on the road constantly, as his riders and knights, maintained stability and peace. Once he had gone, she returned to Avalon in her carriage and headed back to the cottage, to pick up her life again.

From that moment, Morgana's life changed, she had a lot to do, the orb like dream that she had been given by Branna, she hid away until she needed it, and her first task was to sneak out in the night, and head to the cave of crystal. In order to make sure she was completely protected, she raised a partition in front of the cave entrance, and it was exhausting. The following night, having created a wall as you stepped into the cave, she did the spell taught her by Merlin that would make those who came close, divert their path and walk away. Then began the week long task, of using her mind to smoothen the crystal, and polish the walls. It put a great strain on her mind, and she found for several days she had bad headaches that made it impossible to do anything, which created frustrations, and she found herself lying on her bed in the dark, and sleeping more.

Her progress was slower than she expected, as she needed to take a lot of breaks to rest in between large tasks. Branna became concerned, when Morgana did not appear at the market, and sent Rosamund to check on her, as Lothar had been assigned to stay at Tintagel, to help run the estate with Igraine. When Rosamund arrived, Morgana was in bed with a fever, she staggered out of her room to unbolt the door, only to collapse in Rosamund's arms. Her fever burned for four days, and when she woke up, she was in her bed at Berengar Castle. Branna had risked everything, and jumped to her cottage, and sweeping her up in her arms, she jumped back to the castle, and hoped Eve had not been alerted. When Morgana opened her eyes, Branna looked down at her and smiled.

"Good morning, are you feeling better today?" Morgana jerked, and looked around the room. Her voice was croaky and her throat very dry.

"Why am I here?" Branna smiled as she rested her hand across Morgana's temple.

"You have a very high fever, Rosamund was very worried about you, so I came to you and brought you home." Morgana gave a faint smile; she was very weak.

"Thank you, I remember little."

Branna got up off the bed, and lifted a jug, she poured out a water, and handed it to her. Morgana sat up slowly and took it, her face was far paler than Branna had ever seen it.

"I fear the ritual, followed by your work, has drained you. Rosamund said that you complained about your head, then passed out on her. Tell me, have you had pains in your head before?" Morgana swallowed.

"They were just headaches, I have worked long hours, and slept little." Branna understood, but was still concerned.

"Morgana, to protect you from being detected by the Ruling Council, the Fae powers you hold were limited and bound, so you have been using your human side to master the Whitelines. It has placed a great strain on your mind, and I cannot deny, I feared your mind may fracture. Merlin would have been watching out for it, but he is gone now and is instructing the king. Think about what you have done, you mastered the Whitelines almost alone, that feat takes a lot from your body. Stay here a while, and let me help you recover."

Morgana agreed, she was too weak to do much else, and for the following week, Branna cared for her, and made sure she ate proper meals and slept well, and slowly Morgana began her recovery. Most days, Branna would sit on the side of Morgana's bed, and talk of her times living in Avalon with Ariel, and how she too once had a fever, and Ariel had nursed her through it. It was good tonic for both of them, as it helped Branna deal with her loneliness, and Morgana felt close to Branna, and felt that sense of family she had missed after her father died. Morgana also shared her story of meeting Lot and her very first encounter of love making, which came as a big relief to Branna. She had thought it was something Morgana would never do, and that began her tales of the spells she had cast whilst in the midst of her love making with Berengar.

*O*n the seventh day of her stay, she got up and dressed for the first time, and walked slowly down the hallway to Branna's workrooms, where she sat on a stool, as Branna worked. Morgana looked at the crystal box and Ariel within fast asleep, and turned to Branna.

"If it is rude to ask, say so, but I am curious, does sex magic work the same way with a woman?" Branna lifted her head and smiled.

"With Ariel, I found I had a more powerful magic, she also felt the same way. I have often thought of it, and I think it was because she was so dear to me, with her, I think I opened up more, and channelled the energy in a more fluid way. My feelings with Ariel, have always been far more powerful than those I felt with Berengar." Morgana was surprised.

"Really, but if she could not enter you, how did that work?" Branna gave a chuckle.

"Morgana, next time you are alone in bed, slide your fingers down there and copy a man, and then you will understand fully how that works."

She looked down and felt her cheeks go pink, she had never done that, her matron, who cared for her, told her when she was young it was a very wrong thing to do to herself. Branna noted it and chuckled.

"You may be a woman, but you still have much to learn. Who was it?" Morgana looked up.

"Who was what?" Branna smiled.

"The old prude who berated you for it, there must have been someone, tell me?" Morgana breathed in, her cheeks were still quite red.

"I had a matron who cared for me whilst my mother attended affairs. I touched it by accident when washing, and it felt nice so I lingered there, the Matron caught me, dragged me out of the tub, and beat me with a shoe. It hurt so much I had to stand for four days. I have not touched it since." Branna nodded, she understood, there were some in Fae like that.

"My mother told me it was fine, but to go easy, as it could become sore, so I suppose I was lucky, and I learned about myself more. Morgana, you may find at times, it helps, especially if men are scarce."

It felt strange to Morgana that she could talk of things with Branna, she really could not with her mother. Her mother had to a degree been very open with her at times, but Morgana had always felt ill at ease and uncomfortable with those kinds of conversations. Talking with Branna felt different, it was almost as if Branna understood a side of her that her mother had never noticed, and through that, Morgana felt more comfort. In many ways, the bond they had formed was very deep, Morgana looked to Branna like she would a wise parent, and Branna cared and treated for Morgana in a way that felt like she was her own daughter. In an odd sense, both of them needed each other, and it added to their joy to spend time alone, interacting as an infant would with its mother.

*F*or seven days Branna had mixed up a tonic, which was the one Ariel used for her, and so she spent the rest of the afternoon, instructing Morgana on how to make it. She insisted, when she returned, she continued to make it and use it every day, as it would strengthen her, and help her mind focus better. Morgana agreed, and as the evening approached, Branna took her arm, and they walked slowly up the steps to the main hall to join the rest of the family for a meal.

Berengar was delighted to see her up and about, he had visited her room several times, but most of the time she had been asleep. Morgana sat at the table and ate a hearty meal. Maud was quiet and said little, and Otto refused to leave his room, yelling out of the door that he would not sit at a table occupied by a Celt half breed bitch. Morgana heard it and said nothing, she was still very weak and did not want trouble. Branna and Merwig kept the conversation going as Merwig filled her in on how each member of the family was doing in their endeavours. The meal progressed and Morgana was happy, as Maud was behaving, and it fascinated her the way the family worked as one to the soul aim of benefiting the whole family. Towards the end of the meal, Maud looked up and spotted Jarron, sat on the spare perch.

"That half breed bird is unnatural, someone should kill it." She smirked, Morgana dismissively responded, knowing she had to defend the bird that was her lifeline to Branna.

"I am sure Jarron looks at you and feels the same." Maud looked at Morgana with hate.

"At least my blood is pure." Morgana's face was dead pan.

"Pure what… Gargoyle?" Merwig snorted, and looked down, and Rosamund who never smiled, wore a slight smirk. Maud scowled at her.

"You appear brave sat next to the mistress of the house, I do not think you would be so brave alone." Morgana calmly took a drink and swilled out her mouth, and then swallowed as she watched Maud bask in her clever comment.

"When I am fully recovered, let us find out, I am not afraid of you Maud like I was when I first came here. I have been clear all along, I am happy to let you rule, and yet each time you meet me, you insult me more. If it has to come to a matching of skills, let me recover, and then we will meet as equals and settle this, until then, keep your lips sealed around me, for we already know I can beat you verbally."

Branna gave a soft smile as she watched Morgana hold her ground, her eyes moved to Maud who was looking at her with hatred. Her face twisted as she stared at Morgana.

"In order to win, you have to have a fully working mind, and as we all know now, yours is damaged." She sat back with a smug smile, Morgana's eyes lifted up from her plate.

"And yet even with such damage, I outwit you with words, my mind is not so damaged it will strain matching you."

Maud stood up quickly, and Morgana rose slowly with her, her eyes never leaving her, as they both stared at each other across the table. The tension in the air between them was heavy and oppressive. Branna's voice was soft and low, and yet carried caution.

"That is enough, sit down." Morgana lowered into her seat, Branna fixed her eyes on Maud, and her voice rose.

"Now!" Maud looked at her.

"You allow her to disrespect me?" Branna was relaxed and cool, yet her eyes never left Maud, her voice was almost casual.

"You did that yourself when you challenged a weaker opponent. Morgana has been ill, and yet you challenge her, and make threats against her bird. I have warned you before, no one harms my ravens and lives, now sit down." Maud stepped back from her seat.

"I have lost my appetite; I feel sick to the stomach from the stench of half breed filth." She turned and stormed off across the room, Morgana watched her carefully. Branna lifted her glass and took a sip.

"Be wary my little raven, she wants to provoke you while she has the advantage, she will use your weakness against you." Morgana watched as Maud walked up the stairs.

"I know, but I will not allow her to undermine me, even when weakened by illness. Maud will think twice before facing me, weak or strong, I feel it."

"She will challenge you nevertheless Morgana, she feels threatened by you." Morgana turned to Berengar, he too was watching Maud.

"She can be very unstable, and that makes her dangerous, only a fool walks up to a wounded boar. True warriors walk lightly and observe carefully." Morgana smiled.

"It is duly noted grandfather, thank you, I will be cautious." He gave a slight nod, and smiled at her.

*O*ver the next few days, Morgana felt her strength returning at a much faster rate, and she spent a lot of time walking and talking with Branna. They appeared to have much higher spirits, which pleased Berengar, as there had been times in the last months, Branna had slipped back into her old ways of locking her doors and hiding away. The days slipped past, and Morgana found her headaches had completely gone. The rest had done her good, as she sat in her room late one evening and thought back to the last year of her life, a memory flashed through her mind. It was her time at the ritual, shortly before she awakened. She thought of the words, and white face with grey eyes, with long light brown hair surrounding it, as she appeared to look into her dream and smile. her soft words spoke in her mind.

"Shush my little raven, be at peace, rest your mind, for it needs to be healed. I will not let them take you from Branna, she needs you."

It was a strange moment of realisation, she slipped out of bed, and pulled on a long thick robe, and walked quietly down the hallway, as the candles in the brackets on the walls flickered. Morgana gripped the handle, and pushed the door slightly, it opened, and she looked in. The room was empty and almost silent, there was always something distilling and faint bubbling noises in Branna's workroom. Morgana stepped in, and saw the clear crystal box containing Ariel, illuminated by the moonlight. She walked softly over to it and looked down into it, and the face was the same, white, and surrounded by the soft lightest brown hair. Her eyes were closed as if sleeping, so she could not tell their colour, and yet Morgana expected they would be grey. She leaned over to look closer and softly spoke.

"Was it you, were you the one who came to me, did you watch over me? How did you know, or even do that, why did you save me to help Branna?"

"Branna the Raven needs you."

Morgana jumped out of her skin, and clutched at her heart, as she spun around to see Roack on the window ledge. The bird bobbed up and down.

"You are good for Branna the Raven; the woman of light knows that." Morgana regulated her breathing, and spoke quietly as she took several deep breaths to calm herself.

"I do not understand, why me, I am no different to any other family member?" Roack stared at her.

"Branna and the woman of light are as connected as I am, we share her." Morgana frowned.

"Is that even possible, won't her light kill you?" The raven bobbed its head.

"She is no risk to me, as I am no risk to her, our bond is the same, we both protect Branna the Raven." It felt like a curious thing, and Morgana did not really understand it.

"That does not explain me though, why would Ariel come to me, and tell me to heal?"

"Because she loves me deeply, and even though she is in a box, somehow her powers still reach out. Morgana, I care for you as I would a daughter, your mind was straining and I was worried. As I explained, the effort you have used has been vast, and it has put pressure on your mortal side. Mortals fall quicker to the Merle, and yet you have managed to withstand a power equally as strong in the Whitelines. I was concerned and spoke to her, as I do often. If it was Ariel who appeared to you, then she knew you were in need and came to you, for she knows how precious you have become to me, and so therefore protected you."

*B*ranna walked into the room from her chamber, and came up

to her side, she leaned over the box, and smiled at the sleeping face of Ariel.

"Did I not tell you she was loving?" Morgana did not fully understand all of it.

"She is encased in crystal, no power can pass through it, what she did was impossible." Branna gave a slight shrug.

"In theory yes, and yet she managed to come to you. I wear a veil, and yet somehow Eve can see it. The powers passed down from the ancients are far more powerful than any of us really know. Think of it this way, Eve is life, and yet to meet her, she is simply a woman of great beauty with a happy heart, and yet, her eyes can see through a veil. Tell me Morgana, how can she do that?" Morgana shook her head.

"I honestly do not know, Merlin told me I have still got much to learn, but that now is my task alone, and so for now, you ask a question I cannot answer." Branna smiled, and took her hand.

"Come, I will walk you back to your room, it is late and you still need sleep." Branna held her hand, and walked slowly up the hallway back to Morgana's room.

"Morgana, Merlin taught you the language of the ancients, and in doing so, unlocked many powers you have yet to discover. You have years of work ahead of you, and in time as you start to understand all of the ways of men and Fae, you will find you have more abilities than you realise, that is why your mind strained. A time will come soon, when I will be able to unbind your Fae gifts, and when that happens, more things will flow naturally to your mind, and you will achieve great things. The process is not unsimilar to that of a Fae. My mother taught me much, and then sent me out into the world to discover more, and even now after all of these years, I still study, and improve on all I have done. It is the way of our lines, and it is a long road."

"Why soon and not now, if it will take away the risk, why not unbind them now?" Branna stopped at her door.

"Now is not the time, but soon you will have everything in place, and when you do, you will come to me, and we will embrace your gifts and release them. It is time to prepare, for there are challenges to come, and now is the time to work towards them." Branna took her hand and gave it a squeeze.

"The ritual you undertook did to a degree, place more strain on your mind, but that was not all, for the dream sequence was your mind accepting the power, and it also opened deeper aspects of your inner self. It awakened much in you, it is a ritual all Fae go through as children, and we have found that there are lines of men that can also be opened and appreciate our conscious levels of thought, and as it now appears, you are one of them. Morgana, your abilities will be enhanced by this, for your entire being has opened to accept the real truth of who you are." Morgana suddenly understood, and looked her in the eyes feeling the moment of realisation wash over here.

"Is that why I have felt such great desires to take a man, did the ritual awaken that within me?" Branna gave a soft smile as she nodded.

"Yes, Morgana, you have been so focused on your studies, you neglected important parts of yourself, and the ritual reawakened them, so that you will live a more fulfilled existence." It made a strange sort of sense.

"I have been working my mind and neglecting my body, and that is what has caused the headaches. So, it is alright to feel these great desires, and act upon them?" Branna gave a little chuckle.

"There are many pleasures in life Morgana, walking under trees, long deep conversations, eating fine food, and yes, sharing the joy of connecting with someone and acting out your desires. These are all things that sustain the life we live, and all of them are of equal importance to us as people, and the care of our body. Remember, your body has needs, and in that you must allow them." Morgana gave a sigh of relief.

"It pleases me to know this, although in Avalon I am not certain other people will see it that way." Branna turned back to the corridor.

"Trust me, what they call you for, they also enjoy, they are just less truthful about it… Sleep well my little raven, we will talk more tomorrow."

Morgana smiled and walked into her room, she slid back in her bed, and snuggled down, sleep was coming, and she needed it.

*T*he following morning Morgana rose and dressed, and she walked down the hallway towards Branna's workroom, where a guard stood on guard. As Morgana approached, he turned and smiled.

"Lady Morgana, Lady Raven has had to go to the kitchens, there are problems and she was required. She asked that I accompany you up to the main hall where she will meet you." Morgana gave a nod.

"That would be fine, thank you."

He offered his hand to lead the way, and she walked onto the steps up towards the upper floor, and the large main hall of the castle. She was feeling a lot better, certainly stronger, well stronger than she had been when she first came here. His feet made a loud clunk as they hit the steps, the metal studs of his boots really did ring and echo up the stairwell.

She was feeling hungry, and although she had drunk a glass of water on waking, she hoped there would be tea served. The stairs wove round, and were quite narrow, as the guard trudged behind her, and she smiled to herself, as her soft slippers, given her by Branna, made hardly any sound at all.

The door came into view, and there was little sound in the hall, which was normally very busy, although she was a little later than normal, as she had risen later due to her late night talking, and then lay in bed thinking. Morgana walked through the door, into the main hall, lit by the large overhead windows, as shafts of light beamed down onto the floor.

The hall was empty, and the large table had just one place setting, which she assumed Branna had left her. She walked up the hall towards the table, the guard behind her watching over her, as she approached the seat, she heard the familiar squeak of the metal wheels, which she knew was Otto's wheel chair, and gave a sigh. High above her she heard his guttural roll of his throat. She stopped and looked up to see the wheels of the chair, and then Otto's scowling face, with his long white hair and wrinkled expression. He stared at her with his narrowed eyes.

"What are you doing still here, is there no peace from the stench of the Celt?"

Morgana decided to ignore him, until she heard the pronounced 'Tut' that marked Maud's arrival. Realising who it was with him, she turned to face them, as Maud looked down at her with hatred in her eyes.

"We have times for meals, and you may think you are superior with your fancy words and cosying up to my mother, but we have rules here, and meals are served at the right time. I might have known a brain damaged half breed would be incapable." Morgana gave a sigh.

"I was told to come here to meet Branna, not that it is any of your concern, haven't you got a peasant to torture or kill, and just leave me alone?"

Maud gave a snort, and lifted her hand, she gave a sinister smile, and flicked her wrist, Morgana had no idea what she was doing, she had never seen anything like it, Maud looked at the guard.

"NOW!"

Morgana turned to look at the guard, not quite understanding what was happening, when she felt his hands grip her tightly by the neck. His face tensed as he squeezed, and she suddenly realised what was his intent. He pushed, and she stepped back, as her hands came up to his as she tried to grab them, and pull them off her as the air restricted to her lungs. She felt the table against her bottom, as his face screwed up even more, and he pushed harder as his skin turned red. She gasped feeling her throat close, to try and get air into her lungs, which were starting to strain, and heard the sound of Maud as she screeched with joy.

She could just see Maud high up on the balcony, Otto at her side, as he smiled with happiness willing her to die quicker, and Morgana struggled and kicked out at the guard, as panic started to engulf her. Maud was holding out her arm, almost as if she was controlling the guards' arms to squeeze harder. Morgana felt her lungs desperately trying to pull air into them, and she was starting to feel dizzy, but she was not strong enough to pull his hands from her throat, her eyes were starting to fill with tears, and her body was starting to feel even weaker.

The guard pushed her harder, and she fell flat against the table, the crockery behind her pushing into her back, as she fought for her breath, kicking and twisting, as the guard pushed. She looked at him, and realised, his eyes had rolled into the back of his head, she understood he was no longer in control, but knew she did not have much longer, as her head started to feel woozy. From nowhere, in the back of her mind, Merlin spoke.

"Morgana, the following years will guide you forward onto your true path. Now more than ever it is important that you maintain your focus, for the path you follow must be a straight one, even when everything around you, tells you to leave it."

It was a moment of clarity, as she understood his meaning, no matter what she faced, or how bad it got, she had to keep her mind focused. Morgana tried to clear her mind of the panic, and she moved her mind to Maud, and through her tears, she could see the blurry outline of the vile small fat figure. She did not have much longer, as she lifted her hand, and with her palm up, gasping for air, she focused her mind on a spell Merlin had taught her, to move large boulders or trees.

As her body started to fail, in her mind, she focused on the blurred shape of Maud, who was smiling with sadistic joy, whilst Otto egged her on with yelps of appreciation. Morgana closed her eyes, and said the words in her mind, and there was a bright flash, followed by a squeal, and suddenly her throat was free, and she drew in a huge breath, and slid to the floor gasping and spluttering. The guard reeled backwards and crashed onto the floor hard. She breathed in deeply and swallowed hard, as her lungs went into overtime, drawing more air between her coughing and choking. Above her Otto was yelling and screaming, but she could not understand him, as her head pounded in rhythm with her fast heart beats. Morgana felt weak, as she breathed in, her legs were shaking, and eyes streaming with tears.

As she sat on the floor trying to regain her sense, Maud who had been blown completely off her feet by Morgana, dragged herself up on the rail, her face twisted with rage. She pulled herself onto the rail top, and leaned forward, her mouth twisted and disfigured with anger, and lifted her hand to the defenceless gasping Morgana. From nowhere, there was a flash of white, as Jarron, swept through the air, and hit Maud's hand sinking his beak into her wrist. Maud squealed out in pain, and her hand shot up, as a flash of red light shot out of it, Jarron screamed in pain, as the curse from Maud impacted, and passed through his wing.

Morgana, understanding she was still being attacked, shot up her arm, and another streak of white fired out of her, it hit Maud hard, she fell back in shock across Otto. There was an ear splitting scream, as Otto's chair rocked backwards with the force of the spell, and crashed into the floor, with Maud sprawled across him.

Jarron was injured and unable to fly, and dropped out of the air like a stone. Rajani lifted off her perch, and swooped through the air, and caught the bird before it hit the floor. Morgana took a deep breath, as Maud and Otto tried to untangle themselves, and Otto raged with anger. Morgana bent over on her hands and knees, gasping in air and coughing. Maud clawed herself free, and crawled to the rail, and saw Rajani holding the white raven, Jarron.

"KILL IT, KILL IT RAJANI!"

Morgana lifted her head and saw the large black raven holding Jarron in her beak, and she felt an ice cold chill run through her, as she feared the worst for her only solace and companion in Avalon. She sat up and watched, feeling the pain of knowing Maud's raven had to obey her, and yet as she watched, Rajani lifted a foot into the air, and swooped low across the hall towards Morgana.

Rajani landed with a soft click, as her feet hit the wood, and walked the few paces towards her, she watched feeling nervous, unsure of what would happen, as Maud screamed at the top of her voice.

"OBEY ME, AND KILL IT!"

Rajani looked up at Morgana, and then very gently lowered Jarron to the floor, and opened her beak to release him. Jarron lay on his side with blood on his wing. The large raven, looked up at Morgana and their eyes met, the bird gave a slight nod. Understanding the gesture, Morgana spoke with a quiet hoarse voice, through her gasps for air.

"Thank you."

Rajani spread her wings wide, and took off as Maud screamed with hatred at her bird. Morgana had no idea of what just happened, and reached out to lift Jarron, and cradled him in her arms. There was more movement as her heart felt broken seeing her bird injured, and as she looked up, Branna had entered the room and was watching, and it was clear she was very angry. She looked up at the balcony where Maud raged insults at her raven sat on its perch, and had not noticed her. Branna walked slowly down the room towards Morgana, her face on her daughter, who stood screaming at Rajani.

"ENOUGH!"

*M*aud's head snapped round, and she saw Branna, her pupils flickering with red light, her face paler than it had been in a long time, Branna raised her hand towards her daughter.

"HOW DARE YOU DISOBEY ME!" Morgana lifted her head, and saw Maud up above her looking terrified, Branna flicked her wrist as her eyes flared red.

"HOW DARE YOU INJURE MY RAVENS, I WARNED YOU DAUGHTER, YOU WERE TOLD TO LEAVE THEM ALONE!"

Maud gave a startled scream, as she was dragged into the air, and pulled over the edge of the rail, Branna's eyes burned a deep red with her anger. Maud, thinking she would die, defiantly stared at Morgana.

"You do not belong here, we do not want your infected blood in this family, you have no place being here." Branna was furious as she glared at her daughter

"YOU DARE TO CHALLENGE MY COMMAND IN MY OWN HOME? I TOLD YOU, THOSE WHO TOUCH MY RAVENS DIE."

Maud squealed, as she bobbed in the air directly above them, floating around, Branna looked down at Morgana, her voice was soft, but also cold.

"She broke our rules, and tried to kill you… You have the right… Kill her."

Morgana gasped and looked up, Otto had gone silent and stared down from the floor, his face pressed against the rail. Maud looked terrified, as she bobbed in the air, her face white as snow, with wide terrified eyes as she whimpered. Branna's hold was tightening on her, and she was struggling to breathe. Morgana turned to Branna and looked at her, then slowly shook her head. She spoke with a very quiet rasping voice.

"No… Branna, this is not right… Regardless of what has happened, she is still family, she is blood, she is my father's mother. I will not kill her, as much as I hate her, she is still my grandmother." Branna gave a smirk, and her eyes faded back to her black, she softened her tone of voice.

"You have the right, she tried to kill you, and she will again." Morgana sat back holding Jarron in her arms, and looked up at Maud, hanging in the air.

"If she tries again, it will be face to face and fair, and then I will kill her. If she leaves me alone, she will live."

Branna gave a nod, and then swept her wrist left, and Maud flew back over the rail, and went crashing into the wall with a wail.

"So be it." Branna walked over and crouched down to Morgana, and looked at Jarron in her arms.

"How is he?" Morgana looked down at the white raven, she felt hurt, and heartbroken.

"He is badly hurt, can I borrow some of your things, I need to help heal him?" Branna held out her hand.

"Come, you can use whatever you need."

Chapter Twenty Seven.

Another Raven to Rise.

Jarron's wing was badly wounded, and holding her breath, Morgana did all she could for the bird, but it was clear, the wing was very badly damaged. She looked up with tears in her eyes, her throat was painful, and she also felt a pain in her heart. She gave a sniffle as she looked at Branna.

"He is my contact with you, he carries my words to you, and he is the only friend I have in Avalon."

She gave a deep sob, and her sadness and pain flowed out of her. Branna turned, and pulled her close as the injured bird sat on the table, its wing slightly extended and unable to fold in. Branna held her close as Morgana wept.

"Morgana, Jarron will stay with me, and I will ensure he is well cared for and protected. Dry your eyes, he will be fine, and we will have no need of a messenger now, as we will meet in the forest to talk." Morgana lifted her head.

"I will still miss him sat in the tree, or on my window, he has been with me ever since you gave him to me. I know it sounds strange, but I would talk to him and tell him all my thoughts and feelings. Jarron knows me better than anyone." Branna understood.

"I can choose you a new raven, but he was the only white one I had, and the men of your realm fear the black raven as a bird of ill omen, which is precisely why I picked Jarron." Morgana shook her head.

"No, I do not want another, I will never give Maud the chance to hurt me again."

Branna understood Morgana, and she felt it was wise of her to not give Maud another chance to hurt her again, and she was worried that Maud had become so blatant in her opposition to Morgana. She had never thought Maud would go so far, and her use of the spell to control the guard, showed that she was further along than Branna had realised.

"I think you are right Morgana, but you know she sees you as a threat, don't you? She will not stop, you threaten her." Morgana wiped her eyes and sniffled.

"But I am not a threat, I have no wish to rule. Branna, I just want to live a normal life in my cottage, and then hopefully when my mother moves on, I want my father's castle back, and will live there in peace." Branna understood that, but she knew it was not going to be easy.

"Morgana, I feel your Fae powers struggling to break free of their bonds. You may not realise it, but as you have grown, so have your powers. I bound them to prevent them from showing, when they come forth, they will be detectable to some. Eve will see them, and possibly Rhiannon, and when that happens, because of the way you look, they will link that to me. Morgana, I have built a family line here, but in order to protect it from being destroyed, I have had to veil the whole of the realm. You have a personal veil over you, because you cannot walk freely, and a time may come, where here, like it is for me, this may be the only place you are safe. If that happens, Maud will move to destroy you, no matter how you look at it, at some point, you will either face, Eve, Rhiannon, or Maud."

Morgana stood frozen, her eyes so dark and filled with such a powerful spirit, although slightly reddened by her pain of losing Jarron, who would remain forever at the castle. She had always had an air of defiance to her, it was clear she held a great intelligence within her mind, but at this moment, Branna sensed her feelings of helplessness. She took a breath and blinked, and her voice which was strained was lower.

"Then what is the point, what do I do Branna? All I have ever wanted was to live my own life my own way, and on my own terms, and I have been. If they take that away from me, what do I have left?" She gave a small smile.

"All is not lost, I speak of things that could pass, although they may not. Morgana, you have to prepare for every eventuality, you have to look forward and ensure you have the tools to help you survive. Merlin has taught you many of his gifts, but he is still a more skilled opponent, and should you be revealed as of my line, he will come for you. Now is the time to get ready, for very shortly, your Fae powers will be unleashed, and when they do, you will have to be ready." Morgana gave a nod.

"So how will I do that?" Branna reached out her hand.

"Come, and I will show you."

Branna took her hand, and led her up to the higher battlements of the castle. She walked her out onto the wide walkways, and stood in front of her.

"I know Merlin has the gift of passage; Ariel told me of how she saw his white tunnel open. It is a gift used by both Whiteline and Green Circle, as we Fae transform when need arises, as I did to come to you in your sickness. You are part Fae, but not full Fae, you will not transform to move, although you may be able to transform your appearance. Tell me, did Merlin teach you the right of passage?" Morgana gave a nod, as she tried to understand why Branna would want to know this.

"He taught me, but I am still very new to it. He did say in time I would be able to move great distances, but at the moment, I have not gone further than a few yards." Branna understood.

"The tunnel is complex, because it is visual, which is why Fae use something different and not as identifiable. Morgana if you can use what Merlin taught you, and mix it with Fae, you may have a simpler and fast means of passage." Morgana frowned.

"How would I do that?" Branna gave a giggle.

"I will teach you, the very same way my mother taught me."

Branna's lesson started with Morgana showing her what Merlin had taught her, which was she created a pale circle, and walked into it. Five yards ahead the circle reappeared and she walked out. Branna explained how it took great mind power, but the Fae had simplified it, and she talked Morgana through the process, exactly as her own mother had taught her. Her method was simply to consider the point to travel to, and instead of visualising a circle or tunnel, to simply make it a fine smoke.

It took a little practice, but within the hour, white smoke swirled up around Morgana, and as it broke apart, Morgana had vanished. Ten yards away the white smoke came up through the floor and swirled into a cloud, and as it dissipated, she stood smiling. She was delighted with her progress and excitedly talked of how amazing it was, and Branna was happy to see the sadness within her fade away.

As they walked back to the workroom, down the stone stairs, Branna talked to her.

"You must practice, and the more you do, the further you will be able to travel. It is less taxing to your mind, and as a result, it is faster, and will allow you to move with ease and not become tired. Morgana, if you get into a difficult position, you will be able to move quickly and leave no trace. The problem with Merlin's tunnel, is there is always a risk another will try to follow, the way I have shown you, makes it impossible, because as the smoke thins, the door is already closed. Such is the speed of this, it is but the tiniest of moments, and those around you, even if they try to act, it will be too late. This was Enaria's gift to both races of Fae, it has just been adapted by us, to match the Whitelines."

It was an important moment for Morgana, for she had plans for revenge, the problem was, she was the primary suspect in Avalon for everything that went wrong. Her new ability would allow her to move so quickly, she could not be tracked, and would create the appearance of being in two places at once. All she had to do, was jump and be in a different place in full view, and Branna knew that to a degree, it would help her defend herself against Rhiannon.

For four more days, Branna and Morgana practiced and talked. Morgana discussed ideas for the realm of the Chimerical Forest, and what she would like to do there. Branna helped her understand the charm made with the essence of Sandlings, and taught her the Fae skills of collecting the essence of creatures to use as spiritual enhancers of her spells. Morgana as always learned very quickly and adapted the new knowledge to mix with her Whiteline powers. She had much in mind, as her final day arrived.

Branna carried her to the Chimerical Forest, and there she said her farewells for now, and left Morgana to head back into Avalon. As she made her way back to her cottage home, Morgana was stronger and healthier than she had been in many years, which was due to the tonic Branna had made for her, and her mind was sharper than it had ever been. Her powers were growing deep within her, and soon it would be time to begin her rise out of the poverty of her current life, to a greater status.

*O*ver the year that followed, Arthur continued to finish off his castle, as he re-tied the links with his Pendragon line, and the Sachsen survivors of the first landings, built up their lands, which were fertile and their ability to farm, gave them a great advantage. Their influence spread all around them, and their beliefs and customs seeped into those tribes who were considered the true people of the land, and had helped repel Rome. All the while the Christian belief spread, as due to its similarities to the Earth Faith beliefs of the peoples, it made it easy to convert, and with it came more unity under Arthur. Rhiannon, just like Branna, felt concerned that the men of the world, were turning against the beliefs of the council, and her influence began to wane.

As the word spread, Branna's people found those from the lower levels of the Germanic population, moved and spread across the sea, and landed on the shores of what was now being referred to as the Britannica Isles. Christianity spread like a virus, and tribes began to be united by it, as the land under Arthur a new Christian king flourished. Morgana settled into her life and worked away slowly filling her cave with work benches, and the herbs and minerals to mix up and give more power to her spells.

All appeared to be going well as the country prospered, until gossip started. Morgana was met when she visited the castle by Tor and Lot, both of them loyal to Arthur, and escorted to her rooms, where she met with representatives of her family, one of whom, was Gerta. Morgana met her in private.

"My Lady Berengar, we are here because your brother has ruled that our faith is a sin against his God. We are to be spread out, and our site of worship wiped away." Morgana listened carefully.

"Tell me more of this." Gerta explained.

"Our belief is twinned with those of the druids who were there before us, and the similar beliefs brought to us by your late father Victor. Those stones that we pray at, have been here for many generations, and yet we are told our belief is wrong, and we must bow down to your brother's god. We cannot do this, for we do not hold a belief in this being." Morgana understood.

"Your queen is my mother, have you spoken to her about this?" Gerta gave a nod.

"She has not the power to do anything, she has lost much influence, especially since the debts at Tintagel have built up. My Lady, she needs the revenue of the king to keep her going."

It made no sense to her, the lands around Tintagel to which she managed were fruitful, and the income from it were plentiful. The grain stores made a good income, and their trade from the sea, of which many sailed up from Gaul and Hispanica, made a large revenue for Tintagel. She spoke at length to Gerta, and discovered much of what was happening around the court of the king, including one tale, that interested her greatly, as it involved the queen. Gerta explained.

"Some say, they have seen the way the queen looks at Lancelot, and it is the same look worn in the eyes of the women on the day of the gathering. My Lady, people say she temps the knight, and he longs for her also, and she has taken to looking away from the king in disinterest. They say because she has no heir, she looks for one who will provide her one, and Lancelot stays away because he lusts after the queen, and her, him."

It sounded strange, she knew Arthur was devoted to Guinevere, and she was uncertain, although, she remembered many years back, and the moment she had noted the way Lancelot looked at her. She spoke of many things, and gave her word she would talk to her mother and brother, and when she had gone, she changed her clothing and headed out to find Arthur. As she came onto the top of the steps, she heard her name and turned to see Merlin.

"I am surprised to see you here." Morgana walked towards him.

"Why, my brother is the king, and my mother his supporter? It is not unusual for me to visit here; I have been several times." Merlin gave a nod, and looked over the balcony rail.

"Your brother is not here, he is in the east, meeting with chieftains of loyalty to the new Christ." Morgana stood looking at him with wonder, not really understanding why Merlin was so calm about it.

"Why have you not stopped him, his new faith denies the existence of Avalon and all the ruling council, is it right a king of this land turns his back on generations of belief? Merlin, even you were revered by the druids of the lands of Pendragon, you know they are the spiritual guides who follow the faith of the earth, as taught by Hearne and Eve." Merlin considered the question.

"Simply put, they do not threaten us, this land has had many masters, the Romani, the Saxon, and even the Viking, who even as we speak build their small empire in the middle of this land. Times are changing Morgana, and this belief in this Christian is the one thing that unites them with the king. I fear it will spread much wider, and one day it will be the only belief of this land. We cannot prevent the freedoms of thought of the men of this realm." Morgana shook her head.

"Why not, it was you and your council that murdered my father and took control, with men of the Earth Faith? My brother only has a seat as he was backed by the druids of his line, how can you advise the king to be so disrespectful to those who gave his father and now him, his seat?" Merlin sighed.

"Even now you cannot see further than the past, Morgana you must open your eyes and embrace the new." She gave a snort.

"I may not agree with them always, I most certainly do not agree in the way they took my father's home and seat of power and handed it to a brute and rapist, but if what you are saying is true, then you are saying Gwendolyn, Hearne, Eve, Rhiannon, and even you, are now meaningless in the world of men. How can you turn your back on the Lord of the Whitelines, when you have lived with his power to help you seat a king, who is now destroying all that we all have stood for?" Merlin gave a nod; he understood her point.

"Morgana, the world of men has grown, which was our plan, but our time is coming to stand aside and let them rule with freedom. We cannot hold back a line because they believe in something new, and I may add, runs parallel with the faith of old." She could not accept it at all.

"So, what do we do, simply give up and fade away, and allow my brother to force people of the Earth Faith to worship his new god?" He gave a smile.

"Morgana, you are of the line of men, but we are not, we have our own lands, and the places where we will prosper. There are many realms, why do you worry such, there is much we can do, but not in this realm?" She shook her head, and backed away.

"Not me, Tintagel is my home and place of birth, and no matter what he does, he will not tarnish that sacred place with his talk of a god no one has ever encountered." Merlin looked at her.

"Morgana, you have spent too much time alone in your cottage, Tintagel is falling into disrepair. It has seen its day; it too should fade into the past." She could not believe what she was hearing, and felt angry and betrayed by him.

"You may have given up Merlin, but I will never give up on my home. My father built that castle, and not Arthur or you have the means to take it from me, or allow it to fall." She spun on her heels and walked out, as Merlin called back to her.

"MORGANA!" It was too late, she had gone.

$\mathcal{S}$he headed to her room, packed, got into her carriage and headed to Tintagel, and was shocked to see it when she arrived a day later. The lands all around were all fertile, and the fields were filled with a bounty of crops, it made no sense to her that her mother who was the owner of all the lands surrounding, had allowed the castle of her father to suffer.

She stormed into the castle to be met by Lothar sat with her mother. She was angry and it showed as she stood before them fuming inside.

"How could you do this, how could you let his castle become in such a state of disrepair, the fields are full and flowing with bounty, how could you allow this?" Lothar got up from his seat, and held out his palms.

"Morgana, yelling is pointless, sit and listen to us, things are not as simple as you think." She nodded, Merlin had already informed her, but she was not interested in what he thought, all she cared about was preserving her father's legacy.

Lothar sat her down, and began to tell her of what had happened whilst she was in Avalon, and how Arthur had ruled from the castle for many years, as his new castle was built in the kingdom of the Pendragon clan. The funds of Tintagel had been drained, as the expense of a new place to rule mounted, and more and more of the land's earnings had been taken to cover the increasing costs. Igraine looked saddened, and added as Lothar finished.

"Morgana, it is a small price to pay for the peace we have lived under, he is our king, and we are loyal subjects, every kingdom has contributed to his rule." Morgana shook her head.

"I do not care, this castle was not his to steal from, it is mine by right after you are gone. You are queen to a celt line that still supports you, why did you not reach out to them for help, they would have come to your aid?" Igraine smiled.

"And do what Morgana, start another war? Look at us, we have no funds for an army, or wish for a war, we are only just living the meagre life we now have." Lothar agreed with her mother.

"I have done the best I can Morgana, but a silken purse cannot be fashioned out of a sow's ear, he is the king, what choice do we have?" She understood, and calmed down a little.

"I am not sure, but it bothers me that he is filled with this Christian worship and wiping away the beliefs of our people. Even the Ruling Council who I despise are giving up, and they will fade away and leave us alone in this land with a brother ruling who has no control of his purse strings, we have to stop him." Lothar gave a smile.

"I admire your loyalty to these people, but Morgana, he is a king, how can we stop the man who rules all of this land, with the loyalty of every lord from sea to sea?"

"I cannot answer that yet, but I will… I need time to think this out, and then I will try."

Igraine loved her daughter dearly, she stood up, and walked over, and embraced her, with great affection, her voice was soft.

"Morgana, your father would be so proud of you, for you are very like him, but I fear, our time is now over. Things are changing, and a new world is growing, the time for us to fade are upon us as the new powers rise up." Morgana looked at Lothar as he watched on.

"I wish people would stop telling me that." He simply looked at her.

"But it is true Morgana, our time is over." She stepped back from her mother.

"Not mine… If they really want a new power, then I will give them one. I will give them one they will never forget." Lothar gave a sigh.

"How, he has every lord of this whole realm eating out of his hand? Morgana, you can only do this with a war, and there is no stomach for it, the lords grow richer by the day under the rule of Arthur? Morgana you will be completely alone."

"That is fine by me, I have always been alone, but you mark my words this day Lothar, I will stop him. He is not the only power that can rise, and I will prove it."

Without waiting, Morgana left immediately and would not listen to either of them, she had only one thing in mind, and that was to stop Arthur. She travelled back to the castle of Arthur to await his return, and settled in her room to wait and confront him. Over a week passed as she sat alone each day, separated from all of the other women, who appeared to look down on her, but she stayed close enough to hear the gossip.

 Word soon came that Gwendolyn was indisposed of, as her daughter Una was with child, it was the scandal of the realm of

Avalon, as a Lord Kane had taken advantage of her and promised her marriage after he left his wife. He had fooled the young Una and left her with child, and so Gwendolyn had taken her away to birth the child in secret. Morgana smiled, she knew of Una who was supposed to be intelligent, and yet Una had fallen for his fake charm, something she had not, many years ago.

One of Gwendolyn's other daughters had married Tor and had a son, and yet Tor had said nothing when he escorted her here, although to be honest, why would he, none of the Fae elites, had anything to do with her, everyone saw her as lesser than them? As she sat listening, she began to formulate a plan that could help her influence Arthur quicker, and she knew that in order to do that, her priority was to get her new domain established in the other realm of the Chimerical Forest. She had not been fast enough, her cave was set and ready, and she had been practicing and had greatly improved, but with her Fae powers bound, she knew, the only way to stop Arthur destroying Tintagel, was to be released from her bonds.

*T*hat evening Lot arrived back with a smile, he was with Gawain, and Percival, Morgana left them to feast knowing Lot would visit her later. She ate alone in her room, and when all her plates had been cleared, she decided to walk up to the battlements for air, she was killing time, as she knew Lot would be at least another hour. On the battlements, Gawain stood watching out across the countryside, he had a lost look in his eyes, as he stared into space. Morgana knew that the one thing she had that few did, was she understood the minds of fighting men, especially their pride, and in regard to Gawain, that was his weakness. Gawain was a great knight who had proved his worth many times, and yet the king only recognised Lancelot for his valour, and that irked Gawain. She walked up, and he noticed and turned.

"Lady Morgana, I am surprised to find you here, is this not too high for the sensitivities for a lady?" She gave a courteous smile.

"I have heard the gossip; few think I am worthy of the title of Lady. I like it up here, I like to take the air, and enjoy the peace, I find the castle too busy and too filled with idle gossip, it distracts my thoughts." Gawain appeared to understand.

"Tongues wag too easily these days." Morgana leaned on the wall and looked out.

"If there was not a cause, they would be forced to remain still." He turned his head.

"You feel there is just cause in the things being spread?" Morgana stared at the stars.

"I think in some cases, they are not wrong." She knew exactly what she was doing, and Gawain was falling for it completely.

"In what way is there truth in what the ladies discuss?" She smiled.

"When a queen looks at a knight as she once did her husband, it is noted by the women, after all, we read those signs far better than the men of this land ever have." Gawain leaned off the wall.

"I know nothing of this, of what do you speak, for if there is gossip of the queen, we should know?" Morgana turned, and looked at him.

"What good would that do? The king is heavily dependent on Lancelot, they are loyal friends… Well, Arthur is, I am uncertain as to Lancelot, he draws the eyes of the ladies. Although, he has stayed away a lot from the table at times, maybe he hides his shame for coveting something he should never ask for." Gawain looked mortified.

"You know there is truth in these rumours?" Morgana simply smiled at him, knowing the seed has been planted.

"If you do not believe me, watch for yourself, you will see the ladies speak of truths in amongst their fantasies."

It was enough, and the spark to burn down a kingdom, and she had just handed it to the one knight she knew was envious of many things. Guinevere was indeed a beautiful woman, and it was no secret that everyone was smitten with her, but Gawain would never be able to accept that another man had taken her, and she looked into his eyes and saw he was already feeling jealous. He had the very same look she had seen in Uther's eyes as a child, when he looked at Igraine sat at her father's side. Men were so easy at times to predict, and all she needed to do was give just the slightest hint, and she knew it would eat away and fester inside Gawain, for it was no secret, he wanted more authority, and the kings second, was the highest he could rise, but Lancelot prevented it."

She left Gawain, and walked down to her room, and soon after, there was a knock on the door. Lot had arrived, and she intended to amuse herself, after all, she had a busy time coming, as she moved to save her father's castle, and prove Arthur was not the mighty honourable king he had pretended to be.

Chapter Twenty Eight.

The Turning Tides.

Morgana was waiting when Arthur returned, and she confronted him. Arthur smirked in front of his men, as she made it clear, not one more penny, would flow from Tintagel to his castle. Her temper was more than evident, as she threatened him, and told him to stay away from her father's castle, she was powerful, and quite a few who observed were terrified of her. She stormed out of the castle, and in an explosion of white smoke she reappeared at Tintagel, which was the longest distance she had ever travelled, which she attributed to her temper.

At Tintagel castle, she met with Gerta and gathered all the men from the Druid and Woad lines who had sworn to back the queen, and make a stand against the Christian God. Having spoken with them, riders were despatched to spread the word to others, and Morgana ordered the guards loyal to her, to throw out all of Arthur's men and seal the gate. Tintagel had made a bold move against the unity of Arthur, but Morgana knew, that even though the castle may be a little in a state of disrepair, it was still an unbeatable stronghold. She could hold off anything Arthur sent, just as her father had held off Uther. This time, she would not make the same error as her father, she would keep the castle closed to anyone from Arthur's court, or military, and she would never ride out after a king she no longer respected. Arthur was angered by her action, and spoke at the table with his men, and it was agreed, some example was needed to be made of her, the only question was what?

Two weeks later, calamity hit the court of Arthur, as Gawain, backed by Sir Meliaguant and others, called out Lancelot, and asked why he never came to the round table? He then suggested it was because of the attentions of a married woman, and accused Guinevere of being a temptress and hiding her desire. Arthur exploded, and demanded satisfaction, to reclaim the queen's honour. The news went fast around the country, as the accusation had been made and could not be retracted. Guinevere pleaded her innocence, but many of the ladies of court spoke to their husbands and admitted, Gawain was not far wrong. Morgana was right, and Gawain had been the perfect choice to sow the seeds of discontent, and while Arthur struggled, and having instructed Lothar, she made her way back to Avalon and her cottage, to prepare for what came next. Merlin arrived shortly after.

Merlin pushed open her door with force, and stormed into her cottage, as she sat at her table reading her notes, surrounded by bottles and bags of dried herbs. He looked very angry as he turned to face her.

"This has your stamp all over it, I know it was you, do you realise the damage that has been done in the court of Arthur?" Morgana looked up unconcerned.

"Do you always barge into the houses of others without knocking, I was studying the runes of the taking spell… I still struggle to remember it?" He gave a sigh.

"Do not play games with me Morgana, I know it was you who started the gossip that accuses Guinevere of misconduct with Lancelot. Why… Why destroy his kingdom, for what, an old relic of a building built by your father?" Morgana bit her lip, and tried to hold back her anger.

"You call it an old relic, well it was certainly good enough for you to send that rapist into it, and he as I remember, had no problems living there in a luxury he never deserved. You have a nerve accusing me, the gossips were talking long before the accusation was made. I will not deny, even I heard those wittering women, as they sat like pheasants at a feeding basket chirping away. You point the finger at me when there are at least a hundred in that castle, whose tongues have been wagging for months, you are just the same as Rhiannon." He seemed to ease up a little.

"Are you telling me the truth?" She looked offended.

"What… Are you seriously saying you cannot tell, ask any of those wilted old prudes, I am sure a big brave wizard like you can extract the truth out of one feeble woman?" Merlin appeared to calm down, as she watched him, and gave a snort.

"So much for loyalty to your student, I understand we do not agree on a lot of things, but that is because I struggle to understand why you would sell out everything you and the council have built. You all planned to seat him, and his father before him, and yet he has betrayed you and turned to the other side and his new God. Why Merlin, tell me, why let him just walk away after all you have done?" Merlin gave a slight nod; he understood her struggle with her understanding of this.

"Morgana, why does it matter, why are you of all people so angry about this, you have expressed your objection and resistance to the council since the death of your father?" Morgana stood up, and placed her notes on the table.

"Yes, I will not deny, had all of you not conspired, my father would be alive and my life maybe could have been better. I despise the council for their part in his death, but I have always understood the symbols they are to their people. I do not care what any of you think, allowing this new god into the head of the king and forcing the people to believe something that their lives can never touch is wrong Merlin, why can you not see that? All of us in this land have ancients who walked before us, it is who we are, and when the tribes of the Romani came, we resisted them, and yes, Uther and Arthur have both played their parts in pushing them out. I may not like the council as people, but the people of this land believed in all of you, and they looked to you for guidance, and for what, to be told they are no longer relevant? Generations of belief are to be simply snuffed out, because precious Arthur has a cross around his neck. We are of the earth, not Romani, that is our identity, and yet Arthur and his new god call us heathen, pagan, peasant, how could you let that happen?" He gave a slight laugh, and looked at her.

"I find myself quite surprised Morgana, and such passion for your conviction, I do believe you have matured well. Morgana, ask any of us, we will all tell you, this Christ is spreading like fire on dry plains, we cannot hold back change, if we try, we will lose everything. The realm of men is destined to follow their own will, yes, we will at times be called upon, but many will follow this new god and leave the beliefs of the past behind, it was always destined to happen. The lines of Fae will continue, as will our line of white and the green, but ultimately it is up to them." Morgana shook her head.

"No, it is not, Arthur has already told many of my line they can no longer meet in their sacred places. Arthur intends to kill all of it, and I am sorry, but I will not allow that. My family have the right, as my mother did to follow their belief, and no king has the right to stop them. My mother is a highly regarded and respected queen of her people, and yet she was treated as lesser by Uther who saw her as a mere prize to warm a king's bed, and now his son is doing it again, by wiping away the memory of her people. Merlin, I will defend them to the death if I have to, isn't that what you have taught me, to stand beside the people under our protection?"

In many ways he admired her, this was the first time he had ever seen her speak with such passion in defence of any people. She had always been so isolated and alone, and yet as he watched her bright dark eyes shine with her conviction, he actually felt very proud of her. He nodded his head.

"Alright Morgana, you feel connected to these people, argue their case to the king and protect them, for that is what a fellow of the Whitelines should do. Now tell me, why do you study the spell of making?" She shrugged.

"It is the one spell I could never truly master, I have done all the others, I suppose it is pride, I want to be fluent in them all. Saying it all in my head and reciting it, is difficult, the lines always get mixed up in my head, and I get the spell wrong. I guess I just want to master it, as I have all the others." He could understand that.

"It is the phrasing, belief, and the order of the words that are important, it is not easy, it was never meant to be, come, whilst I am here, sound it out for me."

Morgana looked at the parchment for a few moments, and then turned it over. She took a deep breath, closed her eyes, and then started the spell.

"Nowled nay destraught, draw be mitt hanta… Nowled nay craf devow mitt…" She opened her eyes and stared at Merlin, and bit her lip and squeezed her fist as if struggling to remember, he gave a weary sigh.

"It's POW."

Morgana smiled, and lifted a bottle off her table, as Merlin realised what he had done. He had spoken the end of the spell, and in doing so, given Morgana the power to take his essence. He stood frozen unable to move, as a wind began to swirl at his feet, and he felt himself sucked up into the air, and drawn into the bottle in Morgana's hand. Merlin was now her prisoner, she pushed in the cork, and smiled, as she looked at the bottle of swirling mist.

"All that work and boasting, and look at you now, defeated by flattery and pride, the very things you warned me of. What an old fool, caught in your own web of the deceit you spun. That is the price that you pay Merlin for the death of my father, and the desertion of my people, sleep well old wizard."

It was a defining moment in her life, and she could not help but feel the joy. She had thought of this for a long time, and had prepared this for over three years. Now she had him, all she needed to do was make sure no one could find him. She slipped the bottle into her pocket, and grabbed her bag, and then headed for the door, on route to her cave.

*T*he disappearance of Merlin was not noticed at first, after all, it was normal for him to go off and attend to other things. Everyone carried on regardless without him, including Arthur, who had his hands full with the growing problem of court, and the speculation as to whether Lancelot would come back, to face a trial by combat to prove his queen's innocence. One of his accusers who had backed up Gawain, Sir Meliaguant, fought Lancelot, and was beaten in brutal combat, when Lancelot cleaved his head into two parts, and Guinevere was spared from the accusation of adultery. All of this was done without Merlin to advise Arthur of what to do, and Arthur felt angry at the wizard, but he had no idea of the scheme of his half sister, Morgana.

Lancelot was wounded during the fight, and left the castle, and headed to his small camp in a sacred woodland to take care of himself, and pray. When word was received of his injury, Guinevere went to him in an act of thanks to help care for his wound, and as she tended him with great care, she was overcome, and she slid into an embrace of him, and they kissed. That night in the sacred woodland, Guinevere and Lancelot made love under the stars, and Morgana had been proven to be right on the day when she pointed out to Gwendolyn at the castle that there was an undercurrent of adultery.

Arthur was informed of his wife's decision to go to give medical aid to Lancelot, and he headed to the woodland, where he found them both naked and curled together, after their lovemaking, asleep. He was so heartbroken, he pulled out Excalibur, with every intention of killing them, but the truth was, he loved Guinevere with all of his heart, and saw Lancelot as a brother. In his devastation, he pushed the tip of his sword into the soft earth next to their heads, and left, leaving the gleaming blade behind him, and headed back to his castle a broken man. The dream of Arthur was dying, the circle of friendship and honour that had been the basis of his dream of the round table, lay shattered, and Arthur slipped into a deep melancholy.

The following morning Guinevere awoke to find the sword of her husband, and after waking Lancelot, she fled the scene in heartbroken guilt, for in truth, Arthur had been a good and loving husband, and she did love him and realised her folly. Lancelot was filled with despair and guilt, and rode off on his horse, and was not seen again for many years. Guinevere entered a convent at Amesbury, and through all of the months that followed, Morgana worked in the hidden realm clearing the way to begin work on her own castle, one no king would ever try to steal.

*F*ar away from everything, living on a boat on the rivers and inlets of the country, the Magpie sailed side by side with the Harebell. Dorin had done a great deal of work to the boat, and it was looking much better, as the life of transporting goods up the estuaries was a good way to earn money. Dorin and Ena had joined in handfast, and within six months, Ena had become with child, and as they sailed towards the old city of Londinium, two months prior, Ena had given birth to a small female child, whom she named Ursula.

It had started out as a joke, she was small and dark haired, and yet appeared to be filled with life, alert and adventurous. Ursula stood for 'Little She Bear.' Dorin had come up with it, as he had heard of a great warrior named such, who had led a thousand female warriors into battle, and he knew at some point, she would be involved with her mother's plans to battle the dark lands and free Ariel.

Ena had grown strong and powerful under the watchful eye of Bella, and she had undergone a full education of the powers of the Fae, and had learned many new skills. She also had learned a great deal about the Berengar line, both under and outside of the veil. Ena and Bella had access to news and gossip in every dock and mooring they arrived at, and between them, they had a full picture of Lothar, Rosamund, and Morgana. News of Arthur and the gossip over his wife and best friend were rife, but the news that capped everything, was that there was a rumour that Merlin had disappeared.

The boats were tied up and Dorin had gone for supplies, Ena held

Ursula as she slept in her arms, having just finished feeding, as Bella sat at the table with her drink of flowery tea.

"It cannot be Morgana, Merlin is too powerful, she is but part Fae, I find it hard to believe she could overpower a wizard such as him." Bella sipped as she thought about it, her eyes lifted from her cup as the boat gently rocked.

"What if it was the both of them, what if the Raven helped her?" Ena frowned, and shook her head.

"She never leaves the realm, and I doubt she could go to Avalon, if she did, wouldn't Rhiannon see her and kill her? Rhiannon is a powerful queen; you could not hide in her realm." Bella shrugged her shoulders.

"Who then? The Druids have spoken out against Arthur and Merlin defended him, they are very unhappy about that and have said Merlin betrayed them. The Woad's also said the same, do you think they had something to do with it, after all, there are many at Tintagel according to Dingle, he travelled around the coast from over there?"

Ena sat back, and slipped her breast back into her dress, she smiled at the tiny dark haired figure in her arms, and looked back up towards Bella, who was also smiling.

"I am sure the Druids or the Woad's would announce him as theirs, they would not hide it if he was their prisoner, and I cannot believe it is Morgana, so who else could it be?" Bella shook her head, both of them were at a dead end.

"I am not sure, but know this, whoever has taken him, they hide a mighty power to have overcome him." It felt like a sobering moment for Ena, something was not right, she could feel it, and that really did bother her.

*O*n the steps of the House of Scribes at Florae, there was a blinding flash, and Gwendolyn appeared with Madeline her eldest daughter beside her, she walked at a fast pace up the steps, as the guards snapped to attention. Gwendolyn walked quickly through the doors and into the house, not stopping as Bade jumped to his feet. Before he could speak a word, she was in the hallway down to her private apartments, Bade gave a little skip, and hurried off after her. When he arrived at her rooms, Gwendolyn was already at her table leaning over, trying to discover the whereabouts of her husband.

Bade stood in the doorway and watched, as her hand moved

quickly and her eyes flared with blue light, he wanted to speak, but knew this was not the right time. Madeleine leant over the table at her side, watching the images flow across the surface.

"Mother, there is no sign of him, the last time he was seen was at home." Gwendolyn leaned back from the table.

"If my table cannot see him, then he is in grave trouble. This is hopeless, Rhiannon has so many protections on her realm, it is impossible to see anything, the detail is mixed up, and nothing appears to be as it was." Madeline gave a nod.

"You know what she is like, Sequana talks of shadows in the realm, and how Tideguyde will return, and Rhiannon is becoming so obsessed with her fear of being killed like Eleanor, she has endless new spells cast to hide all from her realm?"

Gwendolyn turned at her table and walked to her seat, she sat down to think, her mind was in turmoil, and she was becoming afraid, she leaned back and closed her eyes.

"Something is deeply wrong, and yet I feel I am blind." Madeleine walked over, and sat in the seat beside her, and took her hand and squeezed it.

"You are upset, Father is everything to all of us, you know him, he will resurface." Gwendolyn gave a long sigh, and opened her eyes.

"I have such a deep fear within me, oh how I wish Ariel was here, she would see through it all." Madeleine smiled.

"We will find him. We know his last destination was Avalon, so where would he go when he was in there?" Gwendolyn did not need to think.

"He always visited Rhiannon, and Morgana, and then at times the green lord or Lady Eve. The green lord is in the north with Opal, so he would not have met Merlin. On occasion he would speak with the maker, but it has not been that often since Morgana completed her training." Bade stepped forward.

"I beg your pardon, your highness, but as you know, there has been a great deal of speculation of late, and we do know that Lord Merlin felt Morgana was involved in the accusations of the queen's disloyalty to the king of that realm. I am sure he would have gone to see her to find out what her role was." Gwendolyn looked at him standing in the doorway.

"Bade I am sure Morgana was no threat, she was a good student, and has surprised all of us, but I doubt she would have the capabilities to do harm to my husband, he was very powerful, far more than I feel she is." Bade gave a nod of his head.

"Has anyone spoken with her?" Gwendolyn gave a sigh.

"I hope not, because the only one who would, is probably Rhiannon, and if she is aware Merlin is missing, she will have her in irons and chains before we know it. If this was her husband, the odds are no one of dark hair would be alive in Avalon now." Madeline turned to Bade as he stood in the door pondering the problem.

"The problem is Lord Bade, finding her. The Queen of the Moon made her life so hard, she cast a veil onto her person to stop the queen tracking her. No one really knows where she is." Gwendolyn considered the point.

"Finding her will be hard, especially if she is not at the cottage. Be honest, if word reaches her Merlin is missing, she will panic as she is aware Rhiannon has not forgotten her, Morgana could very well go into hiding. She may be with her mother, they have grown closer in recent years, I doubt she will be with Arthur. He has not forgiven her for challenging him, although to be honest, I did feel Morgana had a point, his spending has drained most of the Tintagel estate of funds. I felt she was right to defend her father's castle and estate." She gave a long sigh.

"Madeleine, I want you to go to Una and take her the supplies we have for her, her time is close. Will Maurice be alright with your daughters a while longer, I need to talk to Melanie? If so, I will try and find Morgana and talk with her." She nodded.

"He will be fine, he has two maids to assist, although I will need to return to Carnac, as soon as Una has delivered her child, Maurice is not good with young children."

Morgana was in Avalon, having hidden Merlin, stored in his essence form, she was out near the water's edge of the large lake collecting cuttings of plants to grow, in what had become her thriving garden. She was on her knees clipping small leaf stems, when she looked up and saw Eve watching her. Morgana stood up slowly and gave a bow.

"My Lady of the Woodland Realm, my apologies, I did not see you there." Eve gave a slight smile, as her violet eyes studied Morgana, who felt a little worried.

"Why do I feel the shadow of this realm around you?" Morgana frowned.

"My Lady, I have no knowledge of what you speak." Eve did not move; it was almost as if she was feeling everything around her. Her eyes moved to each side of Morgana, as if she was looking for something.

"Your veil is good, it will certainly keep the Queen of Fae from seeing you, but I see many other things than my Fae sisters, and I feel something more to you than most others, what is it I feel?"

Morgana felt apprehensive, was Eve seeing something within her no other could detect? She gave a shrug and felt more than a little nervous, and alarmed there was something following her.

"I feel concerned that you think there are shadows with me, do you mean from the past, do I have a spectre of the dead with me?" Eve smiled.

"No… It is not that sort of shadow, it puzzles me so, for your power is white, and yet I sense something similar, something I have encountered before. What does the name Branna mean to you?" Morgana felt a small jolt of panic, but did her best to try and remain as casual as possible, under the scrutiny of Eve.

"They say that the story of her is exaggerated, and that she was made a scapegoat by Rhiannon and fled the realm to live in the world of men. They say Rhiannon blamed her for crimes against the throne. Some say it is all rubbish and just an old wife's tale to frighten children." Eve gave a small chuckle.

"Branna was real, I once saw her with Ariel. Do you know that you look like her?" Morgana could not help but gasp out loud, and tried to cover her reaction.

"Do I?" Eve nodded.

"Very much so, I am sure you could pass for her daughter." Morgana had no idea what to do, her mind moved quickly to try and find a quick answer. One that would convince Eve that she had no connection with her.

"If the myths are as true as you say, from what I understand of the gossips, Branna lived at least two hundred years ago, and I am but thirty eight summers, born of Victor and Igraine. This Branna would also be of Fae, of which I am not." Eve tilted her head to one side.

"Are you so certain, the shadow I feel is Fae?" Morgana gave a quick nod.

"I am quite certain; I am born of a man, and a woman of high standing in her druid line." Eve smiled.

"Yes, I knew your great grandfather well, he had a powerful spirit, and was a dedicated servant of his people, until the Romani cut him down. I was saddened by that." Morgana took a breath, hoping she had distracted Eve away from her line of questions.

"My mother talked of him often when I was a child, she loved him dearly." Eve turned on the path.

"The flowers of your garden bloom white and often, it pleases me to see it." Morgana felt the relief of the moment.

"Yes… I am very happy to see it grow so large; I have helped many in the realm of men with the flowers." Eve walked on a little, then stopped and turned to look back.

"Keep it white Morgana, for then you know you are on the right path." Morgana nodded.

"I will My Lady."

She smiled, turned back and disappeared, and Morgana took a very deep breath, Branna was right, Eve could see through far more than both of them realised. It really worried her, if she talked to the others, it could bring her great trouble, and Merlin was no longer around to protect her.

*M*organa picked up her bag, and hurried as fast as she could, she felt nervous, if there was going to be trouble, she wanted to be as far away as possible. She felt like maybe she should seek out the advice of Branna, after all, they would be meeting in the forest, and she needed to warn Branna that Eve suspected something.

Having a father who was part Fae was her greatest secret, and she had managed to keep it hidden for all of her life, the last thing she needed was Eve discovering her secret, but she had no idea what to do. Eve was very powerful, she came across as being innocent, but there were many who thought highly of her, for she sensed a great deal in the realms and could talk with ease about most lines. She was the one who gave life to all things, and even though Branna had mentioned she knew of secret ways to deal with her, Morgana had always feared harming her.

She did not understand the power of Eve, she just knew she was the sister of the high lord Albanlin, and to harm her, would bring devastation in the form of his vengeance. Morgana had no plans to do anything to Eve, it was far too dangerous to even contemplate, and yet, she felt threatened. She had no idea what she could do, but the one thing she did know, was Branna needed to be alerted, because Eve was quietly on the trail of Branna, and if Eve found her, not long after, Rhiannon would know.

Chapter Twenty Nine.

Light and Shadow.

Gwendolyn smiled as she looked down into the basket woven crib of Sapphire, as she slept, she turned to the smiling Melanie.

"She is strong with sight; I can feel it." She stood, and turned to young Jasper, and smiled as she looked down at him.

"Your new sister is beautiful, I hope you will protect her as a knight, like your father does?" Jasper gave a hearty nod of his head, and Melanie giggled, as Gwendolyn turned to her.

"I have such joy in my heart for you my precious daughter, you have two beautiful children." Melanie took a deep breath, and breathed slowly.

"Mother I am so happy, and Tor is such a good man, he works hard on the farm, and is a tower of strength to his king. Mother we have talked, she will be named Sapphire. It is not a violet stone, but in the right light, it will shine in the hue of a mighty queen of our line."

Gwendolyn took a huge breath, as she thought of her grandmother, and her eyes filled with tears.

"She would be so happy to know that, she was an inspiring woman, and I hope your daughter favours her, for if she does, she will be loved deeply and a saviour of her people." Behind them, there was a loud pop, and Madeline appeared in a flash of light, she looked panicked.

"It is starting, and I have never done this before, having them, and delivering them are very different things. I need you Mother, I fear my hands shake too much, and I may drop the baby." Melanie giggled, never in her life had she seen Maddy so flustered, out of all of them she was normally the calm one.

"Maurice watches your daughters, go to my twin and tell her of my happiness for her." Gwendolyn turned and gave a sigh as she looked at Maddy looking terrified.

"Come… Morgana can wait, Una and I feel, your need, is greater." There was a bright flash as Melanie laughed, and leaned over the crib to watch her daughter sleep.

*S*tenlow held out the paper to Rhiannon, and she lifted it up to read.

"Lord Alder is absolutely certain, it is not a rumour, it is a fact?" Stenlow looked very uncomfortable and nodded.

"He is quite certain My Queen, the wizard has completely vanished with no trace, and Her Majesty, Queen Gwendolyn, is very upset and concerned for his well being."

Rhiannon read carefully, her soft grey eyes moving along the lines of his report, it was very detailed and precise, and there was no denying, in many ways it pleased her. She flicked her wrist at Stenlow.

"You can go, I will look into this, and make my appreciation for your speedy delivery of such news, but speak to no one of this matter. For now, I wish to keep this news quiet, this will alarm certain parties." Stenlow bowed and turned, he started to walk away toward the door.

"Commander Stenlow?" He stopped and turned.

"Yes, My Queen?" Rhiannon lifted her eyes from the note.

"Where is the girl?" He frowned.

"The Girl, which one?" Rhiannon gave a sigh.

"You know full well, his assistant, the dark haired girl, you know, the sister of Arthur?" Stenlow understood.

"I presume her cottage; she hardly leaves it unless it is to walk in the meadows and pick flowers." Rhiannon nodded.

"Find out, from now on, I want to know her every movement." He bowed again.

"Yes, My Queen." He turned and hurried out of the hall.

Rhiannon looked back at the report sent to her by councilman Alder, she turned lost in thought, and then lifted her eyes to Sequana, who had been standing behind her looking into a deep golden pan that gave off a strange odour.

"What do you see?" Sequana took a deep intake of breath, and breathed in the fumes from the pan, her eyes rolled back in her head, and her voice was almost ethereal.

"Shadows walk within the realms, and the light of white diminishes, darkness comes and the realms will burn. There is a creeping death that walks from the sea, and lays to waste many. The guardian has faded, he will not walk here again for many generations." Sequana twitched, and her eyes rolled back into view, and she blinked and then looked at the queen.

"Seal the realm to all the lines of men, I feel the lines of Fae are at threat."

She was not wrong, the realm of men was burning, under a sun hotter than many years, and water was becoming scarce, illness was spreading and people were dying. The realm of men, was about to feel the pains of a very powerful drought. Arthur sat on his throne lost and broken, his mind filled with the pain of seeing Guinevere lay naked and sleeping, curled around his best friend, the country was starting to suffer.

Crops were failing, and the grain stores were only half full, and the bite of hunger was starting to be felt. The druids preached this was a result of the realm turning its back to the earth, and the worship of the new god, and unrest was brewing, yet Arthur sat helpless unable to clear his mind, and focus on his subjects.

$\mathcal{M}$organa waited in the Chimerical Forest for Branna, she felt impatient as Eve had worried her and she really needed to talk to her. For weeks she had cleared a large area to site her new castle, and she stood in the centre and looked around it, counting the minutes and waiting, feeling nervous. Branna arrived in a swirling cloud of black smoke, and smiled, Morgana gave a sigh of relief.

"I am glad you are here; I was worried, things are not good." Branna walked slowly towards her with a questioning look.

"You appear scared, what is happening?"

For over an hour Branna sat on the grass covered floor with Morgana, as she talked of Arthur, her meeting with Eve and her capture of Merlin. Branna could feel her fear, and understood why Morgana was so nervous, she smiled as Morgana finished.

"Morgana, Merlin is taken care of, although that may create a problem with Gwendolyn, and the Ruling Council. It was Gwendolyn's sword that she gave to Uther that changed my grandson, your father's mind that brought him to his ultimate death. No matter how you look at it, they were the ones who actively encouraged Uther and seated Arthur, who now steals the money meant for your mother and you. It is their interference that has shaped all the sadness and pain in your life. I have talked of this time, and how a day would arrive when all of us would be faced with a choice, fight them, or surrender to them. Now is that time Morgana, and whether you have decided or not, soon, you will have to choose." Morgana looked at her, her eyes were filled with her intelligence.

"Branna, I am made of two lines, I am of your line, and I am of my mother's line. Both lines are based in the belief of the earth faith, they are my people, I am one of them. I may think differently at times to them, but all of my loyalties are with them. I cannot believe that the Ruling Council has allowed Arthur to erase what for both of my lines has been the culture of my people for endless generations before us. I told Merlin, I could not believe he has supported Arthur in this new god he has adopted, and he told me that our time is over. Branna he was talking about the council, but why does it have to end, why must you and I give up everything we are, and surrender to this Christ God?" She leaned forward, and took Morgana by the hands, with a smile.

"Morgana, we don't have to, just because they do not agree, does not make them right. Answer me this, was it right to choose one man out of the many to rule, was it right to arm him with superior weapons, who then slayed the man who was actually benefiting his people most? Your father did much to support and protect the people of his community, and yet they took him from not just you, they took him from everyone." Morgana shook her head.

"I do not think it was right, and I have struggled with it a lot, because I know these people, and they have done things of great kindness, and yet they allowed my father to be slain. Branna, when I was young, I wanted to kill Merlin, and yet he took me under his wing, and he showed me kindness, educated, and helped me. Branna, he gave me the cottage, it is mine now, and I have lived happily there for years, because that is what I desired, and he gave it me. I tricked him, and he is now stored in essence, but the truth is, I do not want to kill him, I know it sounds odd, but I do actually admire him." Branna understood that, and gave a soft smile.

"Morgana, he was going to be a problem to you, but you do not need to kill him, and in that you are lucky, because you can choose what you do. There was a time in my life where I was not given a choice, and I took a life I did not want to take, and I have always regretted it Morgana. He was called Halbrand, there are nights I sleep and still see his face, I was forced to kill him, and I did, but it was not my choice. Ariel taught me that it is I who have the choice, and she was right, so the way I see it, Merlin is now removed and no longer a problem, you achieved your goal without taking a life." Morgana gave a sigh of relief.

"I know how you feel about losing my father, I know he is your blood, and I will never tell you what to do, but I have no wish to kill if it is not needed. If I can imprison Gwendolyn as I have Merlin, I will. I know Rhiannon will be different, and if she attacks me, I will defend myself, and if I kill her, then so be it."

Branna leaned back on the grass, her hair hung tatty and black behind her, her face pale and her eyes as dark as blackberries, as she looked at Morgana.

"Morgana, you must never forget, we live in a world mainly ruled by men. It is not easy to be a woman and stand up against them, as you have seen with your brother, he took over and drained your father's castle of all its resources. The way things work in many realms is that men control everything, and the woman are held back. Both of us are lucky that we had one man who stood up for us and allowed us to take the lead, for that is what Merlin did, as did Berengar for me. That is a rare case, and there will be times, no matter what you may feel, where you will have to stand your ground, and kill to survive. It is not pleasant, but it is the reality of the realms we walk within, you will be faced with choices, and in some cases, you will not have time to think, you will have to act or die." Morgana understood that, but she did not really want it either, she took a short breath, and nodded.

"I know… I have never done it, and I know I will have to, but if I can avoid it, I will." Branna smiled.

"It is sad we must have to talk about these things, but that is the path we have chosen. We can rule, we are strong enough, but the men of the world do not see it, and yes, where possible mercy is a better path. Ariel taught me a great deal, and I have over the years done what I can to spare people, I have also taken life and created life. I swore an oath to kill the golden queen, and I still aim to do so, what she has done to my people is unforgivable, and she will account for it when she meets me. In that one aspect, even Ariel understood there would be no other way." Morgana nodded softly, and she looked at the floor in thought.

"We have much in common, more than I realised. Arthur aims to wipe away our lines and replace them with this new god he has, and I swore to his face I would stop him. It is not unsimilar to your fight with Rhiannon. Branna, he is my brother and I have no wish to kill him, but I know in my heart, if I have to, I will. I cannot allow him to wipe away all that my parents stand for, and all they have built, I must stop him."

"Then Morgana, we share a cause, and we shall work to that ends. It is my wish that a day comes, where we both hold dominion over our own free kingdoms, and they flourish. That starts now, for here you will establish your domain, and I already have Berengar Castle and the lands that surround it." Branna got up off the grass, and looked around at the large cleared site.

"You have done well, within one full cycle of the moon, I will unbind your Fae powers in a ceremony I am preparing for you. Morgana, when that time comes, a part of you may be revealed to those of deeper sight. Eve and Hearne will see you as you truly are, and they will turn against you, and you will have to act."

Branna slipped her hand into her pocket, and pulled out two small glass bottles with cork stoppers on them, she handed one to Morgana, who held it up to look at it.

"What is it?"

"This is the liquid created by the spell of the golden queen, which I found in her library. Two drops in a drink will tear Eve and Hearne from their human forms, and prevent them from ever wearing another form of these realms. They will be trapped as spirit and their powers will diminish, or at least that is what the golden queen thought as she created the spell. She is supposed to be the most powerful member of the Fae, and she has achieved a great many things, and so if she is as wise as they say, this will work. Morgana, we have to find a way to stop the council, and this I fear may be the only real weapon we have against them. It must be done before the next full moon, so we can complete your ritual of Fae, and bring you into your full powers once and for all. I fear the pressure the Whitelines places on you could in time fracture your mind, and so I wish to act soon to ensure that never happens." Morgana understood and slipped the bottle into her pocket.

"It will not be easy, she already suspects me, but I will try." Branna looked at her own bottle.

"In this task you will not be alone, I will be beside you, I will reside in your cave for a while, and be on hand ready when you need me."

Morgana frowned at her.

"What about Ariel, will that not leave her unguarded?" Branna shook her head.

"Roack will watch over her, she knows the value of keeping her around me, and she understands it. If Maud tries anything, Roack has the means to deal with Maud. My daughter has never understood the bond of the connection when tied to a raven, and as a result, she will never know the loyalty it brings."

Morgana had not forgotten, she still could not fully understand why Rajani had saved Jarron, and yet she felt in a small way, that she owed the raven, for Jarron was very precious to her.

"I have to ask, because I do not fully understand it. Why did Rajani save Jarron, when Maud ordered her bird to kill him?" Branna smiled, as she thought of the moment, her voice was reflective and soft.

"Morgana, as we bond as people, so does the raven. They are an exceptional breed of bird, they are highly intelligent, and they are also very loyal. Maud is not kind to Rajani, and I think at times Rajani resents being tied to the cruellest member of my family, for she has become darker than any of us ever thought she would. Rajani saw the depth of the bond between you and Jarron, and I think in a strange way, she wanted to protect that. As a result, she defended Jarron against her mistress, and she has paid for it since."

It made some sense, she remembered the way Rajani looked at her and bowed to her, and she felt at the time, the bird understood her pain at seeing Jarron so badly hurt.

"Rajani is connected to Roack, who is connected to the merle, which has been seen as being evil, and yet Rajani showed compassion, which in a way is not evil. I find that curious, because it does not back up what I have been told of the merle. Has Maud been very cruel to her, I would hate it, if that was because of me?"

"Maud has always been cruel to her, and that also played a part in why Rajani came to Jarron's aid. It was not so much about you, and more about the relationship between her and Maud. Morgana, I will not deny, there has been darkness in my family, evil things have been done, and as the head of the family it is I who carry that responsibility, even when I oppose the things they have done. The Merle seeks only what we have, which is a body and a life, I have studied it with Roack, and at times Ariel. I feel it is primal, maybe our races were once like that, they embraced all of life and lived it by their instincts to thrive and survive? Ask yourself, is your desire to eat, breathe, or embrace your sexual desires wrong, for there are some who would say that they were. Today there are many who talk of this new god, but from what I have read, and I have read a lot, they enforce rules on people stating they are unnatural in their desires. Ask yourself, is there even such a thing as something unnatural? I believe to feel is to live, how can that be unnatural, and yet this new god says it is, it says I am evil, but am I? Think about it." Branna turned, and looked back at her.

"The time to build is soon, and you have prepared well, what I want you to do now, is picture every aspect of this castle you aim to build in your mind. Over the next few weeks think of every detail, for you will need all of it in your thoughts when you create it, so let that be your main focus. Merlin will be missed, be ready to be questioned, they will look for him, and they will look to you. I must go, I have things to prepare, we will meet at the market in three days at the same time." Morgana gave a nod.

"I will, and thank you, it has helped to talk with you." Branna smiled at her.

"I am always here my little raven; you will never be alone… Three days, until then."

The smoked billowed up around her, and Branna wearing a smile faded from view, and when the smoke cleared, she was gone. Morgana slipped her hand into her pocket, and felt the glass of the bottle, she had no idea how she would get anyone to drink anything she made, but in that, she knew she had to find a way. She turned and walked towards the path, she felt happier knowing that Branna was on her side and behind her, and as she walked back towards the realm of Avalon, she thought of her plans, and the way she would help her mother protect her people, somehow, they had to stop Arthur destroying the history of her lines.

*M*organa made her way back towards her cottage, she turned onto the path and wandered along her mind lost in thought. Walking, and not really paying attention she did not at first hear the sound of the horses that raced up the track. By the time she understood it was the Marshals, it was too late, they had spotted her and approached her slowing their horses. Morgana gave a sigh as she saw Stenlow, he slowed his horse, and looked down at her, she stood still and waited for his pompous address to her.

"Where have you been, we have been looking for you, the queen wants to know where you are at all times?" Morgana shrugged.

"Why does she have to know where I am at all times, does she know the exact whereabouts of every resident? I live in this realm and like to walk and gather flowers for my home. If you must know, knowing the queen wants to track me, I walk where I know she won't look." He looked at her, it was clear he did not like her answer.

"If you must know, the wizard Merlin has gone missing." Morgana frowned.

"He is always missing, he just wanders off to all places, I hardly see him, and never know when he will show up. That is who he is, a wizard, they are sort of like that. Have you asked with his family, you know, he does have four grandchildren and if the gossips are right, as shameful as it may appear, it appears he is about to have another?" Stenlow leaned forward in his seat, and lowered his voice. His voice changed, and he sounded concerned.

"This is serious, he is really missing and everyone is worried, powerful people do not disappear, even you must be careful. It may surprise you to know, but I also look out to ensure you are safe. Take heed, things are not as they should be, and the queen feels there is danger for all." It felt a little comical to think he would worry about her safety, but she took it in the spirit it was given, and smiled and changed her manner.

"I am sorry. I took a walk, I do actually love this realm, it is why I live here. Thank you, Commander Stenlow, to be honest, I am not that powerful, but I will be extra careful. Merlin is a wizard; I am sure he will show up and wonder what all the fuss was about." Stenlow sat back up in his seat.

"Stay close to home, and stay vigilant." She smiled; he was a strange man.

"Thank you, I will."

He kicked his horse and rode off, and she gave a small giggle, maybe Fagan was right after all, most of what he was ordered to do, did not sit well with him. As he rode away, she continued to walk up the road and see her cottage in the distance, and gave a smile, a tea was needed and she felt, it was a rose hip sort of day. The path was dusty and she felt her spirits had risen, as her mind pondered her conversations in the past with Branna. One particular moment came to mind, as she walked back home along the path, and her thoughts drifted to her last visit, where she had walked in the trees with Branna.

"Morgana, they talk of being in the light, and powers of light, and yet as we all know, when the sun rises, shadows are cast. When I was a girl, I would dance and make my shadow do funny things, and it made me so happy, light and dark working together brought joy to me. I have thought often of this, and I came to the conclusion that you cannot have one without the other. The Golden Queen sits on her padded seat and talks of the powers of white, and yet in her shadow there lies the stain of injustice. The building of Avalon was seen to be a wonderful achievement, and to look at it, I am sure even you will agree it is. I will not deny, to be a part of that, as I was with Ariel at my side, is the happiest time of my life. I would even say that with her I lived fully in the light, for the love I felt for her, even to this day is as strong as it was then. But there is a shadow cast over all of it, she was taken from me to appease the queen of this so called light, and my life was left in the darkness of the pain I felt without her. All my friends have either fled, died, or are back on the Moon realm with my family imprisoned. So, you tell me, who is darker, the Golden Queen, or the woman who stands before you?"

Branna stopped and stood before her as she thought of the words of Branna, it was an interesting question, and one she found not the easiest to answer. Branna smiled at her, but her face held a sincerity to it, as she looked deeply into Morgana's eyes, her voice was soft.

"I love Ariel, I love her in a way no one will ever understand, and I suffer everyday seeing her in that box and not being able to hold her and talk to her. My greatest desire is to open that box and pull her into my arms, for my love for her is pure, and it is the whitest of them all, and yet I am called Dark Fae. Morgana, I am not perfect, I have many flaws, my temper being one of them. I do not deny, I have taken lives to survive, and I do not excuse myself for my actions, some of them haunt my dreams and fuel my regrets. I will ask you this, how many lives has the Golden Queen taken, how many have suffered under her rule, and yet she is perceived to be of the most powerful light?" She smiled.

"I do not believe in dark or light, for after years of study, I have found it is the intention we hold in our acts that are the true measure of power. I work very hard to find the balance Merlin has, for he has full control, and it is my wish to emulate that, so ask yourself, am I right or wrong?" Morgana understood her perfectly, and shook her head.

"I do not see you as evil, and I have suffered what I consider to be an evil act as my father was killed when Merlin conspired with the council and Uther. You have shown me great kindness, and from what I know, which I admit is less than most, I do not think Ariel could love someone truly evil, and I believe as she did."

Morgana arrived at the gate, and stood for a moment as her thoughts lingered with her memory of Branna. She had never forgotten the moment, maybe it was something to do with her face, her sincerity, but at that time, and even more so now. Morgana felt that Branna contained a great pain inside her for the way her life was seen, and how she was treated. She unlatched the gate and walked along the worn dirt path, and slipped out her key, she knew that she had a lot to think about, and also, she had a lot of new thoughts that she wanted to write down. The door opened and she stepped inside the cottage, and gave a sigh of relief, as her mind tumbled over everything that had happened, and Branna's words resounded in her mind.

The truth was, she did not see Branna as an evil person, she understood the wrongs of Rhiannon, and Merlin, and in her mind, she felt the Ruling Council were at fault, and hypocrites. How many other lives had they simply crushed in their need to have things done their way, and to their demands? It appeared that many had suffered for the pretence of their positions. Branna was right, power was not light or dark, it was controlled by intention, and she was really starting to understand how that worked.

In truth, she could have killed Merlin, after all, he was responsible for the death of her father, and yet as she had considered his actions since, she kept him alive, even if it was in a state of sleep. Merlin had told her that the council was stepping back to give man the rights of free will, and that made no sense to her. He was basically saying their time was over, and yet it wasn't they were still here. Even if the lines of men had turned their back on them, and were starting to deny their existence in the name of a new god, it changed nothing, they lived here in and around Avalon. She leaned off the door and walked slowly into her living space, and saw the fire was out, as her mind slowly ticked around, and voiced her thoughts quietly.

"If you are so determined to wipe away your memory from the

lines of men, why do you still linger? You have hurt people, caused chaos, and have helped bring this new god to this world. If you are no longer useful, maybe I should just take out my vengeance and get rid of all of you myself. I can say one thing though, I am going nowhere, I am staying, and I am fighting for my ancestors and the beliefs that they honoured, my mother is my queen, and I shall serve only her purpose from now on. If that puts me in the shadow of their light, then so be it."

Chapter Thirty.

Understanding Others.

*F*or two days Morgana sat alone in her cottage writing and thinking, it was clear that to a degree Stenlow was right, Merlin was powerful, and yet he had fallen to her trick. It was clear, that the council and those connected to it would be cautious, and on their guard, and that meant scrutiny. All of them protected Arthur, which she still felt was strange, because in a strange way, his new god denounced them, which meant he did. It had given her a great deal of thought; she would never denounce Branna who had helped her so much.

Gwendolyn was Merlin's wife, and it was clear that she would at some point work things out and come looking for him at the cottage. The problem was, she also had three daughters, and it was obvious they would support their mother, of which Madeleine she knew was quite advanced. In order to make her plans work, she would have to find a way of taking care of Gwendolyn's daughters, but how, that would not be easy? The following day was market day, and she had goods to take to market, and so for now, she had to busy herself and prepare.

*M*organa stood her stall next to her usual trader of cheese, called Meg. She liked Meg, she was useful as she was probably the biggest gossip in the village. Morgana always traded wearing a headscarf with her hair tied back, and also used the name le Fey. No one knew of her real identity or where she came from, in her early days, she had told them she had travelled far from Bristol. Meg was pleasant and they talked a lot as they traded, and through that she got a lot of the news she wanted to hear. All of the country was starting to suffer, even Meg was worried, as the pasture for her cattle was drying up, and she feared that the milk of her cows would stop.

The country was facing hard times, and many were questioning why Arthur had not acted yet, dissent was growing, and that played well into Morgana's hands. It was late afternoon when a group of knights came riding through the market, Morgana noticed Tor and looked down at her stall, as they passed by, all of the others watched on. Once they were riding down the track heading away, Meg gave a tut.

"It is alright for some folks, I bet his crops do not suffer." Morgana frowned.

"How do you mean?" She pointed.

"Him… You know, Sir Tor. Mr high and mighty, it is alright for him and all of his fancy knights, they will not starve, will they? His farm is big enough, but he will not be selling his crops to us, no he will keep it for his family and rich friends." Morgana looked back down the road, but he had gone from sight.

"I did not know knights farmed; does he farm around here?" She nodded.

"Aye, him and his family all have that big farm down there, although, I doubt him and his wife do anything, you know they have us lot to work for them. They have a good few men, and they do not pay them enough if you ask me, he never pays the full price for the cheese either, always knocks me down. I need the income, and he knows it, I have six kids to feed." Morgana's mind was working overtime, she looked at Meg.

"Does he not buy from the market?" She nodded over the way to Jenks the butcher.

"He buys meat and milk off him; Jenks is always complaining he never pays a fair price. Bloody rich, that is how they stay rich, they exploit us lot."

It did not take long to get the gossip, Meg always did the rounds towards mid-afternoon, and it was not long before she was back, as Morgana began to clear up for the end of her day. Meg slipped up to her and smiled.

"No wonder his Lordship was in a rush, it appears they are gathering as a family at mid summer, and he has given orders to clear the hall for a feast. Apparently, one of her sisters has had a child, and they aim to celebrate with a big family reunion." Morgana smiled.

"I suppose for them that is possible, us lot would never be able to do that, we don't have the money." Meg agreed and they spent the last part of the day, mocking the rich.

*T*hat night Branna came to see Morgana, and she told her all of the news, they sat for a while and thought about the situation. Branna considered everything as they ate in Morgana's room, and she lifted her wine, she thought of something.

"You say they will feast in the great hall of Tor?" Morgana nodded.

"Yes. The family will gather and they will hold a large feast, and then shortly before midnight, they will head to Florae, where they will offer the children up to the world, as is their tradition." Branna knew of the ceremony.

"I know the ritual well, it is one thing all Fae and Green Circle do, and that could be our moment to strike." Morgana gave a frown; she was not sure as to how that would be the moment.

"Branna they will all be together, and they are all of the line of a Fae queen, we cannot face all of them at the same time, we will not live." Branna smiled.

"We will not have to, there are many ways my little raven to subdue a gathering, especially when you know the sort of herblore I have studied. Yes, I think we will have our moment, with no Merlin, this could be our greatest chance to strike hard at the Ruling Council." Morgana narrowed her eyes.

"We are not going to kill them are we, most of them were not even born when my father was killed?" Branna smiled.

"Morgana, trust me, I know how you feel about unnecessary death, I have many ways of dealing with this, and in that I will teach you what I know. We will have work to do, and you will need a place to hold them all, times slips through the hour glass, we must work fast to prepare." Morgana nodded, and noticed Branna watching her.

"What?" Branna sat back.

"Do you still aim to go through with your other plan? I admire your resolve to get vengeance on Arthur, but what you propose will not be an easy thing for you." Morgana took a deep breath, and swallowed.

"It is unsavoury, but yes, I have thought about it a great deal, it is time his line understood what it is like to be robbed of a life." Branna gave a nod.

"Alright, I will help you in your preparations."

Rhiannon grew more worried by the day, as did Gwendolyn, and Marshals were sent out to find word of Merlin. Albanlin was nowhere to be found, and Eve tried to sense all of the realms in hope of tracking down the wizard. Tensions began to grow all over Avalon, and Morgana found that there were more and more riders passing her cottage each day, and she was feeling nervous as she walked with her basket collecting flowers along the dusty roads. Four nights after their meeting at the tavern, Morgana walked into the marshes, and in a cloud of light white smoke, she jumped to the Chimerical Forest, and met Branna.

Branna walked to the centre of the front of her cleared area of the forest, and lined her up ready for the start of a new era for Morgana. She stood behind her and instructed her.

"Close your eyes and think of the castle you wish to build. Allow every detail you have thought of to flood into your thoughts. When you have everything held fully in your mind, go down to your knees and touch the floor, and I will help give you the power you need to flow into you."

Morgana stood silent, her eyes closed tight as she breathed slowly in and out, and in her mind, she pictured a tall castle of black stone. Every detail flowed into her thoughts, every chamber, the dungeons, the kitchens and the main hall. Her body felt calm and relaxed as Branna touched her temples, and Morgana lowered to the floor. Branna lowered with her, her eyes flickering with a red light, as her breathing matched the rhythm of Morgana's, and when they were in sync, she closed her eyes and whispered.

"Morgana, do the spell, and raise your castle."

It started softly, as the blades of the grass vibrated, and Morgana focused on the building she had been building in her mind for over a week. In front of her the earth shook, and an aura of red light flowed out of Branna, and surrounded them both. In front of them, the ground collapsed and fell into a huge crater, and as it hit the bottom and compacted, the wall of black stone rose up out of the floor.

The aura around Branna intensified, and suddenly, the building shot up at speed. Shaping and moulding itself, the huge black castle with a large stone raven on the very top rose out of the floor. It towered above them as windows appeared, steps ran up and down to the battlements, and doors fitted to frames in the walls. Trees around the edges of the castle fell and splintered into finely cut wood, and slithered up the walls and in through the windows, and assembled themselves. Iron ore glowed white as it left the ground, and shot like arrows into the air, moulding and shaping itself, to nail and fix, the hinges and furniture, and as it all came to a shuddering halt, Branna took a large deep breath and relaxed.

She opened her eyes and looked up at the tall gates, and smiled, Morgana was still on her knees breathing in air, she was tired, and swooned a little. Branna offered her hand and helped lift her up, and together they stood and viewed their work, and Morgana was lost for words. Branna nodded with great approval.

"I think for a Fae with bound powers, you did well, very well indeed." Morgana was stunned and could not believe her eyes; her voice was quiet and filled with awe.

"I cannot believe it is real, I could see it in my mind, but this, I cannot believe it is real." Branna gave a giggle.

"It is real alright, and it is yours. Morgana, I gave you the power, but you built this. You created this in your mind, every brick and every nail, and it shows the true power of your mind, because look at the detail, look at how well crafted it is. Morgana, this is your new start, from here you will be able to spread your wings like a true raven, and take whatever you want as your own. Here you can live free and create the world you want, as I have with mine. This is one castle that will never fall into disrepair, or be taken over by another."

Morgana felt emotional, and overwhelmed, as she looked at the raven high above her, where she knew in its head there would be a study room, and a large room to work in, although there was one flaw to all of this.

"Branna, no matter what, it will still be empty with no other people within its walls."

"For now, in time I will show you how to create loyalty in those that surround you, and they will willingly come here to live and work in your service. This realm is hidden, and will never be discovered, here you will find the peace you seek, and here you will start your life all over again. The Council will lose control and you will rise up, and others will run to your aid, and Arthur will fall." Morgana swayed a little.

"I am so tired." She lifted a hand to her face and Branna understood.

"Go… Head to your cottage and your bed, this is yours and no one will enter without your consent, it will be safe enough here. Go, sleep, and rest your mind, you have used a lot of power. Take the tonic, and grow strong again, and I will see you soon." Branna lifted her hand and pressed a finger into Morgana's temple. The smoke swirled up, and Branna stood alone in the forest and looked to the castle with a smile.

"My little raven has proven herself more than she realises, another castle of the raven in this family, it was wise to watch over her. When her powers are unleashed, she will be mighty indeed, I feel Maud should be wary, she may have found her match." The smoke of black swirled up around her, and as it faded away, the forest stood empty.

Morgana woke up two days later, to knocking at her door, she slid out of bed and pulled on a cloak, which she wrapped tightly around herself as she walked to her door. She unlocked it and opened it to find Lot, as she covered her eyes, as the sun burned down brightly behind him. She gave a sigh, as she peered through her blinded half closed eyes.

"What do you want?" She turned, and walked back into her cottage, and he followed her into her living space.

"You have not been at court, and I wanted to see you." Morgana sat at her seat, and leaned forward rubbing her temples.

"I have been busy, but why would I? All my brother cares about is his table, and robbing my family of the inheritance left by my father."

"Your brother suffers the loss of Guinevere, it weighs heavily on his mind, and the country is suffering." She leaned back on the wall she was not even fully awake.

"Guinevere yearned for a child. If my brother spent more time loving his wife, and less time robbing his family and building unneeded castles, maybe Guinevere would have what she desired, and not have sought out affection elsewhere, and he would have a grip on his rule of the land. Why has he not gone to her and stated his love and tried to win her back, that to me appears the obvious choice?"

She closed her eyes, just enjoying the darkness from lack of light on them. Lot looked around the room with its shelves of bottles of tonics and herbs. There was a slight chill to the room, as he looked towards the fire, filled with white ash.

"Do you have ailments?" She rubbed her temples.

"I have a bad headache."

He knelt down and collected some wood and dried moss from the large woven basket, to make up the fire, she opened her eyes and saw him.

"What are you doing?" He looked back at her.

"I am making the fire up, if you are unwell, I will make you something." She closed her eyes.

"I am fine, it is just a headache, nothing more, and I hate to point out the obvious, but I am versed in plant lore and make tinctures. I am more than capable of making myself one." He struck the flint, and the spark landed in the moss.

"You should take more care of yourself; you deserve something better than this." She opened her eyes and sat back.

"I prefer this, I like the solitude. I hope you are not implying I belong in court with all those other useless pampered women?"

The fire was starting to smoke, and small flames licked at the kindling and twigs he placed on it. He built up the fire around it, and stood up, and looked at her.

"Would it be so bad to live in better surroundings?" She gave a sigh.

"Lot, I have told you again and again, that is not the life I want, why do you have to constantly bring it up? Can you not understand, I chose this as my life, it is what I want."

He stood staring at her, and it was clear that yet again he was going to lecture her on living and the appearance of a lady.

"Morgana, you are the sister of the king, and yet look where you live. Why do you refuse my offers, I have a large hall with rooms that stand empty, and have a need to be filled?" The light was too bright and she closed her eyes again.

"Please listen to me, I have told you before. Lot what you desire is not the life I want. I have told you, pick another from the countless maidens you have bedded, I am not the woman to furnish your halls, I have never wanted that." He gave an exasperated gasp.

"But why not, I have much to offer?" She had a really bad headache, and did not want this.

"Lot, I like you, but what you offer is not for me, I do not want to be owned and treated secondary to jousts, war and court, that is not the life I choose. I have a headache and not the will to explain this all over again. I know you do not understand, but I have my own ideas of what I want in this life, and they are not hanging from the arm of a knight." He shook his head.

"I can offer you much, even the freedom to do this… Whatever it is that you think you are doing. I have rooms Morgana, you could fill them with bottles, and whatever these things are. Would it be so awful to share your time with me?"

Morgana opened her eyes, and leaned back on the wall with a frustrated gasp. Lot stood looking at her, and she really did not want to do this, not now.

"Lot, I hate to point it out, but I have freedom already, I come and I go as I please. What you want is not for me, I would not be happy in the way other maidens would be. You think you know me; you assume you know what I want, but apart from living here and being something to liven up your bed, what else do you really know about me?"

He stood staring at her as she watched him, she was right, he knew nothing about her. He took a deep breath, and looked a little hurt.

"I care for you; I am happy when I am with you. I have means for a life of comfort, and would share them with you."

She smiled, and slipped from her seat, and walked over to him, and took his hands in hers. He towered above her, and he had a chiselled, yet kind face as he looked down at her. Morgana smiled again.

"Lot, you are a good man, you are honourable and brave with a good heart, but I have chosen a life of solitude dedicated to my studies. If I had made a different choice early in life, then maybe things would be different and I would be flattered by your offer, but I did not. I understand you see no value in this life, but be assured, I want this, I chose this, and this is how I intend to continue." She could see the hurt deepen in his eyes as he tried to smile.

"You are an amazing and beautiful woman Morgana, and I do not ask this because you liven up my bed. I ask because it is heartfelt to me, I care for you deeply." She smiled at him, he was so sincere, and she knew he meant it with all his heart. She squeezed his hands.

"Thank you, it matters to me that you said that, but I still cannot take what you offer. Lot, you deserve better than me, and if you knew the truth of my life and my feelings, you would understand better. Just know, that for a time I felt cared for deeply with you, and it made a big difference, but trust me when I say, you will thrive in the arms of another."

He stepped back, and was clearly emotional, Morgana could feel the surge of emotion swirling within him. He swallowed hard and gave a slight nod.

"If that is your last word, I have no choice but to accept it. I shall leave you to your solitude, and ask you pardon my interruption. Goodbye Morgana."

He turned abruptly and walked towards the door, and she felt the sadness mix with her frustration, creep up inside her. She walked slowly to the door, where outside he pulled himself up onto his horse. Morgana stood at her door, wrapped only in her cloak, and watched as he gave a nod, sadness painted across his face.

"Live well."

She nodded, he pulled round his horse, and bolted off up the track at speed, and she felt the two tears at the bottom of her eyes, even though this was her choice, watching him ride away was not easy for her. Quietly, she turned, and walked back in, locking the door with a long heavy sigh. As the fire crackled in the hearth, she entered her bedroom, slipped off her cloak, and climbed back into bed, pulled the blankets up over her, where she gave a faint sob.

*F*or the next few days, Morgana felt it hard to be motivated, Lot's visit had left her with a lingering sense of sadness, which she did not fully understand, and his words kept echoing in the back of her mind.

"You are an amazing and beautiful woman Morgana, and I do not ask this because you liven up my bed, I ask because it is heartfelt to me, I care for you deeply."

She muttered to herself as she tried to sort out her herbs and mix up her potions, but her mind kept dragging her back to that moment stood looking into his eyes. Was she starting to doubt her decision? She put down her mortice, and stared at the crushed herbs in the stone pot.

"This is ridiculous, how could he even ask me, can you imagine living in a hall filled with people, constantly questioning my work? It was the right choice, that is no life for me. I would die of boredom, I cannot sit and look pretty all day, trussed up like a boar on a spit, gossiping about who bedded who." She paused and took a breath and looked at the bottles.

"That is the problem, if they stopped gossiping and bedded more of the men they would be content, no one should have to live all their life with one person, sat in a corner dressed like a doll. Their days would be better spent exploring each other and writhing with desire. You made the right choice, that is no life for you Morgana." She gave a resounding nod, and felt better, then thought again and her face dropped.

"I will miss him so much, I learned things of the pleasures I did not know were possible, he was good, whoever he takes will not be bored under his blankets. He was also kind and caring, I know he meant what he said, I feel it too, but what is the point? They would hurt him to get to me, and he deserves better." She gave a long sad sigh.

A memory of them together on the floor came to mind, as she writhed on top of him with absolute pleasure. She swallowed hard and stood up straight as she felt parts of her womanhood throb. She gave a frustrated sigh, and turned to the fire.

"STOP IT, STOP MORGANA, YOU CANNOT HAVE SUCH THINGS IN YOUR HEAD!" She gave a naughty smile, as she crossed to the fire to pull off the water.

"That was such an amazing night, oh lords of the lands, will I ever know such pleasures again?"

*B*ranna walked down the steps into the lower dungeon, where silent mutterings rose up from between the glass bottles, with the scratching of a nib. The clatter of Branna's feet on the steps caught Maud's attention and she looked up from her book, wearing a scowl.

"What do you want, you rarely come down here?"

Branna stood on the bottom step and looked around the place, it was unkempt and dusty. Her eyes moved to Maud, as she stared up from her table.

"I am here out of courtesy nothing more. I aim to unbind the powers of Fae within Morgana, and I felt it was only right to inform you before I do it. Morgana has created a castle of her own, it is impressive, I feel even you would approve of it." Maud curled up her lip and sneered.

"Nothing that half breed does would impress me." Branna understood that, she lowered her voice slightly.

"Daughter, listen carefully to me, she does not desire the power you crave, Morgana has other plans, she was telling the truth, she has no interest in the affairs of this castle. To her it is simply a place to walk freely, a place where she is not spied on. You really should have no fear of her, she has only ever wanted to be part of a family in whom she has similarities."

"I have no care what she wants, or what she does, I will never see her as family, not whilst she has the blood of an inferior within her. She is not now and never will be one of us. I neither trust or like her, she is bad news for this family, and the sooner you stop pandering to her and focus on this family, this blood, the better." Branna gave a sigh; she had no idea why she even tried.

"She will be a powerful asset to this family outside of this realm, I have told you this. You know, you crave good wines and foods, and have the best of everything, even your choice of men to pervert in your deprived conquests. Morgana will help us extend our reach and gain more to the benefit of this line; you are foolish to keep attacking her." Maud spat on the floor, her eyes defiant and filled with hatred.

"I care not what you think, she is a risk to all here, and if she steps out of line, I will kill her for the sake of every one of us." Branna turned on the step.

"Are you really so certain you could kill her?" Maud wrinkled her face.

"Get out of my way and stop defending her, and I will show you. The line of this family will pass into my hands one day, and she will not live past that moment, it is I who will take this family forward after your time, not her." Branna walked onto the next step.

"I came here out of respect to warn you, and now you know. When her powers are unleashed, she will have more than just what the wizard taught her, be wary Daughter, you may meet your match." Maud gave a snort as she watched Branna.

"I fear no one, and she will have to work hard to match me, I have studied far deeper than any of you realise." Branna started to walk up the steps.

"So may it be, we shall see what becomes of it all in future days." Maud scoffed and looked down at her book.

"You will see my Raven Queen; a day will come when even you will not match me." Branna smiled on the steps, she was amused, she had no idea of the powers that flowed from Roack, should she require them.

Branna came up to the main hall where Otto was being wheeled towards the table, Berengar looked up and smiled from his plate, he had aged and yet she still saw that young warrior with a fierce stare, and an impulse to laugh freely when prompted, she stopped by his chair and leaned down to kiss his cheek, he smiled.

"You are happy today." She smiled as she walked around to her seat.

"I am, I am preparing the rooms for Morgana, and I am looking forward to her visit." She sat down at the table, and Otto scowled across it at her, she watched him as she sliced into her food.

"Maud knows Otto, I just told her, and I will remind you that in this house, she is a visiting member of the family, here at my invite. Be warned Otto, as I told my daughter I will tell you, I intend to unbind her powers of Fae, and when I do, you would show wisdom to guard your tongue around her. Morgana has built her own castle, and it is from there she will rule over her own domain, she has no interest in here, apart from her times of visit. Morgana is powerful, you would both be foolish to challenge her."

Otto looked down at his plate with a frown, and muttered something quietly to himself, Branna smiled as she watched him, he was no match for her, and she knew should he try without Maud, he would fall foul of her. Branna started to chew, in her mind her thoughts filled with the size and detail of the castle, Morgana was gifted, even more than she had realised.

Chapter Thirty One.

Seed of Destruction.

*B*ranna looked Morgana in the eye, and she gave a nod as she handed the small bottle over to her.

"Are you sure you want to do this, it will not be easy? This will change your appearance, I am unsure about this, but if this is what you desire, I will help you." Morgana nodded as she took the bottle.

"There is no heir, and that line has stolen enough from me, now, it is my time to steal back what is rightfully mine. I have thought long and hard about this, it is not pleasant, but it is the only way I can force their hand." Branna nodded.

"I admire you, think of this as just any other man, and do what has to be done, and if the gods are with you, nature will take its course and provide you the means to succeed." Morgana took a deep breath.

"I will see you soon, keep watch for me, I should return before Gwendolyn leaves." The white smoke rose up, and Branna stood on watch across the field, in the trees.

*I*n the large hall of Tor's farm, Arthur's closest knights gathered, to discuss matters in private. Bedivere looked across the table, as Lot told of Morgana's attitude.

"She is angry and upset with him, because he took all the revenue out of Tintagel for his castle. She has said often he had no need of a new castle, and could have ruled from there as Uther did." Galahad appeared disappointed.

"He has always talked highly of her; I had hoped he would listen to her. Why can she not let the old castle go, she has no real right to it under law?" Gwendolyn turned from the window.

"Morgana is no fool, and try telling her that, she will just tell you Uther had no right to steal what was not his. She is highly intelligent, it was foolish of Arthur to provoke her, she could have advised him well, as she did in the first days of his reign." Percival frowned, and looked up at her.

"Surely you jest?" Gwendolyn smirked.

"You find that comment far fetched? Morgana advised him very well in his management of Rhiannon, it is why she is not here now ordering you around. Never underestimate her loyalty to family, she has seen much, there are a good number who wanted her to be given the chance at pulling the sword. I am not convinced it would have been that hard for her." Percival could not comprehend what Gwendolyn was saying at all, and stared with utter disbelief.

"But only the rightful heir could pull free the sword, are you seriously telling us she could have ruled, she is a woman?" Gwendolyn raised her eyebrows.

"What are you suggesting Percival, a woman is not fit to rule, because if you open your eyes, you will see you address a Queen of her own race?" He gave a nod and looked down.

"I meant no disrespect, but the whole country was at war, we needed a strong arm to lead us into the battles we had." Gwendolyn gave a little titter.

"Morgana made a valid point, why has Arthur not spoken with his queen? She sits in the convent at Amesbury repenting her sins, which at least shows some remorse, he would be a fool not to at least try to recover the love he once felt. This nation needs a strong queen to back up her husband."

They all sat and looked at each other, it was clear none of them had actually thought of it, Gwendolyn rolled her eyes, Una stood quietly in the corner and gave a small chuckle.

"Please tell me at least one of you has tried to talk to him about it?" They all put their heads down and shook them, and Gwendolyn gave a frustrated sigh.

"Then that is what you must do, Arthur must at least try to make things right, not just for his sake, but for the country. Bedivere without Lancelot, you are closest to him, talk to him and try to convince him he should talk with her." He shifted in his seat, and looked uncomfortable, Gwendolyn sighed and turned to Una.

"I know you have Mac to care for, but could you go with him and help him talk to Arthur, this country will burn before this group plucks up the courage to talk of love and affection." They all turned to her and looked scandalised, she gave a giggle as she walked towards

Una.

"What was that they said about women not ruling?" She gave a chuckle as they all looked even more outraged, and yet said nothing, Una gave a nod.

"It is not a problem, it is possibly better I go, Arthur will need to know if there is danger, especially after father's disappearance. I am concerned he has not appeared anywhere." Gwendolyn looked worried, and Una could feel it within her.

"He will appear mother, he is the guardian of the Whitelines, they will not hold him for long." She took a deep breath and tried to smile, but it was clear she was hiding much of her fears.

Arthur sat slumped in the chair, his hand out holding his cup, which was empty having drunk all his wine. Morgana slipped in quietly and stood at the doors, as the latch clicked, he looked up and gave a sigh.

"Why are you here, have you come to yell and scream more? Go away Morgana, I have no wish to fight, I have no wish to do anything." She leaned off the door.

"I did not come to yell, Lot asked me to help you as I once did, before you decided you knew better. You know Brother, there was a time when you looked to me for advice, had that continued you would not find yourself in this place." He gave a sigh, and his head lolled back on the seat as he looked at her with faded blue eyes.

"There is no point now, all is lost, I found her naked with him, he had sated her desire, something I failed to do." Morgana slipped the cup from his hand and walked to the table, where the large jug stood and refilled his glass, she turned.

"You could win her back."

She slipped the bottle from her pocket, and without him seeing, she pulled the cork and five drops fell into his drink. She put the bottle back in her pocket, and turned swilling the cup in her hand.

"Tell me, what would you do if she came to you, would you yell, or do something different?" She walked towards him, as his eyes fixed on the cup of wine.

"Tell me Brother, would you take her into your arms and kiss her?" He took the cup and drank from it; she smiled as he swallowed.

"Would you untie her laces and reveal her small white breasts, and crave them with a desire no animal has ever known?" He took another drink, and she could see his breathing increase, she smiled.

"You would like that, wouldn't you?" His head lolled back, and his eyes opened wide, he gave a gasp.

"Yes." She smiled, as she could almost feel his thoughts, and knew in his mind he could see her. Morgana gave a little smile.

"She would like that too, to push you back on the bed and slide her soft white skin over you, and you would feel her womanly flesh burn with yours."

He gave another gasp, as Morgana reached out, and pushed the bottom of the cup closer to his lip, he tilted it and greedily took a swig, she smiled at him.

"She would want you to take her and hold her, and run your lips all over her, and you know where she would want you to taste her, don't you?" He was breathing faster, and she knew where his mind now was, he breathed out a long hard breath.

"Oh yes." Morgana pulled at her laces, she knew the drops were working as his eyes rolled as his breathing increased, she took his hand and pulled, her voice soft and alluring.

"Arthur… Come to me."

Arthur blinked his eyes, and his blurred vision cleared as he saw Guinevere. He felt a jolt as she lifted his hand, and slipped it inside her loose top, and he felt the warm softness of her breast, he gasped out loud.

"Oh Guinevere, I want you." Morgana smiled as she pulled, and he came forward, and her dress fell to the floor, and Arthur gazed down at her naked body filled with desire, she guided him softly towards the bed.

"Arthur… Arthur." He walked towards her, his need becoming more than apparent.

"Guinevere, oh Guinevere."

$\mathcal{S}$he pushed him onto the bed and he lay back, as she pulled his pants slowly down, Arthur watched as Guinevere came forward onto the bed and smiled, he gasped at her body with awe, as she slid slowly up towards him, her sex ready to take him. He sounded breathless as he looked at her.

"Oh Guinevere… I have been such a fool." She smiled at him, and lowered herself down onto him, and he lay back with a gasp and moaned.

Arthur watched as Guinevere slid backwards and forth, smiling and groaning in a way he had never known, each thrust sent him into oblivion, as she made love to him in ways, he had never felt possible. It was mind blowing, as he panted and gasped, and approached that moment of desire and climax. Guinevere smiled.

"Arthur, give me your seed, give me your heir."

"Yes."

Her hips thrust hard and he shuddered, and then she started to push faster and faster and he felt she was wild. It was more than his dreams and desires could handle, and he felt the rush, as his hips bucked upwards, and he released with a groan, then flopped back to the bed. Guinevere smiled, and leaned forward as he relaxed.

"As your father used powers to hide his face, and plant a seed in my family, I do the same, and take back the seed to use against you. How does it feel Little Brother, to know your seed will take, and it will bring forth your heir, but it shall not be hers, it will be mine."

Her laughter echoed in his ears, and then everything went black. Morgana grabbed her dress, and in a swirl of grey smoke she was gone, the deed was done, and she had finally stollen what she knew Arthur desired the most, the future of an heir.

*A*t the hall of Tor, Gwendolyn stood outside with Una as the horses were brought round, and the knights gathered. Gwendolyn smiled.

"Mac will be fine with Mel, and Una, make him understand, make him see the love he holds and tell him, she made a mistake, and she has paid a high price for it. No matter what, get him to her, no matter what the nuns say, if you have to, barge your way in." She nodded.

"I will not be long, and I will make sure they talk."

"Good, it could save this nation. Keep him safe and any problems, grab him and bring him to me at Florae." Una smiled as she hugged her mother.

"He will be fine, and they will speak. Take care, and stop worrying so much, he will appear, I know it."

She took a deep breath, and released her mother, then hugged her sisters and Mac. Una was aided to her horse, and the knights all turned, and rode off to meet up with Arthur, and hopefully convince him to talk with Guinevere. Gwendolyn had to get back to Florae, she looked at Madeleine and Melanie.

"I will be back later, once I have taken care of the days affairs in the house, there is much to do, and I want to check with my table, and see if anything has come to light."

Branna watched as Gwendolyn faded into a light and disappeared, Morgana was not back yet, and already two had left, she had no choice, she had to act, and hoped Morgana would catch her up.

Inside the large hall, Maurice organised the children with Melanie, as Madeline took care of Malachite. The column of smoke rose up from the floor on the upper balcony, and Branna appeared in the shadows, she was set and ready. She stood very still and quietly recited the charm as she held out two fingers and spun them round slowly, and a light breeze picked up. With her right hand controlling the spin, she reached into her other pocket, and lifted out a vial of blue powder, and placed her thumb on the top ready.

Madeleine gave a shiver and looked at her arm, the hairs on the back of it had risen with her goosebumps. She had her back to the balcony, so did not see the pale figure of Branna as she stepped up to the rail, and stretched out her hand, and the spinning breeze dropped, and expanded into the hall below.

Melanie stood up quickly from the children, as she sensed something wrong, and was engulfed in the spinning whirlwind. Her head snapped round, as she saw Madeleine snatch up Mac, and pass him to Maurice, as her children huddled together, and there was something about Madeleine's face that told her they may be trapped, then Maddy winked. On the wall at her side, she saw Tor's hat flapping in the spinning breeze which appeared to hold her legs to the floor, and not understanding why, she snatched it towards her. Maurice was looking pale, as he held the baby, and his other hand on his daughters, and she looked down to see Jasper take Treen's hand, there was nothing they could do, and suddenly she understood her fate, she looked up as Branna tipped the blue powdered contents out of the bottle, and her eyes met with Madeleine.

"I love you… All of you…"

She flopped to the floor with the others and there was a flash, the wind instantly stopped. Branna walked slowly towards the stairs, and a plume of grey smoke came out of the floor, as Morgana tied the front of her dress.

"Sorry, I arrived at the meeting spot, and had to get dressed, he lasted longer than I thought he would."

Morgana turned and looked down, where Maurice lay on the floor where he fell, the children were close to him, Morgana turned to Branna.

"They are just sleeping, aren't they?" Branna walked onwards towards the stairs.

"They are sleeping, but we must hurry, before others come, collect them up and then we must return to the castle as fast as we can. How are you, were you successful?" Morgana swallowed, and pulled a bottle out of her bag.

"I have felt cleaner, and have disgusted myself, but I did what was needed, and I have taken what Guinevere yearned for. I want this done, then I can wash myself, I feel my skin is crawling with his touch, and I want it off me."

Branna understood, she had sexually pleasured one or two in the past for no other reason than she wanted to get rid of them.

"There are pools in the marshes where the water flows warm, bathe your whole body, and you will feel better, for they contain many minerals of cleanliness."

They both hurried as they did the charms required, and one by one each of the members of Gwendolyn's family were sucked into the bottles. They worked as fast as they could, and yet Melanie and Maddy were not there, Morgana looked around.

"Where are her daughters?"

"We do not have time, now hurry, we have to get this done, there will be other times."

*S*ide by side they disappeared in a cloud of smoke. By the door unnoticed by the two of them, one of the nurse maids who was on her way to collect the children, lay fast asleep on the floor.

Both of them appeared in the large empty space at the top of the castle built by Morgana, the fire in the large open grate burned, warming the room, which contained very little apart from two very long tables, which contained three racks of vials of which only one had contents, which was a swirling mist of gold and white.

Branna grabbed one of the racks and replaced the bottles with the vials of swirling blue and white, these contained the children of the Fae sisters, and then Maurice into the next rack at it's side, Morgana looked at the three empty vials.

"Her daughters got away, and I had really hoped to get Gwendolyn, it is going to be dangerous until we have them all." Branna eyed the contents carefully.

"She will not be easy, you will need your Fae powers before you face her, but you are closer to removing them, the loss of her son in law and grandchildren will weaken her." Morgana frowned and looked at her.

"How so?" Branna stood up straight.

"When your father was taken from you, how did it feel?" Morgana shook her head.

"It is not the same, he was dead, these are not." Branna shrugged at her.

"Gwendolyn does not know that, does she?"

It made sense to Morgana, she knew how she felt in the weeks after she discovered her father was dead, and it did take its toll on her. It made sense that Gwendolyn would suffer, and she had to ponder if that would give her an edge, she looked at Branna.

"Merlin did the charm to help that beast rape my mother, Gwendolyn gave him the sword that convinced my father he should make a pact, that Uther broke. Rhiannon's weapons killed my father's soldiers, and it was one of her swords that killed him, and the rest of them conspired to seat him and let him rule with my mother as a prize and my father's bed as his. The world of men is turning their back on them for a new god, and so now they are no longer a part of my realm. I shall seal all of them away for eternity, and let man live by his own folly and destroy everything they built."

"You achieved much, now you must return, for you know she will look straight to you." Morgana gave a nod, and lifted her bag.

"Will you be alright; you know what to do?" Branna smiled, as she looked at her.

"It is the box I made that Ariel sleeps within, I will be fine, and all but Merlin will be encased in crystal before I return back to Roack." Morgana smiled.

"Sorry… Yes, I forgot, it was Ariel's box that gave me the idea, I know the charm, I have not done it yet, but I know what to do." She prepared to leave, and Branna spoke.

"Morgana, say the charm as you walk, and the seed will take. Remember, second bridge, turn left, follow that track and you will come to the heated pools, avoid the ones that bubble, for they are far too hot." She smiled at her.

"I had some wonderful evenings there with Ariel many years ago. Relax your mind and soak away the king, and then walk between the two large pools and stay straight, it will bring you back to your cottage." She nodded, as the smoke swirled up around her, and as it faded Morgana was gone.

*T*wo hours later, Morgana sat up to her neck in the steaming water and rubbed her skin, as she relaxed. One of the pools had a large rock in the centre, and as the sun slid down in the sky, she felt clean, but still disgusted with herself. She had done the charm and hoped done it right, and as she got in the pool, she washed frantically at her womanly bits to wash away the stickiness of them. She closed her eyes and relaxed, and breathed in slowly trying to calm her insides, and push the memory of what she had done with her brother out of her brain. The water was so nice and warm, and lapped up the bank in the peace and quiet, she heard a horse pant, and opened her eyes to see Stenlow watching her.

Morgana gasped and panicked, and tried to cover herself to hide her nakedness in the clear water.

"COMMANDER STENLOW…. I AM UNDRESSED!" He realised, and turned his head quickly.

"Oh… Er… I apologise, I can assure you, I was not staring, I am not a man like that."

He flustered on his seat, as Morgana looked back for her dress and cloak behind her, she was right in the middle and afraid to move. Stenlow flustered even more, as Morgana slipped off her rock and tried to crouch down behind it to hide, with the water touching her chin.

"I am most sorry, and I deeply apologise, one of the villagers saw you turn on this path, I did not realise you came here to bathe." She was crouched low, with her hands hiding her breasts.

"I may live alone in a small cottage with a small well, but I can assure you I keep myself very clean. I like to soak, and I was enjoying sitting back for an hour or two, and watching the world in peace, even that is not a crime in this realm. Close your eyes, as I am caught in view, and I have a need to get to my garments." He shut his eyes tight, looking even more flustered.

"My young lady I assure you, I only had to check things out for the queen." Morgana eyed him carefully, her cheeks reddening, as she stood up.

"Well, you most certainly did, I am sure you… Well, I am sure you checked all of my things out." He felt offended, opened his eyes, and turned to her.

"I am not like that."

His words died in his throat, as Morgana stood frozen completely naked right in front of him. She saw his eyes open, gave a slight squeal, and dropped back in the water behind the rock, disappearing for a second, before coming back up spluttering, and coughing. Stenlow had his head turned away apologising profusely.

"I am apologising my dear lady, I thought you had exited the water, oh … Dear, I am most certainly very sorry…. Very sorry indeed." Morgana stared at him.

"Stay still, and do not move until I say so."

She turned, and as quick as she could, she waded to the bank, and snatched up her dress and fought her way into it. She was wet and it stuck to her, which made the whole task much harder than it had to be, as behind her Stenlow continued to give apology after apology. She lifted her cloak, and pulled it tight around herself.

"Alright, I am dressed, and very embarrassed."

He took a deep breath and turned to see her stood on the opposite bank, her long black cloak pulled tightly around her, and her hair dripping. Her cheeks burned brightly with her embarrassment, as she regulated her breathing, and tried not to look him in the eye. He looked at her feeling very awkward.

"I really am so sorry, I was making sure that you were safe, there has been more troubles, and I wanted to ensure that you were in this realm. I had no idea you would be bathing, had I known, I would have called from a distance to alert you. Please accept my sincerest apologies." She nodded keeping her eyes down.

"It is fine… Well, it is not fine, I do not wish it to be known I display myself to others so freely, and I feel quite scared at the moment." He nodded, he understood.

"I can assure you; I will not speak of this to any, you can be assured, I would not say ill of you. My only aim was to make sure you were safe in the realm when it happened." She looked up.

"When what happened?" He looked awkward.

"Of that I cannot say, I have been sworn to secrecy."

She nodded, but she already knew, Branna was right, Rhiannon sent him immediately to check up on her. It was clear that Rhiannon still suspected her of everything, although in this particular case she was actually right. She worked out Stenlow would have to report this, and she thought she would risk it, and asked.

"Am I in danger… You know, if I am, you would tell me, wouldn't you? Merlin is still missing, and I am his assistant, does that put me at risk?" It worked better than a charm, Stenlow leaned forward in his seat, and she could feel the concern in his voice.

"I really do not know, but as I have already told you, please be careful and stay alert. Strange things are happening young lady, and I fear for many at the moment, and it is not just in this realm, it is in all the realms. To be cautious at the moment would be very prudent." She nodded at him.

"I understand, and I am being careful, I am watchful, I lock my door at all times and have stayed home more, but I do love to walk in the wild places of this realm. There is such beauty here, and the cottage is small with just one window." He sat back up.

"If you are finished bathing, I can escort you home safely." She gave a nod, and picked up her bag.

"That would be comforting to me, I find myself a little shaken." He nodded, as she walked between the pools onto the path, and he dismounted to walk his horse.

*M*organa walked back at a slow pace, and he walked at her side. Having calmed down a little she did see a little of the funny side, although she had no intentions of commenting. The sun was slipping down, the sky was turning a deep fiery red. She looked at him as he walked at her side, hoping he was not thinking of her naked body.

"It is beautiful here isn't it. It must be strange to live on the Moon Realm, and then come down here and look up to see home?" He took a deep breath, she felt he was enjoying the walk.

"I think Avalon suits me better, I have a desk with a window, and most nights I see the sun set in the sky. It is funny really; my younger sister often told me of how she would sit there and watch as I do now. I think of her most nights as I watch it, in a way, I feel I am watching it for her. We never had much in common growing up, she was always far more organised than I was, and very grounded, which is why when she told me of the sun sets, I felt there was a hidden part of her I had never seen. It probably sounds foolish, but watching as I do most nights, I feel closer to her, and I miss her." Morgana smiled.

"I do not think that is strange, you clearly love your sister a great deal, I think that is nice." He looked at her.

"You do, you think I love her, for I must admit, I have often wondered, we are so different and find it hard not to argue with each other, it makes me wonder?" Morgana could see the hope on his face, it was clearly very important to him.

"Maybe the next you see her, talk of the sunset and tell her how you watch it and think of her. Let her see that part of you, I am sure she loves you too, but maybe like you; she hides it. I would say it has to be worth a try."

It made a great deal of sense to him, and he smiled. The path widened and Morgana could see the cottage, and was feeling much less embarrassed now. Stenlow came to a halt with his horse at the end of her fence line.

"You are home safe now, I have to go this way, so I shall wait until I see you enter, and then I will be on my way." She turned with a smile and started to walk along the fence. He climbed up onto his horse, she turned to look back and waved.

"Thank you, Commander." He nodded.

"It was my pleasure." Realising what he said, he started to fluster.

"You know, to walk back, not the other… Oh dear, no not the other."

Morgana gave a giggle as she opened her gate, and walked down her path, she pulled out her key and unlocked the door and stepped in. She closed it leaning back on it and gave a sigh of relief, she had done it, for a few seconds there, she had thought she had been caught out. As Stenlow rode off back to Avalonia, she locked the door, feeling clean and free of the touch of her brother, and that the first big step of her plan was almost complete, she walked into the room, where the fire still glowed red, and swung her boiling pan over it.

Morgana crouched down, and lifted some wood from the basket, laid it on the embers, then softly blew until it ignited. For a moment she stared into the flames, and thought of her day, and realised just what exactly she had done. She blinked out of her thoughts and stood up, and looked down at her stomach, and placed her hand on it, and breathed out.

"Am I really ready for this, am I ready to be a mother, I always swore I would never have children, and yet, here I am? Was Branna right, is this what you really want Morgana?"

Chapter Thirty Two.

Clash of Powers.

Rhiannon looked at Stenlow as Gwendolyn stood to one side, he looked sheepish, and had been evasive, and Rhiannon could sense he was holding back, and she was not having any of it. She glared at him.

"How can you be so sure she was here all the time, if I find out you are hiding something from me Commander, I can assure you, you will find yourself with your sister faster than you can blink?" He shuffled his feet.

"My Queen, it is delicate, I do not know how to say what I want to." Gwendolyn looked at him.

"Delicate, Commander Stenlow, in what way could this be a delicate situation, half of my family has disappeared?" He turned and looked at her, as Rhiannon paced.

"I know she was here in the realm, I did find her, but I do not want to compromise her." Rhiannon turned looking very surprised.

"Commander, are you sleeping with her?" He stepped back looking absolutely shocked.

"NO!" He then realised who he was addressing.

"No, I am not My Queen." He looked at both of the women who were staring at him with renewed eyes. He gave a sigh, and tried to find the right words.

"It is where and how I found her… This is a delicate situation, please let me assure you, she was most definitely in the realm when it happened." Gwendolyn gave him a sly glance.

"Where and how, could you elaborate Commander?" He took a deep breath in.

"She was in the marshes at the hot springs, and had been there for two hours when I found her." Gwendolyn smirked.

"You saw her naked?" He looked at the floor and felt embarrassed.

"Yes." He lifted his head up.

"It was not deliberate, I rode up and before I realised, she was there in the water, undressed, and she was very embarrassed and distressed, because I saw her full body." Rhiannon looked unconcerned.

"Is that all, how on earth does seeing her naked take precedence over your queen?" Gwendolyn understood, and she smiled.

"You saw what she does not show, I understand now, you were trying to protect her modesty, I feel that is admirable of you. You say she had been there soaking for some hours?" He gave a nod.

"Yes, your Royal Highness. I gave her my word I would not mention the incident, she was most upset and shaken by it. I feel guilty I made her feel that way, it was not my intent, a lady should have her privacy. I spoke with her, and she is afraid, she fears as his assistant, she may be a target next, I felt she made a valid point. As I said, I felt for the young lady, this is a terrible business that has everyone afraid." Rhiannon snorted.

"She is no lady… Alright, you can go." Stenlow bowed and left the room, Gwendolyn sat down on the marble steps.

"It confirms what I thought, the patterns on the floor, and the maid's description, both fit the gust funnel charm, as described by Maddy. That is a Fae spell, Merlin would not have taught her that. Whoever took Merlin and my grandchildren is Fae, or has Fae knowledge. Morgana uses a combination of druid herblore and the Whitelines. My daughter did not really see who did it, and Mel told me she could not clearly see, as she was too concerned over the children."

It was a difficult moment, and she had never suspected Morgana, but for the first time since becoming queen, she was afraid and very worried, she had no leads and no means of finding out where her family was.

𝒦nowing Rhiannon was looking her way, and she had every intention of scapegoating her for every problem she had, made Morgana nervous. Knowing that Branna wanted to unbind her true powers, she decided that leaving Avalon and going to the castle with Branna would be safer. She hung her bag on her horse and walked it around the lake, as she skirted the lake and came on to the bottom end of the Queen's Road towards the gate of light.

As she walked at the side of her horse, she saw Fagan on his cart, he looked down at her and smiled.

"Off on yer travels again I see." She gave him a smile; it had been sometime since she had seen him.

"I feel when all eyes are on me, it is better I stay out of sight. The way I see it, she cannot blame me if I am not here." He gave a chuckle.

"Tis wise Little Dark Eyes, there are dark deeds indeed at this moment." She agreed.

"To be honest, everything said about me is dark, since the day I came here, I feel I have been under suspicion. All I want is a quiet place to study, but I fear this may not be the place." He whipped his horses, and the cart lurched as the queue cleared.

"Study well and take care." She smiled as he went one way, and she walked the other, towards the outer gate.

*I*t was good to be outside of Avalon, Morgana had arranged with Meg to have her horse cared for, and once she had met and handed over the horse, she walked into the deep woodlands and followed the river to a sheltered spot. Once there she jumped to her castle in the Chimerical Forest, where Branna stood waiting. Together they arrived outside Castle Berengar, and walked towards the long bridge, Branna appeared concerned.

"Times are getting hard, this realm is now sealed as illness is sweeping everywhere, our grain stores are full, but we cannot risk trade, the lowlands are suffering. Yesterday I got one of the guards to drive a wagon of grain through the forest near the river, and I sat hidden in the back under the canvass, and pushed three sacks off the back." Morgana looked at her, not understanding, Branna smiled.

"I know of the tribes stuck in this land; Ariel told me they were good people who took care of her. I have always been grateful to them for that, yet they hate me and call me the Dark Raven." Morgana suddenly understood.

"You made sure they had enough food?" Branna gave a nod as she chuckled.

"I am sure they will never see the irony of it, they will find food and survive whilst the realm is closed, and because it is closed, they will be protected from any illness. In a strange twist of fate, they are my people too, and I will watch over them." They walked onto the bridge, as Morgana thought about it.

"Otto shoots them, does that not bother you?" She gave another chuckle.

"It is rare he hits one, most of the time he misses, his pride does not allow him to admit that, but we all know." They both giggled, as they walked under the large archway and into the castle.

*I*t felt nice to be back in her room, in many ways she felt like this was her home from home, and she unpacked her bag and hung her few clothes up in the large empty cupboard. It was fascinating to compare her life wherever she went, it was well known that the Fae were far more advanced in the way that they lived. They were masters of many skills, which they had taken out into the world of men and helped them to learn. Morgana sat on her bed and remembered her first trip here, sitting in Branna's workroom listening to her talk of her surprise when first encountering how people outside of Avalon lived.

"I was shocked to see a hut made of mud and branches, I still now think back and cannot believe it. The fire was just a pit in the middle of the house and the floors were dirt. They slept on sacks of fern and grass, with rough woven blankets, filled with fleas. I had no idea at all, I had lived with Ariel, in what was considered a simple dwelling, but we had wooden cabinets and beds, and a mattress stuffed with duck down. Something as simple as tiles on a floor suddenly felt like such a luxury, and I think that was the first time I ever realised that as races we were so completely different."

The world of men had come a long way since then, although it still had a lot of catching up to do. It made such little sense to Morgana, even now there were villages that were the same as that first village Branna encountered, why had the Ruling Council not done more to progress the lines of men? Arthur had talked of equality between all men, yet the money he had spent had created a lavish paradise based on Fae design. Nothing in his kingdom was equal, or fair, the lords who were also knights had everything, and people like Meg struggled. Had Lot not told her she deserved better, and yet her cottage was her home, the place she had always loved.

She finished her unpacking, and headed back to the great hall to meet Branna, to find Rosamund alone reading, she looked up as Morgana entered.

"There are problems at the gate, times are becoming dire, my mother has gone to sort things out, there is water, wine, and freshly pressed fruit if you wish to partake."

Morgana turned to the table and lifted a pewter goblet, and poured the juice of lemons into it, then added some water. She walked up the table and looked down at Rosamund.

"What are you reading?" She looked up at her.

"It is the book the Christians preach from, I thought I would try to understand what is the appeal, but I cannot deny, I see nothing in it that appeals to me. I do not understand the men of your world, or why they would favour this over our rituals." Morgana shrugged.

"I do not understand it either, and yet my half brother is smitten with it, none of it makes sense to me."

She heard the tut behind her and knew straight away, she sighed, as she turned around to Maud at the top of her steps. She walked slowly into the hall with her usual scowl.

"I am told by my mother I have to leave you alone, and that soon you will have your full powers. I must admit, I am looking forward to it. I am curious as to what a half bred Fae with gifts will spar like." Rosamund watched as Morgana lowered her goblet to the table, Maud walked with a smirk of satisfaction, Morgana stared at her.

"It will be interesting to find out, I must admit, I am looking forward to it, and if you wish to spar, I will face you, but again as I have said before, I am no threat to you Grandmother. I have no desire to rule here, I have a realm of my own to build within." Maud walked right up to her and looked up at Morgana, who was a good foot taller.

"Not trying to back out, are you?"

Morgana smiled, as she realised Maud was going to face her as soon as her powers were unleashed, she turned slightly and reached for her goblet.

"If you insist on fighting, I will accommodate you, as I have told you, I do not fear you." Maud smiled a wide ugly smile, as Morgana's hand cupped the goblet.

"GOOD!"

Morgana felt the impact on her side and looked down, and saw the knife as Maud pulled it out, and screeched with laughter, it took a moment to understand, as she dropped the goblet. Morgana cupped the wound and saw the blood run onto her hand, it shocked her, and she slid to the side and leaned on the table. Maud took a step back and gave a wild howling laugh, Otto on the balcony was laughing, she could not believe this was happening, as she pushed her side hard, as the blood ran over her fingers.

Rosamund dropped her book and grabbed a towel, as Morgana breathed in, not believing Maud had just stabbed her. As Rosamund pulled her hand from the wound and pushed the towel onto it, and pressed hard, Morgana looked up and saw Maud laughing hysterically, as Otto laughed and cheered from above, and it was simply too much. She breathed in as her anger rose quickly and she gritted her teeth, Rosamund was on her knees trying to stop the blood, and Morgana had taken as much as she was going to, and her instincts kicked in with her temper.

She looked down as her eyes flickered with red light, and pulled off the towel, pushing Rosamund out of the way, and her right hand exploded in white light, as she stared at Maud with hatred and cupped the wound in her side. Morgana felt the power surging within her, her Fae powers were fighting inside her to be free of the bond that contained it. Her words came out through her gritted teeth, and were cold and filled with her hatred.

"I have had as much as I am going to take from you." They were ice cold, and Rosamund slid backwards away, as she saw Morgana healing her own wound.

"Tell me Maud… If you are so powerful, why do you only ever sneak up on me?" Morgana with her hand glowing bright white, took a step forward, and Maud smirked.

"I hate and despise you; I hate your filthy mixed blood and your poisoned line, that corrupted my son. I will never accept you, and you will never rule as long as I live." Maud took two paces backwards as her hands came up like lightening, and there was a bright red flash.

Morgana lifted her left hand to block, and it hit her hard and burned through her top, jolting her slightly, and she staggered to one side. Her head turned as another flash hit her, and she found herself lifted off her feet and was thrown backwards. She crashed into three chairs, and felt the stars as her head collided, she had never sparred, and was not sure how to, but she had no intention of losing, and her anger rose even more as her left hand lit up, and a wave of power shot down her arm.

Maud screamed with delight as she dodged the shot, and fired back two more, as Morgana tried to pull herself free from the chairs.

"YOU WILL HAVE TO DO BETTER THAN THAT HALF BRAIN!"

Morgana felt the impact as it slammed into her, and she was sent flying backwards through the chairs as they shot in the air and crashed either side of her. Morgana slammed into the wall, and her anger rose to an even higher pitch, she had no intention of losing, but Maud was getting the upper hand. She shook her head as her anger boiled and her eyes flickered with red light, Rosamund had gotten out of the way, she had no powers and knew to stay well clear. In her mind she spoke as Maud squealed with delight and Otto above her yelled out and cheered, he was enjoying this more than anything else in years.

"Morgana, calm yourself, think of Merlin and what he taught you, keep your head and focus." Maud was laughing and jeering, and too busy enjoying thinking she was winning, Morgana tried to clear her mind, but she was angrier, not at Maud, but at herself.

"Why, why drop your guard, you are a fool, you should have been wary, you know what she is like, Branna warned you?"

She was so angry, but her thoughts were clearing, the bleeding was stopped, and she felt her strength was no longer draining. Inside her, she felt the anger swirling, and she did not want to lose control, but it was hard, Merlin yelled in her head.

"YOU LOST CONTROL, AND LET YOUR ANGER GET THE BETTER OF YOU, YOU MUST STAY FOCUSED!" She understood that, it was just a lot harder than Merlin thought, she was absolutely raging with hate for Maud.

Maud lifted her hand as Morgana tried to get off the floor, and Morgana saw her, this time she was not putting up with it, she flicked her wrist and spun it fast, and huge bolt of white light came flashing out of it. Morgana sprang to her feet as the lightning bolt rocketed into Maud who tried to deflect it, but missed, and it hit her head on. She screamed and sent flash after red flash firing in a hail at Morgana, who stood shakily on her feet.

As Maud was slammed into the wall scattering armour and tapestries, as they tore everywhere, Morgana stood and deflected shot after shot from the hail that was coming at her. Her temper was now at fever pitch, Otto had gone quiet, as Morgana's eyes flared with red light engulfing all of her face.

"I AM DONE WITH YOU MAUD, I HAVE HAD ENOUGH, HOW MANY TIMES DO I HAVE TO TELL YOU?" Bolt after bolt of lightning shot out of Morgana, as her temper ratcheted up even more.

"I HAVE HAD ENOUGH, WHEN WILL YOU LEARN?" Maud screamed, as she was pinned to the wall, and Morgana walked slowly forward screaming at her.

"JUST LEAVE ME THE HELL ALONE, I DO NOT WANT TO RULE HERE. I HAVE TOLD YOU, AND I AM SICK OF HAVING TO DO THIS." Maud screamed at the top of her voice.

"I WILL NEVER STOP UNTIL YOU ARE DEAD!"

Rosamund watched feeling terrified, Morgana's eyes had so much light coming out of them, the whole room was lit up with a fiery glow. Morgana's temper was now at fever pitch, and her powers inside her were straining at the bond placed around them by Branna. Maud fired from within the hail of spells coming out of Morgana, both of them were out of control, but Branna was not here to stop either of them. Morgana opened her hand and then snatched at the air, and there was a death defying scream, as Morgana pulled back her arm, and then thrust it forward fast, she was no longer in control and running on instinct.

Maud shot forward as if held by an invisible hand, and then slammed violently back into the wall, as Morgana stood still in the middle of the room the light engulfing her. Maud was flicking her wrists and sending more shots into Morgana, but lightening shot from her hitting all of the spells that were fired from Maud. Maud was screaming and yelling her hate, but Rosamund could clearly see she was losing, Morgana was firmly in control.

"I WANT YOU TO STOP, YOU CAN RULE HERE, JUST STOP, AND LEAVE ME ALONE."

Maud slid down the wall, she was bleeding, and Morgana stopped, and the light around her started to fade, as she breathed in and tried to calm herself. Her dress was covered in blood, and her sleeve was torn, her arm was bleeding, she had a cut in her hairline and the blood ran down the side of her face. Morgana stared with flickering eyes at Maud as she breathed in, her voice was calmer.

"Just stop… I am sick of this, we are family, can you not see that?" She lifted a limp arm and pointed.

"Out there, past that bubble of protection, they hate us, and they want to destroy us. They killed my father and raped my mother; do you even understand that? My father was your son, and they took his life and his land, because a beast of a king wanted it. The Ruling Council sat back and let Uther do whatever he wanted, because he was their chosen one and we were nothing to them. We are family, this is all we have left, why is it so hard for you to understand that Grandmother?" She swayed, as Branna watched from the doorway in silence.

Maud looked up at her and it was clear, she would never accept Morgana, she scowled at her from her bloody face.

"I hate you; do you understand that? He left here and went to her and had you, and that is why he is dead. You are the reason, and I will never be satisfied until you are dead." Morgana shook her head.

"That is insane, that is not the reason he died, he was happy. He was a loving father to me; he was kind to his people and loved by all of them. Your son was a man with the power of a king and loved for it, I know, I loved him deeply, like all of us did. Grandmother you have it all wrong." Maud slid herself back up the wall, and Morgana gave a sigh.

"Grandmother stop… You are wasting your time, please stop this." Maud sneered at her, and lifted her hand.

"NEVER!"

As her hand came up, Morgana raised her wrist, and clenched her hand in mid air, Maud gasped, as her face contorted. Morgana swayed as she watched Maud, a small pool of blood on the floor beside her right foot, her eyes fixed on Maud as she breathed slowly. Her face looked so sad as Branna watched, and Morgana softly shook her head.

"I do not want to do this grandmother; you have to stop." Maud gasped in feeling the tightness of her lungs, but gasped out her words.

"I will… Never stop… Until you are dead." Morgana sighed, and lifted her left hand.

"Grandmother it is over… WATCH." She lifted her left hand, and then clicked her fingers.

"RAJANI!" Maud's eyes opened wide, as Rajani lifted off her perch and flew to Morgana, and landed softly on her wrist. Morgana looked back at Maud, as she looked on in horror.

"It is over Grandmother; you cannot win this." Morgana dropped her hand, and Maud crashed to the floor, and Morgana turned her head to Rajani.

"Break from her, you deserve better than her." Maud screamed out in a terrifying wail.

The bird gave a loud screech, and Roack swooped in, and flew low over the room and then up to her perch, landed, and watched the scene below.

"Your bonds are breaking Morgana, your power fights inside to come out, Rajani feels them and knows who is the stronger." Morgana swayed forward, her legs felt weak, as she focused on Maud.

"I can take this bird if I so choose, can you see? We can end this now, live, and tolerate each other, or we will have to take this to the end, and I do not want that, there has been too much death in this family."

One of Maud's arms hung limp and useless as she sat on the floor, and she shook her head slowly.

"I will never tolerate you, and I will never stop until you are dead." Morgana sighed.

"WHY CAN YOU JUST NOT ACCEPT THAT WE ARE ALL A FAMILY, AND THAT IT IS ALL WE HAVE?" Maud lifted her good arm, and pointed it at Morgana.

It flashed, and Rajani lifted into the air, as Morgana screamed at her with all her might, and there was an enormous explosion of red light out of her.

"JUST STOP!"

Everyone ducked, as a huge ball of white light flashed, and then turned deep red, and the whole of the room was engulfed. Even Branna looked away, as the light thundered out of Morgana, and up into the roof like a burning inferno. Her Fae powers had broken free, and she was engulfed as they met, and mixed with the Whitelines.

Maud's screams wailed through the light, and Roack lifted off her perch and flew right into the centre of the light, and it went out. Morgana was as white as chalk, covered in blood with tears in her eyes as she swayed. Her knees buckled, and she flopped to the floor, and Maud lay dead against the wall. Her body was crumpled and broken, her eyes dull and lifeless as they stared at the ceiling. Her connection to Rajani had been severed by the power of Morgana.

Branna gave a sigh, and walked into the room, as Rosamund got up from the floor where she had been blasted. Otto was lay on his side, his chair several feet away and smashed, as he stared through the rails at his dead wife.

Branna knelt down and looked at Morgana, and placed a hand on her chest, she gave a sigh, as her hand moved to Morgana's head, and she looked up at Rosamund with sad eyes.

"This is what I feared, the Whitelines meeting her Fae powers fractured her mind. Her anger magnified it all, it is why I wanted to do this alone with her, it had to be done with great care." Rosamund looked at Morgana.

"Will she live?" Branna looked down with great sadness.

"I really do not know, I understand her Fae side, not fully the Whitelines. Time will be the only way to tell." Rosamund could not believe what she had witnessed.

"She healed her own stab wound. Maud stabbed her, which is how it all started and she just put her hand on it and white power pumped into it, and she healed. I have never seen anything like it." Branna smiled.

"I taught her that, I did it to heal Berengar, it was Ariel who taught me. Come, we will get her to her room, she will need time to heal." Otto looked down as he lay on the floor pressed up against the rails.

"What about my wife, that half breed bitch killed her?" Branna looked up at him, and her eyes narrowed.

"Had your wife listened to me she would be alive now, and had she won, I would have killed her for disobeying me. You know the rule, you are supposed to be Varisci. Maud challenged and lost in the fight, that is the rule, Maud died because she was not a good enough warrior, now hold your tongue, or you will join her."

*M*organa was taken down to her room, where aided by Rosamund, Branna washed her and healed her wounds, and then lay her in bed and sat by her side. Rosamund then took care of Maud, who was laid out on a slab in her workroom. She would be seated in her seat in the room of the gathering, preserved and then sealed inside a crystal box, as was the tradition of the family. Once everything was cleaned up, Rosamund returned to Branna and sat in the room, as Morgana lay lost in her mind, and her powers swirled inside her. Rosamund looked at her mother as she sat holding Morgana by the hand.

"She reminded me of you as she fought to defend herself. I felt her power and it was yours, Morgana should rule, she has earned the right to." Branna smiled, as she lifted her eyes to her daughter.

"She was never the one to rule, I have only ever felt I could trust one to replace me, and understand the way my mind had thought of the future, and it was Ariel who showed me who it would be."

"She did… Who?" Branna smiled.

"You… Rosamund, you do not have my powers, but you have the strength of my mind. Ariel told me she hoped you would be born without powers, because if you were, Maud would never try to kill you. When you were born, we talked and she pointed out that you had a great mind, I knew then I would only ever trust you, and having watched you, I can see that Ariel was right. I am tired my dear daughter, when Morgana recovers, she will leave, she has much to do in her own kingdom. At that time, I have a spell to let me sleep safe for a long time, and as I sleep, it will be you who takes on Berengar Castle and this family, for you are the only one who understands this family as Morgana does." Rosamund looked at Morgana.

"Will she recover?" Branna sighed.

"Her body will heal, her Fae powers are now free, but she is part line of man, and the question now is, will Morgana heal enough to heal her mind? I cannot answer that question at the moment. Until she wakes up, we will not know. She is with child, I feel it, and so I am hoping that alone helps her mind heal."

*L*ay in her bed lost to the world, Morgana dreamed, living her life sat by the bedroom window, holding her book open, as she looked out across the cliff tops.

"MORGANA… MORGANA WHERE ARE YOU?" She looked around at the door, and smiled.

"I AM COMING FATHER!"

Chapter Thirty Three.

Awakenings.

Deep in the Chimerical Forest, the small grey and dull little figure of a Sandling, hid under a log and shook with fear. All around the forest was quiet, and nothing stirred, as she lay quaking and feeling lost, alone, and unsafe.

A few feet away, a bright light illuminated, and she shrunk back further under the log, her large bright dark eyes wide open, showing the terror within her. As she watched, a woman bathed in bright white light crouched down in front of her, and smiled. She had the most beautiful grey eyes filled with life and love. She reached out a soft delicate pure white hand, and the little drab Sandling jerked back more, pressing herself into the underside of the log. The voice of the woman bathed in light was soft and caring and filled with love.

"Do not be afraid, I will not hurt you. Come, it is time your days of loneliness ended, it is time to meet who you belong to, and your days of being separated will end. It is time to be complete again."

It was late, and the candle flickered in the holder casting a small amount of light on the snow white face of Morgana. It had been two weeks, and yet Branna sat holding her hand as she sniffled quietly, lost and alone and feeling the pain of losing yet more of her family. Morgana's words echoing in her ears.

"We can end this now, live, and tolerate each other, or we will have to take this to the end, and I do not want that, there has been too much death in this family." She sniffled and squeezed Morgana by the hand.

"I am sorry, I never should have left you alone, I knew her better, it is my fault and hope you can forgive me? This is not how it was meant to be Morgana, I wanted to protect you. My life is cursed, everyone I have cared about has been ripped from my life, and all because I was so stupid and chased the darkness for approval of a queen who hated me."

Branna dropped her head, and wept deep bitter sobs, as Morgana lay unaware of where she was, or what she had been. Trapped in her mind, living a life that had never existed, as she walked with her father and talked across the tops of the cliffs in Tintagel.

By the open door, a small orb of white light appeared and hovered for a moment. It slowly entered the room and hovered at the end of the bed, an increase of light alerted Branna and she looked up, as she felt a familiar presence, and she inhaled, her word, almost a whisper.

"Ariel?"

The orb floated over the bed, as Branna watched not knowing what to make of it, feeling a power she knew well. Lost for words, she rose slowly to her feet, her hand slipping out of Morgana's. Branna watched as the orb hovered over Morgana, and then expanded out, and in the centre of the bright white light, stood a small figure. Branna gasped as she began to realise what it was, and stood frozen, watching, as the small figure stepped out of the light and onto the bed. Tears filled Branna's eyes, as the tiny creature looked down at Morgana, and smiled, and Branna understood, this was Morgana's own personal Sandling.

The sandling bowed as she smiled, and then screwed up her eyes, and there was a loud 'Pop!' She turned into a bright white orb, and slowly lowered down to Morgana's forehead. Branna was holding her breath, as the tears dripped off her cheeks, as she watched the orb slowly sink inside Morgana. As it disappeared, the bright light that surrounded them both, went out, and Morgana mumbled in her sleep.

Lost in her dream as she walked at the side of her father, following the path back towards the beautiful castle in the distance, Morgana felt something take hold of her hand, and she looked down. Smiling up at her was a tiny creature with large eyes and long black hair, Morgana smiled, as if she knew her. She stopped walking and turned to her father, as he smiled at her.

"I have to go; will I see you again?" Victor of Berengar smiled, but shook his head.

"We have said what was needed, what was lost between us, go

with the knowledge that I am proud of the daughter I created. I will always be there in your shadows and heart. Go Morgana, go with my love."

In a strange way she knew this would happen, she had sensed it all along, and yet now was the moment she knew would come, and she did not want it to.

"I want to stay, but I know I cannot. I have missed you so much, and have loved these moments we have shared." He smiled at her.

"It is time for you to grow up Morgana, and time to walk in my footsteps, and build something that will last as I have. Walk tall Morgana of Berengar, and know you walk forth from a line of great warriors." The tiny hand squeezed her, and suddenly she felt she was dragged backwards into the spiralling darkness, mixed with streaks of light.

Branna watched with hope in her heart, holding her breath, as suddenly, Morgana lurched her chest upwards, her head lolling back on the pillow, as she took a huge, gasping, intake of breath. Her body froze for a second, as if held up by a string, and almost as if the string was cut, her body flopped to the bed, and her eyes snapped open, and she breathed out a long rush of air. Branna could not believe her eyes, and smiled as her tears dripped onto the blankets, Morgana's eyes moved towards her, and Branna smiled, and wiped her eyes.

"Welcome back, I was so afraid, I thought I had lost you."

Morgana was weak, and her mind was still cloudy, but it was enough for Branna as she sat on the bed filled with relief. There was confusion, and little understanding when she found out she had been in bed for two weeks, as Branna slowly told her the story of her confrontation with Maud. For Morgana it was difficult, all she remembered was walking with her father, and yet she was an adult, and he was the same age as when he had died, it made so little sense to her.

The news of her awakening was not as well received as one would have thought, if anything, the family were divided over what had happened, Otto was obviously, firmly against her. Ulric had arrived with his new wife Amalina, Gundobarld and Dagaric were home which was a rare occasion, and Merwig wandered around talking to Lothar. Morgana's survival unsettled all of them, Rosamund had been very precise in the abilities of Morgana, and how it made her afraid.

Lothar who knew Morgana well had no problems with her, Dagaric and Merwig were undecided, they had both had many run-ins with Maud, and did not have that much of a liking for her. Gundobauld and Ulric both felt that she could become dangerous, especially now she had seen her true powers, and the one fact everyone feared, was that on her command, Rajani broke her connection to Maud. That frightened all of them, the thought of one word from Morgana and their life force could be severed was their greatest concern.

Whilst they all sat and talked, Morgana slowly came back to normal, or as normal as she could do. From the moment she awoke, it was clear, a little of that almost innocent sparkle had left her, she appeared calmer and more focused, and probably more precise than she had ever been. In all other regards she was still Morgana, and yet Branna noticed she smiled less, there had been a change, and Branna was interested in working out just what they were.

*I*t took a week before she dressed and managed to stand up, but with each passing day, she grew stronger, and soon appeared above in the hall to sit and share a meal, although she was a lot quieter than normal, and mainly sat and listened as they all spoke of the world outside. Towards the end of the meal, she looked at Lothar.

"What news of Avalon?"

Branna noticed; it was the first time she had mentioned it since her recovery. Lothar leaned on the table.

"Not much has changed, the realm is still sealed to none residents, they say Gwendolyn grieves for the loss of her family in Florae, and the Golden Queen is adamant it was the work of a dark shadow, and ruled those of dark hair are not to enter Avalonia. Arthur has done little, it is said Una the daughter of Gwendolyn is trying to get him to do more to repair the kingdom, although how she will achieve that, no one knows, the whole country is in tatters."

Morgana nodded, her face was paler than it had ever been, and it concerned Branna that her colour had not returned to her cheeks. Otto refused to eat at a table with a Celt, and stayed in his room. After the meal Branna and Morgana walked back down to their rooms, Morgana was still very quiet and withdrawn, she sat on her bed as Branna leaned on the door.

"Are you really alright?" Morgana gave a sigh.

"I am struggling a little with coming to terms with things." Branna nodded as she watched.

"I do understand Morgana, I know this, I have been there." Morgana looked at her, her voice cracked a little and was low.

"I killed your daughter… I have no understanding of how to accept that, I lifted a hand and all my anger came out. Merlin warned me to not let that happen, and yet I lost control. Branna, I looked at them all tonight, and it is there in their hearts, they feel it, they feel threatened by me. I have to go, I cannot be here, I need to be alone until I can figure this all out." Branna gave a soft nod.

"I do understand, but Morgana, remember, to me, you are as a daughter, never forget that. Maud was wrong to attack you, and you gave her plenty of chances to stop. If I am honest, I was surprised by the things you told her, and I did believe that she could have found common ground with you. Morgana, in the end, you had no other option, the result was always going to be the same, we all knew it, only one of you could live, never forget that, for that was Maud's plan."

*T*he following morning, Morgana woke early and dressed, the castle was silent, as the sun was just about to rise. She walked out of her room with her bag on her shoulder, and made her way to the large hall, where the steps parted, one flight rose to the upper room, and one went down to the deeper parts of the castle.

Morgana walked slowly down the stone steps into Maud's workroom, which was utterly silent, the slab she had been laid out on was still there. Morgana looked around, it appeared more cluttered and fuller than she had remembered it on her only visit down here on her first trip. In her mind the voice of Maud echoed back from the past.

"You should not be down here; I share my work with no one."

"I am not here to pry, Branna told me you were very skilled in plant lore, and I have a deep interest in it, I make tinctures to cure people."

"Typical… Celts have no real understanding of the power of the plant world, you make tinctures, whilst I stretch the knowledge of the universe, and bend its will to mine."

*M*organa walked along the long stretch of table filled with dust and bottles containing the many plants she knew. Her main work area was cluttered, and yet there lay open was her thick book, of all she had learned. She stopped and looked down at it, and read her notes on how to transform the flesh, using roots and leaves, she had never heard of such things, and leaned forward to read more.

A flutter sounded into her ear and she looked up to see Rajani watching her. Morgana stood up straight as she looked at the bird, not understanding why it was still here.

"You are free of her now, why stay?" Rajani just stared at her, and she knew that without a connection, she could not speak to the bird. Morgana gave a sigh.

"I aim to leave, like you, I feel my actions have cut me free of the ravens who live here. I no longer belong here; they hate me for killing your mistress. It appears we have that in common, both of us are once again alone in this world. Rajani, I will never understand why you saved Jarron, but I will always be grateful, I hope in some small way you understand that. Maud was cruel to you, and if any good has come of this, for I do feel a wretched guilt, my actions have freed you. I did not want to kill her, I just wanted her to stop, it was never my intent and had I not lost my temper, you would not have lost your mistress. Fly free, for I aim to."

Morgana lifted the book off Maud's work table and slid it into her bag, then turned and walked back towards the steps, as she did, Rajani lifted into the air and flew to her shoulder where she landed softly on it. Morgana gave a small smile, as she walked up the steps with Rajani perched on her shoulder.

"We shall leave together, and both of us can be companions as we wander into a changing world." She walked slowly up the steps and heard voices.

"She is dangerous, you said it yourself mother, her mind fractured, how can we trust her now?"

"You are wrong, she is loyal to this family, Morgana wants nothing from any of you. Maud should have learned, Morgana never wanted my seat, that was why I grew close to her. Tell me, can I trust any of you compared to her, all of you would rip out my heart and take over if for one moment you felt you had an edge?"

"Mother, she commanded Rajani to break her link, and the raven did it, how can we risk that, she is a threat to us all?"

"You are fools, Rajani hated Maud, she was tired of being beaten and suffering the cruelty of a mistress that should have cared for her.

You should thank Morgana, there is a lesson there to be learned about your treatment of your ravens. If Rajani had wanted to stay connected, she would have, none of us can force the loyalty of the ravens, all we can do is earn it, and Morgana showed that clearly."

"Tell us Mother, she showed a great deal of power, has she risen to even challenge you?" Branna laughed.

"What fools you all are, Morgana would never challenge me, she is the most loyal of all of you, she is powerful, and she has earned it, but she is not tied to a raven and never will be, she has no need, she has the power to rule free of the darkness that eats at all of you."

When Morgana walked out of the stairwell into the hall, all of the family were sat at the table, the room went instantly silent, as they all saw the large raven on her shoulder. Branna stood up from her seat, and walked towards her.

"You do not have to go so soon; you still have a way to go to recover." Morgana nodded.

"I know… Thank you, I owe you my life, and my loyalty will be forever to you and the line of this family. Branna, you know as well as I know, I cannot stay, if I do, they will rise up and kill me. I have a kingdom of my own to build, and debts to settle, and like you, I will help add more to this line of ravens to continue its growth. I owe you so much and have no way of understanding how to thank you. I am sorry you lost a daughter, I truly am." Branna smiled, and her eyes teared up.

"It was not your fault, and I still have a daughter in whom I hold great pride, for you will always be a daughter to me Morgana. I understand that this time is needed, and I hope your path has the answers you seek, and it pleases me that you will not be alone, for Rajani will be a good companion to you. Morgana, I will always be there in your shadow, take care my young raven." Morgana nodded and took a deep breath, and Branna nodded at her.

"Just promise me one thing Morgana… When the time comes, return to me, and give birth to your child here with me." Morgana nodded, and spoke quietly.

"I will."

Branna stood, and watched from the top of the tower, as Morgana with Rajani on her shoulder walked out of the castle, and across the long bridge of stone. On the far side, she saw Morgana stop for a second and look back, and then she continued, a tall, slender woman of power with a large raven on her shoulder, she truly was the exact image of a younger Branna. Branna took a deep breath and wiped her eyes.

"Good luck my queen of the Celts, stay strong my Countess of Darkness. Be the Raven, I know you to be."

As Morgana walked into the trees, dark grey smoke funnelled up from the ground, and surrounded her, and as it drifted away on the breeze she had gone. Branna continued to watch, and felt the sadness in her heart, for she knew of the pain Morgana had felt in the taking of Maud's life. Like she did with Halbrand, she knew that Morgana would carry that inside her forever, it was the one life, she had never wanted to take, but had been forced to.

*M*organa travelled back to her castle, where she showed Rajani the perch high up on her wall, above her work tables. The racks of bottles were empty bar one, down in the lower levels of her castle, a row of crystal tubes stood, within which, were encased the son in law, and grandchildren of Gwendolyn. Rajani flew up to the perch, and Morgana gave her a nod.

"I have to travel to my cottage, there are things I need, but you must stay here, for that is one realm where they will hate you and try to kill you. The doors to the raven's mouth are open, you can fly free if you need to hunt." She felt the bird understood her, and turned for the door.

"I will be back in a few days; I need some time alone, and some time to heal."

The dark grey smoke swirled up around her, and the raven watched her disappear. Morgana walked slowly along the path from the marshes towards the road of her cottage, and stopped. There were many riders on the road, and she was wary. She stood in the shadows for a long time, until she knew the road was completely safe, and then made her way as quickly as she could to her cottage. Once inside, she built up the fire, feeling a sense of ease as she felt in a space that was familiar and safe. She stood in the centre of her room, it was small, cluttered and not very well furnished, and in her mind, memories flooded into her.

"Hello Jarron, I am Morgana, we will be looking after each other from now on."

"My father has been dead for years, Uther was never my father, he was your husband. I am sorry he has left you, but do not ask me to grieve the man that killed my father, for I never will."

"You are right, you are the queen of the Fae of Moon, I am Morgana, daughter of Igraine, widow of King Uther, the one true king. I am a countess, and by right of birth, Queen of the Britons of the realm of men. I am apprentice to Merlin, guardian of the Whitelines, as appointed by the White Lord himself, who by rights, is a superior within the ruling council. It appears we are equals, queen of Fae."

She walked into her room, and sat on her bed with a sigh, as her mind swirled, and pictures flowed almost as if they had been lost, and were only now finding their way back.

"Will being a man of this Christ help, there is also great wisdom in the old ways of this land?"

"So, you gave him Excalibur, a sword you would not even allow his father to hold."

"Morgana, we don't have to, just because they do not agree, does not make them right. Answer me this, was it right to choose one man out of the many to rule, was it right to arm him with superior weapons, who then slayed the man who was actually benefiting his people most? Your father did much to support and protect the people of his community, and yet they took him from not just you, they took him from everyone."

"You are an amazing and beautiful woman Morgana, and I do not ask this because you liven up my bed. I ask because it is heartfelt to me, I care for you deeply."

"That is insane, that is not the reason he died, he was happy, he was a loving father to me, he was kind to his people and loved by all of them. Your son was a man with the power of a king and loved for it, I know, I loved him deeply, like all of us did. Grandmother you have it all wrong."

"I will never tolerate you, and I will never stop until you are dead." Morgana sighed.

"WHY CAN YOU JUST NOT ACCEPT THAT WE ARE ALL A FAMILY, AND THAT IT IS ALL WE HAVE?"

"I killed your daughter… I have no understanding of how to accept that, I lifted a hand and all my anger came out. Merlin warned me to not let that happen, and yet I lost control."

"It was not your fault, and I still have a daughter in whom I hold great pride, for you will always be a daughter to me Morgana."

All she wanted was to go back, go back to that place where she walked with her father along the tops of the cliffs. She did not want these feelings, or the anger she felt, she did not want the hatred from Rhiannon, suspicion from Eve or Gwendolyn, why had no one ever understood, all she had ever wanted was to be left alone as a child with her parents. Why had Uther wanted the power, why had the council helped him, and why did they have to kill her father and defile her mother? They had interfered and destroyed everything she had loved, and they had no right, and had never given a justifiable reason, apart from it was their will, it is what they desired, she felt the anger bubbling inside of her as she looked up at the ceiling of her room and screamed.

"WHY… WHY COULD YOU NOT JUST LEAVE US ALONE, WHY TAKE MY FATHER, WHY ALLOW THAT BEAST TO RAPE HER!?"

She lifted her hands and pulled them to her face, as she looked down and wept, her voice low and filled with pain. Her sobs were deep and bitter, as she held her face, and powerful emotions of hurt ripped through her.

"You should have left me there Branna, locked inside, free of it all, left alone with my parents, and the only part of my life that was happy." She gasped a deep sob, and breathed out her words, and it was clear how badly hurt she was.

"He was my father, the man I loved and adored, why did they take him from me, why Branna, why are they allowed to do that, and yet they call you and me, for what, for what Branna, defending ourselves?"

As Morgana sobbed, and grieved into her hands, outside on the other side of the wall, the heavily veiled figure of Branna stood silent with tears in her eyes. She knew Morgana was right, but who would listen, they had all conspired together, and it had changed Morgana's life forever?

Branna stood vigil for a long time, as Morgana settled down, and when she felt she had fallen asleep, she faded away and returned to her castle. The reaction of Morgana she had expected, in many ways she felt it was a turning point, as this would fuel her awakening, and her time to act would be soon.

Chapter Thirty Four.

The Finger of Blame.

*F*or the next week Morgana stayed in her cottage, wept, drank her tonic, and began a process of understanding on a much deeper level, of the powers she held. Branna's confirmation that the seed of Arthur had taken, in a sense brought her back to herself. She was with child, and had to take better care of herself, so she rested and grew stronger, and her mind began to clear more, as her thoughts could focus better. No one knew she was in Avalon; she had entered unseen by the paths of the marshes, and yet Sequana spoke of shadows in the realm, and Rhiannon became more and more suspicious.

She made a few trips back to the castle, to check on Rajani, and also took some of her things with her to make more room in her small cottage. She had more clothing, and she felt that to busy herself would help take her mind off the pain she felt over her confrontation with Maud. It had helped a little. She left Maud's black book at the castle, with a few of the books that had been left her by Merlin, she knew that she would spend many days there, now she had Rajani to talk to as she studied, and she enjoyed her quiet time away from Avalon.

A little over a week after returning, Morgana ran out of wild chamomile, and lifted her basket, and went for a walk. She wandered over towards the Giant's Shoulder, where she knew it grew in great abundance, and yet was clear of people. She breathed in the clear air, and smelt the scents of the grasses and flowers, and felt more like the person she was before her confrontation with Maud.

Lost in her enjoyment, she collected enough chamomile to supply her teas for some time, and sat lost in thought on a log drifting in and out of her thoughts, unaware that she was watched over by two figures. Onc was a shadow, high above her, and one a woman of great beauty with violet eyes, and long red hair. Morgana sat and held her stomach, and looked down at it, her act to gain the seed of Arthur had repulsed her, and yet knowing within her was a child that would be her own, she felt a feeling of happiness and joy.

"You will live in my father's castle, and you will grow to be like him, a man of great honour, and good to his people. One day you will take the throne, and rule for the true people of this land, those who follow the ways of earth, not this god from across the seas."

She smiled as her hand gently rubbed. Eve stepped out from the trees across the way, and the rustle of the branches caught Morgana's attention, and she looked up startled. Eve smiled as Morgana rose to her feet.

"You have changed Morgana, for within you, things are very different. Is the child you carry of Fae descent, for I feel the powers of Fae are strong within you?" Morgana took a breath.

"It matters not, the father will not raise this child, I will." Eve tilted her head, and smiled.

"I was not aware you had returned to these lands; I feel the queen of the realm is also unaware. Merlin schooled you well, if you can slip in and out without the queen knowing. I feel you have matured greatly in the short time since we last met, and wonder if the flowers of your garden still grow white."

Morgana did not feel as nervous as she had in the past, maybe she had just gone through the point of no return, where she no longer cared. She looked deep into the eyes of Eve, and gave a slight laugh.

"What does it matter, nothing I do will ever be good enough for the Ruling Council? All of you have watched me, tracked me, and found criticism in every aspect of my life. I have to live under a veil just to have what everyone else alive has, privacy to just be me. All I have ever wished for is to be left alone, to live my life making teas and tinctures, and helping those I meet. I am Whitelines, yet when the golden queen has a problem, she points the finger at me, and all of you simply believe her." She gave a slight laugh, as she looked at the Ruling Council member.

"You are a hypocrite Eve, you play the role of purity well, but you and all of the council have blood on your hands, you accuse me, and yet your crimes are far worse. All of you murdered my father because he stood in the way of your so called, 'One True King.' It makes me laugh. I lived with Uther, I saw the way he treated my mother and bedded the women of the village. I lived with the stench of his vomit from his excessive drinking all over the floor, I saw the way he taunted and bullied those who were weak. Yet in your eyes, he was perfect, so perfect you armed him with a sword of high honour." She gave a loud laugh.

"What honour, tell me Lady Eve, high ruler of the forests, tell me, where was his honour when Merlin helped him rape my mother? You all sit in judgement of me, and yet it is all of you who should be judged. You destroyed my life, and took away my father who I loved deeply, and never once, has any of you, apart from Merlin, ever shown the slightest bit of sympathy, or regret. None of you, why can you not just leave me in peace to live my life of grief, remembering the only honourable man I have ever known?" The tears filled her eyes.

"My Father." Morgana lifted her basket, and walked off at a fast pace along the path crying, and left Eve watching filled with sadness.

Eve stood and watched Morgana walk away, her mind filled with turmoil, was Morgana right, had she played her part, or was Merlin and Rhiannon, right? They rarely agreed on anything, and yet in this one thing, both of them had been adamant, Victor of Cornwall, was cruel and sadistic, and wielded far more power than any before him. Her mind spun, as Morgana's words held grit and truth to them, she spoke with a power of conviction she had never felt before.

She hurried onto the path up to the high shoulder, she needed to get to her pool and look within the waters of her garden to see what had truly befallen, and reach out to her husband to talk. In her preoccupation, as she felt the power of Morgana's emotions within her, she did not see the shadow stood next to the tree as she approached. Her soul focus was to find the truth, and she could only achieve that at her pool. By the time she became aware of the dark shadow in her realm, it was too late, as Branna stepped forward, and revealed herself as she came in to focus, and Eve stopped in utter shock.

"Branna!" Branna wasted no time, and plunged the tainted knife into her.

"It is Raven… Lady Raven to be precise, you should have left Morgana alone." Eve looked down, and her blood ran red, she looked up at Branna in shock.

"I am Eve, I am life, I have no mortal life, I am life." Branna nodded, and then smiled.

"Queen Rhiannon knows that, which is why she created the means to defeat you, and I found it." Eve frowned.

"Rhiannon is my sister." Branna smirked.

"Rhiannon is evil, she is the darkness in all the realms, why could none of you ever see that, didn't Enaria tell you that?"

Eve shook her head and then flinched, as she felt pain for the first time in her long life, the liquid on the blade was working.

"This is not true; she is the Queen of this realm." Branna jerked her hand, and pulled out the knife.

"You should have listened to Bridget Violet, and Ariel, they were the truth, and yet all of you forced them to make peace with the evil they knew her to be. You helped her kill my grandson, imprison my family, and take Ariel from me, and you sided with that golden traitor to her people. It is time you all paid, now is the time of the rising of the raven, your time is over, and you are not as full of life as you think, Rhiannon has assured it."

Black smoke swirled up around Branna, and she was gone, and Eve dropped to her knees, and clutched her stomach and winced in pain. She looked down, as her hands turned to clay, and began to crack and splinter. She looked up to the sky, and out of her came a wail such as no one had ever heard, and red light exploded out of her, and streaked into the sky.

Morgana wiped her eyes, as she hurried along the path past Merlin's cottage heading back to her own cottage. She had been fine, and now she felt the turmoil swirling inside herself, and all she wanted to do was lock the door and hide away. Up the track came a horse, and she saw Stenlow, and gave a sigh as she stopped, and he rode up to her, and looked at her with surprise.

"When did you get back, I know nothing of this?" Morgana shrugged.

"I have been home for a week, is that wrong, I do live here you know?"

In the distance behind them came a mighty wail, and the sky exploded in red light, Morgana jumped, and moved close to the horse, as she spun around to see the light flowing into the sky.

"What is that!?"

Stenlow watched and felt fear, such was the devastation of the wail, and the horse became erratic, and jumpy. Morgana stepped back looking frightened, her eyes fixed on the horizon, as both of them saw the sky filling with the light. Stenlow slid down off his horse and pulled at the reins to steady the horse, and he could see the fear on Morgana's face. She moved closer, as if for protection.

"What is it Commander, for I fear it, what sounds like that?" He shook his head not understanding any of this, he turned to her white frightened face, looking serious.

"Hurry home and lock your door, I will have to find out what this thing is." Clouds were billowing into the sky, and it was growing darker, she gripped his arm tight.

"Commander, I am afraid to be alone." He looked at her, she was shaking, and he could not deny, he was also afraid. He gently pulled her free, and lowered his voice, speaking in a gentle caring tone.

"Lady Morgana, I can see your cottage, hurry now, and I will watch from here. Go… Run, and lock your door and stay inside until we know what this is. You will be safe, I can assure you, now hurry."

Morgana stepped back, and with a fast nod, she turned, and ran for her life to her home.

*T*here was an almighty flash of white, and out onto the top of the large rocky mount, Rhiannon walked out, to see Eve on her knees and the light of her spirit billowing into the air. Eve was slowly crumbling as her eyes looked to Rhiannon.

"The shadow, it is a raven, she looks like her…" She fell forward, her last whispered words only Rhiannon could hear them.

"Branna is the shadow of Morgana."

Eve crumbled, and fell to the earth as dust. High above Avalon the dark clouds swirled as Rhiannon's head snapped in the direction of the cottage, and she saw Morgana running down the road. The heavens opened and the rain came pouring down, and Rhiannon's face twisted.

"I knew it."

There was a bright flash of white, and she disappeared, and the lightening shot down, striking trees, and cutting them clean in half. The winds rose up, and the clouds rolled in to the sky covering the land in darkness.

*M*organa gasped as she ran, the winds came up the road, howled in her ears, and the rain poured down and lashed into her face. She could just about see the cottage up ahead, and gave a sigh of relief as she reached her fence line, and slowed to walk and gather her breath. Morgana reached the gate, soaking wet and violently shaking, she had no idea what had happened, but never in her life had she heard a wail so terrifying, and she did not deny, it scared her to her core.

As the gate swung open, there was a flash of bright white, and she felt herself lift into the air, and was flung backwards on the road with a crash. The pain shot up her back as she landed in shock not understanding anything, and then she heard her.

"I have you, finally I have you, running from the scene assuming no one could see you. Did Merlin not teach you that in plain sight your veil was useless to the eyes of those who watched?" Morgana scrambled, and got up quickly to face Rhiannon, as she fumed on the road in front of her.

"I am running from the rain, and the fear of whatever that was, for it terrified me." Rhiannon fumed.

"Liar… Always lies, do you honestly think you can fool a Queen of the Fae the way you did Merlin? I was there, I saw her body, and you running away from your treacherous act, and for the crime of the death of Eve, I will kill you." Morgana gasped in utter shock.

"Eve is dead, but she is life, she cannot die."

Rhiannon screwed up her face, and lifted her arm, and as she swung it back, and then threw it forward, understanding her peril, Morgana acted fast. Dark grey smoke funnelled up from the floor and Morgana disappeared, and the spell shot into the trees and exploded, tearing many down and splintering them into bits.

Behind her, Morgana reappeared with a bottle in her hand.

"You missed bitch!"

Rhiannon spun around, and Morgana cast the bottle end forward with all her power, as the smoke funnelled up, and as the liquid hit Rhiannon's arm, Morgana disappeared. Rhiannon wailed out in pain, as it burned into her flesh. Rhiannon's screams echoed all over the realm, and people fell to the floor, and covered their ears in terror.

Morgana flew around the inside of her cottage, as outside the screams of Rhiannon wailed into the air. She grabbed her black book, and some of her journals, replaced the floor stone, and pulled the rug over it casting a charm on it that Branna had taught her. She grabbed another bag, and pulled small jars from her shelves, dropping the most important things she had collected into them.

With one bag slung over her shoulder, and one across her other, she turned to her chimney, and grabbed the carved figure she had done with Branna, it was her most precious possession. Turning quickly to see if she needed anything else, she heard the shouts outside, and then her door exploded open, and Fagan stormed in, and she jumped, dropping the figure.

For a moment their eyes connected, and she looked deeply into his, she shook her head slowly, as the smoke funnelled up around her.

"She is wrong, it was not me Fagan, I would never do that, I believed in Eve, I am innocent."

He swiped with his blade, but she was gone, the smoke parted as his scythe blade came through it with no contact, and Fagan swooned slightly as his mind filled with pictures of the life of Morgana. Behind him, the marshals poured into her cottage, as Fagan turned, and stormed towards the door. Outside, marshals were appearing in small flashes, and the queen was gone. He walked to the road where Stenlow rode up through the chaos of marshals and the heavy swirling rain.

Fagan watched as the flames burst out of the windows, and a great fire roared inside the tiny cottage that had been the home of Morgana of Cornwall. He leaned on the fence he had built all those years ago, his mind filled with many thoughts and pictures as he tried to make sense of them. He had no idea that he would spend the rest of his life thinking about his final moment, as he connected with Morgana, his voice was soft.

"She dropped her veil, and she let me in, why?"

His eyes looked across the garden as he thought, and there in front of him was the old apple tree filled with fruit, and under it flourished a tall plant. As he stared at it, he saw hundreds of white flowers open, the White Star, a plant so sacred and cherished. It was a plant known only to grow in the Forest of Time, and yet it flourished in Morgana's Garden, he stared at it not truly understanding.

"Well blow me, aint that something, ye grew that all on yer own."
Stenlow walked up to him, and looked at him with angry eyes.

"What in all the realms is going on?" Fagan gave a sigh.

"I wish I knew, tis said Little Dark Eyes tried to kill Eve and Rhiannon." Stenlow stepped back, and looked at him with complete shock.

"Are you insane? She was with me, and she was terrified, I told her to run home and lock the door." Fagan leaned off the fence.

"What?" Stenlow looked at the cottage as the flames ravaged at it, and lifted his arm and pointed at it.

"Did you do that, because if you did, you are a fool?" Fagan shook his head.

"Tis the orders of the Queen, they has to burn all traces of her away. Now Stenlow, talk proper, did ye just say she was with ye when Eve was killed?" He nodded.

"Is there something wrong with your ears brother? I told you; she was on the road just past the cottage of the Master of the Whiteline. We both saw the lights and she was scared; I was too, we had no idea what was happening, I told her to run home and lock the door. Where is she, is she safe?"

Fagan stood in the pouring rain, and stared at the white flowers, as his mind filled with the pictures of her walking with a raven on her shoulder, and Branna watched from behind her, and he did not understand at all. Morgana knew he was a mystic, and she had dropped her veil to let him deliberately see, but why, what was she trying to show him? Stenlow stared at him as the water ran down his face, and he blinked.

"WELL?" Fagan looked at him seriously.

"Ye needs to go to the queen an tell her what ye knows, go… Go on Brother, and hurry."

Rhiannon was lucky, not much of the liquid had hit her, most of it was dampened by the rain and washed to the floor before it hit her. The small amount that had, was mainly on her clothing and although it did burn through her sleeve, the small amount that touched her skin was not enough to destroy her. It burned her badly, but Sequana acted fast, and saved her arm.

Two hours later, Stenlow reported to his queen and gave a full account of his actions and his meeting with Morgana. Rhiannon screamed at him and refused to believe any of it, calling him a liar, and accusing him of secret liaisons with her. He was shipped immediately to the realm of the moon, and placed in the same prison to work with his sister, Luminaria.

*G*wendolyn only ever heard Rhiannon's version of events, and Fagan said nothing, but his mind was troubled and his heart heavy, for he loved Eve dearly, and had often spoken with her on his many travels into the Forest of Time. Not understanding his thoughts as he wrestled with doubt, as he did not believe the version of events told by the queen, he took to working less and spending more time alone in the Forest of Time thinking, and found his loyalties to his queen questioned.

He met his mother many times in the forest, and would sit for hours talking with her, and she revealed that she felt that the Moon Goddess, Tideguyde, had left her a message in the form of a thread to follow, and she talked of her visions of a bridge that would take her out of the realms, to meet with the goddess of their line.

Sequana spoke of Morgana, and the accusations made by the queen, and how she did not believe them, and she found herself suffering great doubts. She sat in the centre, deep in the heart of the Forest of Time and looked at her son.

"I see your doubt, you cannot hide from me Fagan my son. Tell me, do you believe that a young woman such as Morgana could kill Eleanor, Uther and Eve, and not be detected, could anyone hide that truly from you? Fagan my son, she took down her veil and you saw inside her, did you see the deaths she is accused of, for your words have more power with me than any queens?" He looked up with sad eyes.

"I have struggled with the load this has placed on me. She showed me the death of her grandmother, as Little Dark Eyes begged her to stop, and I saw the pain she had in her heart. But I saw no other deaths, just the pain she felt for the taking of a life that she did not want to, and it weighed heavy on her." Sequana smiled.

"Listen to me my son, for I have seen much. My teacher was the great and powerful Enaria, and she was the purest thing I have ever known. This Branna who Rhiannon accused; I feel is the same line of blood as Morgana. To me, there is no doubt in that, for she was the double of Branna and no mistake. Nevertheless, I have to ask, do you really think this Branna was a Fae of darkness?" He gave a long sigh.

"I cannot say, I only met her once, and that was as brief as a butterfly passing, as she waited for Ariel." Sequana smiled.

"There my dearest son is your answer." He frowned, not understanding, but she smiled and got up from her seat.

"I have to go, I am leaving the service of our queen, and I will serve a higher power. I will be here one more day, and then my son, I will leave you and Avalon for good, stay a while in the forest and think over my words, for I feel in time, they will become clearer."

Fagan had no idea of the years he would spend, sat in the forest going over everything he had seen and heard. It would stay with him in the life he faced, and become the preoccupation of a time of great solitary living, and it would be long after the days of Branna and Morgana that he would truly realise what part he played in the scheme of everything.

Months later, the grieving Hearne, pulled from the bottom of the lake of Avalon a great white mound of stone, and on it's top, he stood with Albanlin and Opal. From inside his cloak, Albanlin pulled a small red glowing orb and looked down at it, with deep sadness.

"She rests in spirit, it will be many generations before she will summon the strength to appear in her true form again, but she will never wear the garment she fashioned at the start of the days of life. Sleep well my sister and recover, for I shall miss you dearly."

Albanlin handed the orb to Hearne, as Opal wept, and Hearne lifted his woody lined hand, and below them a hole in the floor appeared. He held out his arm above it.

"Sleep well my love. I shall remember always the joy of the life you gave me and softness of your heart, my world will be forever darkness without you."

Slowly the orb descended into the white stone, as she lowered to the bottom, it sealed with a star of silver. Tears were shed, and grief was felt by the many that looked out across the water, and the white island was thus named, 'The Isle of Tears' for few could visit and not weep for the loss of Eve. From that moment on, Opal named the large lake of Avalon, 'The lake of Passing.' For no one could travel it without passing the monument built to honour Eve.

Time passed as Morgana settled in her new home, which was her castle in the forest. Branna, true to her word helped her understand the realm, and showed her how to win the loyalty of men to work for her, and her castle became a hive of activity, as her stomach expanded, and she felt the life that grew inside her. She was a frequent visitor to the castle in Tintagel in secret, as her mother grew old, and Lothar took good care of her. The time to return for the first time since her last visit to Castle Berengar, for the birth of her child approached, Branna prepared, and in Florae, Gwendolyn and her daughters hunted for the truth.

The world changed as Una tried everything to try and get Arthur to listen to her, and finally after almost a year, he agreed, but only after setting his knights to search for a grail, that he was convinced would save the land and unite the country, which had suffered famine and illness, and lay wasted and barren, as the people fought to survive.

The day arrived, and even though the nuns objected, Una forced her way in, and she sat outside Guinevere's room, as the young Opal waylaid the nuns. Guinevere had saved Excalibur, and handed it back to him, so he was once again reunited with the sword of kings. Arthur stayed the night, and as they confessed their feelings, they made love, and Una cried for such was the beauty of the moment as she sat not listening, but hearing their love as they spoke to each other.

Two days later, Arthur returned to his castle filled with hope of finding the grail, but the world was changing, and things were starting to pass into secret. People grew fearful of the rumours of dark deeds that passed around the country, and became secretive and untrusting. Sian of Good Hope who had married Lancelot in his exile, and built a church, smuggled Guinevere out of the convent in the night, aided by Opal. She travelled to her church, where Guinevere was hidden from everyone, under the protection of Hearne. In secret, Guinevere, who had conceived of a child, would live and raise Arthur's son, without him ever knowing.

$\mathcal{M}$organa arrived at Berengar's Castle, and alone in her room, with Branna's assistance, she gave birth to a son. She named him Medraut, which was in the original language of her mother, but when translated into the common language, it became Mordred. It held the meaning of 'within bounds, or controlled,' which in an ironic way, Morgana named him to reflect the life that had been forced upon her in Avalon by Rhiannon, surrounded by a fence, living in her cottage.

She stayed for a week, never leaving her room, and then travelled back to the castle in the forest, with a nurse maid picked by Branna. Morgana grew a deep bond with her son and loved him deeply, she was a doting mother, and for the first time in a long time, she felt her life had great meaning. Branna visited her often and saw the change in her, and power of the love she held for her child, and it pleased her to see it. One evening, as they sat by the fire, Branna smiled as she sensed the feeling of happiness and contentment within Morgana.

"Is this the life you wanted; will you leave the past behind you now?" Morgana gave a sigh and relaxed in her seat; her eyes moved to

Branna's.

"I have not forgotten, how could I? I have a son to raise, my pace has changed, but my plans are still in play."

Shortly after, Branna headed home, and a few weeks later got the message that Igraine was dying, and so she travelled to Morgana to give her the sad news. When Morgana arrived in her mother's castle secretly, Arthur was in the castle at her bedside. Morgana stood by the door and saw her mother lay in her bed, her long grey hair splayed on the sheets, as Lothar stood at her side, and spoke quietly.

"She has not suffered, age has caught up with her, she has asked for you."

In the corridor ten men stood all aligned to Igraine, and the ways of the earth. Morgana pushed open the door and stepped in, and Arthur looked up from where he knelt at her bedside. Morgana entered the room, and looked at him.

"Call if you must, but no aid will come, everyone here answers to the command of the Queen of this house, and that is her, this is her request." He gave a nod, and spoke quietly.

"I have no intention of calling, she is our mother, you have the right to be here." Morgana sat on the bed, and took her mother by the hand, and Igraine opened her eyes, and gave a weak smile.

"My daughter… My beautiful and precious daughter." Morgana swallowed hard, and her tears filled her eyes.

"I am here Mother, My Queen, I am here." Igraine breathed in hard, as she looked up at her.

"Morgana, listen to me, he was so proud of you, he loved you dearly, and you have no idea how like him you are. He told me, build a strong foundation, and it will outlast everything, and you are mine. My foundation, for like him, it was your strength that gave me the courage to continue, I admire you, for you are a true queen of your line. I love you daughter, I did not always show it, but I love you dearly." Morgana breathed in, and swallowed hard as her tears dripped on the covers.

"I love you too Mother, I wanted to be like him for you, and I have tried to keep true the lines of both him and you, I always defended you both." She smiled.

"You did, and you were glorious in your role. His castle will rise again, I know it will, and it will mark the world to show we were here, and we did what was right." Morgana smiled.

"It will, I will ensure it." Igraine took a deep breath and smiled.

"I go to Victor now, for he is waiting."

She closed her eyes, and breathed out, and it was long, and her last. Morgana closed her eyes, and wept still holding her mother's hand. Arthur quietly got up and moved to the door. He looked at Morgana as she wept, and felt great sadness.

"There will be peace between us Morgana, and we will honour her." Morgana sat up, and turned to him, her eyes wet from her tears.

"There will never be peace between us, until the people of my mother and father are free again. Tell your god he has no place here, for here the old ways are ruled by a true queen of this land, and her name is Morgana." Arthur nodded.

"I am saddened to hear that, I truly am."

"GET OUT, YOUR LINE HAS DEFILED THIS CASTLE ENOUGH. LEAVE US ALONE, THIS IS OUR LAND, OUR HOME, AND THERE IS NO PLACE FOR YOU HERE NOW!"

*T*he following morning Morgana had to leave, as both Gwendolyn and Rhiannon arrived to pay their respects. Morgana felt it was an insult and stood on the cliff tops out of sight, grieving alone and heartbroken. She stood watching with the wind blowing through her much longer hair, just as she had so many years ago as a young girl. Igraine's body was lifted and carried out of the gate, and in a great ceremony organised by Rhiannon, Igraine was taken to Avalon to be placed at the side of Uther. Morgana felt it was an insult, as she stood watching the long line of marshals walk out of the gates of her castle in the distance. Behind her, Gwendolyn appeared in a faint flash, and Morgana felt her presence the moment she arrived, she gave a sigh.

"Come to kill me have you, well my back is turned to you, so take a shot, that is the usual way the council act?" Gwendolyn stood still; her bright blue eyes focused on her.

"I did not come to fight you Morgana, your mother has died, and I believe that is a time of truce. You are not easy to find, and yet I knew you would be here, and I want to talk." Morgana turned, and faced her.

"I would not tell your sister the golden queen, she will curse you for not killing me the moment you saw me." Gwendolyn looked her in the eyes.

"All I want is the truth, every lead I have, crosses the path of you. I know that you know something, and I need to know how to find my family members, my daughter's need their children back." Morgana gave a small laugh, as she looked at Gwendolyn in her long thick white robes, her blue cloak, and her long golden hair flowing behind her in the wind.

"You talk of truth, which truth, the facts as they are, or the words of the great golden queen, for it appears to me, only her words matter, and my voice is silenced?"

"Morgana, all I seek is the full truth, your words do not have to be silenced, tell me."

"Then what, you will go to the golden queen and set things right?" Morgana laughed.

"You look at me and see evil, would you truly believe anything I say? The golden queen has smeared my name, and accused me of every wrong in the kingdom. Just because it is the great and glorious golden queen, everyone bows down and agrees with her. Are you honestly telling me anything I say will be believed, for if you are, then you know you speak lies?" Gwendolyn stared at her with hope in her eyes, she took a step forward.

"I know you know something, and what you know can help me, Morgana, please talk to me, and I will listen." Morgana shook her head.

"Gwendolyn, I know you to be a reasonable person, but have you any idea of what my truth will do? She will destroy your kingdom, and tear down everything to hide what the truth of her is. If I told you what I know, you would not live long enough to listen, do you not think she is watching you now, and is ready to pounce the moment you leave? I already sense her guards approaching." Gwendolyn looked around, as Morgana smiled.

"Her hand is long, and even you are not safe. I am not guilty of the sins she has given me, but that matters not to her." The smoke swirled up from her feet, and Gwendolyn reached out to grab her.

"Please Morgana no, I need to know what you know!"

It was too late she was gone, and Gwendolyn gave a frustrated sigh, as marshals popped out of the air and surrounded her, she spun around her eyes blazing with blue light.

"WHY ARE YOU HERE, HAVE YOU ANY IDEA OF THE DAMAGE YOU HAVE DONE?"

There was a massive burst of bright blue, and all of the guards were blown over, and Gwendolyn was gone, as the marshals of Rhiannon lay on the floor stunned and bewildered.

*R*hiannon oversaw the parade through Avalon, as Igraine was carried up to the top of the Citadel Mount, and taken to the rest where she was laid in a stone tomb next to Uther. She gave a great speech of how Igraine was a queen of her people, and served them with high honour. Sadly, none of her people were present, as only residents of Avalon were allowed to attend. She stood there as the Queen to all, and basked in the glory of her magnificence, and her tribute to a great queen, and when she was done, she walked to her rooms feeling the glory of her humility.

Darkness fell over Avalon, and the quietness of the night descended with the mists of the marshes, as Gwendolyn stood at the half burned gate of Morgana's cottage. She looked at the burned out ruin, blackened and charred, with just the fire place and chimney left standing, and talked quietly to herself.

"Did you come here my love, did you come to see her, and then left, or is Rhiannon right, was it all Morgana's fault, was she really that strong to take you, for I cannot believe that to be true?" She looked at the ashes and lumps of charred wood and gave a long sigh.

"I miss you, I miss my family, I miss Eve, she always had the way of making things clearer, like she did with my grandmother of understanding all. Merlin my love, I feel so alone and afraid, and I know somehow the truth is all here in this realm, but my pain of loss blinds me and I feel I am losing my way."

"You all fear the truth." Gwendolyn looked up, and saw a dark black hooded figure in the mists.

"Who are you, do you know of what I speak?" Gwendolyn strained her eyes, as the mists swirled around the figure.

"Is that you Morgana, will you not speak to me?"

"I am not her, but I know of what you wish, and this I will tell you; Morgana is far more innocent than has been said. Like another before her, she was the victim of the golden queen, if you truly want the truth, you have to go back to the start Gwendolyn White Circle. You have to look to the past, and this time, learn from your folly."

The figure turned, and Gwendolyn raised her hand, she felt desperate, and had spent too much time looking for answers, and she knew whoever this was, that they could answer them all.

"I WILL NOT LET YOU LEAVE; I NEED YOU TO TELL ME WHAT YOU KNOW!"

She focused her mind, but from nowhere a bolt of red light came at her, she turned to deflect it, but was not quick enough, and it hit her full on and lifted her off her feet. She felt the impact and power, and gasped in pain, as she crashed back into the floor. Gwendolyn lay on the floor gasping for air, feeling the pain all down her side. As her eyes blurred, she heard the soft footsteps on the rough dirt floor, and the voice spoke as if close to her.

"You are a fool, I should have killed you, but Morgana does not want you to die. If you want the truth, look to Ariel, for in her words are the answers to all that you seek. Open your eyes and ears Queen of Fae, for you have allowed the golden to deafen and blind you."

"MOTHER!" The patter of feet came down the path, and she felt Una, she gasped out, and everything went black.

"Morgana?"

Chapter Thirty Five.

Cruel Twists of Fate.

As Gwendolyn lay injured and suffering, and Rhiannon rushed to her aid, Morgana walked into the rest and knelt before her mother's tomb, where she laid a small bunch of wild flowers and wept. Behind her the faint outline of a tatty hooded figure watched on, and as Morgana quietened down, he moved forward slightly, Morgana sensed him and she sat up.

"Have you also come for me, to punish me for the sins of my accusers?"

"No… I am merely a spectator in all things, although, you stand on a fine edge young Morgana, and it interests me in what you will do next."

Morgana gave a sniffle and stood up and wiped her eyes, she turned to face the shadowy outline of Albanlin.

"I am whiteline, so you are indeed my master, as you are Merlin's. Do you wish also to command me?" His hood moved slightly, as she looked at him.

"It may surprise you to know, that to this date, you have honoured your oath that you undertook as a student of my guardian. I see only one life that weighs heavy on you, and in that I feel you judge yourself harshly, for it appears your life was in great peril, and your need was to defend yourself."

"My belief is to preserve life, I am not so casual in the way I deal out death, unlike others you are allied to."

"Indeed, I admire the sense you hold for the injustice you see. My interest now lies in the path you shall walk, as I see many roads, of which some are shrouded in darkness." She gave a slight laugh.

"You care about me whilst your council destroy whomever they choose to get what they want. What about those who have suffered at their hands, tell me Lord, what of the deaths and wrecked lives that grieve for the actions of your so called superiors who wield the power?"

"That is exactly my point young student, I have given free will to all, even you, and I will not step in to stop you. You have the power of your own choice, and it is in that, the way forward is paved. I see the choices you have and the lengths you have gone to, I am not as blind as you think, but I will add, that you alone took it upon yourself to act, and speak out against the injustice you see. That was the path you started, all I ask is will you continue straight, or deviate onto darker roads?"

"All I can do is fight for what I have seen as unjust, and yet I fight the corruption of those you support, and you stand here and question me?" She gave a slight laugh, and turned and pointed behind her.

"There lies my mother, laid out in a box, next to the man who raped her, tell me wise lord, can you not see how insulting that is to her memory? She was a queen of those dedicated to the faith of the earth, a faith that celebrated you, and those who came with you. She was a woman of the highest standing in this realm, and yet you have sat idle and allowed Arthur and this rapist to bring forth a god who betrays her and all of us. You seat a queen in this first realm and call her glorious, whilst she hurts the very people who have toiled in this land to create her realm of power. How can you stand before me and request what path I take, when you have never cared of the path of those you have aligned yourself with?" His hood twitched.

"Yours, young student, interests me the most." She gave a sigh.

"Your priorities appear to me to be somewhat off balance, for I am meaningless, as all I want is to live in peace, and yet no matter how hard I have tried, since the day I was born, I have been attacked for a reason I still do not know. My Lord, do not waste your time on me, I have nothing left, my father and mother have gone, and I feel empty like a barren wilderness." The White Lord turned and walked slowly towards the door.

"The time to choose your path will soon come, and the choice you make will be of great importance. You have never been meaningless young student, the path you take will be a great bearing on everything. Think with care of your road from this day, for if I am right, you will bring about great change." He faded away and she stood alone, and lost, filled with grief, and shook her head.

"You know it all, and still do nothing, does everything have to burn down before you finally take note?" Her voice echoed off the walls, he was gone. Morgana turned and looked one last time at her mother's tomb.

"You are better off now, you can be with father, and I must continue this miserable existence here in this dying realm." The smoke swirled around her, and she was gone.

*F*ar away on the edge of the Shrouded Lake, Rhiannon lay Gwendolyn down on the bed, inside the small one room cottage. Una slipped onto the bed at her side, as Rhiannon stood back.

"She will recover, it will take time, Morgana may think she is powerful, but she is no match for a queen. She is lucky, she could have been killed, I have to return, there are things that must be done to seal this realm, your sisters are in Florae and guarded." Una gave a nod and looked up.

"I am grateful Queen Rhiannon; we have lost much of late, and I could not bear to lose her. Morgana will pay for this; I will see to it." Rhiannon gave a slight nod.

"Your father should never have taken her as a student, it is clear now, she planned this in her twisted head to enact revenge for her father, from the start. Be wary Una, we have lost too many and the list keeps growing, killing Eve was an evil act, she will think nothing of destroying you." Una looked down at her mother.

"I am grateful to be where she will never find us, I need to recover my mother fully, and then I will inform Master Elgin." Rhiannon walked towards the door.

"I fear no realm at the moment is safe, it is best she stays here."

*M*organa returned to her castle and sat in her chair as her son was taken to be cared for by the maid, as her thoughts drifted around inside her head. Lost in thought as the fire crackled and sparked in the hearth, she felt tired and weary. Her voice was soft as if spoken only for her ears.

"I have the choice to choose my own road, that is the problem, I never have. Even now I am forced away from a home I love and forced to live where no one will find me. I have never picked my own road, they always have, it is why I want to remove them." She closed her eyes and felt her body relax, she needed to rest, and to try to focus her mind.

Una was forced to travel to Florae to meet with her sisters, and could sit with the Council of Elders and speak with them, for now Maddy had the role of speaking for the queen. Una spent many hours talking with Maddy and Elgin in private, and then retired for the night as it was very late.

Morgana woke late in the night with a start, and groggily walked to her table, she needed to sort out her things, her days had been busy with her son, and her workspace was cluttered. In the centre of her table was Maud's book, and she slid it to the side, out of her way, Rajani swept down from her perch and landed next to it. Morgana stopped as she saw the raven push it's beak into the book, and try to flick it, she leaned over, and lifted the book open at the page the bird wanted, and read the line.

The spell was an advanced containment charm, she looked down at it and could see Branna had corrected Maud's work, by changing some of the wording. She looked down at the page and read it very carefully, reciting the words in her head. This was a spell of Fae of Moon, and it was a powerful one, was this what she needed to finally remove all of them and clear the way for her son to rule? She practiced the spell over and over in her head, Maud had the pronunciation wrong, but she had no trouble correcting it.

As the sun rose over the Forest of Time, Morgana slipped on a plain black hooded cloak, and headed to the forest, looking out for Hearne. She had heard of his rage and anger, and was wary as she hid in the shadows sensing all of the area around her. It was not long before she felt something, and it was powerful. Morgana hung back and watched on the edge of the long road that led up the centre of the realm, where he stood waiting. It was her best chance to strike, and she prepared, as hidden in the trees under the deepest veil taught her by Branna, Morgana recited the spell in her head, and lifted her hand to point at the lord of the woodland.

As she spoke clearly in her mind, and willed the spell of containment, something unexpected happened, there was a flash, and Una appeared, and Morgana finished the spell and it was cast. With a flash, Hearne stood frozen, as a crystal tube rose up from the ground, and sealed him in, but Una was nowhere to be seen. Feeling nervous she looked around, but there was no sense of her.

It was still a stroke of great luck, and without taking another moment, she cast the spell of movement, and the tube lowered into the floor to take him to her dungeon in her castle. Morgana stepped out of the trees, and watched as the tube disappeared, she looked up the long road, why were they meeting, what did they plan to do here? She had no idea, she just knew that Hearne was now held her prisoner, and all that was left, was Rhiannon, Opal, Gwendolyn, and her daughters.

She returned to her castle feeling happy, she was closer than ever to her goal of completely removing all of the Ruling Council, and that would leave Arthur exposed, as he searched for a relic of his new god, she now had time to prepare and plan, and felt excited that she could share her thoughts with Branna.

The spell of Maud had worked well, and on her return, she looked at the book, and slipped it back to the first page and began to read. The study of Maud's spells became a preoccupation of hers, as she raised her son alone in the forest. Time gently slipped past as she lost track, and Branna saw less and less of her.

Alone in a cottage out of sight, Gwendolyn slept, held in her state of sleep, as Una was busy with her sisters and continuing to hunt for their children, and there was no one to come to her aid. The days slipped into a week as she burned with a fever in her bed, and then, on the night of the full moon, she got a visitor.

Outside, the whole of the lake lit up with white light, and the door to the cottage opened and the light flooded in, Sequana turned, and looked at the moon goddess at her side.

"She is the future I saw, and yet she ails in a state of darkness, help her."

Sequana stood smiling as a being of the brightest blue light walked over to the bed, and lifted her hand over Gwendolyn, and then lowered it slowly, and placed it on her chest. Tideguyde spoke slowly and softly.

"You are wise not to trust, a queen taught by Enaria was a mighty queen, and her wisdom has guided you well. Your eyes are blind to the truth, and they need to be opened. Never doubt that the power that consumes others is given as friendship, for those of power fear everyone. Take this knowledge to your table and learn from it to protect your line, as your sight grows stronger into the future, you will need it. The present is tainted, and the one chosen to bring the renewal is the most unlikely, follow this guide to its end, the future now lies in others, this time will soon end when a king falls." The Moon Goddess walked back to the door, and looked at Sequana.

"She will wake soon, speak nothing of this, and I shall wait for you at the start of the bridge." Sequana bowed, and turned to see Gwendolyn stirring in her bed.

*A*lbanlin had talked of choosing the right path, and at that time, Morgana had balanced out her powers and was seen by him to be correcting the imbalance created within the council. He knew of the crystal tubes with their sleeping inhabitants, he watched from high up, and he could see how the fates were changing.

"There are some who see us as gods, there are those who think they are gods, and those who yearn to be gods, and then there is you Little Morgana. There are times my child, when in order to get the simplest of things, you have to fight, and the weapons you choose are what makes all the difference. Choose wisely, for in just three pages, you will find the longest and darkest path, and if you pick that one, know this, it is the same path to the one that guides you, but her mind is stronger. Her struggle for balance to undo the wrongs is equal to yours, but to walk her path behind her, that will take time, and bring about the same end. I have time, I have always had time, and I feel I will have need of it."

*M*organa turned over the page and scanned the text, then flipped over the next sheet and stared down at the one thing she never expected to see. Maud had copied Branna's charm of connection, so she could tie others to the raven. As she read the lines, Rajani landed at the side of her, and Morgana's eyes moved to look at her.

"Did Branna know she had this?" Rajani gave a low squawk. Morgana looked at the page and read on.

"Will this give me what I need to match them, or beat them and end all they have started, will I have the ability to finally be free of them?" Rajani gave a loud squawk, and Morgana nodded.

"In time, this may be my only choice, and yet I feel, it is the one choice I will never make." She closed the book, and Rajani lifted off the table.

*T*he days morphed into years, Gwendolyn returned to her realm still weakened and took time to heal, Rhiannon kept her realm sealed and sent out riders to search for any traces of Morgana, and Fagan slowly reduced his stock of weapons and made more effort to visit the forest. Many times, he sat in Eve's Garden and spoke to her, just as he always had, even though he knew she could not hear him. The years moved on and Arthur tried, but all his attempts to try and overcome his falling popularity failed. His knights returned after years of searching, all them empty handed, and Rhiannon grew weary of him, and looked less and less into the realm of men.

Morgana often had those days where she remembered her past, and at times she felt melancholy. When it happened, she would walk quietly back into Avalon under her veil, and sit in the marshes hidden from view, and stare at the burned out remains of her home. Even now it was painful to see it burned to the ground, Branna had many times warned her not to go back, but she found herself drawn to it.

Sat in the grass she remembered her first day, her lessons with Merlin, Lot's proposal of marriage, and the strange encounters with Stenlow, or the happy smiling face of Fagan. She had hoped he would understand why she dropped her veil that day, but she could see now it had not been long enough for him to see all of the real truth. She sat there with small tears in her eyes, her impulse to be here was stronger than normal, she gave a sniffle and wiped her eyes, and spoke softly to herself.

"Why do I still torture myself so, that life is gone, I can never be the happy person I was living here in those early days?"

She took a deep breath, being here was not helping, and she made to get up, when she saw a faint flash, and strained her eyes to see, and gasped with surprise, it was Gwendolyn.

Gwendolyn stood once again at the burned out gate, and stared at the ruined building. Her instincts told her the answers were here, but how she did not know. She slipped past the gate and walked down the path, littered with debris from the day it burned, no one had ever wanted to clear it away.

She walked slowly looking at the floor, it was strange, as she could remember sitting in this room talking to Morgana and giving her advice. Slowly she looked around remembering everything, the long line of smashed and burned glass which were the shelves filled with bottles of herbs, some of which were still intact, and filled with charred contents. The stack of wooden beakers on the shelf, all burned, apart from the one at the bottom which was black from the fire, and the dirty old rug filled with holes where it smouldered.

She stopped and looked down, and looked through a hole to see a cracked stone, had the heat been so fierce it could shatter the stone under the rug, yet had not all of the stone floor been exposed? It made no sense, and she bent down to examine it, Morgana stood up to watch from under her hood, Gwendolyn had her back to her, so she would not be seen. Gwendolyn peeled back the mat, and it broke apart, as she pulled it away to reveal a stone with a blackened ring on it.

"What is this?"

She reached out, and took hold of the ring, and gently pulled it back, expecting some sort of trap. Nothing happened, she drew back the stone and looked down into the hole, and there was a book. It was a book Merlin had given to Morgana on symbolism, she had no idea, but Morgana had read it many times during her life in the cottage. Gwendolyn smiled as she saw the neat handwriting and felt a tug at her heart.

"You believed in her, when even I doubted her."

"He did, yet you never shared his faith in me, and let her talk you out of the truth." Gwendolyn jumped in surprise, and turned to see Morgana ten yards back, in what used to be her neat garden. She took a breath and held up the book.

"I admit, I never understood why he would take on and teach a mortal from the world of men. Especially one in which he accidentally brought about the death of her father, you are right, I did not understand him." Morgana nodded.

"When I was young, I wanted him dead for that, but here in this house, a house that gave me everything I ever dreamed of, I learned from him, and I learned to care for him in a way that even now I do not understand. I did not kill Merlin, I know she says I did, but she is wrong, he lives." Gwendolyn took a deep breath, and felt her heart beat faster.

"He does?" Morgana nodded.

"It is why I did not take the book, I left it so others would see that the symbolism proved he was alive. Read it, and you will see." Gwendolyn looked down at his small hand written book.

"How do I know this is not some trick to lure me to my death, Rhiannon is convinced as are many others that you are responsible?" Morgana shrugged.

"I have no need to lie, I never have, you of all people should know that. Look at the title, open the first page, it is there right in front of you, are you really so blind? I always felt you were far wiser than Rhiannon, was I wrong? Read it." Gwendolyn looked down at the front of the book, it was plain and bound with leather as all his books were, she lifted the cover and read the words out loud.

"Symbolism, the means to hide in plain sight."

Morgana smiled as Gwendolyn froze, and a crystal tube rose up from the floor to encase her, Gwendolyn stared at her unable to move, as Morgana looked at her.

"I have killed only one person, I tried to avoid that, it was no one of this or the realm of the Britain's, even now I deeply regret it. Your husband sleeps safe, and is very much alive, as will you be now. Next, I will face and defeat Arthur in battle with my son."

𝓜ordred grew to be a strong boy, and Morgana shared her time between her castle and Branna's, where Berengar rejoiced in being allowed to train Mordred in combat. On his sixteenth birthday, Morgana took him to the castle at Tintagel, where she had kept on a small staff to keep the place running, it was still in a bad state of repair, but many had died in the famine and the fields around the area, and it had grown wild and untamed. There was still good trade from the sea, which kept up the revenues. On one of the nights of the gathering, having seen the dissent of the people, Morgana, called all the followers together, and addressed them in the great hall of Tintagel.

She offered up her son to replace Arthur and bring better times, and asked who would support him. Cheers rang from the rooftops, and Morgana began in earnest to raise an army and march against Arthur. Mordred was equipped with armour, and with ten thousand men they moved towards Arthur, news went out fast, and Arthur was alerted, and gathered his army, and rode out to meet the advance.

It was the middle of Winter, and the ground was hard, as the two armies faced each other on the battlefield, and Mordred rode out at just age eighteen, in golden armour with a spear of toughened steel. Morgana watched alert, as she looked for any signs of interference from Rhiannon, but none came.

The battle was fierce and raged on for three days, and it was brutal as men fell on both sides, but Morgana sensed victory with Mordred, as Arthur's fighters had grown old and tired, and the young men were unskilled after years of peace. Wave after wave of Morgana's army flooded the field, and by the fourth day things were getting desperate as Arthur joined the fight brandishing Excalibur. Mordred picked up his spear, and rode at the king with speed tasting victory, he was Varisci trained, and enjoyed the lust for blood. He charged onto the field screaming with Arthur in his sights, and Morgana watched with pride, and then she noticed another enter the fight.

Out of the trees rode Lancelot, she smirked, she could not believe her eyes. He had a fatter stomach, and a long beard of grey, and instead of his armour, he wore leather protectors. Morgana watched amused, as he dropped from his horse, and waded into the mass. She was impressed, as he was still a mighty warrior, but he was greatly out numbered. He screamed to gather around Arthur, and Arthur noticed him and called out his name, both men saw each other and smiled, and started to fight their way towards each other. Lancelot battered, smashed, and sliced his way to Arthur, and then Mordred rode between them, and sliced through the top of Lancelot's arm with his spear. His arm fell limp as he still swung out with his sword, but it was in vain as he stumbled within feet of his king.

Mordred saw Arthur and dropped from his horse, he was trying to cut his way towards Lancelot, who had been cut down and lay bleeding in the mass. Mordred ran at Arthur, and as Excalibur came up, Mordred drove the spear clean through his side with a smile. Lancelot screamed from the floor unable to move reaching out as his king crumpled to his knees.

Arthur looked down as his breathing became laboured, and up into the eyes of his son, it was only in that moment he realised what Morgana had done. Mordred leaned in towards the dying king and laughed.

"Your throne is mine to rule now Father, I will rule in your stead."

Arthur reached up his left hand, gripped the spear, and pulled it hard. He felt the pain as the spear slid through him, but with Mordred still holding, he lifted Excalibur, and thrust it forward with his last dying might, straight into Mordred, who looked up into his mother's eyes in shock. Morgana screamed out as her son fell, dragging Arthur with him, and Arthur crashed into the floor, and looked into the eyes of Lancelot.

Lancelot thrust out his hand, and Arthur reached out and took it. Lancelot gave a gasp, and he spat out the blood.

"My King, my friend, always My King."

Lancelot breathed his last, and died still holding the hand of his king, and the call went up that Arthur was dying, as Morgana broke down and wept. The fight was over, as the battlefield cleared, and Morgana wept over the recovered body of her son. Arthur gave Excalibur to Sir Percival, and ordered him to ride to the nearest lake, and cast the sword back into the water. As it left Arthur's hand, Rhiannon sat up, as the image flashed through her mind. In a flash she was gone, and after two failed attempts where he could not do it, he rode back through the night, and finally did it, and as the sword fell towards the water, an arm dressed in silver came up through the surface, and caught the blade, and pulled it down into the depths.

As dawn rose, Arthur was lifted up from the field, as the hand of Rhiannon touched the hilt of Excalibur, he breathed his last breath, and understood, that even though he brought unity and years of peace, like his father, he had failed. Sir Percival rode back with speed to inform his king, but he was too late. He was told that the handmaidens of the Fae had taken his body to Avalon, and so he mounted his horse and rode as fast as he could. On the outskirts of Avalon, he saw the barge, on which Arthur was laid out, and he jumped from his horse, as it sailed towards the opening to Avalon, a realm that was now sealed.

He fell to his knees, and wept knowing the king of whom he had learned so much, was gone forever. On his knees a figure stepped out of the trees dressed in white, with a hood up over their head.

"Good Sire, tell me why you bow to the dawn mist?"

"I mourn the passing of my lord, for there will never be another as kind or fair and even handed as he."

"Know thus Good Sire, for there are those who can see what will come to pass in the times ahead. This I tell you today as truth, for another will come, for his line has not been broken. Throw down your sword good sir, and pick up thy quill and write down what has been said here today."

"How can this be my young lady? No man knoweth what will become of the world?"

"Believe what has been spoken of here today, and tell the world to watch for the bowman, for he will herald the start of new days."

*F*or Percival it was a revelation, and he rode off to write down what he had been told. For Morgana, it was one step closer to finally ridding the world of those who meddled in all affairs. The one thing she knew, was the daughters of Gwendolyn would have to leave Florae, and attend to the king. As Arthur's casket was carved from a mature oak by Fagan, alone at the tomb of Uther and Igraine, Gwendolyn's daughters wept as they prepared the body of their king.

Morgana appeared in the upper chamber and could see the lights below, she was grieving for her son, and was angry, this time she was not going to lose them. As she quietly descended the steps, she said the charm, and without hesitation she walked in the chamber for Arthur and cast it. They had no time to react as the crystal tubes slid through the floor, and with one last glance at Arthur laid out dressed on the table, she was gone in a twist of smoke. She finally had all of them bar Opal and Rhiannon, and now it was her time to grieve her lost son.

Mordred was not taken to Berengar Castle, Morgana took him to Tintagel, where next to her father, he was buried, and a stone placed, on which she wrote, 'Medraut, Prince of Cornwall.' She knelt long and wept, before standing and looking at the grave of her father who she knew was not there, and tried to compose herself, and the pain she felt.

"What am I to do now father, they have taken you, and my son who I loved dearly, and once again I feel the emptiness within me? It feels like the cruellest twist of fate, as I am again alone, is this my destiny?"

She gave a sniffle, turned, and walked onto the cliff path. Morgana walked as she once had with her father and mother, in the days long before the pain was brought to her life. It had taken such a long time and she was weary, but she was closer to her goal. She meant for them to sleep forever, so no other would ever suffer as she had. The wind blew gently through her hair and she breathed in deep, and as she walked, she saw the figure waiting, just like she had done for her in the beginning. Morgana walked up to Branna, and Branna pulled her close as she buried her head into Branna shoulder, and wailed out her pain.

"He was my son, and I loved him so dearly, and I have lost him too, what do I do now, how can I carry on without him?" The dark smoke surrounded them both, and as Morgana quietened, she found herself in Branna's workroom, looking at Ariel's crystal box. Morgana lifted her head.

"How do you do it, how do you sit here day after day, knowing you have lost her?" Branna smiled, and looked at the box.

"I cry, and I talk to her, it does not take the pain away, but it helps." Morgana understood.

"I know you mean well, but I want to be alone tonight." Branna gave a sigh.

"I know you do, I just wanted you to see that I am here, you are not alone Morgana, I am here, we are family, and it counts."

Morgana tried to smile, as the smoke funnelled up around her, and she arrived at her castle in front of her red padded seat by the fire. In many ways, sat in the flickering light of the flames, reminded her of the cottage, and it was her only comfort at sad times. She sat back and closed her eyes, and the weariness of her grief overcame her.

Chapter Thirty Six.

A Last Act of Vengeance.

As Morgana mourned the loss of her son, Rhiannon was ratcheting up towards hysteria, she glared at her advisors, things were looking very bad for her reputation.

"HOW… HOW DO THE DAUGHTERS OF A FAE QUEEN GO MISSING IN AVALON, HAVE YOU ANY IDEA HOW BAD THIS LOOKS?"

There was nothing she could do, Sequana, had disappeared, so had Gwendolyn, and now her daughters were taken right from under her nose on top of the Citadel Mount. She seethed through her teeth.

"The realm is sealed, no one can enter, and yet Morgana can just walk in and out at her ease. All of you, scour this realm and close every door into it for good."

Councillor Alder was briefed, and despatched to Florae with the bad news, and the Fae of Earth sealed the realm to all, until any news could be found of the whereabouts of Gwendolyn and her whole family. Sir Bedivere took over Arthur's castle, which was partly paid for by his family under the agreement it was Arthur's for his entire reign, but now that was over, it entered into the family, and Opal, who was the only serving member of the council, apart from Rhiannon veiled it from all.

Opal had taken to sleeping in the garden of Eve, as she missed her parents. Her mother was gone, and Hearne was a captive, and each night she would dream walk in the Chimerical Forest. In her grief, Morgana like Branna, had taken to sitting high up on the top of her castle, on the balcony that extended in the mouth of the stone raven. One night she noticed as Opal came down the wide path between the trees, and stopped in front of her castle. Normally dream walkers were miles away, and did not stray this far, but Opal was not like others, and

Morgana worked out very quickly, that Opal was asleep and off guard.

Thinking to her days after the death of her mother, Morgana had often sat on her mother's bed to talk and feel close to her, as she had as a small girl. Morgana acted quickly, and jumped to the Forest of Time, and found her sleeping on her mother's bed. With a fast snatch, she jumped to the forest and laid Opal out in the grass. She placed the charm of protection of some of the Sandling dream over her, and left her to wake up, knowing there was no way out, it was up to Opal now to try and survive. When Opal awoke, she had no idea where she was, and found that she could not escape. The only way to move in and out or live, was with the death of a Sandling, and Morgana knew full well, that would never happen. Opal had no idea that Morgana had already used the charm from the sandling given to her by Branna, and was now another prisoner, free to roam forever.

When Branna arrived, Morgana was feeling much better, and they sat by the fire and ate together and talked. Branna looked up at her.

"Morgana, how are you, you have all of them out of the way, you have achieved your goal without taking a life? All there is left is the golden queen, tell me, was it worth it, is your revenge sweet or bitter?" Morgana sat back in her seat, with a sigh. Her eyes lifted to Branna, and her voice was quiet and reflective.

"All I wanted was to stop them acting like gods and meddling in the lives of others, and I have. I listened to Merlin and I used my mind, not powers, simple thinking, and it outsmarted them all. Now I have them, they will never do to another what they did to my life, my parents and me. It matters not how I feel Branna, someone had to do it. It may sound crazy, but I miss my cottage, I know I have this castle, but that tiny little house, was all I had ever dreamed of, and Merlin gave it to me. I hated him for such a long time, but I am glad I did not kill him as I had planned. He was kind to me Branna, he taught me the powers I hold, I am now a fellow of the Whitelines because of him, with this pendant to prove it. I have thought a great deal of late, I aim to finish his work, I have nothing left now my parents and my son are gone, and I do not want to rule an empire like the golden queen. I will go out into the world and bring help to those who suffer, and for as long as I can do that, I feel my life from now on will have value. It is what I wanted when I was twelve summers old, and I will do that now." Branna understood that, and she was happy for her.

"You have balanced the two powers together well, and it pleases me that you achieved what I wanted without the use of a raven. You have given me hope Morgana, that I can achieve the same, I had lost it, and you have restored it for me. It is right Morgana, you have seen too much darkness, live in the light from now on." She smiled.

"I will, I shall wear a white raven as a symbol in all I do, maybe I will be the Lady White Raven, to your black, and I will help you research and find balance, because I want to see you reunited with Ariel. You know, I am not sure if you know, but I am sure she came to me and helped me, I am sure she wanted us to be together, and it was through her, I came back after… You know?"

"You can say her name Morgana." Morgana shook her head.

"No, those nightmares still walk my dreams, I will not give them my life as well."

Branna looked in to her dark shiny eyes, they did appear to have more life than they had after her long sleep, when the Fae inside her was released. Branna lowered her voice and spoke softly.

"Morgana, the golden queen is sealing her realm and leaving, Avalon will be hidden forever, no one will be able to walk there again." She smiled at Branna.

"I know, I get news here when I need to. She cannot seal me out, I own land there, I will always be able to walk there if I need to. She never understood the power of what Merlin has done for me, it is why she could not stop me from coming and going, even when she closed every door, she could not close them on me. I shall not be returning, that time is done."

"I am glad to hear that."

*F*or the rest of the evening they talked, and laughed with each other, and it felt very much like the days when Morgana first came to the castle. Branna embraced her as she prepared to leave, happy to see her looking healthier and happier.

"I will see you soon, until then."

In a cloud of smoke Branna faded away, and Morgana walked along her table, and looked at the bottle containing the essence of Merlin. She lifted it up and looked at it, as the mixture swirled inside, and an idea came to mind.

*T*hirty minutes later, Morgana stood and looked at the ground, at the opposite end of the forest, to the one she had placed Opal in.

She looked down at Merlin, having used the last of the liquid from the charm of the Sandling on him.

"I owe you Merlin, you took away one life and then gave me another, and so, in one day you shall awaken whole, trapped, your powers bound, in this realm forever. You will be free to live as you choose, and wander where you wish, it is not the life you planned, but it is a life all the same. It will be interesting to see if you two can find each other, that I will leave to you both, but I will warn you, I will never allow another ruling council whilst I live. Should any of you try to create another, I will destroy it as I have this one. The lives of men are not yours to destroy, learn from this lesson."

Morgana felt good when she returned, as she talked to Rajani up on her perch, whilst she filled a large steel bowl with water. She slipped off her dress, and began to wash all of her naked body, and it made her feel clean and refreshed. Morgana hummed as she washed, and in another realm, millions of golden lights rose into the sky, as Rhiannon stood high on the Citadel Mount next to Fagan.

"You watch this realm, it is the only reason I let you stay, watch over the forest, and keep this realm free of shadows." He gave a regal bow to her.

"I will watch over ye realm always, tis also my home, and I will keep my sense with me at all times. Fare thee well My Queen." She nodded.

"You have two days, and then all of my protections will activate, make sure you are not on my roads when they do." He looked seriously at them below the mount, bright white and standing out from the green of the grass and trees.

"Aye My Queen."

Fagan stood and watched as Rhiannon rose into the heavens, and travelled back to the moon realm, Avalon was empty, and all he had to do, was grab his packed cart, and walk down the Queen's Road into the forest, for he already had a site picked out, and he had plans for a lot of good quality woodwork.

Branna sat in her seat with her glass of wine, and smiled at the crystal box.

"She is over the worst and will heal now, the golden queen has gone, and it irks me my love, but time can and will fade all into the past and memory. Morgana needs that now, she shall finally have her time for herself, and have time to study again, it is needed my love, we all need the break." She gave a sigh and sat back in her seat, and relaxed, it would soon be time to prepare for a long sleep.

*M*organa lifted her towel and rubbed her thighs, and between her legs to get dry, she felt so much better, above Rajani dozed on her perch, and the castle was silent, it felt perfect as she rubbed her clean body.

Behind her on the table, Maud's book opened, and a soft cold almost whispered cackle rose from it.

"Ha… Ha…Ha!" Morgana frowned, and turned around.

"Whose there?" She stared into the dim darkness of the room, lit only by the candle on her work table. She dropped the towel, and walked slowly forward.

"Ha… Ha… Ha!" Morgana scanned the darkness.

"Show yourself, reveal who you are?" The page on the book turned over, and she saw it and frowned.

"What is this?" She came closer staring at the book as another page turned, the quiet voice whispered behind her.

"Steal my spells, will you?" She spun around, but the room was empty.

"Where are you… Show yourself."

"Te, hee, hee, Poor little Morgana lost and alone, a damaged brain, and a burned out home."

Morgana felt a cold prickle run down her arms, as she scanned through the dim corners of her room, she knew that voice, but it was not possible.

"Maud?"

She felt the ice cold grip on her shoulders, lifted into the air, and was dragged backwards, and slammed spread eagled into the wall, and winced with the pain. Morgana felt panicked, she was stuck five feet off the floor. She looked at her arms, nothing was holding them, but they were pinned, as were her legs. She tried with all her might, but she could not move, and then movement caught her eye, and she turned to face forward, and saw it.

The candle on the table flickered illuminating the open book, and black smoke was rising out of it. Morgana pulled with all her might, as she watched it forming, and it slowly crept off the table, she knew exactly which form it would take. Maud appeared in a dusty smoky form, her black elongated form, stretching back to the pages of the book, like a writhing snake. She smiled that sick smile as she approached, and Morgana pulled with all her might, and struggled frantically, but she could not move. Maud advanced with a face filled with hatred.

"Take my life, take my book, steal my spells and use my magic, little perfect raven, Branna's perfect pet, a half breed bitch who thought she was better than the rest. You pride yourself on your intelligence, well tell me now, who is the smarter one?"

Morgana looked down as Maud lifted her left hand, and Morgana's silver dagger slid off the table and flew into her hand. She gritted her teeth, and fought to free her bonds, and could feel the fear growing inside her, she was caught and could not get free, and she was starting to panic, as Maud came closer.

"So perfect, so pure, so unattached to a raven, Branna's pride and joy. She named you daughter, and replaced me, you owe me half breed, you took my bird."

She smiled another ugly smile, and then her face wrinkled as Morgana watched on helpless, unable to move. Maud gazed up at her with utter hate.

"You want my bird, take her, but take her as all of us have."

She leaned back and laughed, as she lifted the knife, and held it up to the roof, and then started to chant. The words were dark and corrupted, and Morgana could not work them out as her mind panicked and struggled to try and get free. Above her in the tower, black clouds appeared and thunder rumbled, Morgana looked up, and suddenly understood what Maud had in mind, and she screamed.

"NO…. BRANNAAAAAAAAAAA!"

Rajani was dragged off her perch, and thrown into the top of the tower as Maud continued to chant, and Rajani stretched out and grew, as lightening flashed, and Morgana saw the huge black bird, and tears of panic filled her eyes.

"No… No, I do not want that, I am whitelines, I do not want any more darkness. Maud please, I do not want any more, I have had too much already."

She fought with all her might, as the smoky figure screamed more of her chant into the air, Morgana looked down with tears in her eyes and shook her head.

"NO… NO MAUD, DO NOT DO THIS, YOU KNOW OF THE LIFE AND THE PAIN IT CAUSES? PLEASE, I BEG YOU, I DID NOT WANT TO KILL YOU, I WANTED YOU TO STOP. I WANTED US ALL TO WORK TOGETHER, BUT YOU GAVE ME NO CHOICE."

Her tears streamed down her cheeks, as Maud screamed with laughter, and the knife shot out of her hand, and stuck into Morgana's left naked breast, and carved out the first rune. Morgana screamed with all her might, but she knew no one would hear her, she was in a realm where no one ever entered. The lightening flashed again, and a strong wind howled downwards into the room, tossing all the glass off the table, shattering it against the walls. Morgana closed her eyes and forced her mind, and with everything she had, she screamed into her brain.

"BRANNNNA!" Branna jerked up off her seat.

"Morgana!?" Roack landed, and looked at her.

"The raven Rajani has opened the darkness." Branna panicked.

"It is not possible, how?"

Her instant reaction took over, and in the blink of an eye, she was stood in Maud's dirty workroom, and looked around. Roack landed on the window, and Branna looked at her.

"Her book is gone, oh no, Roack, Maud has put herself inside it, and Morgana is alone." Black smoke funnelled into the room.

*M*organa screamed, as a fourth symbol was cut into her skin, the whole of the room had a swirling mass of clouds, smoke and smashed furniture flew around the outer walls. In the centre, Morgana was screaming pinned naked, and spread eagled above Maud, as the raven above her got larger, and the lightning pounded down to the floor. The figure of Maud still connected to the book cackled with delight, and began to recite the final words of the spell.

At the end of the room, the doors exploded open, and Branna entered, her eyes blazing red, and Morgana looked up through eyes filled with tears, and screamed for help at the top of her lungs, as her tears rained down out of her eyes.

"BRANNA HELP ME, I DON'T WANT THIS, PLEASE STOP HER… BRANNA DON'T LET HER DO THIS!?"

Branna advanced at speed, but Maud lifted her other smoky hand, and a wall of smoke rose up in front of Branna, and she bounced back off it. Morgana screamed out in desperation.

"NO…. PLEASE… DO NOT DO THIS… THIS IS NOT WHAT I WANT!"

Branna could see Morgana, naked, pinned to the wall unable to move, blood running down the front of her torso, and she recognised the crude runes carved on her flesh. They were the same runes as she had carved with a feather of Roack, into Berengar.

She lifted her hand, as Maud chanted the final incantation, and with a blast of light she cut through the smoke, saw the book, where Maud stretched back, and connected to it. The silver dagger shot into the air, as Branna lurched for the book, grabbed the page, and tore it out, as Maud yelled into the tower.

As fast as she could, she swept it into the flame of the candle, and the page ignited, Maud snapped round with a scream, and then laughed out loud.

"Too late… My Queen of the Ravens, not fast enough, not this time."

The paper flared in Branna's hand, and Maud screamed, as flames shot up through the smoke, and she exploded with a high pitched laugh. Morgana gave out a terrifying wail, there was an explosion of white, as a ball of pure white light, exploded out of her. It hurled across the room, and smashed through the window, and shot down into the trees below. Morgana slid down the wall and crumpled to the floor, the knife stuck out of the front of her chest. The storm stopped instantly, and Rajani fell to the floor, and Roack swooped in, and caught her.

Branna rushed over, and knelt on the floor, she lifted up Morgana's limp body, and pulled free the knife, then lifted her into her bosom, and held her and wept.

"I did not want this, not for you, you were a perfect balance, you had what I was seeking with Fae and white. I did not want more darkness for you, not you, who were as a daughter to me. I never want anyone to have my life."

She pulled Morgana close, and wept into her hair, deep bitter sobs of pain, as Roack laid Rajani on the table, and looked at Branna cradling the limp Morgana in her arms.

"It is done Branna the Raven, we cannot undo this, she will rise tomorrow another Raven of Berengar. The spell is cast, she is now like you, and Rajani is hers forever." Branna gave a sniffle and looked to Roack.

"I made my choice Roack, and we have been joined and been true to each other. This was not hers to choose, she has no choice, and I know, this was something she never wanted. Morgana wanted to do good in this world with light, not darkness." She turned back to Morgana and wept.

"I am sorry, I am so sorry Morgana, you do not deserve this for all you have suffered. I should not have left you tonight, I should have stayed and protected you."

She pulled her close and wept long deep bitter sobs, but the truth was, there was nothing left now to do. The choice was made and her path was set, Maud, in one last act of vengeance, had chosen it for her. Morgana of Berengar, was now one of their ravens.

Outside the castle, hidden under the leaves of the thick undergrowth, a small quiet voice, echoed as it wept bitter tears of pain in the empty forests of the Hidden Realm.

$\mathcal{M}$organa would sleep, and then awaken tied to Rajani, it could not be undone, not without killing her, and Maud knew that. In her last act of vengeance, knowing she would attack Morgana, she left a trace of herself in her spell book, thinking Branna would place it in her workroom. She had planned for it to be opened there, at which point she would be released to attack Morgana, and her dark devious and evil plan worked perfectly. Branna had two choices, kill Morgana, or suffer to watch her live slowly being corrupted by the darkness. Both she knew would torment her mother for the rest of her life. In Maud's warped brain, that was the price Branna must pay, for not teaching her from her black book.

$\mathcal{M}$organa awoke the following day in her bed in the Castle of Berengar, she was healed completely, strong and healthy, probably stronger than ever before, but she was very angry. Branna tried her hardest, but Morgana in a fit a rage, exploded out of the room, and headed back to her own castle, where in a temper she smashed up her workroom, and screamed into the tower in heartbroken rage. Morgana had no choice but to accept her fate, and she knew that.

It was over a year later, when she returned to see Branna, she was calmer, but colder. In every way she looked like Morgana, and they walked and talked in the forest, but she was not the same, not the Morgana she had laughed and joked with. Morgana stayed for the week, and was rude and insulting to Otto, and he got more than his match, and hid in his room. Once she headed back to her own castle, Branna sat in her seat with her wine, and felt the tears in her eyes, and the pain in her heart, as she looked at the crystal box containing Ariel.

"It is not her my love, something is missing, and what she has gained, does not fit the woman I know her to be. Morgana had an innocence, almost a naivety to her, a goodness, and that has gone now, and I miss it."

She closed her eyes filled with sadness and remembered Morgana as she was, sat at the desk framed by the window, her eyes shining with life, as Branna held up a cloak of black feathers for Morgana to admire.

"When I arrived here in this castle, I created two just like hers, but made from the feathers of my ravens. Here, take this one, it is a little short on me, which is why I made a second. If you are to be the Countess le Fey, you should have a presence when you enter a room, and this cloak will do exactly that." Morgana rose from the desk looking awestruck.

"It is beautiful, I can see the glints of blue in the daylight." Branna smiled, as she slipped it over Morgana's shoulders.

"The long feathers on the collar I collected when Roack lost them, so these are very closely connected to me and precious. Wear this when you leave Avalon, and be a countess in the shadows."

Morgana smiled, her eyes dancing with delight as she examined herself in a tall polished plate of silver. She turned to look at Branna, and lifted her arms with joy.

"This truly is fit for a countess, a countess in the shadows."

Branna walked up to her with a slight chuckle, and helped straighten the collar, and then she stood back to admire Morgana, with her long cloak of feathers, and her dark eyes and hair.

"Yes, I do believe you are right, in that, you truly are the Countess le Fey."

Morgana gave an excited giggle, and lifted her hood on the cloak to hide most of her face creating an air of mystery to her, she lowered her voice tone and spoke, with an air of mystery, and giggled.

"Good evening, Lady Branna, I am the Countess of Darkness." Branna wiped the tear from her eyes.

"I was so foolish, so stupid, I let the golden queen play me, and in a moment of utter stupidity, I have wrecked everyone's lives." She bit down on her lip, and tried to stifled the scream, as she looked at Ariel in her box.

"WILL THIS PAIN EVER END?" She buried her face in her hands, and wailed.

*T*he years passed, and Branna entered her first time of sleep, as she sealed her rooms, and Rosamund took over the running of the castle. Branna lay in her dream state, dreaming of Ariel, and also a little of Morgana.

Morgana was drawn more and more into darkness, as her anger at being tied to the raven tore at her, although she did fight to keep as much as herself as she could. She was part Fae, but not Fae enough, and her human side succumbed slowly to the darkness, and it corrupted and twisted her mind. Her manner was more abrasive, and at times she was malicious and hateful, all of which was driven by her anger and heart break. Branna often felt that the girl she knew was still in there fighting, but it was a fight she would never win. In an interesting twist, as Branna saw a few times, a small part of her could still connect to the fear of others, especially young children. In many ways, such was the power of the pain and hurt she had felt as a small girl grieving for her lost father, that a strong sense of the young Morgana remained within her, and at times, in a strange way, it showed.

Dorin grabbed her, and pushed her up the wall, she was frightened, as she saw the soldiers dragging people out of their boats and beating them.

"Ursula go, run to your mother, she went to the eastern market, now hurry."

"I am scared father." He smiled, and gave a nod.

"I know… But you have to be brave, you need to get to your mother, and tell her to get away from here, and I will head for the viaduct over the east river. Now go, hurry they are getting closer and I have to untie the boat."

Ursula scrambled up the wall onto the top road, and looked back, her father was untying the boat as fast as he could, the Harebell was already in flames. She ran as fast as her legs would carry her, gasping in air as she dodged the carts, swerving from left to right with great speed.

She reached the alley, and flew down it, and came out into the mass of people, there were shouts down the alley, she had been spotted, she looked round quickly, the street was packed, and she was gasping for air, and started to walk as quickly as she could towards where she knew the east market was. Panting for air she could hear the voices behind her, and she looked around and spotted a shop door.

As fast as she could, she headed towards it, and as she reached the door, she felt a firm hand grip her, she spun round and looked up into the dark eyes of a woman, with a pale white face. She smiled a crude smile.

"Come with me little Fae, I will take you where no one will harm you." Ursula did not know what to do.

"I have to find my mother."

"Is she Fae too?" Ursula nodded, and the woman smiled.

"I am also, here, hide under my cloak, no one will find you there, what is your mother's name?"

"It's Ena… Ena of Ariel and Enaria." The woman's eyes opened wide, and she smiled another crude and disfigured smile.

"I am Morgan, Morgan le Fey, some call me the Countess of Darkness. Come, you are safe, no one would dare harm you with me around. Come, I have wanted to meet your mother for a long time. Fear not Ursula, I will protect you, I know what it is like to be alone in a world of evil people."

*A*valon was silent after one hundred years of isolation, and now deserted, as Branna stood next to the gate, and looked at the charred remains of Morgana's cottage. It was strange, it had not changed at all, not even the weeds that swamped her garden grew on the stone. She walked through the gate onto the old stone floor, and looked at the devastation. At the base of the chimney where the wood was piled up burned and charred, she noticed something and bent down to look. She moved the wet black lumps of burned wood, and lifted up the thing she had seen, and wiped off the grime with her fingers, and smiled, as she looked at the small rough carved figure of Branna.

"Not as good as the one I made you, but you did well for a beginner. Do you remember the girl you were when you made this, is she still in there fighting like she did for justice? She should have left you alone, all of this was so unnecessary, so pointless. Oh Morgana, she has no idea of what her self obsession in her own myth has created, but somehow, I think you do, and I wonder at times how all this will end." She slipped the small figure into her pocket, turned, and gave a sad sigh, and looked up at the mount.

"The jewel of Rhiannon, a golden queen glowing aloft to the glory of the Fae and man, and carried on the backs and deaths of many." She shook her head, and laughed softly.

"And she called me dark and evil, no one knows how dark she runs below the gold. I have more to do, I have to find the balance, and also save Morgana."

She walked back to the gate and closed what was left of it behind her, and turned to have one last look, and saw the apple tree, with its thick red apples, of which Morgana had brought her many. Below it, was the bushy growth of the white star blooming with small stars of bright glowing white, and she smiled.

"At least the truth grows somewhere, my white raven." With a chuckle she disappeared.

*M*organa of Cornwall, was born a half Celt, half Saxon princess. She was spoilt and pampered a great deal, but that was because she was showered with love. Morgana was always bright and intelligent, and she idolised her father. There are some who would call her, and some who would praise her, for she grew up in a time when men ruled their world, and as a woman, that made life difficult. She was at heart a good natured girl, and driven by her ambition to be something no other woman wanted at that time, she wanted to be free.

Her life in Avalon was not easy, her day to day living was toil, living alone chopping her own wood, making her own shoes, growing and cooking her own food, and selling her goods to earn her own money. Morgana learned about the people the hard way, she struggled as they did to survive, and it gave her an insight into life, none of the elite members of Fae ever had, and that made them very nervous.

Her manner of being from the way she was raised, gave her the voice she needed, and she stood her ground for what she believed in, and fought the injustices she saw in the way the poor were treated. She called out the Ruling Council for what she saw as their interference with the natural way, and yet in many ways, she was loyal to them in her belief that the old ways should not be wiped away so easily. She was powerful, the daughter of a queen, but that was in a way what became the thing that brought her down, she drew the attention of

Rhiannon.

Morgana used her intelligence, not great powers from the lines of old, and in doing so, she outwitted them and out smarted them. She ultimately removed them from the lives of the rich and powerful, and in doing so, she removed the one thing all those who craved power and greed needed most, the support of the Ruling Council. No matter what her future holds now, in that one thing, she should always be remembered, for she was without doubt, an unsung hero of her people. She was the daughter of a great queen, and it showed.

Morgana never wanted the darkness she has now within her, or to be seen as evil, she never wanted to act evil. All she wanted was justice for the murder of her father, and the rape of her mother, and to most, if it was any other person, that would appear to be fair and proper. She wanted the truth, and questioned all who confronted her, for she saw two truths, the facts as they happened, and the stories told by those of influence who craved greed and power, but which truth was right? She fought for what she thought was right, as did Branna, Rhiannon, and even Maud, all of them believed in the truths they held.

Morgana had many choices in her life, and she chose what she felt was the right path, which was to become a white raven for good. In her lack of understanding of the hate she faced, she suffered a cruel last act of vengeance, and it cost her the very core of whom she was. Morgana became in the eyes of others, the very thing she hated the most. Today, she is still called evil, and yet as I sit here, knowing her as I did, I have to ponder, and I do have to ask… Was she really? Branna closed the book with a sigh, it had been many years in the writing, but was now complete, she lifted her eyes to the crystal box.

"It is done my love, a day will come when others will read this, and I hope they judge her less severely."

*H*igh above the realm of Avalon, in the heart of the Realm Ofmoon, in the centre of the maze of work camps and mines, Stenlow walked with his meal tray into the Guards Dining area. He was worn out and tired, and for the first time in the age he had been here, he saw his sister, and walked over towards her. She looked up at him as he sat at her side, as he laid out his plate of food and utensils. She sat chewing, and glanced his way.

"I heard she sent you here too, how are you?" He placed down his tray at the side in an unoccupied place, and turned to her, and looked her straight in the eyes.

"I used to sit at the desk every day in the office, and look at the sunsets, and as I did, I would think of you Sister." Luminaria stopped holding her fork, and looked at him, looking shocked.

"What made you say that?" He smiled.

"I once told a very sweet girl about you, and she told me, I should tell you if I ever saw you, and this is the first time I have seen you since that time. I told her I cared for you, but did not know how to say it, and so she told me to not hide my feelings and tell you, and I am glad that I have." Luminaria took a sharp breath in, and then smiled.

"I am glad she told you, I also loved to watch the sunsets over Avalon. What was this sweet girl's name, do I know of her?" Stenlow sat back, and he smiled for the first time in years, and his eyes gave a slight twinkle.

"Morgana… She was a very unique, and yet a kind and gentle girl." She smiled at him.

"Nice name, she sounds like she was indeed a sweet girl." He smiled, as he remembered her, to him she was possibly the nicest, and prettiest young woman he had ever met.

More Author's
From
Violet Circle Publishing

Mike Beale. (Children's Book)

Crumble's Adventures.
ISBN: 978-1-910299-06-7
Digital ISBN: 978-1-910299-08-1

Colin Smith (Play)

Heaven knows I'm Miserable Now
ISBN: 978-1-910299-16-6
Digital ISBN: 978-1-910299-23-4

Ted Morgan. (Poetry and verse)

Wordsmith's Wanderings.
ISBN: 978-1-910299-04-3
Digital ISBN: 978-1-910299-09-8
Peregrinations of the Wordsmith
ISBN: 978-1-910299-18-0
Digital ISBN: 978-1-910299-21-0
Silhouette Soldiers
ISBN: 978-1-910299-19-7
Digital ISBN: 978-1-910299-22-7
A Menu of Memories
Digital ISBN: 978-1-910299-32-6
Digital ISBN: 978-1-910299-33-3

Robin John Morgan. (Fiction/Fantasy/Slice of Life)

Heirs to the Kingdom.

Book One, The Bowman of Loxley.
ISBN: 978-1-910299-00-5
Digital ISBN: 978-1-910299-10-4
Book Two, The Lost Sword of Carnac.
ISBN: 978-1-910299-01-2
Digital ISBN: 978-1-910299-11-1
Book Three, The Darkness of Dunnottar.
ISBN: 978-1-910299-02-9
Digital ISBN: 978-1-910299-12-8
Book Four, Queen of the Violet Isle.
ISBN: 978-1-910299-03-6
Digital ISBN: 978-1-910299-13-5
Book Five, Crystals of the Mirrored Waters.
ISBN: 978-1-910299-05-0
Digital ISBN: 978-1-910299-14-2
Book Six, Last Arrow of the Woodland Realm.
ISBN: 978-1-910299-07-4
Digital ISBN: 978-1-910299-15-9
Book Seven, Bridge Of Sequana.
ISBN: 978-1-910299-17-3
Digital ISBN: 978-1-910299-20-3
Book Eight, The Circle of Darkness.
ISBN: 978-1-910299-26-5
Digital ISBN: 978-1-910299-29-6

The Curio Chronicles.

Part One, Abigail's Summer.
ISBN: 978-1-910299-27-2
Part Two, Curio's Summer.
ISBN: 978-1-910299-34-0
Digital ISBN: 978-1-910299-35-7
Part Three, Curio's Christmas.
ISBN: 978-1-910299-38-8
Digital ISBN: 978-1-910299-39-5

Other Works.

Rise Of The Raven
ISBN: 978-1-910299-30-2
Digital ISBN: 978-1-910299-31-9
The Countess Of Darkness
ISBN: 978-1-910299-40-1
Digital ISBN: 978-1-910299-41-8

Han's Cottage.
ISBN: 978-1-910299-36-4
Digital ISBN: 978-1-910299-37-1

Find out more about our authors and their books at
www.violetcirclepublishing.co.uk